Wedding bells and Christmas bells!
What a perfect match! And speaking of perfect matches...

*Toni's divorce would be going fine except for one thing.
She was stuck in a narrow bed with her soon-to-be ex,
unable to tell her sweet old aunt that Derek was about
to be her former husband. And she was unable
to tell Derek that he was about to be...a father!*

Christmas is indeed the season of miracles
in Marie Ferrarella's *Christmas Bride.*

"Ms. Ferrarella holds reader interest at...fever pitch."
—*Romantic Times Magazine*

* * *

*He could go from daring detective to darling dad—except for
one thing. When Holly found out what Jake was really after,
would everybody's dreams of a happy holiday fall apart?*

A new family finds its future threatened by the truth, in
Suzanne Carey's *Father by Marriage.*

"Suzanne Carey's touching storytelling
will warm your heart...."
—*Romantic Times Magazine*

MARIE FERRARELLA

sold her first contemporary romance to Silhouette Books seventeen years ago. She is part of Silhouette's exclusive Five-Star Club, having sold more than five million copies of her books. Recently she had a ten-part serial launched on Harlequin's newly remodeled Web page, www.eHarlequin.com. Her romances are beloved by fans worldwide and have been translated into Spanish, Italian, German, Russian, Polish, Japanese and Korean.

She has earned a master's degree in Shakespearean comedy, and her writing is distinguished by humor and realistic dialogue. Marie Ferrarella describes herself as the proud mother of two and lucky wife of a man who still knows how to make the room fade away for her. This multi-nominated, RITA Award-winning author is thrilled to be following her dream of writing full-time, and loves nothing more than to entertain her readers.

SUZANNE CAREY,

a Phi Beta Kappa graduate of Lake Forest College, Lake Forest, Illinois, and a former reporter who covered local politics and criminal courts as well as undertaking investigative and feature assignments, has been writing novels for Silhouette Books since the early 1980s. Though she was born in Illinois, she has been a resident of Florida for many years. She and the man in her life, a clinical psychologist who is now a university professor, reside in Sarasota, on Florida's Gulf Coast.

YULETIDE BRIDES

MARIE FERRARELLA

SUZANNE CAREY

Silhouette Books

Published by Silhouette Books

America's Publisher of Contemporary Romance

SILHOUETTE BOOKS

ISBN 0-373-21724-2

by Request

YULETIDE BRIDES

Copyright © 2001 by Harlequin Books S.A.

The publisher acknowledges the copyright holders of the individual works as follows:

CHRISTMAS BRIDE
Copyright © 1996 by Marie Rydzynski-Ferrarella

FATHER BY MARRIAGE
Copyright © 1995 by Verna Carey

Printed in U.S.A.

CONTENTS

CHRISTMAS BRIDE   9
by Marie Ferrarella

FATHER BY MARRIAGE   251
by Suzanne Carey

Dear Reader,

Whenever I begin a story, I make sure that I am writing about people I would personally want to know, people I enjoy being around, because writing is a very intimate experience and I am very picky about the people I allow into the worlds I create. I love all my couples, but some stand out in my mind more than others and I have to admit I love them just a tad bit better. Such a couple are Toni and Derek. There's just something about their relationship that seemed to click for me from the very start. Maybe it's because they'd known each other forever. Maybe it's because they fell slowly in love with each other without even realizing it. Or it could be because I have a weakness for couples who engage in snappy banter. But whatever the reason, Toni and Derek have remained close to my heart, and I hope, if you're picking this book up and reading their story for the first time, that they will find a soft spot in yours. I just know you're going to love them as much as I do.

Now, as always, I wish you love,

Marie Ferrarella

CHRISTMAS BRIDE
Marie Ferrarella

To my family,
who always made Christmas
the best time of the year for me

Chapter One

Dear God, what had she just gone and done?

Antoinette D'Angelo Warner stared at the telephone receiver just beneath her hand on the cradle. She had just lied to the sweetest little old lady in the world. Either that, or she'd made a promise that she hadn't a prayer of keeping.

Cradling the telephone in her lap, Toni pushed herself deeper into the cushions of her sofa and sighed.

Well it certainly was the season for prayer, she thought. It was less than a week to Christmas, even though the Southern California weather just outside her window was warm and balmy. When she thought of Christmas, it never involved palm trees. It always brought up images of snow-covered pines and knee-deep drifts of cold, white powder, stinging cheeks and bright fires in a redbrick fireplace. Those were the kinds of Christmases she'd experienced as a child in upstate

New York, where winter, like a long-lost relative, always arrived early and stayed late.

The past two months had been rough, and Toni had really been looking forward to going home for Christmas. Going home to her roots. Most especially, going home to her beloved grandmother. In a way, Nonna meant Christmas to her the way nothing or no one else ever could.

Toni wanted to be enfolded in that loving, soft embrace just one more time. Nonna had a magical way of making everything bad disappear. Problems, inadequacies, unfulfilled dreams—nothing seemed to matter whenever she was around Nonna's wonderful, sunny smile.

Moving heaven and earth, Toni had arranged her schedule at the research laboratory so that she could take two weeks off and fly home. She had been just about to call Nonna with the news when Nonna had called her, beating her to the punch.

And sweetly, lovingly, blowing her completely out of the water.

Wrapped up in preparations and anticipations, Toni had been taken completely by surprise. But she shouldn't have been. And it was her own damn fault.

She'd never told Nonna about the pending divorce.

She couldn't.

The ebony coffee table, newly polished, bounced her image back at her.

"Coward," Toni muttered to her reflection as she replaced the telephone on the table. She should have told Nonna right from the beginning.

But it had been so hard. She'd searched desperately for the right words and, in the two months since she had thrown Derek out and filed the papers, she hadn't found them. How could she find the words that, gentle or not, would break Nonna's heart? From the first moment Toni had brought Derek up to the house to meet her, her grandmother had been completely enamored with him.

Just the way she had once been.

Over the next year, while Toni and Derek were dating, Nonna had all but adopted Derek. All her conversations with Toni seemed to begin and end with his name and center around inquiries as to how things were going between them. Nonna, Toni mused, was a hopeless romantic who adored happy endings. And believed in them.

Nonna was eighty when they got married, and she actually danced at their wedding, leaning heavily on her grandson's arm. It was difficult for her, but Nonna swore that the joy bursting in her heart negated any pain. She danced once with each of Toni's brothers, and twice with Derek.

She started hinting about great-grandchildren a month into the marriage.

Well, at least she could use that as a Christmas surprise, Toni mused, mechanically cupping her hand about a belly that was as flat as the rink at the Ice Follies. It would be a hell of a surprise for Derek as well, if he knew. Her mouth curved with a tinge of bitterness. It would probably make him run to his lawyer and urge that the divorce be somehow sped up. As much as she wanted children, he didn't. Something else she hadn't known about him.

She fervently hoped that the good news would offset the bad for Nonna.

Toni could still hear the old woman's whisper-soft

voice in her ear, bubbling with quiet excitement about the coming holidays.

"I cannot wait to see you and Derek." Toni's mother had called earlier and told her that Nonna was ill. It was her heart. Fearing the worst, Toni had made the decision to come home for Christmas, even though she could hardly be spared at the laboratory. There might not be other Christmases for them to share.

But when Toni had asked about her health, Nonna had lightly shrugged off Toni's concern.

"What will be, Antoinette, will be." Her voice gained enthusiasm. "But this I promise you—I am living for the day I can see the two of you standing before me, holding hands and making me feel young again."

Three times Toni had started to tell her grandmother that there would be only one of them standing in front of her. She hadn't gotten beyond a sharp intake of breath.

Nonna had interpreted the sound as concern and laughed softly. "Ah, Antoinette, the doctor, he tells me that my heart isn't strong, but what does he know? I was an old woman years before he was even born. Seeing you for Christmas will be all the medicine I need. You and my handsome Derek. How is he, Antoinette? You have not mentioned him."

So what could she say? Could she tell Nonna that she didn't know? That she hadn't seen Derek for almost two months? Could she tell her grandmother the truth—that if she never saw that two-faced tomcatting womanizer again, it would be too soon?

No, she couldn't say any of that. Instead, she'd said, "He's fine. Just very busy."

"But not too busy to come, I hope."

It was her loophole, her one chance to save herself

gracefully, and she had choked. She could have told Nonna that Derek was rarely home before evening, that building his practice was his driving concern and that everything else, including her, had gotten lost in the shuffle. That much would have been the truth, at least, for that was how it had been before she'd caught him in his transgression.

It was the perfect way out.

But she had gotten tangled up in the hope she heard in her grandmother's voice and let the opportunity slip away.

Toni damned herself as she heard her own voice say, "No, he's not too busy to come. We'll be there, Nonna. Derek wouldn't miss seeing you for the world."

She'd said it because she knew that was what Nonna wanted to hear. She'd said it and instantly cast herself headfirst into a bog of quicksand.

We'll be there.

The words mocked her as they echoed back in her head. Darkness crept into her small living room on large, woolly feet, blotting out chunks of light with it.

She felt as if the blackness was seeping into her soul.

We'll be there. Yeah, right.

Toni sighed and restlessly dragged both hands through her mop of raven hair, at a loss as to what to do about the situation.

She knew her choices. It was either walk into Nonna's festively decorated house and look into that sad little face when she told her that she and Derek were no longer living together, that they were getting a divorce, or...

Or.

Toni looked down at the telephone again. It seemed to have grown in size, like a demon in a small child's nightmare. There was another way open to her. The ultimate sacrifice. It meant calling Derek and throwing herself on his mercy.

She'd rather eat nails. Rusted ones.

"Your grandmother is very ill, Toni. I want to make this the best Christmas ever for her." Those had been her mother's exact words. And all Nonna wanted for Christmas was to see her.

With Derek.

It was like asking her to perform her own appendectomy and then go out dancing afterward.

Toni chewed on her lip. If she asked him, he'd probably say yes. Derek really liked Nonna. He'd become genuinely fond of her when they lived in New York. They'd visited frequently, and when they had moved to California he'd been the one to suggest flying home whenever they could both manage it. It definitely wouldn't be that difficult to convince him.

But that meant talking to him, and Toni didn't want to. Oh, God, she didn't want to!

Toni stared at the telephone again, a sinking feeling taking hold.

She really didn't have a choice. She had to ask him to come.

Provided he could tear himself away from his sex-starved nurse, Sylvia, who conveniently doubled as a receptionist and a paramour.

The thought of the curvaceous woman who had once professed to be her best friend had Toni's mouth hardening as the sting of hurt still vibrated through her.

Annoyed with herself, Toni struggled to get her thoughts under control. This wasn't about her, this was about Nonna. About giving the sweet old woman what she wanted most. Toni's determination strengthened as she visualized Nonna in her mind. She was going to let Nonna see her and Derek together even if it meant skinning him and wearing his pelt around her shoulders.

Still, when she began to tap out his phone number, part of her was hoping that she'd get Derek's answering machine instead of him. Funny how his new number remained embedded in her brain, even though she'd seen it written down only once. Derek had given her the number the last time she'd seen him in case she ever needed anything.

What she had needed was a loving, faithful husband who'd be there for her, who wanted to be the father of her baby, not a gorgeous, six-foot-three, blond hunk who had an equally gorgeous woman stuck to his side. A gorgeous woman whose mouth was hermetically sealed to his. A woman who wasn't her.

Toni burrowed herself farther into the cushions on the sofa with each number she tapped out. She was almost completely entrenched as her finger slid off the last button of Derek's number.

It was ringing.

She braced herself, suddenly realizing that she hadn't a clue as to how she was going to phrase this. She always sounded so squeaky on answering machines that—

"Hello?"

Oh, God, it wasn't his answering machine, it was him! She almost dropped the telephone receiver as she scrambled out of the layers of cushions and sat up ramrod straight, a soldier facing a firing squad and wanting to make one last attempt at pride.

"Derek?"

There was a long pause on the other end of the line. "Toni?"

Why, after all this time and especially after what had happened, did the sound of his voice still send shock waves over ninety-eight percent of her body? "Yes, it's me."

"Is anything wrong?"

Derek wondered how he had managed to be so busy as to miss the news that hell had frozen over. That was the specific weather condition that was to have occurred, according to Toni, before she ever deigned to use his telephone number.

"That depends on your point of view," Toni answered guardedly.

He heard that familiar defensive tone in her voice. Same old Toni. He sighed. "I don't have a point of view about this, Toni. I just said hello. You called me, remember?"

Her fingertips were getting clammy. How had she allowed herself to get into this? And now that she was "into this," what did she say?

Half of her was tempted to slam down the receiver. She should have rehearsed this before she'd called. Or better yet, she should never have called. She should have had enough nerve to tell her grandmother the truth.

Too late.

Staring into the darkness, Toni forged ahead. "It's almost Christmas."

"Yes, I know, I have a calendar. It's one of the few things you let me keep." He couldn't help recalling the scene when he'd last been home. She'd run out of his office, after cursing his lineage down through several generations. He'd finally disentangled himself from Sylvia's grasping arms and hurried after Toni, to reason with her and calm her down. It was like trying to calm down an earthquake. When he'd reached home, he'd found that, like the hurricane he often likened her to, she had completely upheaved his life. His possessions, what little of them he had, were all strewn on the lawn in front of the house. It was her way of saying it was over.

She had stubbornly and staunchly refused to listen to anything he had to say in his own defense. She'd been judge, jury and executioner, convicting him on circumstantial evidence rather than believing in him. Trust had died that autumn day. But for it to have gone so quickly, he knew it had never really existed to begin with. And love had no breeding ground if there was no trust to make it fertile.

He still hadn't gotten used to it.

"Let me guess—for Christmas you want to pick up where we left off and argue again? I'm sorry, Toni, I've given up arguing for good."

He made it sound as if it was all her fault instead of his, but then, he'd always been good at twisting things around. What she had done had been completely out of character for her, but people did strange things when they had their heart run over by a tractor trailer.

Derek had actually tried to make her believe he was innocent. It might even have worked, but then Sylvia had come to her and confessed everything. In graphic detail. It left no room for doubts. Or forgiveness.

Nonna. Think of Nonna.

Summoning a calm she didn't know she was capable of around him, Toni attempted to sound brisk. "I didn't call to argue. I have a favor to ask." She bit off each word as if it was dipped in lemon juice.

"A favor?"

The amusement she heard on the other end didn't

help. "It's not for me," Toni said quickly. She didn't want him getting the wrong idea. "It's for Nonna."

"Your grandmother?"

His voice had taken on a softer tone. The soft spot in his heart for the frail woman was his one redeeming quality. There'd been a time when she thought all his qualities were wonderful. But then she'd painfully learned otherwise. And she'd grown up. "Yes, it's for my grandmother," Toni finally said.

The last time he'd seen Gina dePauli, she'd been a wisp of a woman in a fuzzy pink bed jacket, housed in a four-poster bed. She'd just gotten over a bout of the flu and looked very frail. The idea of a world without her saddened Derek immensely.

Was Toni telephoning about funeral arrangements? That would explain the sudden call out of nowhere. He braced himself for the worst.

"How is she?"

"Not good." Toni could have sworn she heard a sigh of relief on the other end of the line. Or maybe it was impatience. He was probably dying to get back to his love life. "My mother says that this is probably going to be Nonna's last Christmas. Which is why I'm calling you now."

Toni licked her lips. Suddenly dry, they absolutely refused to moisten. As for her throat, the dust bowl could make a comeback there, she thought. She had to push the words out.

"I'm flying home for Christmas. Her home," Toni clarified. Nonna's old three-story house had always been home to her. She, her mother and brothers had moved in the year she had turned ten, after her father had left them.

She paused, temporarily out of steam and out of courage, waiting for Derek to take the hint and make an offer to come see Nonna with her.

Toni couldn't be asking what he thought she was asking. That would have been wishful thinking, left over from a time when he had actually had great dreams for their relationship. Well, he wasn't going to fall into that trap and be put in his place again.

"Give her my regards."

Damn the coldhearted bastard. How could she have been in love with him once? He was purposely making this difficult for her. He knew exactly what she was asking. "Nonna wants more than that from you."

"Meaning?" he asked cautiously.

If she had any sense, she'd hang up and forget the whole thing.... Toni swallowed her pride for Nonna's sake. It stuck in her throat as she made the request. "She wants to see you."

"Even though we're in the middle of getting a divorce?" But even as he asked, he knew it was typical of the woman. She might have been small in stature, but he had never encountered anyone larger than Gina dePauli in soul and spirit.

Toni really hadn't wanted to get into this, but she knew that there was no recourse left to her. Curling her toes, as if that could help her brace herself for this, Toni began.

"That's just the trouble...."

It came to him in a flash. "You didn't tell her, did you?"

Her cheeks grew hot at what she took to be an accusation.

"How could I?" she demanded. "For some strange reason, Nonna dotes on you." Once that had made her very happy. But that was when she had foolishly be-

lieved in wedding vows. "If she knew what kind of a
person you really were—"

Derek felt his temper being nudged awake, but he
held on to it. He knew that it would be far more irri-
tating to Toni if he was just amused at what she said,
instead of indignant. Or hurt.

"You certainly know how to sweet-talk a man into
doing what you want him to." He heard her angry huff
and smiled to himself. "You called me asking for the
favor, remember?"

He was making it sound as if she was the one who
wanted to see him. The only way she wanted to see him
was on a skewer, over a barbecue pit. Turning slowly.
Damn, he wasn't supposed to affect her like this anymore. She knew him for what he was, a coldhearted,
self-centered bastard who didn't have time for her,
didn't have time to begin a family, but had time to
snuggle up to a hot little number in a white uniform
one size too small for her body.

He didn't deserve her tears.

He had them anyway.

Toni clenched her teeth together. "I said it wasn't for
me. It's for Nonna." Taking a deep breath, she forced
herself to calm down. Derek had to be made to see
reason and it wasn't going to happen if she was yelling
at him. "It amounts to her dying request." Surely he
had an ounce of compassion in him.

"Let me get this straight. You're actually asking me
to come back to New York with you for Christmas?"

She hated that amused tone of his. *Oh, Nonna, why
did you have to have such poor taste in men? And why
did I?* "Yes."

"And pretend like nothing's happened?"

God, he was getting a kick out of this, wasn't he? "For her benefit, not mine."

"That's understood. But you do realize that she's going to put us in the same room." If he knew Toni, she hadn't gotten to that part yet in her mind. She had a habit of rushing off without thinking things through. Her refreshing impetuousness was part of what had attracted him to her in the first place. How could he have known that it would lead to the end of their relationship, as well?

No, she hadn't realized that. Toni hadn't thought of anything beyond the request and what an awkward position she was in. And how it was beyond her to deny her grandmother anything that she wanted, because she always asked for so little. And her silence gave her away.

"You didn't think of that, did you?" He gave a dry chuckle.

It was the last straw. "Forget it," Toni snapped. "Forget I said anything." Angry tears spilled down her cheeks. She thought she'd cried him out of her system. "I wouldn't want my grandmother to die believing a lie."

"That everything between us is fine?"

"That you were worth caring about," she retorted. "Nonna has this huge misconception about you. How you're this big, wonderful man who swept her granddaughter off her feet. That you're this Prince Charming with a stethoscope around his neck...."

She could hear the smile in his voice. "I always liked your grandmother."

"Yes, and every other female who crossed your path." *Instead of just me, you big jerk.*

Toni made up her mind. Calling Derek had been a

mistake. Just the way marrying him had been. She was just going to have to find a way to tell Nonna the truth.

"Never mind, Derek. Forget I said anything. Forget I even called." She began to hang up, but the sound of his voice forced her to place the receiver against her ear even though she knew she shouldn't. "What?"

"I said, when are you leaving?"

"Why?" She didn't wait for an answer. She just wanted to get off the phone. Now. "Tomorrow. Go back to Sylvia."

Then, before he could say anything else to her, Toni slammed the receiver down on the cradle. She placed it on the coffee table, shoving it to the far end in her anger.

Well, that had gone well, she thought. For a disaster.

Toni scrubbed her hands over her face, wishing she could scrub away the past ten minutes. She had no choice left. She had to tell her grandmother that she was getting a divorce. Everyone else in the family knew. But, like a conspiracy of love, everyone had kept it from the eighty-two-year-old woman for fear of upsetting her. Gina's heart was so delicate that the family was afraid any little thing might push her over the edge and hasten her demise.

So how was she going to drop this little tidbit on her? Toni thought in despair. Maybe she would tell her about the baby first. But that would make the divorce seem even worse.

It seemed hopeless.

Listlessly she crossed to the light switch and turned it on, then squinted as light flooded the room. She still felt as if it was filled with shadows.

Maybe she'd get lucky and Christmas would be canceled this year.

Toni squared her shoulders. Canceled or not, she was still going home. Her mother was right. This might be the last time she would see Nonna.

The thought of that possibility brought with it a sharp, bitter pang. It was all right being here, three thousand miles away, as long as she felt that Nonna would be there whenever she returned home. Sitting in her wide, cathedral-ceiling living room, surrounded by countless knickknacks she'd been given by well-meaning children, grandchildren and great-grandchildren over the years.

A constant to cling to, a beacon from her past.

As long as Toni could remember, Nonna had been there for her, as she had been for everyone. Always dependable. Always wonderful.

Toni frowned as she walked into the kitchen to feed the huge emptiness she felt. With any luck, this time she would keep it down.

For once, Toni had her story rehearsed and down pat. She chanted it to herself like a mantra as she drove her rented car from the airport to the old house she loved so well.

She was going to tell Nonna that Derek was very sorry, but his duties at the hospital prevented him from coming to spend the holidays with her. He was a pediatrician on staff at Harris Memorial Hospital; the hospital was one of the outstanding institutions in the country, specializing in neonatal care. She would go on to say that, at the very last moment, he'd been called on to assist at a delicate operation. His tiny patient was clinging to life by a thread. Being dedicated, Derek felt that he just couldn't leave the baby at such a time.

Nonna would understand and be proud of him. That

was a bitter pill to swallow, but so be it. And in actuality, it was more than a feasible excuse. In the year before the end had come, Derek had spent far more time in his office and at the hospital than he had with Toni. Most of that time, she knew, was actually spent caring for his patients. Whatever else she might think of him, Derek was a first-class physician who truly cared about each one of his patients.

Toni pushed away the thought. She wasn't here to think about Derek. She was here for two weeks to see Nonna and the rest of her family. Two weeks that promised to be bittersweet and produce memories that she would press in the pages of her mind long after...

Today. Long after today.

Besides, she did have good news. Nonna would be thrilled about the baby. It would be a spring baby, making its appearance somewhere around the end of April. It would give Nonna something to look forward to. Something to live for.

She was in familiar surroundings now—long, tranquil, tree-lined blocks that spoke of a peace that had eluded her of late. Toni drove toward the house slowly, enjoying the trip. The trees, in place over a hundred years, were majestic. Denuded of leaves, barren of the snow that had fallen a week ago, the long, thin branches reached out to one another like the fingers of man stretching to touch his Creator in Michelangelo's painting. They formed a spidery arch, allowing only snatches of the blue-gray cloudy sky in between the slits.

Nonna's house was the last on the block. A mass of brick surrounded by verandas whimsically built on by Toni's grandfather whenever he was between jobs, it hadn't changed in thirty-four years.

A warm feeling pervaded her just from looking at it.

She'd always felt safe here. As if nothing could ever harm her while she was here.

Home, she thought.

Her eyes stung.

Damn, where were these tears coming from? She wiped away the streaks with the back of her wrist. Ever since she'd gotten pregnant, her emotions felt as if they were permanently riding on a roller coaster. But Nonna didn't need tears, she needed happy faces. She always said that there was nothing she liked better than a happy face.

Toni struggled to put one on now.

There were cars parked all along the end of the block. Toni pulled up into the driveway and turned off her ignition. She'd forgotten how to parallel park. Newport Beach, with its head-in parking spaces, had spoiled her. Maybe one of her brothers could move the car for her later, she mused. There would be no end to the teasing, but better that than a dented rental car.

Derek could parallel park on a dime. The thought flashed through her mind out of nowhere.

But Derek wasn't here.

She pulled up the hand brake a little too hard. Thoughts of Derek were getting to her. She had to stop this. It would spoil her holiday.

Toni left her luggage in the trunk. There was time enough to get all that later. Right now she just wanted to see Nonna.

She reviewed her excuse in her mind one last time as she knocked on the door. The late-afternoon wind nipped at her face, making her shiver. Toni ran her hands over her arms, waiting.

The coat wasn't warm enough, she thought. She'd

forgotten how cold winters here could be. She should have borrowed her friend Lisa's skiing jacket.

The door opened on her second knock. The next moment she was pressed against an ample bosom and enveloped in a warm hug that brought fresh tears to her eyes. Toni savored the feel of her mother's arms around her for a beat before drawing back.

"How is she, Mother?"

Josephine D'Angelo smiled warmly at her only daughter as she stepped away from the door. Toni had grown thinner in the past few months. Two weeks of good cooking might remedy that. Cooking and perhaps something else. Her eyes shone.

"She's in the living room." Josephine gestured toward the room that was habitually bathed by the afternoon sun. "Why don't you go see for yourself?"

There was something in her mother's voice that created a sense of urgency within her. Toni didn't bother taking off her coat or even unbuttoning it. Instead, she quickly made her way to the parlor.

It had been more than a year since she'd been in this house and she had a sudden need to see the woman. Even if it meant facing up to the lie she had allowed to be perpetuated.

She reached the living-room doorway and then hesitated for a moment.

"Who is there?" Nonna's voice floated through the air, beckoning to her.

Toni moved into the room. Nonna was sitting in her favorite chair, a huge winged affair that had been recently reupholstered in burgundy. She looked like a tiny, regal matriarch. The chair made her look even more frail, more delicate than she already was. Toni drank in the sight and pressed it to her heart.

"It's me, Nonna. Toni."

"Antoinette?" The soft face dissolved into a wreath of smiles. She beckoned her granddaughter to her. "Come, come into the light. Let me look at you."

Toni smiled as she knelt by the chair. "Nonna, how are you?" Not waiting for an answer, she enfolded the small woman in her arms.

"Wonderful, wonderful." The exclamation was slightly muffled, whispered against Toni's shoulder. "Now that you are finally here, Antoinette. Now I have you both with me."

"Both?" Toni leaned back on her heels, confused. She scanned her grandmother's finely wrinkled face for an explanation. What was she talking about? "What do you mean, bo—?"

"Hi, Toni. Looks like my plane arrived earlier than yours."

The voice came from behind her. It was only then that she realized Nonna wasn't alone in the room. Still on her heels, Toni turned and lost her balance.

She would have fallen if Derek hadn't been quick and caught her in his arms.

Chapter Two

Slowly he raised her to her feet. Time froze. The very air turned into crystalline particles around her, holding her hostage to the moment, the place. Toni felt as if she was moving in slow motion as she turned completely around in Derek's arms to face him.

Such a familiar feeling. Such a heartbreaking one.

Her eyes wide and incredulous, Toni stared in disbelief at the man whose child she carried beneath her heart.

The man who had broken that very same vital organ.

"Derek." She had to push his name out over the dry expanse of desert that doubled as her tongue.

What the hell is he doing here?

"Of course it is Derek. Your husband." Affection flooded Nonna's voice. "And how perfect. Look." She pointed vaguely over their heads. "You are standing beneath a mistletoe."

Toni rolled her eyes upward. There it was, beribboned and green, hanging over her head like a withered, leafy bounty.

"Perfect," she echoed without Nonna's feeling.

Nonna's eyes twinkled as if she were an impish young girl. Her exuberance peeled away the years from her face.

"Kiss each other," Nonna urged, then coughed delicately when they made no move to acquiesce. "For me."

There was no choice open to them and no reason they could offer Nonna why they wouldn't do just as she prompted. They'd always freely displayed their affection before.

"This isn't my idea," Derek murmured to Toni under his breath just before his lips touched hers.

Just before the kaleidoscope swallowed her up, taking her deep into the belly of virtual reality, filled with sights and sounds, colors and emotions that she was trying so desperately to purge herself of. It was like being instantly catapulted into a past she had once thought herself lucky to have.

A past, Toni now knew, that had been only an illusion.

The taste of his mouth—dark, sensual—could always disengage her brain in record time, no matter what logic might dictate to the contrary. Toni felt herself leaning into him even when something just beyond her consciousness was ordering her to pull away.

She would.

In a minute.

In a very long minute.

Damn, he wanted to assure himself that he was well on his way to being over her. He'd had enough anger and hurt within him to be over twelve women. Twelve women who weren't his about-to-be ex-wife. Twelve women who hadn't burrowed their way into his heart and left a cavity when they summarily exited.

Who weren't Toni.

She could unglue him the way nothing and no one else could, and he missed her. God, but he had missed her. He'd told himself that he didn't miss a woman who couldn't trust him, who wouldn't believe him above all else, who wouldn't believe *in* him even when the evidence was damaging. But that was a lie.

The single kiss beneath the mistletoe made him very aware of that. He could feel his body aching for her, the sight, the scent, the taste of her. How he missed her!

It didn't seem fair.

When he drew back he was pleased to see that Toni wasn't quite as composed as he knew she wanted to be, either. That helped. A little.

Drawing in air slowly, he took a step back. The bell had rung and they had to return to their separate corners. The next round would come soon enough.

Derek shifted his eyes toward Nonna and crossed to her. "I've just finished explaining to Nonna why we were arriving separately," he told Toni.

Toni felt as if she'd just been torpedoed and was scrambling to see if she was still seaworthy enough to continue her journey. It took a second before his words registered.

"Then she knows..." Toni deliberately trailed off, waiting for Derek to fill in the excuse. She didn't want to be tripped up and contradict him in front of her grandmother.

Derek's eyes narrowed as he deliberately lobbed the

ball back into her court, making her squirm before taking her out of her misery. "Yes."

He was toying with her, damn him. Toni glared at Derek. He was standing beside her grandmother as if the tiny woman belonged to him, not her. "That..." *Say something, damn it,* she thought, conveying her thoughts to him with her eyes.

Derek would have enjoyed the game a great deal more if it were just the two of them involved, but there was Nonna to consider. Nonna, who was the only reason he was here to begin with. It wasn't fair to suck the sweet woman into the quagmire that had once been his marriage.

"That—" he picked up the word Toni had tossed out and built on it "—I was at a medical convention in Connecticut and thought it would be a lot easier to arrive here from there than go home and wait until you could fly with me." He smiled, satisfied with the excuse he had tendered to Nonna to allay her suspicions. "Saved time and money."

"And money's very important." The sarcastic retort left Toni's lips before she'd even realized she wasn't just thinking it.

"Not nearly as much as time," he countered. "I just don't seem to have enough of it." Turning so that he didn't have to look at Toni and have his thoughts scrambled, Derek looked down into Nonna's face. "Otherwise I would have been here a lot sooner to see my girl." Derek leaned over and kissed Nonna's cheek.

Toni could have sworn that there was a pink tinge creeping up her grandmother's silken, wrinkled cheek. She was buying in to his words, and loving it, Toni thought with a stab of jealousy. Nonna belonged to her, not him.

God, she sounded like a five-year-old, Toni thought. Something else to blame Derek for.

Nonna laughed and patted Derek's hand. "Ah, you are so good for me, Derek. So very good. You make me think I am a young girl again."

Derek enveloped her hands in his. "You are, Nonna. A very young girl."

It hurt his heart to see Toni's grandmother like this, a prisoner, with cruel Time a jailer. Nonna was the warmth he'd never really felt in his childhood, personifying the very feeling of home for him.

After Toni.

"Age is a matter of attitude, and that's locked up here." Very gently Derek tapped Nonna's temple. "And here." He touched his own heart as he smiled into her face.

Damn the man, how could someone who could voice such beautiful sentiments to her grandmother, be such a two-faced rat underneath it all?

Because he was good at it, Toni thought. He had fooled her, hadn't he? Fooled her into finally risking her heart and believing that she could be happy with him, that he was different from other men. That she could trust him not to break her heart.

Well, she'd learned the hard way, hadn't she?

I can't come home yet, Toni, he'd said to her when he'd called home from the office. *I'll be there as soon as I'm finished.*

As soon as he finished making love with Sylvia, Toni thought bitterly, replaying in her mind the scene she had walked in on. He'd shattered her that evening. Shattered her so completely that she thought she'd never be able to pick up all the pieces again.

But she had, and she was damn well not going to let

him have any of them again, especially not the piece that was her heart.

No matter how unglued she became when he kissed her.

She was looking at him with the eyes of a jury that was about to deliver a guilty verdict, coupled with a recommendation for the death penalty. Nothing had changed, Derek thought. But then, he hadn't really thought it would. He certainly hadn't come here for that reason. He'd given up that hope after a week of slammed doors, telephone hang-ups and having his clothes thrown on the front lawn. An unreasonable person, he'd concluded, couldn't be reasoned with. And Toni was an unreasonable person.

No, he'd come just to see Nonna again and to experience a family Christmas for the last time, even if it was really her family and not his. But the D'Angelos had been the only real family he had actually ever known. His own had splintered by the time he was twelve.

This small house in upstate New York represented the best memories of his life.

Not knowing what Toni might have said to her family about him, Derek had called Josephine right after Toni's telephone call. He'd asked his mother-in-law if it was all right with her and the others if he came for Christmas. Josephine D'Angelo had been overjoyed at the suggestion. It was all the summons he'd needed.

Josephine, accompanied by her older son, Joe, walked briskly into the room. She'd been listening outside the parlor door and hadn't heard any fireworks. So far, so good.

She looked from her daughter to the man she had been happy to call "son." Both of them had tight smiles on their faces. In Toni's case, the smile was so tight that it looked as if it was going to crack her lips. Josephine was grateful that her mother's vision wasn't what it used to be.

"So, Mama," she said in a voice that was a shade too bright, "now that your Christmas wishes have been fulfilled early, I'm going to settle Toni and Derek into their room." *And pray,* she added silently.

Josephine hooked an arm through each of theirs, keeping herself between them like a human bundling board. Jet black hair that was streaked with gray fell into her eyes as she looked over her shoulder. "Joe, get your sister's suitcases out of the car."

Joe laughed shortly. "Is she going to pay for the hernia operation?" It was a matter of record that Toni overpacked for an overnight stay, much less one that involved two weeks.

Toni felt herself relaxing. The friendly banter eased the tension from her shoulders. "Better than that, I'll do it myself," Toni promised.

"Let you near me with anything sharper than a crayon? Doctor or no doctor, that'll be the day." Joe shuddered as he went out. "Never mind, I'll take my chances."

"Chicken." She laughed. It almost felt like being home again. Almost.

"I'll help you," Derek volunteered. With a nod toward Josephine, he disengaged himself.

"All right," Josephine called after Derek's disappearing back. "I've put you up in the room you stayed in the last time you visited here."

Last time you visited here. The phrase replayed itself in Toni's mind. The last time they'd been here, they had been married. Happily.

Or so she had thought.

"I want to talk to you," her mother whispered, her voice low.

Before she could respond, Toni found herself enveloped in a crowd scene as the rest of her relatives, small and large, came to greet her.

"See, I told you she was here," Karen D'Angelo said, sniffing triumphantly at her brother and cousins the way only a twelve-year-old could lord it over children younger than she was.

Jackie, her brother Alex's wife, ushered her twin sons in before her. She gave Toni a quick hug. "Hi, we were hoping you'd be able to make it."

"Dad didn't think you'd come," her nephew, Dustin, interjected. For his trouble he got a sharp poke in the ribs from his sister.

"Wild horses couldn't have kept me away," Toni vowed. "Wild horses or wild beasts," she amended, thinking of Derek.

"Did you bring any wild beasts with you, Aunt Toni?" Zak's eyes widened with hope. At seven, he took everything at face value, and was far more optimistic than his twin, Nik, or his father had ever been.

"Only one," she murmured under her breath. But she saw that Alex heard her.

Joining the group, he leaned over and gave her a quick kiss. "Feisty as ever, I see."

"And twice as ugly," she ended, echoing a taunt that had originated in her childhood when Alex and Joe would tease her mercilessly. A wave of nostalgia washed over her. She wished those days were back again, days when her largest goal was just to put her brothers in their place.

Nik tugged on her skirt. "What did ya bring us, Aunt Toni?" He eyed her hopefully.

She'd been so busy rehearsing what she wanted to say to Nonna that she'd forgotten everything else. Her natural bent toward procrastination had left her with no previously purchased gifts to bring. She knew she could buy everything here, but that didn't solve her immediate problem.

She tousled Nik's hair and shrugged helplessly. "Um, well, nothing, but—"

Nik pouted. His hangdog expression reminded her of Alex when he was a boy. "Uncle Derek brought us planes."

"Space shuttles," Zak corrected importantly. He was older by five minutes and felt it entitled him to pull rank whenever he could.

Jackie looked at her sister-in-law nervously. None of them knew the exact details of the breakup, but they were all aware of the sensitivity of the situation.

"I told Derek he was spoiling the boys," she began, then realized her mistake. "I mean…"

Toni nodded. So, Derek had struck here, too. She should have expected it.

"I'll get you a space station for the shuttles," Toni promised the boys. "And something for you, too," she told Karen and Dustin. "Just give me a little time. I packed in a hurry." That much was true.

Forgiven her slip, Jackie looked relieved. "C'mon, boys, let your aunt go to her room and settle in."

"The same goes for you, Karen," Annie said when her daughter looked as if she intended to follow Toni up the stairs.

"But I haven't seen Aunt Toni in so long," Karen wailed dramatically.

Annie hooked her arm through her daughter's. "You can see her all you want at dinner. Now let the lady breathe."

Toni smiled her thanks. She winked at Karen. "Later."

Feeling privy to a grown-up moment, the girl instantly brightened. "Later," she echoed.

"Nice to be home again," Toni murmured. With a sigh that was half contentment, half anticipation, Toni followed her mother up the stairs.

The boys' voices wafted up behind her. "Give me my plane," Nik cried.

"Space shuttle," Zak crowed.

On the landing Toni looked at her mother. "He gave them gifts?"

It was a rhetorical question. She knew what Derek was up to, trying to make her seem like the heavy in this breakup. What she didn't know was *why,* but that didn't even matter. What mattered was that she wasn't about to let him get away with it.

Josephine knew that tone. "Came in not an hour before you, presents for everyone," she said, opening the curtains. Bright sunlight spilled into the room, making it cheery, friendly. "He called them pre-Christmas presents."

Toni's eyes narrowed. "Everyone?"

Josephine patted the small circular gold pin Derek had brought her. It was far too extravagant a gift. Her smile faded. It broke her heart to see them at odds like this.

"Everyone," she said with emphasis. "He enjoys it. Especially giving gifts to the children." Her smile, slightly lopsided like her children's, widened with feeling. "He really loves children."

Toni moved to the window and fiddled with the curtains, adjusting them. "Yes, but only if he doesn't have to come home to them."

Josephine crossed her arms before her chest. "Meaning you?"

"No—" Sensitive, Toni stopped abruptly. "Was that a crack about the way I'm behaving?" Maybe she *was* acting childish, but her mother didn't have to point it out. Besides, she'd earned the right to be petulant. Derek was undermining her in her own territory.

Josephine slipped her arm around her daughter's shoulders. "What's the matter with you, Toni? It's like you've become like a different person in the last few months."

Toni shrugged, moving away from the haven of her mother's arm. "Maybe I am a different person." She raised her chin defiantly. She didn't want to be analyzed. She was sick of analyzing things. She just wanted to be welcomed and loved unconditionally. "Maybe I've grown up."

Josephine studied her youngest child's face. "Or regressed."

Just whose side was her mother on, anyway? "What's that supposed to mean?"

Dredging up the memory was difficult for Josephine, even over the space of time. But it was necessary. "You're behaving the way you did when..."

Defensiveness danced all through Toni, making her alert and weary at the same time. "When what?"

"When your father walked out on me." As mother and daughter, they had talked about everything. Everything but that. Maybe they should have, Josephine now thought with regret. Maybe if they had, Toni wouldn't be making this huge mistake. "Did Derek walk out on you?"

Toni's body became ramrod straight. "No, I told you, I was the one who walked out on the marriage." *After he had stepped out on it.*

Josephine tried desperately to read between the lines. "Yes, but you didn't tell me why."

And she didn't want to tell her now. But she would have to eventually, Toni thought. She let out a long, shaky breath. When she spoke, her voice was small, distant. "I caught him with another woman."

"Derek? Are you sure?"

Did her mother think she was hallucinating? The disbelief Toni heard in her mother's voice annoyed her almost beyond words.

"Yes," Toni snapped. "St. Derek, the Apostle, giver of gifts—I caught him with his nurse straddling him as if she was the Lone Ranger and he was Silver, about to take her off on a long, wild ride." Toni swung away from her mother, afraid that she was going to cry.

Josephine couldn't bring herself to believe what she was hearing. Anyone but Derek. There had to be some mistake. Hands on her daughter's shoulders, she turned Toni around. "Where?"

She wasn't going to cry, she *wasn't*. "In his office."

Josephine tried to find an excuse and couldn't. But there had to be one. She knew Derek, or at least thought she did. There was love in that man's eyes when he looked at her daughter.

"What were you doing there?"

Toni pulled away. "What was *I* doing there?" The question was entirely inappropriate. "What were *they* doing there?" Of all the people in the world, she would have expected her mother to be on her side, to understand what she was going through. She felt abandoned. Almost as abandoned as she had felt when she had fled Derek's office. "You're taking this awfully calmly, Mother, for a woman who's been through all this herself."

Because it involved her daughter and a man she thought very highly of, Josephine D'Angelo clung to the hope that there was another explanation. "Maybe it's because I've been through all this that I can look at it from another angle."

Suddenly cold, Toni ran her hands along her arms. "I saw enough angles, thank you very much, when I walked in on them." Staring out the window, watching—without really seeing it—the wind toy with the skeleton of a tree, she let out a long, shaky breath. "I went there to tell him something."

Something in her daughter's tone alerted Josephine. "What?"

Toni shook her head, waving a hand at the question. "It lost its significance when I saw them like that." Hot, angry tears gathered just beneath her lids. She pressed her fingertips to her eyes until she felt in control again. Her mother was still waiting for an answer. Well, she'd know soon enough, anyway. She might as well tell her, even though the joy had been siphoned off. "I came to tell him that I was pregnant."

Josephine's eyes widened as her mouth dropped open. Her baby. Her baby was having a baby. "Toni! You're..."

A rueful smile curved Toni's mouth, but lost its way to her eyes. She tried to make light of it. "With child, yes."

Josephine hugged her daughter, instant tears coming

to her eyes. And then she held Toni away to look at her face. "Why didn't you tell me?"

Toni shrugged, helpless. Hapless. "Somehow, the joy just left."

And it had. Everything left the day she felt she'd lost Derek's love. Now it was a matter of putting one foot before the other until she found herself on firm ground again. She was still looking for it.

"I was going to make the announcement Christmas morning. It was supposed to be my big surprise for Nonna. I was hoping it might help counterbalance the one about the divorce." Toni frowned. There was going to have to be some reshuffling now. "But now that Derek's here…"

Of course, Derek still didn't know. Josephine shook her head. "You have to tell him."

All she wanted to tell him was to get lost. Forever. "Why?"

"Because it's his baby." Josephine's eyes swept over Toni's stomach. It was still flat, but that would change, and rapidly. "And it's not exactly something you're going to be able to hide indefinitely."

Toni lifted her shoulder in a half shrug. "Not from people who see me," she conceded. "But Derek isn't going to see me after the holidays are over." Not if she had anything to say about it.

The stubbornness, Josephine thought, they got from their father. "Toni, you have to—"

"—Get through this without any mishaps," Toni declared, her voice drowning out her mother's. "I'll stay after he leaves and tell Nonna then. Everything," she added significantly. "Okay?"

Josephine frowned, but there was nothing she could

do. Toni was a grown woman. "It's not okay, but when have you ever listened to me?"

This time the smile was genuine and did reach her eyes. Toni slipped her arm around her mother's shoulders and hugged her. "I seem to remember a day in 1993. October, or maybe it was in November..." Her voice trailed off.

Josephine huffed as she shook her head. "Or maybe never." A commotion behind her curtailed their conversation as Joe and Derek walked in, five suitcases between them.

Joe grunted as he deposited the ones he was carrying on the floor beside the bed. "I see she's traveling light this time."

"One of them's mine," Derek interceded gallantly. He placed that suitcase by the window. It was smaller than the others. His medical bag he put on top of the bureau for the time being.

Josephine looked from Toni to Derek and then back again. Her eyes silently urged Toni to make a clean breast of it. Toni's expression remained stony. It was time for all good mothers to retreat.

"Well, I'll leave you two to unpack." So saying, she ushered Joe out of the room, all but pushing him in front of her.

Joe raised his hands in surrender. "You don't have to shove, Ma. I don't like being in the war zone any more than you do." He looked at Derek just before he left, a genuine fondness in his eyes. "Don't turn your back on her, Derek, unless there's a mirror available. She likes to kick from behind."

Derek nodded, a smile involuntarily curving his mouth. "Thanks for the warning."

As the door closed, there was suddenly a wall of

silence between them, silence that separated them, yet joined them.

Toni glared at Derek, her hands on her hips. "I see you've been bribing my relatives."

She was being petty. He didn't remember her being petty before. But then, there must have been a lot of signs he'd missed.

"A few simple gifts isn't called bribing. It's called being nice." Because he needed something to do that didn't involve throttling her—or holding her—he picked up his suitcase and placed it on the bed. "You used to like me being nice to your family." He punctuated the statement with the snap of each lock.

"That was when we had joint custody of them. Now they're mine again." She pushed the suitcase lid down, wanting his undivided attention when she was yelling at him. She was through letting him block her out when she talked. "I don't want them taking your side."

He pinned her with a long look. "If your hold on them is so frail that a few trinkets can make them shift sides, then maybe you'd better rethink your relationships."

"I am," she retorted. "Starting with ours." She pressed her lips together. She wasn't going to let him lead her down that road again. "What are you doing here, anyway?"

Was she serious? "I seem to recall a phone call asking me to come."

"If you remember the phone call, you also remember that I said never mind." And after seeing him here, she'd never meant anything so much in her life.

He flipped the suitcase lid open again. "Must have been a bad connection. All I heard was 'come.'" Derek hung up a shirt, then turned to face her. The amused expression was gone. "Look, we're going to be here for the duration and we're both here because of Nonna. Let's make the best of it."

He made it sound like the simplest thing in the world. But then, for a man who had carved out her heart with a jagged piece of tin, she supposed it was.

Chapter Three

Derek could remember when silence between them wasn't this uncomfortable, unwieldy thing. When they could curl up against each other, each studying from a different textbook, and be content just to be together. Now silence was some sort of horrid monster with pointy spikes that drove them apart.

Derek endured it only long enough to empty out his suitcase. Toni had commandeered the closet, leaving the bureau for him. He'd taken two drawers, leaving the others for her and folding the change of slacks he'd brought with him over the chair.

Waiting until she had crossed back to the bed and her open suitcase, Derek deposited his empty valise on the floor of the closet.

"So—" the word sounded casual enough to his ear "—what have you been doing these last two months?"

Toni moved past him without sparing so much as a

glance in his direction and shoved another hanger onto the rod. "Forgetting about you." She paused, then turned toward Derek, unable to suppress her own curiosity. "You?"

He shrugged, a study in nonchalance. If she could be so flippant about what they'd had together, so could he. "Same."

That stung. She'd thought she'd stripped herself to the point where nothing he could say or do would hurt her, but she was wrong. And she hated him for it. "Then we're agreed."

"About what?" She had lost him. They'd exchanged only a few words and already she'd managed to confuse him. That had to be some kind of record.

Toni stood glaring at him. "That our marriage was a mistake."

If it was a mistake to have loved her, then he was guilty. And because he still did, that made him stupid. Guilty and stupid. A hell of a description for an up-and-coming pediatrician.

"Yes." Derek's reply was icy. "We're agreed." He saw the hurt flash in her eyes. The next moment it was gone. He'd probably just imagined it. After all, this was what she wanted to hear, wasn't it? "But for different reasons."

Toni's eyes narrowed. "Only I had a reason," she snapped. She hadn't been the one to be unfaithful, he was.

"No," Derek countered evenly. "Only I had, but I'm not going to stand here and argue with you like a couple of ten-year-olds squabbling over imaginary rules to a game they just made up."

He knew if this went any further, he would really

lose his temper, and he didn't want to risk that. It would push him into a region that was best left unexplored.

"Ten-year-olds?" Toni echoed, her voice rising as she went toe-to-toe with him.

At that moment Alex opened the door, feeling as if he should be waving a white flag of truce. He poked his head into what his brother had accurately referred to as a war zone. "Hi. Am I interrupting anything?"

Distracted, Toni and Derek both turned toward Alex and shouted in unison. "No."

Alex flashed an exaggerated smile. "Didn't think so. I knocked," he added, venturing a few steps into the room, "but apparently not loud enough to compete with whatever it was I wasn't interrupting."

Toni blew out a breath and with it part of her anger. Focusing her attention on Alex, she returned to the bed and her open suitcase. "Stop being the mayor's attaché and tell me what you want."

Behind Toni's back, Alex exchanged glances with Derek. His was filled with compassion. Alex knew what Toni could be like.

"World peace, a raise and a merry Christmas, but I'll settle for you two coming downstairs. Dinner's in ten minutes." Alex was already backing out of the room. "Jackie and Annie sent me up." Raising his hands, he proclaimed himself blameless for the intrusion. "I'd never have come of my own free will."

Derek laughed softly as he watched Alex leave. "What d'you know, an honest politician."

Toni refused to smile. "Someone has to be honest in this world."

Intrigued, Alex paused in the doorway. "Is that some kind of code?" he asked Derek.

At least the rest of her family made him feel welcome, and Derek was grateful for that. "It's more than a code, it's a language all her own. Your sister's perfected it."

Yup, there was definitely a war on here. The sooner he withdrew, the better his chances were of not getting sucked in. Alex shook his head. "Gee, I figured world peace and a raise were out, but I thought I had a shot at a merry Christmas."

The smile on Toni's face was heart-meltingly appealing as she crossed to her brother. For a moment it reminded Derek of the first time he ever saw her. She'd been running across the campus, late for class as usual, and collided with him. Her books had gone flying. When he'd helped her gather them up, she'd flashed that smile at him. He'd been a goner from then on, though he had fought it in the beginning.

Toni kissed Alex's cheek. "You do have a shot, Alex." She patted his arm. "Especially if you get me something to shoot with."

Alex had the good grace to wince as he looked at Derek. "She's gotten more sharp-tongued since she moved to California. I didn't think that could happen."

Derek thought of the words she had hurled at him when she'd thrown him out. "You don't know the half of it," he murmured.

"And he's not going to," she declared. They were close, she and her brothers, but this was something that was far too personal to open to their scrutiny. Telling her mother had been hard enough.

"My exit cue," Alex announced. "Don't forget— dinner, ten minutes. We're having roast chicken. We're all out of fatted calf." With that he gratefully closed the door behind him.

"You're angry with me, not your family. You didn't have to take off his head," Derek commented.

"Don't tell me how to behave with my family," she retorted.

Derek stared at her as if she was some sort of new strain of flu he'd discovered under his microscope and hadn't been able to categorize. "Is it just me, or have you always been this moody?"

Moody was a mild word for it. Her moods had been swinging back and forth with fair regularity like a pendulum gone amok.

Lifting her head regally, she swept past Derek to the door. "Just you."

Derek caught her arm just short of the doorway leading into the dining room and gave her a warning look.

"What?" she said in a semi stage whisper.

"We're supposed to appear happy for your grandmother, remember? She might suspect something's wrong if you look as if you'd rather have me served on that platter instead of the chicken."

"Don't tempt me." But he was right. At least about this. Leave it to him to show her up by thinking of her grandmother's best interests first.

Once, that would have made her very happy. Now it only added to her irritation.

She threw back her head, her hair flying over her shoulder, and smiled broadly. "How's this?"

In response, Derek placed two fingers at the corners of her mouth and gently pushed down, reducing the wide smile by several degrees. "Now it looks genuine."

"At least one of us is," she answered under her breath, tugging him along with her as she entered. "Hi, everybody, sorry we're late. Took us longer to settle in than I thought."

She saw her mother exchange glances with Alex. Only their eyes hinted at the uncertainty they felt. The conspiracy of silence had been agreed upon earlier. No one wanted to be the one to tell Nonna that not only was there trouble in paradise, but there was a full-fledged vacancy sign posted in front of it.

Toni looked around the windowless room and was instantly catapulted back to her childhood. This was the room she liked to sit in, hour after hour, and dream about a perfect home life. A life where her father had been content enough to remain with his wife and his family.

It smelled the same, she thought. Just ever so faintly of vanilla and the lemon polish that was religiously applied to the dining-room set that Nonna had brought with her from Palermo. And to the hutch her husband, Giuseppe, had built for her on their first wedding anniversary. Twenty years had passed before they'd had dishes that Nonna had deemed worthy to be put on display behind the glass.

Nonna was at the head of the table, where she had sat for as long as Toni could remember. She beamed when she saw them, and extended a hand to each. When they moved forward to take her hands, Nonna indicated the place settings on either side of her.

"Ah, now we can begin, you are here. You, Antoinette, shall sit by my right hand, next to my heart. And you, Derek," she said, turning crystal-clear blue eyes up to him, eyes that reminded Derek of Toni, "shall sit by my left."

The left side. Once believed to be the devil's side. "How appropriate," Toni murmured as she took her seat.

It was going to be, Derek thought, resigned, a very long Christmas vacation.

That evening felt as if it would never end. The children were in the dark as much as Nonna was regarding their true situation. Maintaining the pretense of being happily married and in love was even more wearing on Toni than she had expected, thanks to her present condition. She felt so emotional that she was afraid she was going to cry. And then there was Derek, touching her hand, smiling at her, giving a performance of a loving husband that was worthy of a De Niro. It made her want to cry more.

But she managed because it was for Nonna. Managed because she would rather have died than let Derek see her cry. The big dope would have thought it was over him, and she wasn't about to give him that satisfaction.

He certainly wasn't suffering. On the contrary, he looked as if he was enjoying himself. Derek was talking to her brothers and to everyone else as if there was nothing wrong, as if he still belonged in the bosom of this family that had taken him in unconditionally.

There had been one condition, she thought ruefully. That he'd remain faithful to her. And he'd broken that condition.

"What is wrong, Antoinette? You look sad," Nonna observed.

Toni rose from her perch on the heavily upholstered winged chair. "No, I'm just tired, Nonna. I think I'll go to bed."

Nonna nodded. "I am a selfish old woman, keeping you up after you have traveled so far. Forgive me." Before Toni could answer, Nonna had called to Derek.

"Come, take your wife to bed. She is tired and I am wearing her out even more."

Coming as summoned, Derek laughed softly. "That's because you're such a powerhouse." It was obvious that his words pleased her. He brushed a kiss to her cheek. "G'night, Nonna." He turned toward Toni and took her by the arm. "Let's go, 'wife.' I've been ordered to take you to bed."

"Don't get any ideas," she muttered between lips that were barely moving.

"You've got to teach me that trick," he commented. "Talking without moving your lips," he explained when she raised a quizzical brow. "Although that would be the sort of thing you'd pick up. You've already mastered talking every other way. In your sleep. In my sleep…" His voice trailed off.

Hearing them, Alex laughed, then sobered when he caught the look Toni shot him.

"Good night, Nonna." Toni kissed her other cheek. "I'll see you in the morning."

If I survive the night, she added silently as she allowed herself to be taken from the room.

Once out of sight, she yanked away her arm and preceded Derek up the stairs.

"Well, you certainly had fun tonight," she said frostily as she walked into the bedroom.

If it was an accusation, he remained oblivious to it. "Why not? I always liked your family. They're good people." He closed the door behind them. "Do they all know?"

The sounds of the rest of the house were sealed out. It felt as if the door to a tomb had been shut. She'd never exhibited signs of claustrophobia before now, but something very definitely was going on. Her palms were damp and there was a jittery feeling shimmying up and down her spine.

Maybe it was just another adverse reaction to being pregnant. But she doubted it.

She nodded. "Everyone knows. Except for the children. And, of course, Nonna."

"Of course," he echoed. He was glad that the job of telling Nonna the truth wasn't going to fall to him. He would hate to be the one to tell the sweet old woman that they hadn't been able to make a go of it. Especially when seeing them together seemed to make her so happy. "She's going to have to be told, you know."

She hated having him point out the obvious to her, as if she had no brain of her own. She had an excellent brain and it had gone to the same schools that his had. "I know. Do you think I'm a child?"

He turned away from her, determined to get ready for bed without any incident. "I take the fifth." He closed the bathroom door behind him.

Toni stared at the closed door. She blinked back angry tears. Nothing had changed. She was a fool to have hoped otherwise. Though he had broken her heart, she was still attracted to him. Desperately so.

But that was her own personal hell and she was going to have to navigate her way out of it, she thought ruefully. And she would.

Watching the closed door, Toni hurried into her oversize jersey. Only after it was on did she remember that Derek had been the one to give it to her. He'd probably take it as a sign of something.

Well, let him. She was wearing it because it was comfortable, nothing more.

Frustrated, trapped and feeling increasingly more so, she crossed to the window and threw it open. Just beyond was the towering oak she used to talk to at night when she was growing up. Then it had comforted her. She wished it could be that easy now, to derive comfort from talking to a tree.

"Why are you opening a window?"

Toni jumped and swung around to see Derek crossing to her. He was wearing only a frayed pair of jeans that looked like a second skin. He was still the best-looking specimen of a man she'd ever seen.

He slid the window shut. "It's forty degrees outside and dropping."

Determined to have her way, she pulled it open again. Swinging around, she stood in front of the window, daring him to shut it. "It's stuffy in here."

"Is that a crack?" He didn't know whether to be annoyed or to laugh.

It was, but it would have been childish of her to say so. "It's an observation."

Derek began to reach around her to close the window again. With his arms on either side of her, he hesitated and looked into her eyes. Infuriating or not, he had to admit there was still chemistry there between them. That and heat. It was rapidly becoming the only warmth in the room.

"You're perspiring." He tried to lay his hand on her forehead, but Toni jerked her head back. "And you're flushed."

She didn't want him putting two and two together. "I told you, it's stuffy."

Derek backed off with a shrug. "Have it your way. If you want the window open, we can have the window open." He glanced at the four-poster. The one where, for lack of funds, they had spent their wedding night. It had turned out to be an excellent choice. "There are enough blankets on the bed to counteract the fact that you're turning this into a meat locker.''

Toni had to move quickly to get to the bed before he did. She positioned herself in front of it like a picketer daring him to cross the strike line. "There's only one bed.''

He was well aware of that. "Well, at least the stuffy room hasn't affected your eyesight." The next thing he knew, Toni had tossed a pillow and the comforter onto the floor. It was followed by the folded blanket that had been at the foot of the bed. "What are you doing?"

Toni turned down the remaining cover on the bed. "I'm not totally without feelings. I'm giving you the extra blanket you want."

"On the floor?"

His voice was low—she would have even said dangerous, except that she knew him. He didn't have a dangerous bone in his body. Only unfaithful ones. "It's where you're sleeping."

"Oh, no, I'm not." The charade had gone on far enough. He gathered up the blankets in his arms. "I'm not atoning for sins I haven't committed."

She swung around to face him, her eyes narrowing, pinning him. "How about atoning for sins you have committed?"

If he let go of the blankets he was holding, he wasn't sure if he could trust himself with her right now. His hold tightened. "The only sin I ever committed was falling in love with you."

Toni's mouth dropped open. For once in her life, he noted, she was speechless.

Derek released a ragged breath. He didn't want to get into a shouting match with her in her grandmother's house. He was tired and, besides, there was no point in it.

"All right, we'll compromise." He dropped the blankets and began to straighten them out on the floor. "We can each take the bed on alternate nights. Since she's your grandmother, you can have the first night."

"That's very big of you." She'd had absolutely no intention of letting him have the bed tonight. Or any night, for that matter. But for now, she pretended to go along with his suggestion.

Derek lay down and punched up his pillow. "Toni, if we're going to pretend to be happily married, you're going to have to stop gritting your teeth every time you say something to me."

Toni slid her legs into the bed. Derek tried not to notice the way her jersey hiked up her thigh just before it disappeared beneath the blanket.

"Maybe if everything you said didn't set my teeth on edge," Toni countered, pulling the blanket up to her chest, "I wouldn't grit them."

He'd promised himself that he wasn't going to say anything to her. The time for explanations had passed. She was supposed to have trusted him enough to hear his side of the story. Loved him enough not to even *have* to hear it. But she hadn't allowed him to say a single word in his own defense. She'd been too busy throwing tantrums and clothing.

Angry, stunned, unable to penetrate her wall of indignation, he'd resolved to just let it go. And he thought he had.

But during dinner, watching her laugh at something her brother had said to her, Derek had decided he really wanted to at least try to recapture the times they'd had. There had to be something he could do.

Yet, as soon as he'd made up his mind to search for that opening—that crack that would help him cement their two worlds together once more—she'd set him off again, incinerating his resolve and bringing his easygoing nature to a boil.

No one had ever made him angry, except Toni. And no one had ever made him feel as much as she had. But all that was behind them now.

Unwilling to argue any further, he turned his back to her and pulled up the covers. "Good night, Toni."

Toni was amazed. They were alone, with night stretching out before them like an endless black carpet—and he wasn't even going to try to explain himself to her?

Well, what did she expect? She'd been right in the first place. Right to throw him out, right to try to rip him out of her heart.

To try, but not to succeed.

She pulled the covers over her and huddled beneath them. The loneliness was not held at bay. It ate away at her.

"Good night, Derek," she murmured.

When he made no response, she assumed that he was asleep.

He could sleep, the jerk.

But she couldn't.

Toni lay awake, watching the moonlight filter through the gnarled branches of the oak tree and chase shadows in slow motion across the ceiling.

It seemed like hours before she finally dropped off into a fitful sleep that gave her no rest and filled her head with snatches of dreams she was destined not to remember when she woke up.

* * *

Toni peeled her eyes open as consciousness grabbed her. Pressing her lips together, she stifled a moan. She'd hoped it would be different today, but it wasn't. This morning hurtled up to greet her just like all the other mornings had ever since she'd hit her third month. It arrived with combat boots on, complete with a nausea so strong that it threatened to bring up whatever was still left in her stomach.

And, barring that, her quivering insides.

Toni felt subhuman. It wasn't even seven yet. Light was barely sweeping into the room, just touching lightly along the corners. And it was freezing, thanks to the window she'd insisted on leaving open.

Somehow, she thought, that was Derek's fault, too. Just as the nausea she was feeling was. His baby *would* make her feel nauseous. She knew plenty of women who had thrived in pregnancy. Both her sisters-in-law had made it seem like a piece of cake.

The thought of cake had her holding her mouth to forestall what felt like the inevitable.

She had to get to the bathroom. Eyeing Derek's sleeping form, Toni slid out of the bed. Her feet came in contact with the floor and she bit back a gasp of surprise. It felt like ice. Very quietly she stepped over Derek and padded across the floor to the bathroom. She was going to have to buy a pair of slippers for herself this afternoon, she thought ruefully.

If she lived.

Toni closed the bathroom door as softly as she was able, curtailing the impulse to hang on to it for support. She made it with no time to spare. Pooling to the black-and-white-tiled floor, with her fingers curled around the porcelain bowl, she felt her stomach rushing up to join with her mouth.

Toni had woken him up when she had stepped over him. He never slept very deeply, and the slight brush of her ankle along his bare arm had roused him. A hell of a lot more than he was happy about.

Derek lay there for a moment, staring at the closed door. Toni was probably getting an early start on the day, showering in hopes of getting out of there before he was up. That was fine with him. He wasn't sure just how much more of this playacting he could take. Not when he wanted to hold her. To make love with her.

But a man had his pride and his price. His was trust. And Toni didn't have any. He'd known when he married her that her trust was in short supply. He also knew the reason for her distrust of men as a species.

But he wasn't just any man, he was her husband. And Derek would have thought that would have counted for something.

He turned his head, listening. Was it his imagination, or—?

The next minute he sat up. It wasn't his imagination. That was Toni, being sick. He was sure of it.

She probably caught pneumonia because of the damn open window.

Pushing off the covers that had tangled about his legs, Derek rose and crossed to the window. He pulled at the sash, firmly shutting out the arctic breeze.

He heard her throwing up again. Derek knew he shouldn't let that concern him. So she was sick, so what? She wouldn't care if he was ill.

That was a moot point. He knocked lightly on the door. "Toni?"

She was too miserable to hear the light tapping on the door. There was nothing but an infernal buzzing in her head until his voice broke through.

"Toni, are you all right in there?"

Panting, she waited until she could draw breath again. "Couldn't be better."

Whatever was ailing her didn't seem to interfere with her sarcasm, he noticed. He was tempted to just walk away, but instead he remained where he was. "Are you sick?"

"No." She squeezed her eyes tight, wishing away the next wave. There was nothing to throw up, damn it. Why didn't this stop? "Yes." She relented. "Something I ate last night didn't agree with me."

Derek was in the bathroom before she could stop him—as if she had the strength.

"Don't you knock?"

"I did." Coming over, he squatted down beside her. Her skin was ghostly pale. "I thought our conversation through the door was an invitation to come in."

"Well, it wasn't." She didn't want him seeing her like this, but there wasn't anything she could do about it.

"What are you doing on the floor?"

Toni swallowed. Her throat felt as if it was lined with shards of glass. "Communing. What does it look like I'm doing?"

"Being sick."

Today's bout appeared to be over. Maybe. Toni held her hand out to him. "As long as you're here, you can help me up."

Rising, Derek took her hand and pulled her to her feet. Her body bumped against his. She was too miserable to feel anything, but he wasn't. And he did. Derek dismissed it just as quickly as it appeared.

He touched the back of his hand to her forehead.

Toni glared, weakly shifting her head to the side. "I

said it was something I ate. I'm a doctor. Shouldn't I know when I'm sick or not?''

She would probably argue with God, given half the chance. "Maybe not. Maybe that's why they say, 'Physician, heal thyself.'''

She was in no mood for his jokes. She marched out of the bathroom. "They had you in mind when they said it, not me.''

Sick or not sick, he'd had it up to here with her and her thrusts and parrying at him with a dull sword. "That's it. We're going to have this out once and for all.''

"No, we're not, we're going to get dressed, go downstairs and have...breakfast." Her momentum abruptly halted. "Excuse me.''

Pushing him out of the way, Toni ran into the bathroom again, slamming the door in her wake.

Chapter Four

"**Y**ou're pregnant, aren't you?"

Toni had harbored the slim hope that Derek would have left the room by the time she came out of the bathroom again. But he was right there, fully dressed and leaning against the wall beside the door, apparently waiting to grill her.

She didn't feel like being grilled.

Pushing past him, Toni refused to look at Derek's face. She knew if she did, he would detect the truth in her eyes, if not in her greenish pallor. Stubbornly she wanted to hang on to what she felt was her secret.

"No. I told you, I ate something that didn't agree with me."

Toni began rummaging through the closet for something to wear. She didn't see a single article of clothing on the hangers she ruthlessly shoved from one side to the other. All she could think about was Derek standing there behind her. He was dressed—why didn't he just go?

Had she always been this damn contrary, or was this something new? "As far as not agreeing with you, there's a lot of that going around." It frustrated him to address the back of her head, but every time he moved, so did she. She was blocking his moves like a veteran prizefighter. "But I ate the same things that you did. Why aren't I throwing up?"

Settling on a wine-colored jumper and a beige pullover sweater, Toni spared him a scathing look over her shoulder. "I don't know. Because you want to annoy me?" Why couldn't he just drop it?

"No," Derek answered patiently. "Because I'm not pregnant."

She tossed her clothing onto the rumpled bed, then, still avoiding his eyes, took out fresh underwear from the bottom drawer. "A man who's not pregnant. Now, there's a surprise."

He knew she was trying to make him give up and walk out. But this was too big to just walk away from. He'd already made up his mind that she was pregnant. It would explain not only the session in the bathroom but the mood swings and the changes in her complexion. He just wanted to hear her admit it so that the idea could gel in his mind.

"And you *are* pregnant."

And I am. Oh, God, I am. I'm pregnant with Casanova's baby. "An even bigger surprise," she retorted flippantly.

Derek caught her by the shoulders, unwilling to continue talking to a moving target. He could feel his heart hammering in his chest as he asked, "You are, aren't you?"

There was no use in avoiding it any longer. Besides, her mother was right. Derek would probably know soon enough. She'd be showing before she knew it. And in any event, this wasn't something she could keep from him if she continued communing with the toilet every morning.

"Yes," she shouted at him. "Yes, I'm pregnant. Happy now?"

Prepared or not, hearing the words said aloud stunned him. He was going to be a father, something he'd made his mind up years ago that he would never be. His hands slid numbly from her arms.

"I don't know," he answered honestly. He loved children, but one of his own? It was a huge emotional investment that up until this moment he didn't think he was prepared to make.

He was devastated, Toni thought. It was there, all over his face. Though she'd expected as much, disappointment skewered her.

Toni turned away under the pretext of looking for a hairbrush. Finding it, she dragged it through her hair. "Another surprise," she murmured bitterly to herself.

He watched her face in the mirror. "And what's that supposed to mean?"

Whirling on him, she threw the hairbrush on the bed. It bounced and landed on the floor.

"It means I know perfectly well that you don't want children." Her eyes, moist, blazed. "Well, you don't have to worry. I have no intention of asking you for anything. As far as I'm concerned, this is my baby, not yours." And she was going to manage just fine without him.

It wasn't easy, trying to overthrow a twenty-two-year-old philosophy in the space of a couple of seconds.

He concentrated, instead, on sparring with Toni. It was easier than trying to disentangle himself from the pain that the thought of fatherhood dredged up.

"I know it's the season for it, Toni, but as far as I know, there's been only one immaculate conception recorded." His eyes swept over her belly. It was still flat. The way she was throwing up, it was small wonder. She had to be—what—at least three months along by his estimate, if not more. Damn, when had it happened? They'd been so careful. "This is not a do-it-yourself project for one."

He let out a long breath as he ran his hand through his hair. Pregnant. Toni was pregnant. He felt as if he'd just dived out of an airplane and was still fumbling with his parachute while the earth was hurtling up at him at an incredible speed. "Pregnant. Wow. I thought you were practicing birth control."

"Obviously practice doesn't always make perfect." Toni bit her lower lip. "It failed." She looked for some small spark of happiness in his eyes and didn't find any. He looked like a deer captured in the headlights of an oncoming car. Toni turned away. "Nothing's changed."

How could she say that? "*Everything's* changed." He thought of her unfounded suspicions, of the jealousy that had led to their split. That she was still hanging on to. "Well, almost everything." He took a cleansing breath and made up his mind. "In light of this interesting turn, I think we'd better forget about the divorce."

No emotion, no joy, no nothing. She might as well have been talking to a tree.

Her eyes narrowed accusingly as she looked at him. "And you're making this decision all by yourself, thinking I'll just go along with it? What about what I think, what I want?''

Just who the hell did he think he was, some feudal lord who had the power of life and death over her? She wanted him to sweep her into his arms, to beg her forgiveness and swear on a stack of Bibles that it would never happen again. That he loved her beyond reason. She wanted him to be overjoyed about the baby. She might as well have been wishing for the moon.

''The divorce is on,'' she informed him just as he opened his mouth. ''What I had better forget about is you, right after New Year's.''

She could do that? Just like that? Derek was dumbfounded. Maybe they hadn't had the kind of relationship he'd thought after all. Maybe he'd just wished it into existence. But the presence of a child changed all the ground rules.

''Toni, this baby is mine. I have an obligation—''

No mention of love, just responsibility, she noted. He couldn't have chosen his wording more badly if he had tried. ''Take your 'obligations' and shove them, Dr. Warner. I don't want them.'' Scooping up her clothing from the bed, she drew herself up. ''*We* don't want them.''

Storming out, she marched into the hall and went directly to the tiny bathroom next to the twins' room. She fought back tears as she threw on her clothes.

Obligations.

Duty.

He made this baby sound like a stint in the marines. Well, damn it, who needed him? She didn't. She was going to get along without him just fine. It would just take a little adjusting.

She ran her fingers through her hair. The face in the

mirror was crying, she thought. Funny, she didn't remember shedding tears.

She jerked her head up in surprise at the sharp rap on the door. "Toni, are you all right?"

Jackie.

The trouble with having a big family all around you, Toni thought, splashing cold water on her face, was that there was always someone around even when you didn't want them to be.

Toni took a deep, fortifying breath before she opened the door. "I'm fine," she said a bit too cheerfully. "How did you know I was in here?"

"The nice part about having children is that they report everything they see. Sometimes it's something interesting." Jackie searched Toni's face. "Is there anything I can do?"

Toni pressed her lips together, afraid of saying anything, afraid her voice would crack. She shook her head.

Jackie knew better than to press. She hugged Toni and then stepped away. "Well, you know where to find me if you want to talk." She glanced toward Toni and Derek's room. Sympathy softened her expression. "I know you don't want to hear this, but I'm still hoping this'll work out between you. I always liked Derek," she confided.

"Yeah," Toni said under her breath as she walked away. "Me, too."

Until he had given her cause to feel otherwise.

Derek was already in the dining room when Toni entered. He was sitting beside Nonna. The only two in the room, they had their heads together and were laughing over something. Everyone else apparently was either sleeping in or had gone out already.

Toni felt her stomach tightening. The creep was probably bragging to Nonna how the pregnancy had been all his idea. It was Nonna's fondest wish.

But one look at her grandmother's face told her that Derek hadn't said anything about the baby. Well, maybe he wasn't such as creep after all.

Calming down, Toni smiled at Nonna as she sat down. There was a stack of freshly made pancakes on a warming tray, as well as waffles and a good-sized helping of scrambled eggs and toast. Annie had been here. Annie wasn't happy unless everyone was stuffed.

Toni's stomach twisted and threatened to lurch again. She settled on sipping a glass of orange juice and hoped it would remain where gravity placed it.

"Good morning, Nonna," she said. "How are you feeling today?"

Nonna's eyes sparkled. "I have my whole family around me, how should I feel? Absolutely wonderful." She inclined her head toward Derek. "I was just asking Derek what you two are doing today."

Avoiding each other like the plague. "Well, I think that Derek is going to be busy," Toni said brightly. She saw the bemused expression on his face and ignored it as she leaned toward Nonna. "But I want to take you shopping with me. I didn't have time to buy any gifts before I left and I could use your expert input."

Toni could remember going into town with Nonna when she was a little girl. It had been a wonderful adventure. At the time, "town" had been a faraway place. Now the town had turned into a city and had brought with it malls and a myriad of stores she knew her grandmother hadn't had the opportunity to frequent. Toni smiled. It was her turn to return the favor and make the introductions.

To Toni's surprise, Nonna shook her head. Placing a thin hand delicately to her chest, she looked at her granddaughter.

"All that noise, the crowds, it would be too much for me. But do not let me stop you from going." The bright eyes lost their somber look. "Although I think that in your condition, it would be better if Derek postponed his plans and went with you."

Toni's brows rose in surprise. He *had* told her. How *could* he? This was her surprise for Nonna. Incensed, she glared at him, but Derek only lifted his shoulders in innocence.

He did that well, she noted. But then, he'd had practice.

"Oh, Nonna, Derek spoiled my surprise for you." Though she tried to prevent it, it was hard keeping the disappointment out of her voice.

Nonna laughed softly, the smile crinkling up to the corners of her eyes. "No, he is an honorable man, your Derek." Nonna laid a frail hand over his. "He said nothing."

Confused, she looked at her grandmother. "I don't understand. If Derek didn't tell you, then how did you know?" Her mother knew, but Toni was certain she wouldn't have given it away.

"There is a look in your eyes, Antoinette. The same look that was in your mother's eyes each time she was carrying one of you." Nonna thought back fondly over the years. "And in the eyes of Anne and Jacqueline when they were with child. I am an old woman, Antoinette. I see things others do not. It is my reward for a long, hard life. So—" Nonna looked from Derek to her granddaughter, her eyes snapping eagerly "—when is the blessed event to take place?"

Toni had already counted off the days half a dozen times. "April."

Derek looked at her. Then she was five months pregnant. It had to have been that weekend they had gone to the convention together. It was the first vacation they had taken in years. That made the baby one hell of a souvenir.

Nonna clapped her hands together in anticipation. "A baby in the spring. It is a good time." Her smile widened, growing impish. "Any time is a good time to have a baby. Come." Spreading her arms wide, she beckoned to both of them. "Hug a happy old woman."

Rising, Toni allowed herself to be enfolded in the warm embrace that contained so many memories for her. There was a time when she had gotten lost in Nonna's hug. Now she was afraid of holding her too tightly, afraid of hurting her. She was such a fragile little lady.

A lump formed in Toni's throat. God, she hated this deception, hated the fact that she was making her grandmother so happy only to have to disappoint her in the long run.

Nonna cocked her head, studying Toni's face over Derek's shoulder as she embraced him in turn. "Tears of joy?"

Toni sniffed quietly. "I'm not crying," she whispered.

But Nonna knew otherwise. She looked into her granddaughter's eyes and saw. "Yes, you are," she said as Derek moved back.

He looked at Toni and she averted her face as best she could. Damn her stupidity for ever having called him.

"There are tears in your soul, my dear," Nonna was

saying. "This I see, too." Her smile was beatific. "Do not be afraid. Having children is the most wonderful miracle in the world. It is why we are all here. To love each other and create children out of that love."

Toni slanted a glance at Derek. "There are some who would disagree with you."

There was sadness in Nonna's voice as she answered. "Then they are fools."

"Yes," Toni agreed, looking at Derek directly. "They are."

He waited until she was beside him in the car. Being married to Toni had taught him to choose his moments. "I never said I didn't want children," he observed. "I just said not now."

That had been his response to the one time they had actually discussed it. He'd never told Toni the real reason he'd made his decision. It was rooted in the past, years before he'd met Toni, and was far too painful for him to go into. So he had shut it out, shut it out just the way his parents had shut out each other and him. As far as he knew, Toni had accepted his position.

"That was just an excuse," she noted. "Everything about you said 'not ever.' Whenever I even mentioned children, you brought the conversation around to your practice." It seemed that his practice was all-important to him. He was so devoted to the children he cared for, there was no space for any of his own. As the months passed, she found herself wanting children more and more, afraid that the time would come when she wouldn't be able to have them. "You made it sound as if having your days filled with children—other people's children—was enough for you."

With an eye on the road, he felt himself slipping into

yet another argument. They'd been together for almost two years before they had gotten married, and they hadn't argued at all. What was it about their marriage that had changed everything?

"I was struggling to put a practice together, remember? And we were still basically newlyweds."

A van pulled up beside them in the next lane. There was a Christmas tree strapped to the roof and, from what she could see, at least three children inside. That was what she wanted out of life, Toni thought. A Christmas tree on the roof of her car and a van full of love.

"We still are, for all the time you put into the marriage." She had put up with the long hours apart when they were both residents. But it was a surprise to find herself alone so much of the time even after he went into private practice.

He thought of the nights when he was the one to make dinner because she had to stay late at the lab. "And you weren't busy?"

She sighed, staring out the window. Winter had already been here twice over, leaving its calling card. Dirty snow was melting on the sides of the road. "This isn't going to get us anywhere."

No, it wasn't. And he wanted to get somewhere with her. Somewhere where there were no more arguments and things could be resolved easily. It was probably just a pipe dream on his part.

Finally she had to ask. "Look, why are you coming along with me?"

Because I want to be with you and I'm using any excuse I can. He was annoyed with himself. A man was supposed to have more pride than that. "Because Nonna asked me to, remember?"

That excuse would have lasted only long enough for

them to leave the house together. Once out the door, they could each have gone their separate ways. Why hadn't he? For that matter, she thought, why hadn't *she?* She had a car at her disposal, too.

But this wasn't about her, she reminded herself. It was about him. "Nonna wouldn't know if you had decided to go off on your own."

He thought of the future that loomed before him— unless something drastic happened. A future without Toni or the people he had come to regard as his own family.

"I'll be doing that soon enough." He spared her a glance as he drove into the parking structure. "Can't we just go shopping like two civilized people without crossing swords?"

"That would be assuming that you were civilized."

Pulling up the emergency brake, he threw up his hands in disgust. She was hopeless. "Why the hell do I even bother?"

"I don't know," she shouted back at him, "why do you bother?"

"Because I still love you, that's why!" he blurted out.

For a minute the air was knocked out of her. And then she recovered. He was lying. "You expect me to believe that?"

Suddenly he felt very tired. "I don't expect you to believe anything. That would take faith." He got out of the car and slammed the door behind him. "Something you don't have."

She scrambled out and hurried after him. "Oh, faith now, is it? Faith might have worked if I had been struck blind before walking into your office to see Sylvia hermetically sealed to your body."

He swung around so fast that she almost fell over. "All right, that does it." Grabbing her roughly by the arm, he pulled her over to the side and pinned her against a girder.

"What do you think you're doing?" she demanded. There were people around them, but they all seemed too intent on their destinations to take any notice of what was going on.

"You're going to listen to me."

Toni raised her chin. "I don't have to if I don't want to."

His eyes darkened. She'd never seen him like this before. "Oh, yes, you do. I'm not letting you go until I tell you what really happened."

She didn't want to hear any lies. There might be a chance that she would believe him—and set herself up for another fall. "I don't need any more gory details, and I saw what was happening."

"No, you didn't," he insisted. "You saw what you wanted to see."

"And what is that supposed to mean?" Was he going to tell her that she had imagined the whole thing? That Sylvia was only helping him with the filing?

It was all so tangled, he didn't know where to begin. Besides, she probably wouldn't listen, anyway. "Ever since we got married, it was like you were waiting for me to be unfaithful to you."

That wasn't true. It wasn't. Her eyes narrowed. "Didn't have to wait long, did I?"

It hurt to have her think so little of him. "Just because your father stepped out on your mother doesn't mean that I would."

Why was he talking as if this hadn't happened? It had. She had seen it. "But you did."

He let her go before he was tempted to shake sense into her. "Goddamn it, woman, what's the use? You know everything." He shook his head, swallowing a curse. "I swore to myself I wasn't going to bother trying to defend myself. You tried and found me guilty before the case ever came to court."

She blinked back the tears that burned her eyes. "That's because you were guilty. I walked in and she was all over you."

He looked at her. Didn't she hear what she was saying? "Yes, she was."

He'd admitted it. Finally. Why was there no triumph in that? Why did it feel as if someone had just let out all the air in her body? "So what are you yelling about?"

She didn't see. "*Sylvia* was all over *me*. *I* wasn't all over *her*. Get the difference?"

Semantics. It was just semantics. "There is no difference."

Derek began walking toward the mall entrance. He wasn't going to spell it out for her any more than he had. "Then there's no point in even talking to you."

She hurried after him. He was surrendering, giving up. Telling her she was right all along. Damn him, why didn't he show her she was wrong? Show her that she'd slipped into a parallel universe and had seen two different people, not her husband and her friend together.

He stopped at the door and stoically held it open for her. "You're not going with me?" she guessed.

"No, you wanted to do this by yourself, so go ahead." He glanced at his watch. "I'll meet you back here in two hours. Unless you need more time."

She hadn't the slightest idea what she was going to buy. Her mind felt numb. As numb as the rest of her.

"No, that should be enough." She looked toward the center of the mall. The store owners had put up a huge tree. She could see the lights glittering from here. Ordinarily, the sight would have warmed her. She was beginning to think that nothing would ever warm her again.

"I'll meet you by the tree in the center court." She pointed toward it.

He nodded absently and began walking away.

"What are you going to do while I'm shopping?" If she went after him, he'd take it as a sign of weakness. Strength was all she had left to her. That and a shred of pride.

He turned. "I thought I'd get some shopping of my own done."

She frowned. "It might look funny if we each give them individual gifts."

Derek walked back to her. "Why? Everyone but the kids and Nonna know. And I'm not so sure that Karen doesn't suspect." There had been something in the young girl's eyes when she'd looked at the two of them at dinner last night. "Kids can be sharp. Besides, since this is my last Christmas with your family, I'd like to do it right." She couldn't take that way from him.

"Suit yourself," she murmured. She had begun to turn away when she heard him mutter to himself.

"If I was suiting myself…"

She looked at him sharply. Perhaps even hopefully. "Yes?"

Shaking his head, he turned on his heel and walked away. "Never mind."

But she did, she thought. She minded very much.

It was hot.

There seemed to be three times as many people

packed into the mall as the stores were able to hold. The press of bodies had used up most of the air and heated what was left, making it uncomfortable.

Toni couldn't remember ever being this miserable when she was shopping. Especially Christmas shopping. It was something that normally gave her a great deal of joy, but today it seemed like an endless ordeal. She couldn't wait to get finished. As it was, she still had to get some things for her mother and Joe.

Joe was always so damn hard to shop for, she thought. He never really wanted anything she bought.

Not like Derek. Any gift she gave him had always pleased him. She'd seen several things today that made her think of him.

Almost everything made her think of Derek.

Where *was* he? She looked around at the meandering sea of faces that seemed to ebb and flow all around her. It was getting hotter by the minute and she didn't know how much longer she could stand here by the tree, waiting for him. She had to get some air, and soon.

Before...

The world shrank down to the size of a pin.

Chapter Five

Efficiency was second nature to him. Derek made the most of his time, buying all the gifts he needed in one of the four department stores that made up the cornerstones of the mall. All in all, it had taken him a little over an hour. That left him with roughly fifty minutes to kill.

He had no patience with window-shopping. That had been something he'd done with Toni when they'd first become serious. Window-shopping and dreaming about "someday" had been the only indulgence they could allow themselves or, for that matter, afford. Window-shopping now would just dredge up too many more memories.

Passing a small coffee shop, Derek decided to buy a cup of espresso. The extra caffeine might come in handy on the ride home.

He took his minuscule cup of double espresso and

sat down at the only table that was still unoccupied by harried holiday shoppers taking a break. From his vantage point, he had a view of the center of the mall and the tree, but only if he craned his neck. If he remembered to do that periodically, being able to spot Toni shouldn't be too difficult.

He glanced around at the milling crowds, taking stock of the people who were hurrying to take advantage of one last sale, or searching, at their wits' end, for the ideal gift. On the far side he could see a long, twisting line comprised of parents with children in tow, all queuing up for a visit with what appeared to be a very tired Santa Claus.

Someday he might be standing in a line like that, Derek mused, taking another sip of espresso. There'd be a son or daughter beside him, fidgeting impatiently, waiting to tell Santa what they hoped to find under the tree Christmas morning.

No, he amended, he wouldn't find himself in a long line like that. He'd be standing at the head of it, probably an hour before Santa himself was due to arrive. He liked to get things done early.

With luck, the baby would take after him. If it took after Toni, he or she would always be late. He smiled to himself. They might be late, but nobody would care because they'd be so damn appealing. Like Toni.

Sighing, he took another long sip and found he had almost drained the cup. He toyed with the idea of getting a refill. If he did, he'd probably be wired until New Year's.

Derek set down the cup and stared off into the crowd. There'd been so much love there between them. How could things have gone so wrong?

He'd known full well that there'd been a strike

against him going into the marriage. A strike that was there through no fault of his own—he was a man, just like her father had been.

Open by nature, Toni had told him all about her father not long after they'd begun dating. She'd told him about how she had practically worshiped the ground he had walked on and how devastated she'd been when he had left the family, trading their love for the affections of a woman almost half his age. Derek could almost visualize her the way she'd been on her tenth birthday, waiting for her father to make good his promise to be there. And how she'd gone to bed, heartbroken that he hadn't.

It hadn't occurred to Derek then, though perhaps it should have, that she was waiting for him to disappoint her that way, to betray her love the same way her father had. The seed for her mistrust of relationships had been planted early and its roots went deep. Derek had thought that all he had to do was love her and everything would be all right.

He'd thought wrong.

She hadn't been suspicious of him, waiting for disappointment, until they'd gotten married. It was only after they'd exchanged vows formally that everything had begun to change. It was as if she was holding her breath, just waiting for him to do something wrong.

And then Sylvia had poured herself all over him, springing the trap. He hadn't seen it coming.

It had been after hours and Sylvia had volunteered to stay behind to input some patient data on the computer. He'd remained to explain a new office procedure he'd wanted to implement. Before he knew it, when he had turned around, Sylvia was undoing her uniform, intent on donning him in its place. Taken completely by surprise, he'd been trying to extricate himself from her embrace when Toni had walked into the office.

The rest, he mused, was history.

Looking back, he knew he'd been a blind fool to have left himself open like that. He'd known Sylvia had been attracted to him, but he'd shrugged it off. Although he'd found her attractive, too, he'd honestly never given her much thought. His heart and soul belonged to Toni. He'd never dream of violating their marriage vows.

This was something Toni wouldn't believe, even though it was a fact she should have inherently known. It was a given, like the sun coming up in the morning and snow falling in Buffalo in the winter.

He looked down at the dregs in the bottom of his cup. And now she was pregnant.

He still wasn't sure how to handle this newest piece of the equation. He'd never pictured himself as a father—not because he couldn't love a child, but because he could love one too much. He never wanted to go through what his parents had, what he had.

Apparently the choice had been taken out of his hands.

Derek frowned. With a sigh he moved aside the cup and saucer and glanced toward the tree. Well, wonder of wonders, Toni was actually there, waiting for him. Derek looked at his watch. Right on time. Now, that was a change.

Maybe pregnancy agreed with her. He thought of this morning. A small smile curved his mouth. And then again, maybe not.

Derek reached for the shopping bags and stood. He waved at Toni, but she didn't appear to see him. There was the oddest expression on her face. He could see it, even at this distance.

Uneasy, a sense of urgency prodding him, Derek shouldered aside several people who were in his way as he hurried toward Toni. He had almost reached her when he saw her face grow paler than the snow that was forecast for Christmas morning.

He had a bad feeling about this.

Quickening his step, he got to her just as Toni dropped what she was holding and went limp. Packages rained down from his hands as he grabbed her.

"Hey, somebody fainted."

"She okay, mister?"

"Nice catch, buddy."

"Do you want me to call 911?"

"There's a security guard around here somewhere."

Words buzzed around him like bees swarming around a hive as concerned shoppers clustered around them. Holding her against him with one arm, Derek opened Toni's coat and the two buttons on her blouse. Her face was drenched with perspiration.

"No, it's all right," he assured no one in particular, his eyes on Toni. "I'm a doctor and she's my wife." In the back of his mind he thought how comfortable the word felt on his tongue. As if it belonged. "It's just a little hot in here for her."

Lifting her up, he carried Toni over to a nearby bench. He was aware that several people had picked up their fallen packages and were following him. Glancing over his shoulder, he murmured, "Thanks," to a woman and two teenagers he assumed were her children.

The woman looked at Toni sympathetically. "Can we get you anything?" she asked Derek.

"No, she'll be all right." At least, he hoped so, but

his concern wasn't something he wanted to share with a stranger, no matter how helpful.

"I'd get her home," the woman advised. "Well, merry Christmas," she said as she herded her children back into the crowds.

"Merry Christmas," Derek echoed absently, his attention focused on Toni as she slumped against him on the bench. He had her head against his shoulder and she hadn't opened her eyes yet. Derek rubbed her hands. Maybe he should take her to the hospital. "Toni? Toni, can you hear me?"

Someone was calling her name. The voice floated to her across an abyss that was as black as the sea at midnight. A huge abyss that threatened to swallow her up. There was no bottom to it. She had to get across before she fell in. Before it was too late.

Too late. It was already too late.

Derek was gone.

Derek? The name throbbed in her temples. Where was he?

Where was she?

With effort, Toni fought her way back up to consciousness and then struggled to open her eyes. Her lids fluttered as she tried to focus. Toni squinted. The world was fuzzy, swimming in bright colors. There seemed to be lights everywhere. Lights and people.

Someone was talking to her, holding her. She was all right.

Safe. So safe.

The scent of cologne crept into her consciousness. Warm feelings slipped in with it, sensually nudging at her, making her long for the touch of his hand.

Derek's hand.

Her eyes flew open and she straightened, surprised

and confused. Toni looked around. The last thing she remembered was standing in front of the tree, waiting for Derek. What was she doing, sitting here with him holding her? She shook her head, trying to clear the cobwebs away. She couldn't remember.

Toni wet her lips. They felt incredibly dry. The rest of her felt incredibly damp. "What's going on?"

"You tell me," he said softly.

His arm remained around her, as if he was afraid that she would fall again if he took it away. For a moment Toni made no effort to move. She took a deep breath, attempting to reclaim her composure. And allowing herself to enjoy the safe, warm feeling that being in Derek's arms always generated. Just for a moment, the incident in his office had never happened. There'd been no Sylvia, no betrayal, no recriminations. Nothing. Only the two of them.

Concentrating, she tried to answer his question—and her own. "I was standing by the tree, waiting for you." The tree was now off to her right. How had that happened? "It was hot and noisy and then—nothing." Twisting, she looked at him in wonder. She'd fainted. That was it. Her mouth formed a small circle as she silently said, "Oh." And then wonder entered her eyes. "I thought fainting while you were pregnant was just an old wives' tale."

He laughed at the look on her face. "I guess that makes you an old wife." *Just not mine anymore.*

Gently Derek combed his fingers through her hair and pushed it away from her face. Her color was returning. There was nothing to worry about. He felt better.

"Feel up to going home, or do you want to sit here a little longer?"

He was being nice. But then, he'd always been nice, except for...

With effort she shut out the rest of the thought. She didn't want to dwell on that now.

Toni knew she should have said that she was fine, that she wanted to go home, but something within her resisted, seizing the tiny island of an opportunity she'd been afforded. She wanted to sit here in the haven of his arms for just a moment longer. To pretend that nothing had changed between them. That they were still the same two people who had silently vowed undying love while dancing to the Anniversary Waltz in her grandmother's backyard.

"Maybe just a minute more," she murmured.

The smile on his lips began deep within the core of his being and spun outward. "Fine." His arm tightened around her and he leaned his head against hers. "I'm not going anywhere."

She sighed, contentment licking at her from all sides. Memories burrowed their way forward. "Remember when we used to do this? Just sit and watch the world go by?"

It seemed like a hundred years ago instead of just a handful.

He laughed softly. "We did it because we couldn't afford to buy anything and were too broke for any other kind of entertainment." *Except one,* he added silently.

She felt the corners of her mouth curving. "Don't take the aura away. It was a nice time." And it had been. A very nice time. Why had it gone so wrong?

"Yes," he murmured. "It was. In a way, it was a lot simpler than it is now."

And he would have given anything to turn back the clock. To have never hired Sylvia in the first place. But that still didn't change the fact that Toni didn't trust him. With no precedent of his own, she didn't trust him. And that was the core of the problem. He needed that trust, given unconditionally, and she couldn't do it. If it hadn't been Sylvia who had triggered this schism, it would have been someone else.

Yes, things certainly weren't simple anymore. He was talking about the baby, Toni thought, and the impasse they were at. There was no turning back. What had happened had happened. And yet, moving forward was scary. Because she would be moving forward without him.

She turned her head slightly so that her eyes looked into his. "If things aren't simple, that's partly your fault."

"No," he countered quietly, so quietly that she could detect no anger, no hurt, "it's yours."

Business as usual, she thought. Toni tried to twist around in her seat, but he held her firmly, keeping her where she was.

"You're still pale," he reprimanded. "Sit here a few minutes longer."

She didn't feel weak anymore. Just sad. Sad for what they'd lost. "I don't seem to have a choice. You have a half nelson on me."

If she meant him to release her, he didn't make a move to obey. Instead, Derek leaned his head in closer to her. When he spoke, his breath glided along her ear, her cheek. As much as she wanted to tell herself that she no longer reacted to him, she knew she did. The chemistry between them was alive and well. Only everything else was gone.

"And while I have that on you," he said to her, "I want to tell you something." He felt her stiffening, but he maintained his hold. He had to get this out, if for no other reason than for his own peace of mind. "I want you to listen carefully, because I'm only going to say this once. I never did anything with Sylvia." Toni began to struggle to pull away, but he wouldn't let her. Not yet, not until he was finished. "She was the one who had unbuttoned her uniform—I didn't even see her doing it. And *she* threw herself at me bodily—like human flypaper. I guess she thought that if she could show me her 'charms,' I'd take it from there. Except that I didn't."

Derek loosened his hold sufficiently to allow her to turn and look at him. "What you saw when you walked in was Sylvia kissing me, not me kissing Sylvia. There is a difference."

So he had said. Deep in her heart Toni really did want to believe him. But she knew what she'd seen, and what Sylvia had told her. "Derek, I—"

"I'm not through yet," he warned quietly. "When I am, you can say what you want. But you're going to listen."

She folded her hands in her lap. "All right," she said stoically. "Go ahead."

"I fired Sylvia the next day." He'd spent a sleepless night in the doctor's lounge at the hospital after Toni had thrown him out. His first order of business when he'd arrived at the office was to terminate Sylvia. He'd been astonished that the woman had actually thought he would want to have anything to do with her after what she'd done. But then, he'd never been all that good at figuring out women. "And I haven't seen her since."

He didn't look as if he was lying, she thought. But then, her father hadn't, either, when he had made promises to her. Promises he didn't keep.

Besides, there was another reason not to believe Derek. "Sylvia came to me the next day," she told him. She saw the surprise in his eyes. Probably because he heard the nails going into his coffin. "She said that she'd never meant to hurt me but she couldn't help herself, that you'd been coming on to her all this time and that she was only human. She also said that you'd been having an affair with her for six months."

Derek could only stare at her. "And you believed her?"

Toni blinked, her lashes moist with tears she refused to shed. "There were all those nights when you came home late...."

She'd never really thought that he was with another woman until Sylvia had told her that he'd been with her. There had always been that nagging worry, but she had never allowed it to break free.

"I was working, Toni. Working." He couldn't believe that she was serious. "You could have had me paged anywhere and I would have called back immediately. An affair—my God, you thought that little of me that you took her word over mine?" Why was he surprised? "Hell, you let her talk to you, which was more than you let me do."

Toni stared down at her hands. Everything she'd been so sure of fell apart. "She sounded so sincere. She asked me to forgive her."

"She made it up." He emphasized each word. "All of it." Appalled, Derek looked into her eyes. "Don't you see, she said all that because she was trying to break us up. With you out of the picture, she probably thought that cleared the way for our having that affair you thought we were having. Or maybe she just wanted to get even with me for rejecting her." Sighing, he scrubbed his hand over his face. Maybe part of it had inadvertently been his fault. "Damn, it was all in front of me and I was too involved in my work to see any of the signs."

That much she believed, Toni thought. Derek had always been an innocent when it came to women. He never knew when other women were coming on to him. She'd seen it time and again in the hospital when they were residents together.

If then, then maybe…

She wasn't saying anything. He didn't know if that was a good sign or not. But that still didn't eliminate the real problem behind everything. Toni didn't trust him, and without trust there could be no foundation for a marriage.

He squared his shoulders. "Now you can believe me or not, but I wanted to tell you that."

Toni chewed on her lip. "And you haven't seen her since?"

Derek shook his head. "She left a few messages on my machine, but I've never returned them." He laughed shortly. It amazed him how far Sylvia was willing to go without any encouragement on his part. "She even said she'd go to Africa with me."

"Africa," Toni echoed. "Why would she say something like that?"

That's right, she didn't know. Except for the phone call earlier in the week, they hadn't spoken to each other in two months.

"Because I've been offered a position to oversee a clinic there." He saw the surprise wash over Toni's face. Was she glad? he wondered. "You know how I feel about working with children. They have a serious need for doctors in so many regions there." When the offer had come in, it had seemed like the perfect solution for him. To get lost in work he believed was important. But that was before he'd found out he was going to be a father.

And before he'd kissed her again and discovered that he would never be over her, no matter what he had hoped to the contrary.

She didn't understand. "But your practice, all that time you spent building it up." She couldn't help the accusation that entered her voice. "Time you took away from us."

He was guilty of that, Derek thought, of taking time away from developing their marriage. But that was because he'd naively thought their marriage was already built and would remain solid. How was he to have known that he was wrong?

Derek shrugged. "Somehow, the practice didn't matter that much after we broke up." He tried to put his feelings into words. At least, the feelings he'd had when he'd made his decision. "Being one of the doctors you can find in the Yellow Pages doesn't make as much of a difference as being the only doctor for a few hundred miles." He'd already flown there once to look the area over and had been appalled by the need he saw there. He was only one man, but he could make a difference.

She knew that tone, knew what it meant. "Then you've made up your mind?"

Slowly he began to gather together their shopping bags. He shrugged in response to her question. "I told them I'd give them my decision right after I got back from my vacation."

"But you're saying yes."

Derek looked at her. She was all but telling him to

take it. His expression was solemn. There was no hope for them, he thought. "I'm saying yes."

She pressed her lips together to keep the protest from emerging. It was his life, not hers any longer. And his decision to make. It would certainly make things simpler, not having him around.

So why did she feel so awful?

For both their sakes Toni tried to sound cheerful. "It's probably for the best." They had only two weeks left—less, really. They shouldn't waste it bickering. "Look, I know I've been kind of waspish up to now—" When he laughed, she stopped. "What?"

"It's the first time I've ever heard you understate something."

She opened her mouth to protest, then thought better of it. He was right. "All right, a lot waspish. But in light of everything, maybe we should call a truce. Just for the holidays?" she added when he didn't say anything immediately.

"I'd like that." Derek rose to his feet. "You know, I never did like arguing with you." That was *his* understatement for the day.

Shifting the shopping bags so that they were all around one wrist, Derek extended his other hand to her.

Their eyes met and held for a moment. Regret filled her. Regret for time lost, both in the past and to come. And then a small smile crept along her lips. She wrapped her fingers around his hand and stood. They had now. An isolated now. And that would have to do. She could pretend that nothing else mattered.

Taking a step, she felt a little wobbly, but not nearly as wobbly as his news made her. He was leaving. Maybe for good. Forever. Loneliness stood on tiptoes, hovering over the perimeter of her world, threatening to swallow her up. Just like the abyss she'd thought herself on the edge of earlier when she'd fainted. Worse. Somehow, his leaving for Africa brought everything else into focus. It would really be over between them.

It was the way she had wanted it and yet now, with reality facing her, she found the thought incredibly saddening.

He saw the strange expression on her face when she looked at him. Was she going to faint again? "What's the matter, do you want to stay here a while longer?" He nodded toward the bench.

"No, I think we should go home."

"Then home it is." Slipping his arm around her shoulders, he guided her toward the parking structure, taking care to walk slowly.

And Toni pretended that it was last year, when everything was still right in her world.

Chapter Six

Toni glanced toward the curb as Derek pulled the car up into the driveway. The other cars were back. Alex and Joe must have made an early day of it driving back from the city, she mused. The extra-long trips were putting her brothers out, but she knew that they would do anything for Nonna. The holidays had always been a special time for all of them, a time to pull together, to count their blessings and renew their strengths.

It was, she thought as she opened the door, a pretty terrific family.

Derek put his hand out to help her from the car. "What are you smiling about?"

She took his hand without thinking. "It's Christmas. I like to smile."

"Good enough." He slipped a hand around her back, guiding her toward the house.

She looked over her shoulder at the car. "What about the packages?"

He fished out the key Nonna had given him when he'd first married Toni. *"You are family now,"* she'd told him. *"And you may come and go as you please. This is your house, too."* But not much longer, he thought.

"Later." Derek unlocked the front door. "When I'm sure there aren't any questing little eyes around."

She hadn't thought of that. Karen might not peek, but Dustin and the twins would. Toni gave Derek his due. "You're pretty good."

"I always said that." Derek pushed the door open.

Any reply she might have made was swallowed up, as were they. Everyone, it seemed, was waiting in ambush for them.

Jackie threw her arms around Toni and squeezed, then turned toward Derek and hugged him. Toni and Derek exchanged mystified looks.

"What?" Toni looked around for a clue to this demonstration. She met her mother's eyes. Josephine D'Angelo shrugged broadly, casting off any blame that Toni might want to lay at her door.

Alex supplied the answer. He clapped Derek heartily on the back as soon as Jackie moved aside to clear the way. "Nonna told us."

There was no need to ask what. This was the same kind of excitement Toni had witnessed when she'd been told that each of her brothers' wives was pregnant. Now she was on the receiving end, and what should have been an elated moment for her wasn't.

She glanced at Derek to see his reaction to the reception. He looked pleased, but he could have just been playacting again for Nonna's sake.

"Hey, I think it's wonderful," Joe declared. He grinned at his sister from across the room. "Welcome to the sleepless set." Flanked by his own two, he tousled their hair.

Dustin laughed in response and feigned a punch to his father's midsection. Karen pulled away, smoothing her hair and looking at her father with huge, accusing eyes. This was something new for him, but Joe was adjusting as best as he could to the loss of his tomboy. Karen had discovered boys in a whole new light this past school semester.

Joe raised a hand in mock surrender. "Sorry, I forgot." He mimicked a high pitched voice. "Don't touch the hair."

The others laughed. Karen said nothing. Instead, she withdrew to the corner of the sofa in the living room, pulling her legs up and tucking them under her. To Toni it looked as if Karen was trying to make herself as small as possible. Her effervescent personality seemed to have disappeared.

But this wasn't the time to wonder about that, not when Annie was embracing her. "So," her sister-in-law whispered against her ear, "does this mean...?" There was a hopeful note in Annie's voice.

"I don't know what it means," Toni whispered back.

She knew Annie was hoping that this meant the end of any talk about divorce, but it wasn't as simple as that. Not for either of them, she thought, looking at Derek. He'd mouthed a few words about responsibility, but had swallowed them quickly enough when she had cut him short. To her, that indicated that he felt nothing had changed between them. All systems were go, all trains were to continue along the tracks they were running.

And on top of that, he was leaving for Africa. That pretty much settled it.

"What it means," Nonna said in a loud voice, surprising both women, neither of whom thought anyone had overheard the exchange, "is that this is going to be the best Christmas I have ever had."

Guilt pricked at Toni and she looked at Derek. They were living a lie, actively perpetuating it, and even though it was for the best of reasons, there would be consequences to pay. Not the least of which would be Nonna's broken heart if they continued to lead her down this primrose path.

She couldn't deal with this, as well. Toni wet her lips. "Nonna—"

She was going to tell her, Derek thought. He could see it in her eyes. And it would serve no purpose but to clear her conscience while ruining what could possibly be Nonna's last Christmas, as well as throwing a damper on everyone else's.

He couldn't let her do that.

Derek shut her up the fastest way he knew how. Taking her arm, he turned her away from Nonna and kissed her. It was almost a spontaneous reaction, done with little thought on his part.

It resulted in spontaneous combustion.

Whatever altruistic reasons he might have fooled himself into thinking had prompted him to do it, he was kissing her not for Nonna, not for family harmony or world peace, but for himself. Because he'd missed kissing her, missed holding her.

Missed loving her.

Toni was vaguely aware of her head dropping back as she let the kiss course through her body, lighting up each area it passed like a liquid volcanic torch. The heat worked its way down to her toes.

It was hard to remember what had made her leave him. Hard to remember that she was standing in the middle of the living room with her family all around her. Hard to remember anything at all except that she craved this sensation and wanted it to go on forever.

It didn't.

When he drew back, a smile curved the corners of his mouth, as if he knew the exact effect he had on her. She was so dazed, for the moment she didn't care.

"Sorry," Derek apologized. "Just got caught up in the spirit of the moment."

Jackie glanced at Alex. "Try sending some of that spirit this way."

"As I say," Nonna repeated, her eyes shining, "the best Christmas ever."

"It's not much of a Christmas without a tree, Nonna," Dustin observed.

Nik and Zak surrounded her, each hanging on to an arm of the chair like monkeys suspended in flight.

"Yeah, how come we don't have a tree yet, Nonna?" Nik asked. "Is Santa going to bring it?"

Zak leaned over and bopped his brother on the head with his closed fist. Nik wailed.

"He doesn't bring trees, dork. Santa brings stuff to put *under* the tree. Everybody knows that, right, Uncle Derek?" He turned his face up to the man he considered the authority on everything.

"Technically, Santa can bring anything he wants to bring," Derek answered diplomatically.

"Yeah, but really—" Zak began. He'd hoped to be declared the winner in the argument, and nothing short of Derek's endorsement was going to satisfy him.

Nonna held up her hand. Instantly the twins released their separate holds on the chair's arms and sank to the floor, folding their legs beneath them. Peace had been declared.

Annie leaned over toward Toni. "I think she has a patent out on that hand. I pick mine up and the kids just go on squabbling. Maybe if I'm very good, she'll teach me how to do that."

Nonna smiled at Annie, but her attention was focused on the two boys at her feet. "Santa is not bringing the tree, boys. Derek and Antoinette are. This is their year to choose it. Unless you do not feel up to it." Nonna raised a delicate brow in Toni's direction.

Their year. Toni bit her lip. They all took turns selecting a tree. It was a tradition Nonna had begun years ago. This year the duty fell to them. How could she have forgotten that?

Derek shook his head. Toni probably wanted to lie down, not go traipsing around looking for a Christmas tree. He could handle this alone.

"Toni's not—"

"—going to be left behind," Toni assured her grandmother quickly, cutting Derek short. All he had to do was hint that she'd fainted and Nonna and her mother would probably bundle her off to bed like some fragile china doll. Her eyes warned him not to say anything. Elbowing Derek aside, she crossed to Nonna. "Of course I'd love to pick out the tree. I've been looking forward to this all year. Just give me a few minutes to catch my breath and change." She looked pointedly at Derek as she left the room. "Wait for me."

He spread his hands obligingly. "All of my life, apparently." Toni said something under her breath he didn't catch. He laughed as he turned away. Nonna was slowly rising to her feet.

He crossed to her quickly and gently took an elbow. Alex positioned himself on her other side.

"What kind of a tree did you have in mind, Nonna?" Derek asked.

Nonna looked into the center of the room, by the fireplace, where fifty Christmas trees had stood before. "A beautiful one." Slowly she looked from Alex to Derek. "Like my family. Big, bright, cheery—and wonderful." Then, with a small movement of her shoulders, she shrugged them both off and leaned forward on her cane, a dowager queen reclaiming her dignity.

"That's a tall order. It isn't going to be easy," Derek teased.

She turned to look at him. "It never is," she told him quietly. "But the work is worth it. Joe, come, I need to talk with you." Her grandson was at her side before she finished her sentence.

Derek could have sworn she winked at him just before she withdrew from the room.

She knows, Derek thought as he followed Alex into the kitchen, but he couldn't ask without giving everything away.

Alex sat down at the tiled island in the center of the kitchen, the last bit of renovation his grandfather had completed before he died. He reached for the coffeepot.

Derek nodded toward the living room. "That's one cagey little old lady."

Alex nodded. "Keeps us on our toes." Silently he indicated the coffeepot. Derek thought of the espresso he'd already consumed, then decided that a little more couldn't hurt. He took a mug off one of the pegs that lined the wall beside the towel rack and offered it to Alex.

Alex filled it to the rim, then topped off his own mug. There was a plate in the center of the island, piled high with seven different kinds of cookies. Alex took two. Breaking the first in half, he eyed Derek as he ate. "So, does this news change anything?"

Sitting down beside him, Derek slanted a look at Alex. "You mean between us? No offense, but—"

Humor curved Alex's mouth. "It's none of my business?" he guessed. Setting down his mug, he shook his head. "Sorry, partner. What affects one of us affects all of us. You got a package deal when you married Toni." Most men would say that the arrangement ended when a divorce took effect. But that was no longer the case. "Now that you're having a baby together, we stay in the bargain even though a judge might say some mumbo jumbo over you, dissolving the 'contract' between you."

Derek laughed and shook his head. It was a hell of a way for a public official to regard the law.

"You people always jump in and finish sentences." Toni was the worst offender, but her brothers weren't far behind. "I was going to say that any changes are up to your sister." He paused, debating. Oh, what the hell—they were, as Alex had pointed out, family, and he was as close to Joe and Alex as he was to any man. "You know the details behind the split?"

Alex shook his head. "No."

"I'm surprised." Derek was more than surprised. He was amazed. "She talks about everything."

"Not about this." Alex finished the cookie and began on the next one. "I got the impression that she was hurt." He watched Derek's face. "Really hurt."

Derek laughed shortly, but there was no humor in the sound. "She wasn't the only one." He turned on the stool to face Alex. "Condensed version of the story is that she walked in on me and what she thought was an amorous tryst with my nurse."

Alex prided himself on being able to tell when he was being lied to. He studied Derek's face. "And was it?"

"No." The mug met the counter a little briskly. "I've got Toni—or I had her," Derek amended. "Why would I have gone after something else?"

"I dunno." Broad shoulders rose and fell in a vague shrug. "Some guys stray." He sipped his coffee, still watching Derek's face. "It's a hobby."

"Well, it's not mine," Derek affirmed shortly. He realized that the man beside him wasn't sitting in judgment, he was just vocalizing thoughts. Derek blew out a breath, struggling to control the frustration he felt. "All I ever wanted was Toni."

Alex believed him. And pitied him. He'd been on the wrong side of Toni's wrath more than once and it wasn't a pretty thing. "So what happened?"

"She wouldn't let me explain. And the more I thought about it, the angrier I got that she even had to have me explain." He looked to see if Alex understood what he was trying to say.

Alex cocked his head. "Come again?"

Derek drained his mug and set it down again. He tried to put it in terms Alex could relate to. "Don't you feel that there are some things that Jackie should just take on faith? That she should trust you, even if there's damaging evidence to the contrary?"

The man didn't know Jackie. She might look easygoing, but she was volatile. Alex arched a brow. "How damaging?"

"The woman's uniform was hanging open. She'd undone most of the buttons and was trying to take it off."

"Oh, boy." He enunciated the words slowly. Alex could just picture Toni's reaction. "And you?"

"I was just trying to take *her* off." Derek shook his head, remembering. "It was like trying to remove a five-and-a-half-foot strip of adhesive tape."

"Boy, some guys have all the luck." He laughed, then sobered when he saw the expression on Derek's face. "Sorry." He leaned forward, cupping his mug. "So Toni wouldn't let you explain?"

"Not a word. After a while I gave up. If you don't have trust, then there's no marriage." It sounded right, *was* right, he told himself. But it still didn't help fill the emptiness he felt inside. The emptiness that having her in his life had once filled.

"Oh, I don't know. You could let the trust aspect develop slowly. A marriage can be built on other things." Alex gave up trying to be good and picked up a third cookie. "From where I stand, there's a lot of flash and fire between you." A blind man could have seen that in the living room.

Flash and fire, an apt description. "That, my friend, is from the gunfire."

A movement caught his eye and Derek turned on the stool. Toni was standing in the kitchen doorway. He wondered if she'd overheard anything.

Sliding off the stool, he took his mug to the sink. "Ready?" He tossed the question over his shoulder.

She nodded, crossing to the island. Eyeing the platter, she decided to play it safe for now. Her stomach had settled down and she didn't want anything setting it off again.

"What are you two talking about?"

"Upcoming football scores," Alex said without batting an eye.

Not hardly. "There's no football game being played today."

"That's why it's upcoming," Alex countered, swallowing the last piece of his cookie. He took two more from the platter before getting off the stool. "I swear I love this house around the holidays," he told Derek. "I don't know how she does it, but Nonna has this spell over the plates so that there's always food on them, no matter how much you nibble."

"Or scarf," Toni corrected, her disapproval evident.

"Hey." Alex pretended to protest. "I'm a growing boy."

"Your sons are growing boys," Toni noted. "You are an expanding man." She bit her lip. "Want to come along?"

Alex was already backing away. "I told you how I feel about cross fire."

"We've called a temporary truce," she interjected quickly.

Alex looked from Derek to Toni. His grin was broad. "Yeah, I noticed you signing the peace treaty in the living room. You guys should be rated PG."

"And you should be rated Pea Brain." Toni sighed. "Never mind, I take back the invitation. C'mon, Derek, let's go while the pine trees still have needles."

Derek stopped her and hooked his arm through hers. She raised a questioning brow. "In case Nonna's watching," he explained.

She nodded. "Okay, for Nonna."

The sky had turned a grayish color, blending in with the clouds that hung heavily overhead. It looked as if it was going to snow any minute.

He held the car door open for Toni. "What kind are we getting?"

Toni waited until he'd rounded the hood and sat down behind the wheel. "The green kind."

He started the car. "No, I mean Scotch pine, Douglas fir, what?"

With four days left to Christmas, she doubted if there was much of a selection left. She shrugged in reply. "At this late date, whatever we can get."

They left the residential area behind them. Derek debated going left or right and chose left. "We could always get one in a department store."

She looked at him in surprise, trying to judge whether he was serious or not. "A fake one?"

If worse came to worst. "Yeah."

She sat back in her seat, adjusting the seat belt. "Heretic."

"Sorry, I lost my head." He shrugged. "It was just a thought."

When he was growing up there had always been the same tree for Christmas. A small, artificial one that stood atop the TV console. It went up the day before Christmas and came down on New Year's. Except for the year he turned twelve.

He pushed the memory away.

"It was a bad thought." Toni scanned the streets. "Keep your eyes peeled for a lot."

He glanced at her as he slowed down before the railroad crossing. The lights flashed as the barricade came down on either side. "I think I figured that part out."

Toni raised her voice as an Amtrak train rumbled past them. "What part haven't you figured out?"

"The rest of it, Toni. The rest of it."

The bars rose again. Derek stepped on the gas and the car swayed as it crossed the double row of tracks. "What's to figure out?" she said flippantly. "I'm having a baby and you're going to Africa."

He saw a lot on the next block and headed for it. "The two don't have anything to do with each other." Just making the light, Derek pulled up and parked in the street. "And you're not having the baby, we are."

Toni got out of the car. She smiled sweetly as she closed the door behind her. "Okay, when the labor pains get too much for me, you take over."

The lot was a fairly large one. And fairly empty. There were only a few trees left. All of them were marked down. A bored-looking salesman stood off to the side, nursing a thermos of something.

Derek looked at Toni. "If I could do that for you, I would."

Her eyes met his. She'd forgotten how green they were. And how they could look into her very soul. "You really mean that, don't you?"

He never said anything he didn't mean. He thought she knew that. "I never liked seeing you in pain."

"Then why...?" Her voice trailed off and she shook her head. This wasn't the time to start. "Never mind."

He caught her arm as she began to walk off in another direction. "No, finish it. Then why what?"

She pressed her lips together. The words had just come out. She hadn't meant to start something, not here. He was being nice to her. "We're having a truce, remember?"

He remembered, but apparently she didn't. This had

to be put to rest once and for all. "Finish it," he said evenly.

"All right." She told herself that it didn't bother her anymore to talk about it. But it did. A great deal. "Why did you let me think that you and Sylvia were having an affair?"

He stared at her and realized she was serious. If he lived to be a hundred, the workings of the female mind would remain a mystery to him. "I didn't *let* you think anything. You wouldn't let me talk. And besides—" He came to the heart of it all. "You should have known me well enough to know I would never be with another woman. I loved you, Toni."

Loved. Past tense. As in an action that was over. As in not anymore. Toni felt tears sting her eyes and she looked away.

Her voice dropped to a whisper. "It just looked—"

"Looked," he emphasized. "Not *was*." How many times was he going to have to point that out to her? He turned her to face him. "Where was your trust, Toni?"

There were reasons she'd thought what she had. Lots of them. "Any I had went out the window when Sylvia made her confession."

"She didn't make a confession, she made a fabrication. And why believe her and not me?" He wanted to know. She'd never answered that question, he realized. "She was just a friend, I was your husband."

For a second he looked hurt, and he made it sound as if she'd been a fool. Had she been? Was it her fault after all?

"I—"

He didn't want to hear any more excuses. "I'll tell you why. Because you'd been waiting for me to be just like your father. Well, I'm not, Toni. I'm me. A man who handed you his heart the very first time he saw you."

"You did?" She thought that she was the one who'd fallen like the proverbial ton of bricks and that he had been won over slowly.

"Yes."

She touched his arm, her voice soft, low. Apologetic. "I never knew."

He made a show of looking at a tree, to hide his emotions. "It's not the sort of thing a man takes out an ad in the newspaper about." He shook his head. There was absolutely no point in going over this. "Never mind. It's in the past." He turned his attention to another tree.

Toni followed him. "And in the present?"

He didn't want to discuss it anymore. "Is a tree we have to find before it gets too dark to make an intelligent choice." There were several clustered against a makeshift rope fence. He wandered over to them.

Each tree was sadder looking than the last. She smiled. "You remember our first tree?"

His mouth curved. "Oh, yeah. God, that thing looked pathetic."

That was what he'd said at the time. She'd preferred to describe it differently. "It needed love."

She'd always had her own way of seeing things. "It needed branches."

That was true. It had been three feet high and mournfully lopsided. "It was all we could afford." Her expression grew soft as she remembered. "A short, scrawny tree with popcorn chains and multicolored stickers pasted to the branches." Without realizing it, she had taken his arm and tucked herself into the space there. "They gleamed pretty well when they caught the light."

He liked her there, against him. For a moment he could even pretend that nothing had gone wrong between them. "As I remember, so did you. That's one of my favorite memories, you know—you, nude except for those three-inch heels, standing in front of the tree with the light from the candles gleaming along your skin."

She remembered that Christmas. All they'd had to give to each other was love. And they had given it freely. "Really? Your favorite?"

He smiled down into her face. "Really. My favorite."

Her breath caught in her throat. There was so much to say and no way to say it. "Derek—"

Derek roused himself. There was no point in falling into the same trap, no point in getting lost in the same eyes. Releasing her, he looked over her head at a tree.

"Hey, look at this one." Taking it away from its brethren, Derek shook the tree slightly, making the branches fan out. "What do you think?"

Disappointment pricked at her and she called herself an idiot. Pasting a smile on her face, Toni stepped back and surveyed the tree. It wasn't bad. And it was tall. That made up for other shortcomings. "She'll love it."

He nodded. "Sold." He looked around. They were the only ones on the lot. The salesman had disappeared. "Okay, find the guy so we can pay him and let's get out of here. I'm getting really cold."

She grinned. "Your blood's thinned out."

He wasn't about to argue. "Happens to the best of us. I can't wait to get back to your grandmother's house and warm up."

"By the fire?" They'd yet to light one. It was one of the traditions she loved best.

The look he gave her brought forth a myriad of memories she'd locked away. "Whatever it takes."

She let out a breath. "I'll go find the salesman."

Chapter Seven

"They got one!" Nik bellowed the announcement loud enough for his voice to carry to the second floor. "Aunt Toni and Uncle Derek got one! And boy, is it ever big!"

With a deftly boneless movement that could only belong to a seven-year-old, Nik bounced off the chair he'd dragged over to the window in his self-appointed position as sentry and went running for the front door.

Alerted, Zak scrambled off his stomach in the living room, abandoning the television set and the washed out tape of Christmas cartoons he'd been watching ad infinitum since Toni and Derek had left. Belatedly he tossed an invitation over his shoulder in case Karen had missed Nik's announcement.

"C'mon, Karen, let's go." He couldn't understand why she was still just sitting there on the sofa, paging through that dumb old magazine full of skinny, puckered ladies with big lips. "They've got the tree."

"So they've got the tree. Big deal." Karen shrugged, not even bothering to look up. She continued thumbing through the fashion magazine that didn't really hold her interest, although she was convinced that it was supposed to. "So what?"

"So what?" Zak whirled around to face his cousin, his hands fisted at his sides. "So what?" he echoed incredulously. "So that makes it Christmas." Frustration marked his round face. "So Santa can bring stuff now," he added, like a lawyer adding the final coda to his summation.

Annoyed, more with herself than with the pesky cousin she had to put up with for the next week and a half, she blew out a breath. "Shows what you know, midget. There is no—"

"Can it, Karen," Dustin ordered as he walked into the room.

Nik had halted a foot shy of the front door and was watching his cousins with huge, luminous eyes. Something important was going to be decided here. After all, Karen was the oldest and she knew things that they didn't.

Dustin gave his sister a disgusted look, then turned his attention to Nik and Zak. "That's okay, dorks," he affectionately assured them. "She's just in a bad mood 'cause we're all here and Billy Taylor's in Queens and she can't see him."

Her lethargy at an end, Karen jumped to her feet, tossing the magazine on the floor. "I am not!" she shouted.

"Are not what?"

Derek's question came out breathlessly as he entered

through the front door, his arms wrapped around the tree. It was over eight feet tall, perfect for the cathedral ceiling in the living room, not so perfect when it came to bringing it home. He'd just dragged it off the roof of the car and up the five steps into the house. Toni had tried to help, but he had ordered her away, struggling with the tree himself.

"We could hear you guys fighting all the way to the curb." He stopped in the foyer, dragging in air. "What's going on?"

"Nothing." With a toss of her head, Karen flounced out of the room, passing her uncle as she went. She didn't even spare him a glance.

Still holding the tree against him, Derek looked at Dustin for an explanation.

The lanky youth just shrugged. "She's worse than she ever was and man, that's saying a lot."

With Karen out of the room, he was the oldest of the cousins. Aware of the mantle, he assumed his duties and moved around the tree, surveying it with a critical eye. After scrutinizing it from all angles, he nodded his approval.

"Hey, man, not bad."

Derek mimicked Dustin's bobbing and weaving motions as best he could, encumbered by the tree. "Hey, man, thanks."

Taking no offense, Dustin grinned at him. "You sound funny."

"Yeah, well, so do you." Tilting it slightly forward, Derek righted the tree.

It wasn't a bad tree at that, he mused. He glanced around the branches at Toni and met her eyes. She smiled at him. They should have had a lot of moments like this, he thought. Derek felt cheated.

He turned his head toward the children. "One of you get the stand for this. My arms are breaking."

"I will, Uncle Derek," Nik volunteered.

"No, me," Zak cried, scrambling out of the room.

His brother was hot on his tail. "He asked me!" Nik yelled.

Alex laughed as he moved Toni aside and buried his hands in the branches. Taking a firm hold of the trunk, he helped Derek straighten the tree. "How come I can't get them to volunteer like that for me?"

Derek raised a brow in his direction. "How come you weren't around a few minutes ago to help me get the tree into the house?"

"Just lucky." Alex grinned. "Speaking of which, you two got pretty lucky this time. You don't usually find trees this full and symmetric this close to Christmas."

Toni raised her chin, slipping into the game they'd all played during their formative years. One-upmanship that nearly drove their mother crazy. "Looks better than last year's tree."

"Hey," Alex protested indignantly. "I picked last year's tree."

Toni grinned, looking, Derek thought, like a carefree young girl instead of a dedicated research physician. "Yes, I know."

"Your wife's getting pretty cocky," Alex commented before he realized his slip. As far as they were concerned, they weren't really married anymore. He shrugged ruefully, lowering his voice. "Guess I'm getting into the spirit of the thing."

"Which is a good thing." Derek nodded toward the doorway. "Here comes Nonna."

Drawn by the voices and the activity, Nonna made

her entrance, followed by Joe. Josephine followed a moment later to give the tree a once-over before dinner. She wiped her hands on her ever-present apron.

"I heard the boys," Nonna told Derek. "So, you have found one."

She looked tired, Toni thought with a pang. "I'm sorry, were you napping?"

"Napping?" With a wave of her hand, she dismissed the apology. "I was in the kitchen, supervising." She narrowed wispy brows over sharp blue eyes as she looked at Alex. "Your wife does not let me do anything. And yours—" she turned to Joe "—she takes over everything."

"A real D'Angelo," Joe agreed. He grinned, blameless. "Can't help it, Nonna, it's in the blood."

Alex peered out around the branches at his brother. "She's a Fenelli."

"They get it by proxy, right, Derek?" Joe turned to Derek for support.

Derek lifted one shoulder. The position of the tree didn't allow for any other movement. "Hey, don't look at me, I'm easygoing."

"Ha!" was Toni's spontaneous reaction to his comment. She pressed her lips together. This felt like old times. Like last Christmas and the year before, when they had come out to join the family and celebrate. With all her heart she wished things hadn't changed.

Nonna smiled to herself at the various snippets of conversation buzzing all around her. Leaning heavily on her cane, she moved forward to survey the tree. "It is a beautiful tree, is it not, Alexander?"

Alex pretended to shrug indifferently. "Oh, it's okay, I guess."

Toni took off her coat and draped it haphazardly over

the back of the sofa. It was beginning to feel too warm again. She didn't want to repeat this afternoon's incident. Not with a roomful of relatives who would instantly fuss and baby her.

The only one she wanted to fuss over her and baby her was Derek. But it was too late for that. Too much had been said that couldn't be taken back and there were just too many things in the way for them to get back together.

Blocking the thought, she shook off the melancholy feeling that threatened to overtake her. She looked at her brother with an air of superiority she'd developed years ago. She hadn't forgotten his comment about the tree.

"You are such a spoilsport."

Alex returned the volley easily. "Takes one to know one."

Derek blew out a breath. He was still standing in his coat and, while he'd been cold in the lot, he was definitely sweating now. He looked around at the others. "I hate to break up this scintillating exchange, but could one of you get the damn tree stand? Or are Alex and I supposed to hold this thing until Christmas morning?"

"Now, there's a thought," Toni mused.

"I've got it right here," Derek heard Jackie announce. The next minute he could see her entering the room, holding the battered red-and-green stand aloft. She was followed by the twins, who had postponed their squabbling in honor of the tree.

Next step, positioning. Derek looked toward Nonna. "Okay, where do you want it?"

Regally she pointed to the left. "Where it always stands, by the fireplace."

Derek braced his shoulders. "Alex?"

"Ready when you are."

Moving in synchronized harmony, they two-stepped the tree over to the fireplace. Hurrying before them, Josephine pulled away the chair that occupied the space the rest of the year.

His back to the fireplace, Derek was grateful there wasn't the roaring fire he'd fantasized about earlier. He was getting hotter by the minute. "Okay, get the stand in position."

Alex looked over his shoulder at Toni. "Kinda takes over, doesn't he?"

Toni laughed. She felt infinitely better than she had a few minutes ago. She pushed her sleeves up to her elbows.

"It's the doctor thing. It makes him feel closer to the holiday than he should." Her mouth curved as she caught Derek's eye. If there ever was a doctor who didn't have a God complex, it was Derek.

"Very funny," Derek remarked. "Joe, when Alex and I lift the tree, you get the stand in position and start tightening the screws."

Annie patted her husband's shoulder as he took the stand from Jackie. "He's good at putting the screws to things." Annie watched as Joe snaked under the tree. "That's what makes him a good cop."

"Oh, I just thought that's what makes him such a pain in the butt," Alex huffed as he lifted the tree up. "You done yet?"

Joe's voice drifted up from beneath the tree. "I could be if you and Derek held the damn thing straighter. It's in here lopsided."

"Wait, wait." Hands out before her like an artist framing a portrait, Toni stepped back to scrutinize the tree. "Alex, tilt it closer to Derek."

"Closer? I've got a mouthful of tree already," Derek protested.

Toni gave him a look that would have been spared to a man whose IQ rivaled that of string cheese. "Then close you mouth. Tilt it, Alex."

Crossing her arms before her, Annie inclined her head toward Jackie. "Kinda makes you wonder if there'd be a Brooklyn Bridge if these guys were in charge of building it, doesn't it?"

Jackie laughed. "Not me—I don't wonder. I know." She shook her head, contradicting Toni. "To the right, Alex."

Right now Derek was really grateful that Christmas came only once a year. "*Whose* right?" he wanted to know.

Annie cupped her mouth and coached, "The tree's."

"No, it's fine the way it is," Toni argued.

Joe looked toward the Greek chorus. All he could see of his wife, sister and sister-in-law were their feet. "Make up your minds. I don't want to stay down here all night. I've got a bad back."

Alex looked down at what he could make out of his brother's posterior. "You've got a bad attitude," he corrected.

"Children," Josephine called in a loud voice. She clapped her hands together three times to get their attention, the way she'd done when they were younger and the squabbles had been in earnest. When they turned toward her, resplendent in innocent looks, she smiled. "The tree is perfect, right, Ma?"

Content, Nonna nodded.

"Finally," Joe huffed. Quickly turning all four screws at the top of the stand, he secured the tree, then snaked his way back out again. Sitting on the floor, he glanced up. "Somebody get some water."

Nik was at his side, eager to do *something* ahead of his brother. "For the tree, Uncle Joe?"

"No, for me. That was thirsty work." Joe stood, then turned and saw Toni roll her eyes. "Well, it was. You try chasing bad guys all day and then come home to crawl around under a tree while half a dozen people argue which is the tree's right side."

"Aw, poor baby. I didn't know you suffered so." Standing on her toes, Toni brushed a kiss on her brother's cheek.

"Can we decorate it now, Mom, can we?" Zak hopped from foot to foot as he tugged on his mother's arm. Nik mirrored his actions, flanking Jackie on her other side. Even Dustin, who'd tried to maintain an aloof pose, was beginning to catch the fever. He slipped out of the room while the twins negotiated with their mother.

Jackie turned Zak in the direction of the dining room. "Maybe after dinner."

He twisted around, craning his neck at his mother. "Why not now?"

"Because," Derek interjected diplomatically, "we're all hungry." He was relieved to be finally shedding his coat. If he was lucky, he judged that he'd probably stop perspiring in about ten minutes.

"I'm not," Zak announced.

"Me, neither," Nik chimed in. Using their hands and pouty expressions, they held their mother prisoner literally and figuratively.

Alex came to his wife's rescue. "Then you can watch us eat." His words were met with a chorus of *aws*, which he ignored as he maneuvered his sons toward the bathroom. "Wash up, guys."

This added insult to injury. "But we're not dirty," Zak cried as he and his brother were herded out.

Jackie sighed, turning to Annie. "Everything's an argument with them these days."

"Just be glad you don't have a girl," Annie said.

She was smiling, but the look lacked conviction. There was something sad and bewildered in her eyes. Derek was surprised. He'd never heard Annie complaining about her daughter before. "Karen's a wonderful girl."

"Oh, I know she is." Annie was quick to agree. "But suddenly she's this little stranger I don't know. It's like she's crawled into this tiny space and I just can't find the door."

Derek slanted a glance toward Toni. The description could easily be applied to the way he felt about their relationship these days. There was a door between them that he couldn't unlock. And trust was the only key. A key that was missing.

"Want me to talk to her?" he offered. He hung his coat in the closet. "Sometimes an outsider can make headway where a parent can't."

Annie smiled. "Is that the concerned pediatrician in you speaking?"

Derek laughed and shook his head. "No, that's the concerned uncle. The pediatrician comes in handy if there's a medical condition to diagnose."

Her expression sobered. "Anything you can do..." Annie's voice trailed off.

Derek gave Annie's shoulder a squeeze. "No guarantees. But I can try. Where is Karen?"

"In her room," Dustin piped up as he walked in balancing three boxes of decorations. They tilted and fell, spilling their contents just as he reached the sofa. Dustin let out a sigh of relief as the balls dropped, unharmed, onto the cushions.

Annie leveled a reprimanding look at her son. "I thought we weren't decorating."

"Not yet." Dustin gave her a grin that would have made a first-class con artist proud. "But I just wanted to get the stuff ready."

"Now, if I could just get you to look at your homework that way."

"Aw, Mom," Dustin protested, embarrassed.

Derek crossed to the threshold. "When's dinner?" he asked Nonna.

"Whenever you are ready," Nonna assured him.

"Hey, Nonna," Toni teased, "you'd think that he was your favorite." She nodded at Derek's back.

"He is." She looked at the others in the room. "You are all my favorite." She inclined her head slightly. "Sometimes more favorite than at others, but all equal in the end."

The longer Nonna believed that all was right between her and Derek, the harder the news would be for her to take when she was finally told. Torn, Toni hesitated. "Nonna—"

"Come," Nonna requested as if she hadn't heard Toni start to say something. "You can help in the kitchen. Maybe you can convince your mother to let me stir my own sauce, eh?" She hooked a thin arm through Toni's. "Have I ever given you the recipe?"

Toni smiled. Maybe her confession could keep. At least until after dinner. "No."

"It is time that I did." She patted Toni's arm. "Soon

you will be cooking for three. There are things you should know, things I need to pass on to you.''

The idea of continuing a tradition always pleased her. Toni smiled. "Yes, Nonna." With Nonna at her side she followed her mother and sisters-in-law out.

He was winging this, Derek thought, and hoped he wouldn't make a mess of it. But the abject misery in both Karen's and Annie's eyes had goaded him on. Derek knocked on Karen's door.

"Go away." Karen's voice was muffled, as if her words were being deflected off a pillow. "I'm not hungry and I don't want to decorate the stupid tree."

She was covering all the bases, Derek thought. Resourceful. "Karen, it's Uncle Derek. Open the door."

Derek heard her scramble off the bed.

He immediately saw the telltale tracks of tear stains on her cheeks when she opened the door. The tracks were out of sync with the rest of her. Karen was a very pretty girl, with lively blue eyes and a torrent of dark hair.

This was what Toni had looked like as a girl, he thought. Joe had remarked on the resemblance more than once.

Right now she was looking at him warily. Derek left the door ajar. "Hi, kid, got a minute to talk?"

"I'm not a kid," Karen snapped, then bit her lip ruefully. She'd never snapped at him before.

"Sorry, my mistake," he amended. "You're not. Sometimes we get so caught up in day-to-day things, we don't notice the bigger picture." He nodded toward the bed. "Mind if I sit down?"

She shrugged, and he smiled at her. The first step was to rewin her trust. At least here he thought he had a good chance. "First time I saw you, you were so dirty that I didn't know if you were a boy or a girl."

She lifted a shoulder and let it fall. "Yeah, well…"

He could see he had injured her pride, and quickly backpedaled. "No trouble seeing the difference now, though. You've grown up into a very pretty young lady." He wasn't sure if he had chosen the right words. "Or is that politically incorrect to say these days?"

She shrugged again, less indifferently. A smile was creeping along her lips. "I dunno."

He studied her face. "Are you comfortable with these changes?"

"Huh?"

Derek began patiently. "Well, last year you were a tomboy who almost knocked the wind out of her brother playing touch football—"

"I *did* knock the wind out of him," she said indignantly.

Derek grinned. There was still some of the feisty little girl left. He would have been disappointed if there hadn't been. "I stand corrected. But this year you look as if you don't know if you should be doing that anymore."

Sitting down on the edge of the bed, she studied her feet. "I don't."

"It's okay to be both, you know," he said softly. "A girl and a tomboy. They're both parts of you."

It was as if a dam had broken open. Tears filled her eyes as she threw her arms around his neck. "Oh, Uncle Derek. I think I'm going crazy."

He stroked her hair, holding her to him and trying to calm her. "Why?"

She let out a deep breath. "There're all these feelings running around in me. I'm happy, I'm sad. I feel lonely for no reason.'' She turned her face up him. "Am I freaking out?"

"No." He suppressed a laugh, knowing it would hurt her feelings. Instead, he tried to look very serious. "Welcome to the adult world, Karen."

Consternation filled her eyes. "You mean it's always going to be like this?"

"No, it'll level off," he promised. "Right now your hormones are all scrambling around for position. Things'll get better for you. Trust me. These are all very natural, very common emotions to be feeling. It's okay to be confused." He read the question in her eyes. "And it's also okay to want to be a kid and a young woman at the same time. Each have their time. Your aunt still acts like a kid sometimes."

"Really?"

"Really." He squeezed her hand. "And if you want to play with the guys, that's okay, too. Plenty of time to be an adult. Believe me."

Sometimes, he mused, there was too much time. He'd grown up at twelve and had never been able to look back. He didn't want the same thing for Karen.

She let out a huge sigh, looking incredibly relieved, Then she looked up at him shyly. "Can I talk to you sometime, you know, if I get all mixed up again?"

She was going to be all right, he thought. "I'd be hurt if you didn't."

She bit her lower lip. "Even if you and Aunt Toni aren't—?"

He'd known she suspected. It was hard to keep a secret in this family. "Who told you that?"

She shook her head. "Nobody. I overheard Mom and Dad talking."

Having made headway, he wanted her to remain confident. "Listen, whatever happens between Aunt Toni and me doesn't change anything. I'll always be your uncle. Here." He tapped his heart. "Where it counts. Call me anytime." He took out his wallet and handed her a card.

She turned it over in her hand, reading the script written on it. It was the address and telephone number of his practice. She pointed to the last line. "What's that?"

"My beeper number. You can reach me with that anytime."

She stared at the card with awe, then raised her eyes to his face. "Anytime?"

"Anytime."

"Wow." She threw her arms around his neck again and kissed him. "You're the best, Uncle Derek."

He thought of Toni. "Too bad some others don't agree with you."

She was already woman enough to understand. "I can tell her," she volunteered. "I can tell Aunt Toni how neat you are...."

Some things couldn't be told. They had to be felt. "Thanks, kid, but—" He stopped.

Karen waved away the silence. "That's okay, you can call me kid if you want to."

He took it as a compliment. "Still not hungry?"

"Suddenly I am."

"Great, me too. Let's go. Nonna's holding dinner for us." Rising, he took her hand and they left the room together.

Chapter Eight

"How is it they have that much energy?"

Toni felt as if she was literally dragging herself up the stairs. Reaching the landing, she turned and waited for Derek. The past three hours had been spent in what her mother whimsically liked to refer to as organized chaos. Eleven people all trying to decorate the tree, getting in one another's way and having, she supposed, grinning, a really great time doing it. With Nonna supervising everything from her wing armchair.

Derek followed Toni down the hall. With an unconscious movement he passed his hand over his stomach. It ached. As per Alex's observation, there had seemed to be an endless supply of cookies to accompany the tree decoration. Everywhere he'd turned, there had been either a dish overflowing with some kind of confection or someone handing him yet another thing to nibble on. Immersed in the goings-on, and partners with Joe in untangling the twisted ropes that eventually became working Christmas lights, Derek had eaten without thinking.

It was payback time.

He felt that if he breathed in too deeply, he'd explode.

He noticed that Toni had prudently refrained from eating anything. The woman had more willpower than he would have guessed. And a hell of a lot more than he had. But she'd been raised with all this. For him, even now, it was still a novelty. His mother's idea of a treat was a bag of cookies that had been reduced in price because the shipment had been dropped and the cookies inside were smashed.

Toni really did look wiped out. He took an obvious guess at who she had been referring to. "I assume you were talking about the kids?"

"I think they could have gone on forever." Toni walked into the bedroom. It had seemed as if Dustin, Karen and the twins argued over where every single ball was to be hung, what branches the garland should be strung on and who would throw the tinsel and where. Her head still ached. Mentally she apologized to her mother for countless sibling squabbles in the past.

She looked around the room. The bed had been neatly made up and there was an extra pile of bedding at the foot. Her mother had been here.

Derek noted the additional blankets. Well, at least tonight he wouldn't be cold. With a philosophical shrug he picked up the bedding and began arranging it on the floor.

"Better get used to it," he advised Toni, glancing at her stomach. Part of him still couldn't believe that they were going to be parents. "Kids are born with energy and pretty much stay that way until they turn into us."

Which was a shame, because now would be the time when he could really use that extra energy. His days were always so long and yet he felt as if he didn't accomplish half of what he wanted to.

Toni took out her jersey from beneath the pillow. "What are you doing?"

With a snap of his wrists he spread out the sheet on top of the first blanket. "Making my bed, why?"

Toni kicked off her shoes and nudged them under the bed. She padded over to him. "It's the second night," she observed.

"In a long string of nights." All of them without her. He turned to look into her eyes. Without her shoes on, she came up to his shoulder. Perfect for wrapping his arms around. He had to hold himself in check not to give in to the desire that wove through him like a steely thread. There was no point in giving in to it. It would only make things worse. "Yes, I know."

She saw something in his eyes, something that made her pulse jump. Something that told her she was never going to be over him, no matter what she tried to make herself believe.

"It's your turn." Her mouth grew a little dry. "For the bed, I mean."

His mouth curved slowly, sensuously. "Are you being noble?"

Because she could easily be lost in his eyes, she looked away. "I'm playing by the rules."

"That's a new one," he murmured under his breath. He dropped a pillow into position. "Sorry, low blow." And that wasn't his style. He no longer knew what his style was, but he was fairly sure it didn't include being petty. "Okay, new rules. Seeing as how you're pregnant—" he gestured gallantly toward the four-poster "—you should have the bed."

She didn't want favors. What she wanted, she thought, was for the past two months, and what had led up to it, never to have occurred.

"You don't have to baby me."

He shrugged, picking up the last blanket. He arranged it for her. "Okay." He sat down on the bed, making himself comfortable. "You take the floor."

Toni glanced down at the bedroll he'd set up. She bit her lip just the way he'd seen Karen do when she'd been debating letting him in on her secret. It had to be a family trait, he mused, and on Toni, it was damn appealing. On Toni, anything was damn appealing. Except jealousy.

She gave in. "All right, maybe you can baby me just a little."

Because he couldn't help himself, he touched just the ends of her hair, his eyes caressing her face.

Here there were no excuses for touching her. Here he couldn't pretend that he was playacting for Nonna's sake. Here he couldn't pretend that he still loved her. Or pretend to pretend.

"I was under the impression," he told her softly, "that I already was."

It took her a second before she remembered to swallow. The very air stood still around her as her eyes held his. Was it going to be over? Was she going to be free of this horrible limbo she was existing in?

The limbo, she reminded herself, she'd entered under self-exile. "Meaning?"

Better not to start something that couldn't be ended.

He turned away. "Nothing, just a slip of the tongue. You can have the bathroom first."

She could remember when they did everything together. Sharing a tiny sink between them as they got ready in the morning, a tiny shower stall where showering together took more than twice as long but neither of them minded. With a nod of her head, she went in.

When she came out again, her hair pulled back in a red ribbon, the jersey flirting with the tops of her thighs, she looked like his fantasy come to life.

Swallowing an oath, he crossed to the bureau and took out the cutoffs he wore to bed.

Toni wrapped her hands around one of the posts on the bed. "You know, it's a four-poster."

He didn't turn around. The drawer shut with finality. "I'm aware of that."

Her voice sounded just a trifle high to her ear as she continued her thought. "There's no reason why we can't share it."

"Yes, there is." Cutoffs tucked under his arm, Derek looked at her over his shoulder. He told her the truth. He'd always told her the truth, even if she didn't believe it. "If we share that bed, I'm going to be tempted to make love with you, and neither one of us wants that."

"No," she agreed quietly, looking away. "We don't." Still holding on to the post, she slowly sank down on the bed as she watched him enter the bathroom.

Derek was out in a few minutes. He'd always been fast. She was the one who slowed him down, she mused. But they had enjoyed those times. A great deal.

"Why don't we want that?" she asked him.

He hung his jeans and shirt carefully over the back of the chair. "What?"

Feeling self-conscious, she tucked her legs under her on the bed. "What you said before, about—"

"Oh." Mentally he began searching for something to occupy his thoughts. Anything but the sight of her long limbs. "Because it would only complicate things for both of us and I think things are complicated enough with the divorce and the charade...."

He was telling her that he didn't want her. That a moment's thrill wasn't worth it. That there was only lust, not love, left.

Her voice became hard. "And you going to Africa."

He nodded at the addition. "And me going to Africa." He got down on the floor and slid in between the blankets. The sheet was cold against his bare legs and he shivered involuntarily. Lacing his fingers beneath his head, he shut his eyes.

She called herself a fool for not just shutting her mouth and going to sleep, but she couldn't help herself. Toni leaned over the side of the bed and looked down at him.

"Couldn't you just go to L.A.?"

His eyes opened, and he was surprised to be looking up into her face. "What?"

She lifted a shoulder and let it drop, hoping the gesture looked nonchalant. "There are plenty of people who can't afford medical care there. You don't have to fly halfway around the world to be charitable. It begins at home, you know. Charity."

"Yes, I know." Propping himself up on his elbows, Derek looked at her. How could anyone look so damn sexy in just a worn jersey? God, but she could still do it to him. Unravel him until there was nothing left. And she *had* left him with nothing, he reminded himself. He wasn't going to make that mistake again. He wasn't going to get so lost in her that he would ultimately be lost without her. "Maybe I need half a world between us."

She had no idea that hurt could spring up so instantly. Even when she'd discovered him with Sylvia it had taken a moment for the pain to sink in. Now the wound was immediate. And deep.

"You hate me that much?" she whispered.

He wanted to reach out to her. To take her into his arms and ease away the hurt look in her eyes. To tell her that he didn't hate her, but loved her. But that wasn't going to solve or change anything.

"No, I just hate the feeling you generated." He sat up. This was going to take a while. "When I came into the marriage, I knew, or thought I knew, what I was up against with that specter of your father between us. I thought all I had to do was just be me and that would erase any of your doubts." Talk about being an innocent fool—he certainly took the crown. "But being me wasn't enough."

The look in her eyes was defensive. She was up in arms again, he thought. And he was much too tired to fight this out now.

"And you don't think I had any cause whatsoever?"

He never wavered. "Not to condemn me without a hearing, no."

Was he so stubborn that he couldn't see it from her angle? That he couldn't understand her feelings, given what she'd seen?

"Let me get this straight. If you walked in on me and some man—some half-naked man," she elaborated, "was wound around me and I had my arms around him—"

If she was going to spin this story, she was going to

spin it right. "Around his hands, trying to pry them off," Derek corrected.

She blew out an impatient breath and continued as if she hadn't been interrupted with technicalities that hadn't struck her at the moment. "You would see that and just stand there, believing that I was an innocent victim of circumstance?"

"No."

Finally she'd gotten him to admit it. So what was he disputing? "Well—"

"I'd punch the bastard out for being all over my wife. Then I'd listen to your side of the story."

She laughed shortly. "Maybe I should have punched Sylvia out."

Leave it to her to miss the obvious. "Maybe you should have listened," he countered.

She didn't want to fight anymore. About anything. She just wanted her life back the way it had been. "Well, I did listen. And I forgive you."

His expression darkened. Why had he even bothered? Because he loved her, of course. But obviously that wasn't enough. Without her trust, this was a scenario they were doomed to repeat. He didn't want to keep looking over his shoulder, worrying that she would misconstrue something. It would wear away the love between them and leave only ashes.

"There's nothing to forgive."

Toni held up her hand, accepting blame. "Sorry, wrong word." She tried again. "I'll forget about it."

"But *I* won't. That's just the problem, Toni. I won't forget that you didn't trust me. If we can't have trust, what can we have?"

He was drawing away from her. Without moving a muscle, he was pulling away. And it was her fault. But she couldn't reach out for him. Not any more than she had. Because he still might slap her hand away. She couldn't handle that humiliation.

"A baby," she said quietly.

"A baby," he repeated. He'd almost forgotten about the small being they'd created. It made a grave difference in the outcome. "So what are you saying? That you want to give it another try for the baby's sake?"

She wasn't going to use a baby to get him back. Because then she'd never know why he was there. She'd never feel secure.

Suddenly Toni understood what he'd been saying to her. What he had to have felt.

Toni shook her head slowly. "No. I'm not."

He didn't understand. "Then what are you saying?"

It was too late to make amends, too late to fix anything. She was just going to have to accept that. "I'm saying good night." Lying down, Toni rolled over and pulled the covers up over herself.

At least it didn't feel like a meat locker in here tonight, Derek thought. He turned his back to her. Small compensation. It might not be cold in the room, but it was certainly frigid. The temperature had just dropped ten degrees.

Wrapping up in the blankets and cocooning himself like a caterpillar about to begin his metamorphosis, Derek closed his eyes and waited for sleep.

It was a long wait.

It occurred to him that a hundred years wasn't long enough to untangle the workings of the female mind and that Africa wasn't far enough away to go to escape what he was feeling.

He was always going to carry images of Toni in his

mind.

He figured it was his penance.

When the first strong stirrings of nausea woke her, Toni moaned and sat up. At least this morning she didn't have to try not to wake Derek. That was some consolation in his knowing about the situation.

Some, but not much.

With a sigh she looked down, feeling her stomach lurching. The bedding was gone from the floor. Looking around, she saw that the blankets and sheet were neatly folded on the chair where his clothes had been. The pillow was on top. Derek was the child her mother would have loved to have had, she thought. She and her brothers always left a mess in their wake, even now. This man got an A in neatness, but not much else.

Why hadn't he waited for her?

She covered her mouth, feeling tears forming as the spinning sensation went up another notch within her stomach.

Just as well, she thought, stumbling into the bathroom. She hated having Derek see her like this. She felt like something that had been dragged across the bottom of a parakeet cage and left there.

Toni sank to her knees. They came in contact with the cold, hard tile beside the bowl just as she felt a surge.

Almost five months pregnant and she'd barely gained an ounce. The way her clothes felt, she was afraid she might have lost a few in the bargain.

Finished—she hoped—Toni let out a shaky sigh and pulled herself up again. There had to be a better way to have a baby.

"Death warmed over, that's what you look like," she muttered to the bleary-eyed reflection that looked back at her over the sink. "No wonder he's running away. I would, too, if I saw this."

She shut out the thought—all thoughts—and showered. By the time she had dressed, she felt a little more human. Not much, but enough to join the rest of the world.

Voices, laughing and chatting, greeted her as she walked down the stairs. They were coming from the dining room. And from the sound of them, they were all female. Derek had to be somewhere else.

She felt a tad better not having to face him.

Day three of the deception, she thought. Toni squared her shoulders as she walked into the dining room.

Nonna was sitting at the head of the table, sipping her usual cup of cocoa. Toni felt her shoulders sag slightly. Derek was there, sitting with Annie, Jackie and her mother.

Holding court, Toni thought with a stab of bitterness.

No, that wasn't fair. He wasn't the type to bask in female attention. That had been her father. But back then she had been so pleased, so happy that so many people liked her father, it had never occurred to her to attach any significance to the fact that the preponderance of the crowd had been comprised of women. Women lavishing their attention on him, and her father absorbing it like someone who had an insatiable hunger.

She forced a smile to her lips. "Good morning, everybody."

A chorus of *good morning*s greeted her. Toni poured herself a cup of tea, hoped that it would stay down and took a seat on the far side of the table.

"Here, sit closer," Nonna urged, waving her forward. "My eyes are not as good as they used to be and I want to look at you while you and I are still together."

When Toni obliged, seating herself in the chair she'd occupied last night and the night before, Nonna peered at her face. "You are feeling better?"

"I wasn't sick," Toni protested. She shot Derek an accusing look. His expression remained impassive.

"You were pale," Nonna noted. And then she smiled. "But even now the color is returning." She glanced approvingly to her right. "Derek must be taking excellent care of you."

"Excellent," Toni agreed, forcing the smile back to her lips.

Annie couldn't wait to share the news. "Well, he certainly is taking excellent care of my life."

She was so happy, she didn't notice the sharp look that came into Toni's eyes.

But Derek did, and it just reinforced the conclusion he'd reached last night. Nothing was ever going to change. She would always be seeing offenses where there were none. He couldn't live that way.

But the problem was, something within him whispered, he couldn't live without her, either.

Toni looked from Annie to Derek. She hadn't the vaguest idea what Annie was talking about and right now she felt so miserable physically she wasn't sure that she cared.

Annie, sitting beside him, wrapped her arms around one of his. "Do you have any idea how wonderful this man of yours is?"

Annie had obviously forgotten about the divorce, Toni thought. Small wonder, with Derek touching her and kissing her at every opportunity that availed itself. And she...well, she was responding, which didn't help anything in the long run. They were not only fooling

Nonna, but apparently dragging everyone else into this make-believe world they were fashioning.

Including her.

Annie couldn't stop singing his praises. "He talked to Karen." She beamed at the others at the table. "And now Karen's talking. To me." She sighed happily. "I never knew how much I wanted to hear her say something that wasn't hostile to me. It was like waiting for her to say her first word all over again—except much more intelligible this time." She grinned as she squeezed Derek's arm again. "I don't know what you said to her, Derek, but she's my girl again and I have you to thank."

Displays of gratitude had always made him feel uncomfortable. Derek waved it off now.

"Just remember what it was like growing up," he advised. "Remember all the uncertainties you were harboring then."

Annie shook her head. "I didn't harbor any. I took one look at Joseph D'Angelo in the sixth grade and knew he was the one for me. From then on, it was one long campaign to get him to come to his senses and agree.

"I was too busy plotting and scheming to know I was going through any earthshaking changes." As she remembered those days, a dreamy look entered her eyes.

Toni felt a pang. She'd lost all that, given it up because she'd allowed demons from her past to color what she saw.

But it wasn't all her fault, she thought fiercely.

And then she realized it didn't matter whose fault it was—the end result was the same. They'd lost what they'd once had. She'd lost it for them.

"It wasn't that easy for me," Jackie was confiding to the others. "I was a mess. Growing up with three brothers, I had no privacy. When I started to—" She stopped abruptly, slanting a look at Derek. "Should we be talking about this around you?"

"Probably not," Derek said, laughing. He knew an exit cue when he heard one. Besides, the look on Toni's face was making him uncomfortable. It was sad and it made him long to comfort her.

But none of this had been his fault.

Josephine reached across the table, placing a hand on his arm to stop him. "Why not?" she asked the others. "He's a doctor. And the only one of us who got to the heart of Karen's problem."

It was clear Josephine wanted him to remain. Well, if he was staying, Toni thought, she was going. Right now it hurt too much to pretend that everything was just wonderful between them.

Nonna looked at her as she rose. "Antoinette, where are you going?"

Toni began to ease away from the table. "If you'll all excuse me, I still have some more shopping to do."

"But you did not eat your breakfast," Nonna observed.

"I'm not hungry." And if this miserable feeling in the pit of her stomach continued, she would never eat again. The baby was only partially responsible.

Nonna looked expectantly at Derek.

The lady was not subtle, he thought with a fond smile. "Wait, I'll go with you." He might as well, he thought. Besides, yesterday's incident might repeat itself if she went to the crowded mall. She shouldn't be alone.

Toni panicked. It felt as if the very walls were closing

in on her here, and even though she loved them all dearly, what she needed right now was space. "No, that's all right. You have other things to do."

Derek ignored the cue. If she was going to be stubborn, he was going to play dirty. "But what if you—?"

She looked at him sharply, warning him into silence. "I won't."

Annie quickly positioned herself between them. "Look, I've got a few things to get myself," she told Toni. "Why don't I go with you?"

Jackie was quick to pick up the thread. "Yeah, me, too." She linked her arm through Toni's. "We'll make a day of it."

Outmaneuvered and outnumbered, Toni nodded. At least Derek wasn't part of the number. "Sounds good to me," Toni said, trying to muster some feeling.

Chapter Nine

"My God, look at it coming down."

Annie's hands tightened on the steering wheel. The road had turned icy since they'd left the mall.

Jackie peered out through the side window at the snow that was falling relentlessly. The sky was obliterated and there seemed to be no end in sight.

"How could it have snowed so much in just three hours?" Jackie marveled.

"Four," Toni corrected.

"I don't know, but I wish it would let up." Annie squinted, trying to peer through the flakes. "I hate driving on slicked streets."

A red light gleamed up ahead. Annie barely stopped in time. Toni laid a hand on her shoulder. "Let me take over."

Annie let out the breath she was holding. The light

changed and she eased her foot onto the accelerator again. "Oh, right, the Californian."

Blindfolded she could drive better than Annie, Toni thought. "I've only been there for a couple of years. I haven't forgotten how to drive on icy streets."

Toni watched, almost hypnotized, as Annie slowly picked her way through the streets. Cars and an occasional pedestrian all seemed to be on the same mission—to get somewhere warm and dry to wait out this unexpected turn of the weather.

"Quiet," Annie instructed. She stared straight ahead. "You're making me nervous."

"Well, that's certainly reassuring to hear." Toni held onto the arms of her seat. Up ahead she saw a car spinning out. Annie slowed even more.

Annie glanced at Toni. "I thought the snow wasn't supposed to fall until Christmas morning."

"Someone obviously forgot to tell the snow. It's green." Toni pointed toward the traffic light. "You're doing fine, Annie, we're almost there." Ducking her head for a better view, Toni made out a street sign on the right. The familiar name made her sigh with relief. They were only three blocks from home. "Just make a right on the next block and we're practically there."

Eyes trained on the road, Annie inclined her head slightly. "Right."

Toni didn't understand why she was being so stubborn. "Annie, if you don't like driving in this, why won't you let one of us drive?"

Annie swallowed. "Because I like someone else driving even less."

Jackie leaned forward. "You let Joe drive every time you two are in the car together."

"That's different," Annie told her. "He's a husband. He's supposed to drive."

Jackie rolled her eyes at the archaic thinking. "Oh, puh—leez."

Only Toni saw the hint of a glimmer in Annie's eyes. It heartened her.

"Besides, why do you think having someone else drive makes me so nervous in the first place? Joe won't *let* anyone else drive. You'd have to pry the steering wheel out of his hands." Annie leaned forward. It looked as if there was someone standing in the middle of the street. Or was that just another stalled car? They'd already passed two of them on the way. No, that was a person. That was... "Toni, isn't that Derek in the street?"

Toni looked. As fast as the windshield wipers were moving, that was how quickly the view was obstructed. She had to concentrate to make out the figure.

But she would have known that stance anywhere.

"Yes." Derek was at the end of the block. He looked as if he was waiting for them. But why?

Unless...

Toni's heart felt as if it had stopped. She exchanged looks with Jackie before squinting through the windshield again. "Oh, God, I hope nothing's happened to Nonna. Drive faster, Annie."

"Then something'll happen to us," Annie retorted. But she eased down on the accelerator a little more. Holding her breath, she passed Derek and aimed the van for the curb.

Derek pivoted, turning around. He followed behind the van. Thank God they were back.

He'd lost track of how long he'd been standing out in the cold, waiting for her. Drawing his hand out of his coat pocket, he glanced at his watch. A little more than half an hour. They were supposed to have been gone for only a couple of hours. After four, unable to just sit there, he'd gone outside to wait.

And worry. Storm warnings had been upgraded twice before he'd gone out. What was supposed to have been a gentle snow flurry due two days from now had somehow managed to turn into a full-fledged blizzard within a matter of hours. The weather bureau's track record never ceased to amaze him.

But she was back, so everything was all right.

Everything but his fingers. They felt as if they were frozen solid. Shoving his hands into his pockets hadn't really helped. He wished he'd remembered to pack his gloves.

Toni was out of the van first, and ran back to meet him. "Is she all right?"

Snowflakes were alighting on her hair, contrasting with the raven color. Reminding him that the first time he had met her, it had been snowing, too. Her cheeks had been ruddy from the cold and there had been snowflakes on her lashes. He'd probably fallen in love that very moment.

"Is who all right?"

"Nonna."

Taking her arm, he turned her around and walked her back to the van. Annie had gotten out and Jackie was passing the packages down to her.

"Yeah, fine," Derek answered. "Why?"

Toni looked at him, bewildered. "Well, you're standing out here, turning into a snowman. I thought—why are you out here?" She shook her head, getting rid of the snow that was melting into her hair.

He shrugged and started picking up the packages on

the curb. They certainly knew how to spend money, he mused. "Just getting a breath of fresh air."

"Ha!" The observation came from Jackie. She passed down the large box, which contained the twins' new upgraded video game set. "The air isn't fresh, it's frozen solid. Why don't you just admit you were waiting for her and get it over with?"

There was a time Toni would have instantly believed that—would have thought of it herself. Now she wasn't so sure. "Were you?" she asked.

He helped Jackie down, ignoring her knowing smirk. "Yeah, maybe." Outnumbered by the women, he surrendered. "All right, yes, I was. This storm hit practically out of nowhere and they were issuing motorist advisory warnings. The road back from the mall was one of the ones they specifically mentioned was becoming impassable. I was worried. About *all* of you."

"Very sweet of you," Annie pronounced, kissing his cheek. She knew better. Toni had been the only one on his mind and so should it have been. She hoped her Joe was holed up somewhere with a hot cup of coffee and not traveling the roads, patrolling.

She looked at the pile of packages and then at the house. "Kids inside?" she asked Derek.

"No, they're out back, making snowballs and probably swallowing snowflakes." They had begged him to join them. He'd turned them down, wanting to be sure Toni was home before he gave them his undivided attention. "I'll take these in," he told Jackie and Annie, nodding at the packages. "You go on inside and warm up."

Jackie hesitated for a moment, then relented. "Talk about a great guy." Passing Toni, she inclined her head and said in a stage whisper, "If he's really back on the market, let me know. I think I just might put in a bid."

He was probably eating this up, Toni thought. "You're married to Alex."

"Exactly," Jackie murmured as she went inside.

Annie shrugged as Toni looked at her quizzically. Leaving Derek to cope with the shopping bags and packages, Toni quickly followed Jackie and Annie into the house.

This was going to take more than one trip, Derek decided. He looked at Toni's departing back. She could have stayed to help. Served him right for worrying, he thought.

Picking up as many bags as he could, he made his way slowly to the house.

Toni caught up with Jackie just inside the foyer. "Were you serious out there?"

Jackie laughed, waving away the question. "No, just kidding."

There was something in Jackie's voice that didn't ring true. "But something is wrong?"

Jackie shrugged out of her coat. "They call it the seven year itch."

"You've been married eight," Toni reminded her. Concern mounted. She'd always thought Alex and Jackie were great together. Was everything coming apart?

A small, self-deprecating smile appeared. "Yeah, but it started at seven." She hung the coat on the rack. "Don't get me wrong. Alex is still a great guy. And I'm wonderful," she added flippantly. "But together, well—I think the magic's gone."

Annie hung her coat next to Jackie's and slipped a

comforting arm around her shoulders. She nudged her aside as Derek brought in the first load of packages.

Annie lowered her voice. This, after all, was girl talk. "It's not gone, it's just hiding," Annie assured her. "You need to go away some place. Together. Without the kids," she emphasized. "You'd be surprised how that rejuvenates your juices."

For a second Jackie seemed to consider it; then she shook her head. "No, Alex would never go for it."

"Sure he would. You've just got to phrase it right."

"What'll I do with the kids?"

"We'll watch them," Annie promised her. "It's the least we can do. Think about it. In the meantime, a little playacting wouldn't hurt."

Sensitive on the subject, Toni jumped on the word. "Playacting?"

Mischief was written all over Annie's face. "Sure. You know. You're the countess, out on the high seas. He's the lusty pirate who saves you from his men—and for himself." She warmed up to her subject. "You're two shipwreck survivors, marooned on an island." She looked at Jackie. "Use your imagination."

Toni couldn't envision her brother doing anything remotely close to what Annie was proposing. "You're kidding."

Annie's eyes were dancing. "Try it. I guarantee you'll love it. Keeps us going."

"Keeps you going where?" Derek asked, dragging in the last of the gifts.

"Strong," Annie said quickly, winking at the others.

Derek nodded absently. He'd deposited all the packages in the foyer. Despite the cold, he'd worked up a sweat. He rubbed the back of his hand along his forehead in an exaggerated motion. "I'm beginning to understand why the guys go to work every morning."

"Don't you bail out on us," Annie warned, then laughed as she looked at the pile of packages he'd brought in. "Thanks, Derek, you're a dear." Rolling up the sleeves of her sweater, she began to sort out which packages were hers and which belonged to each of the others.

Jackie was beside her, making quick work of it. "We'd better get these out of sight before the kids come in," she urged.

Only a few of the packages were Toni's. She stashed them on the top shelf in the hall closet—all but one. That was still in her hands when she glanced toward Derek. But he was walking away from her, apparently to the kitchen. And he still had his coat on. Curious, she kept her own on as she hurried after him.

"Where are you going?" she called after him.

"Outside." He nodded toward the back door. "To play with the kids. They asked me earlier but..."

A smile blossomed on her lips. "You were waiting for me."

He'd already admitted that and didn't want to dwell on the subject. "Is it a crime to be concerned?"

She liked the feeling his admission generated. He still cared. At least a little. Maybe it was just residue from their marriage, but it still felt nice. "Annie was driving."

"That was why I was concerned." He became serious. "Besides, Annie's van is a high-profile vehicle and the winds were kicking up." They'd died down now, but if the weatherman was right for once, it was just a temporary lull. He turned to go outside.

"Derek, wait."

Now that she was safe, he didn't want to drag this out. "What?"

Why did she suddenly feel awkward, as if she was doing this for the first time? "I brought you something."

He looked at her. This was a switch. "You bought something for me?"

"No, I stole it." She blew out an impatient breath. He was making her feel silly. It had been strictly an impulse thing. The others were buying things for their husbands and she'd seen these on sale. And remembered that he didn't have any. "Yes, I bought something for you. Don't look so surprised. I've bought you things before."

After the way she'd vilified him, he would have thought that buying him a gift was the last thing on her mind. "Yeah, but not since—"

"Just take it, okay?" She didn't want to rehash anything right now, especially not when Nonna could walk in on them. "It's the season for giving. Besides, it's no big deal. Here." She shoved the bag at him as if it had suddenly turned hot in her hands. She shrugged self-consciously, wishing she hadn't said anything in the first place. "Seeing how it's practical, I didn't see the sense in having it wrapped."

Practical. Now there was a word she didn't use very often. Derek looked into the bag.

She'd bought him a pair of dark gray leather gloves, lined with sheepskin. It really was practical, he thought. Looking at her, he raised an eyebrow.

Toni looked down at his hands. They were still red from the wind. "You forgot to pack your gloves," she said as if that explained everything.

It didn't even begin to scratch the surface. "Yeah, but how did you know?"

"I watched you unpack, remember?" she reminded him. He'd brought only a few things with him for the stay. "Sometimes you can be too utilitarian."

He smiled, pulling them on. They felt soft against his hands. Soft, like the feel of her skin. Longing curled through him like smoke from a chimney on a cold winter morning.

"Thanks." He thought of what he'd promised the kids. "Seems a shame to ruin them."

It always amazed her how he liked to save things, as if each thing were to be cherished. It was one of the things she liked best about him.

"You could always put them under glass." She grinned. "They're gloves, Derek. Wear them. Use them." Toni glanced out the back window. Outside, the kids were immersed in building up two separate arsenals, glorying in the snow that was coming down. God, she missed being that young. When something as simple as snow was a cause for celebration. "It looks to me as if you're going to need them."

Just as Derek was about to agree, Zak ran inside. An impatient scowl creased his wind-roughened face.

"Are you coming out or what, Uncle Derek? They're creaming us and we need help." He lowered his voice. "Karen throws snowballs like a regular baseball pitcher."

Derek laughed. "Help is on the way."

Toni followed him to the back porch. "Kind of unfair, don't you think?" She nodded at the two camps with their makeshift snow forts. "You being so big and all."

He grinned in response. "Think so? Then why don't you even up the odds and join the others?"

Tickled at the challenge, she didn't even have to consider it. "Think I won't, don't you?"

His expression was the soul of innocence. "I'm not saying a word. I just remember the last snowball fight." Amusement entered his eyes as he recalled it. "You throw like a girl."

She took pleasure in squelching his confidence. "That was just because I was trying to lose and make you feel manly."

They went down the back steps together, two challengers ready to face off in an arena of white powder. "Yeah, right."

He didn't believe her. She needed nothing more. "I'll show you 'right.'"

Nik had joined their ranks. He looked from one to the other. "You're going to come out?" he asked Toni, oblivious to the fact that she already *was* out.

Her eyes never left Derek's. "You bet."

Nik went running to the others. "Hey, everybody, Aunt Toni's going to throw snowballs at Uncle Derek."

Toni and Derek looked at each other and laughed. From where they stood it sounded like too tempting a proposition to pass up.

"C'mon," Derek urged her. "Put your money where your mouth is."

He was in for a surprise. She'd purposely played the weak female in the encounter he recalled. There was no reason to do that now. On the contrary, she had a side to champion. And a man who needed a lesson in female athletic prowess.

"I don't know about money," she answered, "but I'll put snow where your mouth is, wise guy."

Joining Nik and Zak, Derek was already making snowballs and envisioning the target area. "You and what army?"

"This army," Karen and Dustin cried in unison.

"My soldiers have spoken." Toni laughed. She hurried to catch up in the production of munitions. "You call these snowballs?" she asked Dustin.

"Yeah. What's the matter with them?" he wanted to know.

"The middles have got to be slushy." Rather than explain further, she got busy. "Here, I'll show you."

Dustin and Karen exchanged looks as they watched her quickly pack snowballs together. Dustin stared at her uncertainly. "Hey, Aunt Toni, you used to throw snowballs?"

"Ask your dad." She piled snowballs on top of snowballs. "I used to beat him all the time."

"No way."

"Way." Toni laughed.

"Don't believe anything she says, Dustin," Derek called out to him. His hands moved quickly as he tripled the arsenal. "She's just trying to snow you."

Groans arose from all sides, with Toni's being loudest of all.

"Hey, seemed like the thing to say at the time." Derek's words were punctuated by three flying white missiles launched in Toni's direction.

One of them hit her in the shoulder. "No fair! You were supposed to declare war."

"War!" Derek announced loudly. Two more snowballs followed, smashing into her.

The next moment the air was alive with snowballs flying left and right as soldiers from both sides hurled missiles at moving targets. War cries rang in the air and retreats and advances changed hands over and over again as both sides took turns winning the battle.

Toni got in several good shots, getting Derek back. And then Derek reversed his position, going on the offensive.

One snowball burst right over her mouth. Sputtering, Toni raced over the short battlefield, her hand raised high, and began pelting Derek at close range.

Laughing, he gave as good as he got. "Give up yet?" he called.

"Never!"

Out of snowballs, Toni grabbed handfuls of snow and threw them at him quickly. Ducking his head, Derek grabbed her hands and stopped the onslaught. Weak with laughter, they both tumbled to the ground.

The laughs slowly stilled as the warmth of their melded bodies registered. He looked into her eyes. She was covered with snow and she had never looked so beautiful to him in her life.

"I guess I got carried away," she admitted.

"Yeah," he murmured. "Me, too."

And he wanted to get carried away some more. He wanted to pick her up and carry her into the house and make love with her all night long.

Belatedly they remembered that they weren't alone. There was a human ring forming as four faces looked down at them.

"Is that how you're supposed to have a snowball fight?" Nik asked, bewildered.

Derek rolled off to the side. "If you're married and it's snowing," he answered the boy.

Rising, he offered a hand to Toni. She took it and let him pull her to her feet, then gasped as she found her face suddenly washed with snow.

"Sorry, couldn't resist." The other hand had been behind his back, full of snow.

Bent on getting even, Toni chased him around the yard as the twins, Karen and Dustin cheered them on, changing sides as the whim moved them.

Derek caught her up in his arms and threatened to toss Toni bodily into the puny fort her side had constructed. Just then Josephine appeared in the doorway.

"Children!" Her eyes were on Toni and Derek as she called. "Get in here and change your clothing before you all catch your deaths." Four sets of feet came reluctantly to the back porch. "That goes for the two big kids, too. C'mon, hurry up!"

Derek set Toni down. A strange pang ran through her as she left his arms.

"Seems like old times," Toni commented. She nodded toward her mother.

"Yes," he agreed quietly, his eyes touching her. "It does."

Still exhilarated, Toni pushed him toward the house. "We'd better go in before Mom comes out to get us."

He nodded. "Wouldn't want to set a bad example for the kids." Taking her hand, he led the way back.

Toni smiled to herself as she let him.

Chapter Ten

Having the kitchen to herself during the holidays was a rare thing for Josephine. Everyone, it seemed, was bent on showing off his culinary skills, or contributing to the meals. Even Joe and Alex poked their noses in, although as far as they were concerned, it was usually to snare something to eat rather than to lend a hand preparing anything.

And while this usually pleased her, once in a while Josephine longed for the peace that working alone in the kitchen provided. She did her best thinking while she was cooking and augmenting recipes that had been handed down for generations. Augmenting them and making them hers.

Right now there was no one in here. Just her and the radio. The station was playing traditional Christmas carols. She savored the tranquillity. It was rather, she mused, glancing through the window at the snow that had been falling for the past few hours, like being in the eye of a storm.

Her sons had returned home safely, thank God, beating out the main brunt of the storm by what appeared to be minutes. The wind had picked up considerably in the past few minutes, sending the windchill factor rising, or plummeting, depending on your view.

Toni and Derek hadn't seemed to mind the cold. She smiled to herself as she gave the spaghetti a single, good stir, then replaced the lid on the huge pot. She'd watched them for a long time before she'd ventured outside. It did her heart good to see them like that. Acting as if none of this had ever happened.

And perhaps, if they all pretended enough, it would just fade away and they would get back together.

That was why she'd insisted on sending them both upstairs to change. On the hope that this playful feeling she'd witnessed would continue. And escalate so that it obliterated the hurt feelings that existed between them.

It was, after all, Josephine mused as she listened to Johnny Mathis sensually sing about the holiday, the season for miracles.

A movement at the bottom of the back stairs caught her eye, and she turned.

Toni, her dark hair curling about her head and shoulders like a riot of dark waves, walked in.

Josephine couldn't block out the stab of disappointment she felt. "You're down so quickly."

This really was like old times, Toni thought. How many times had she come down the back stairs to see her mother like this, commandeering the kitchen, overseeing a four-course meal and making it look no more difficult than sticking a frozen dinner into the microwave? Her mother didn't even own a microwave. She preferred doing things the old-fashioned way.

She was an old-fashioned woman, her mother, for all her modern allowances of letting her daughter have the same opportunities as her sons. And that was why her own divorce had hit Josephine D'Angelo twice as hard. She really didn't believe in the institution.

Toni picked up a cinnamon cookie from the plate on the island, debated, then returned it to the stack. Her stomach felt as if it was on the border of rebelling again. No sense in flirting with disaster.

She shrugged in reply to her mother's observation. "How long does it take to change clothes?" She looked down at the blouse and black jeans she'd put on.

"But you went up with Derek."

Was it her imagination, or was that a hopeful note in her mother's voice? "We took turns in the bathroom."

"I was hoping you were taking turns drying each other off."

Toni's eyes widened in surprise. "Mom!"

"What, I'm too old to talk about sex?" It amused her that the younger generation thought that they'd invented it. She knew, because at Toni's age, she had felt the same way.

Toni was mystified. Her mother had given her a straightforward talk about the facts of life at an early age and supplemented it with books, but they had never personalized the subject by actually applying that information to include either one of them. Toni wasn't sure how to handle this new approach. "Um, no, but...well, there's just no point in starting something that can't be finished." She looked up to see if her mother understood what she was saying.

Slotted wooden spoon in one hand, Josephine looked at her in awe. "It takes you that long?"

So much for vaguely skirting the subject. "Mom, I was talking about it not leading anywhere."

Her mother set down her spoon. "Maybe if you started it, it would."

Josephine turned off all four burners and let the pots stand for a moment, steeping. She wiped her hands on her apron and looked at her daughter, debating whether or not it would do any good to reopen an old wound. One that had never properly healed and probably never would.

She decided to give it a try. Mistakes had to have some redeeming value.

"It's your own life, Toni, and I can't tell you how to live it. I can only tell you what I would do in your place."

What was her mother talking about? "I know what you would do in my place." It was certainly no secret. They'd all lived through it. "You already did it. With Dad."

A bittersweet expression played across her face. "Yes, I certainly did." Josephine glanced at the clock on the wall. "Which is why I can tell you I would do it differently now."

Now she knew she wasn't following her mother. "You'd take him back?"

Josephine didn't answer immediately. Instead, she went to the swinging door that separated the kitchen from the dining room and opened it a crack. There was no one in the other room. Satisfied, she crossed back to the island. Getting on a stool, Josephine patted the one beside her.

Puzzled, Toni sat down.

The light overhead flickered. Gene Autry skipped a section of Rudolph's woes before he came back on, stronger than ever.

Josephine began slowly, each word wrapped in a tissue of emotion. "I'm going to tell you something I never told anyone else."

Toni straightened, turning the stool to face her mother. "Not even Nonna?"

Josephine shook her head. "No, not even Nonna." Clearly, this wasn't easy for her to say. "Your father came to me a few years after he ran off with...that woman."

Even now, over the space of twenty years, Toni noted, her mother still couldn't bring herself to call the other woman by name.

"He told me that he was sorry, that he'd made a mistake." A sad smile played on her lips and Toni thought she could see tears shimmering in her mother's eyes. She slipped a hand over the clenched ones in Josephine's lap. Josephine raised her chin. "He missed me and all of you. He was asking to come back into the family."

She paused for a moment, letting the words sink in.

"I refused to forgive him. He begged me, that tall, strong, strapping man. With tears in his eyes he begged me, swore it would never happen again.

"I sent him away. It didn't feel good the way I thought it would, but I sent him away."

She looked up into her daughter's eyes. "There wasn't a single corner of my heart where I could find forgiveness for what he'd done to me and to my pride."

Josephine took a deep breath and then let it out slowly. Her voice was no longer shaky when she spoke. "Your father died six months later. That's all we would have had together, six months. It was six months I didn't have because I let my pride get in the way.''

Toni looked at her, confused, not knowing what to think. What had her mother wanted her to glean from this? "But he cheated on you."

"Yes, he did." There was no denying the facts. "And maybe he would have again, although I don't think so.

"I think somehow he knew he was getting near the end." The bittersweet smile returned. "Or maybe he'd decided that he wanted me after he'd tried all the others. But I'll never have that chance to find out."

Josephine leaned forward, her hand cupping Toni's cheek. The lights flickered again, but she didn't pay any attention to them.

"What I'm saying is that bitterness is a cold companion. It offers no comfort. Don't follow my example. Find your own. If you're just shutting Derek out because I shut out your father, don't," she implored.

Moved, stunned, Toni poured out her heart. "Derek explained things to me."

Hope alighted, warm and vibrant. "Oh?"

She didn't realize until she drew a breath that she was close to tears at her mother's revelation. "He told me that Sylvia had been after him for a while and that what I saw was Sylvia trying to seduce him, not Derek being seduced."

Toni didn't have to say anymore. Josephine clapped her hands together just as the radio behind her squawked and then died. "I knew it. I knew I hadn't misjudged him."

That her mother was so quick to take Derek's word on faith surprised her. This was not your typical mother-in-law, she thought.

"You believe him?"

"Of course I believe him. Toni, I see the way that man looks at you, the way he's always looked at you." Her look of relief was impossible to miss. "He's not the type to stray on purpose. And even if he had been led astray—" she emphasized the word *led* "—no one's perfect. He wants to be with you."

Coming on again, the radio let out a high pitched noise. Annoyed, Josephine reached over and shut if off just as the lights wavered a third time.

"No, he doesn't."

Josephine waved a hand at her daughter's words. "That's just his injured pride talking."

She only wished, Toni thought. "No, that's Africa talking," she said with a sigh. Her mother looked at her, puzzled. "Derek just told me he's taking a position at a clinic there."

Toni could see from the expression on her mother's face that Josephine seemed not at all bothered by this tidbit. "He could change his mind."

Her mother, Toni decided, was a hell of a lot more optimistic than she was. "I don't think so."

"You could change it for him."

She didn't want to maneuver Derek. It wouldn't have any meaning that way. "Mom, I'm not going to make him do anything."

"Just make it easier for him to see the light, that's all, honey. That's what we're here for." The smile was broad and, for her mother, wicked. "To make men see the error of their ways."

The lights flickered again, and then went out. There was barely any daylight left outside and the little of it that squeezed into the kitchen was woefully dim.

Josephine fisted her hands on her ample hips. "Now what?"

All six fluorescent fixtures overhead were dark. "Looks like the bulbs all went out together." Although that didn't seem very likely to Toni.

Josephine looked toward the swinging door. "Looks like the whole house went out." She sighed. "Joe!"

Joe was in the kitchen before she'd finished saying his name. The door swung shut behind him. "Right here, Ma."

Moving slowly, Josephine had found her way to the cupboard and had taken down the flashlight she kept there. She switched it on and held it out to Joe. "See if we blew a fuse."

"It's no fuse, Ma." Alex joined them, a small yellow beam preceding him. "The whole neighborhood's down." He jerked a thumb vaguely behind him. "Looks like the blizzard's knocked out a power line."

"Blizzard?" Josephine echoed.

"The 'mild snow flurries' the guy on the news told us about last night," Alex scoffed.

He pointed his flashlight toward the pantry, where his mother kept a camping lantern. It had been put there shortly after the big blackout of '65 when, she liked to tell him, the entire East Coast had been plunged into darkness.

Alex handed the flashlight to his mother. Josephine frowned. She looked at the already cooling pots on the stove. "Good thing I just finished making dinner. No telling how long this is going to last."

She turned the flashlight toward the window and then drew closer to the sill. "Look at it coming down," she marveled. Then she stopped suddenly. "Is anyone with Nonna?"

"Derek went up to her," Joe told her.

"I can always depend on that man." Josephine looked at her daughter pointedly. Then she turned toward her sons. "All right, round up all the flashlights and candles in the house. I still keep them in the same place."

Alex and Joe left the kitchen. Josephine took down the dinner plates and handed them to Toni. She smiled. "Looks like we're dining by candlelight tonight," she said.

Toni could have sworn her mother looked pleased about the power failure.

As she had every day of her life, Nonna ate sparingly while enjoying the sight of those around her eating well. Six tall candles stood equidistantly placed on the extended table, illuminating the room and the occupants for her.

The children were quiet and wide-eyed, the adults even more talkative than usual, as if by talking they could deny the power of the darkness for the children.

Nonna smiled as she handed her plate to Jackie, who was clearing the table.

"This is just like when I was a little girl in Palermo." She directed her words to the twins, who had looked very uneasy throughout dinner. "We always ate by candlelight. It makes the meal taste special, do you not think so?"

The twins didn't answer, but Joe did. "Yeah, this way you don't know what you're eating." His comment drew a sharp poke in his ribs from Annie. He yelped in surprise. "What?" Annie gave him a dirty look. "Ma knows I'm teasing. Don't you, Ma?"

"Maybe, but compliments are better." Josephine didn't crack a smile.

Joe inclined his head in a formal bow. "We all love Ma's cooking."

Alex laughed. "It's better than Toni's, that's for sure."

Toni had picked at her meal, not because the baby had been acting up but because she was mulling over what her mother had said to her. Singled out now, she raised her head and pretended to take offense.

"What's wrong with my cooking?"

Alex and Joe laughed as they exchanged looks. They had both been her guinea pigs when Toni had decided to try her hand at cooking. Some of it had been miserably unsuccessful. Even now she couldn't hold a candle to their mother.

"Nothing." Alex surrendered his plate to his wife. "Except it's a good thing you decided to be a doctor. That way you can feed them and then treat them."

Picking up Toni's plate, Jackie stacked it on top. "She's in research, remember?"

Alex nodded solemnly. "That would explain the experiment."

Prepared to be the butt of his joke, Toni had no idea what he was talking about. "What experiment?"

Joe took up the thread. "Isn't that what you called that thing you served the other night?"

"It was fruitcake." A little hard around the edges, maybe, but the center had been all right. As long as you had all your own teeth.

"It was an experiment," Alex insisted. "Harder than a brick." He caught Derek's eye, but the latter shook his head. He wasn't touching this with a ten-foot pole.

"If it had been," Toni countered, "I would have thrown it at you."

Using her back, Jackie opened the swinging door. "Don't you just love the holidays?" she said to no one in particular.

Flanked on either side by children who were unusually quiet, Joe tried his hand at taking their minds off the power failure.

"So, what did you kids do today?" Joe asked Dustin and Karen.

"Nothing much." Toying with his glass of soda, Dustin shrugged. Karen echoed his gesture.

"We had a snowball fight," Zak piped up. "And Uncle Derek washed Aunt Toni's face in the snow."

Alex gave Derek a thumbs-up sign. "Atta boy, Derek."

Toni was still smarting from the crack about her cooking. "He's only saying that because I used to get him when we were kids."

Alex leaned over to Derek. "Funny how when they get old, their memory goes."

"Gee, I was just thinking the same thing," Toni countered.

Josephine pushed herself back from the table. "Dessert anyone?"

Joe slanted a look toward his sister. "Depends on who made it."

"I made it," Nonna said proudly. It had taken her the better part of the morning. There had been a time when it would have taken her only half that, but it had still been done with love.

Affection highlighted his face, made that much more dramatic by the candlelight. "Then I'll have seconds," Joe declared.

"You have to have firsts first," Toni reminded him.

His eyes teasing her, Joe shrugged easily. "Okay, give me firsts and then seconds, Ma."

Josephine pushed the swinging door open slowly. "Can't you keep your husband in line, Annie?"

Annie looked at her mother-in-law knowingly. "Just giving him enough rope to hang himself."

"It's a conspiracy, you know," Alex whispered as he leaned in toward Derek. "They fool us into thinking they're the weaker sex, get us to spend our hard-earned money on them, then they outlive us and have a ball, throwing it all away on some hunk half their age."

"Ouch!" Jackie winced, taking her seat beside him. "Bad day at the office, honey?" she asked sweetly.

"You don't know the half of it."

"Poor baby." Jackie kissed his cheek, and her sons squealed and groaned in disgust. "You can tell me all about it later." She caught Annie's eye. The wink was almost imperceptible, given the lighting.

But Toni saw. It looked as if Jackie was going to be taking Annie's advice. Well, they were going to have a nice evening, she thought. A trace of envy wafted through her.

With a sigh she wasn't aware of, Toni rose from the table. "I'll help you, Mom," she called out.

Long shadows, echoing the darkness she felt inside, preceded her as she went through the swinging door.

Zak huddled uneasily against his mother. Wearing their coats, they were all camped out in the living room before the fireplace for the remainder of the evening. Zak and Nik were sitting beside their mother on the floor.

A roaring fire was casting light throughout the room, but it didn't seem to reassure him.

"Is it going to be like this all night?" Zak asked his mother.

She tightened her arms around both boys. "Afraid so, honey."

"I'm scared, Mommy," Nik admitted.

Derek's heart went out to the boy. He could remember feeling like that. Could remember feeling fear's effects when he was a lot older. There had been no one to hold him and make it go away.

There had been no one to really hold him until Toni had come into his life, he thought.

He glanced toward her. Toni was sitting on the floor at her grandmother's feet, the light from the fire trapped in her hair, slipping along her skin like soft pink rose petals.

He felt his gut tighten, and he looked away.

"Nothing to be afraid of," Derek told him. Sitting cross-legged on the floor beside the hearth, he drew closer. "There's nothing here now that isn't here during the day."

Zak looked unconvinced. His eyes were huge in the dimly lit room. "Shadows are here."

Toni laughed and Derek turned toward her. He'd forgotten how much he'd missed that sound.

There was a look in his eyes that made her warmer than the fire did. Toni felt her stomach flip over and almost forgot what she was going to say.

"He's got you there, Derek," she heard herself whispering.

Derek shook his head, refusing to give up for the boy's sake. "Shadows are just like big, dark blankets," Derek explained.

Zak shivered. "What are they hiding?"

Derek approached it from a different direction. "What do the blankets on your bed hide?"

The eyes grew bigger still. "What?" both boys asked breathlessly.

Derek tweaked each nose affectionately. "Nothing. Except maybe the sheets. Or you when you're under them." He made it sound so natural, both boys began to relax a little. "The point is just because you can't see everything doesn't mean that there's something to be afraid of there. No sense in letting your imagination run away with you." He glanced at Toni before gesturing toward the tree. From where he was sitting, it was bathed in golden hues. "See how pretty the Christmas tree looks, even in the dark? It's not spooky, is it?"

"No," Nik and Zak mumbled in unison. But the answer was a little uncertain.

"When I was a little girl," Nonna began, coming to Derek's rescue, "all of the Christmas trees had candles on them instead of lights."

"At least they never got tangled," Joe commented.

Dustin, ever practical, asked, "Didn't the trees burn?"

Nonna shook her head. "I never remember any burning in my village. We were very, very careful not to brush against the tree."

"Was Santa alive when you were a little girl?" Zak wanted to know.

"Zak," Jackie admonished.

But Nonna laughed. "That is all right. He was alive, but he was busy elsewhere."

"So he never came?" Nik's expression was horrified.

"We had La Befana," Nonna told him.

"Who's that?" Zak made a face.

"She was a good woman who some say was a friend to the Three Wise Men. She was unable to make the journey with them to Bethlehem. When she would come, she would have a cane in one hand and a bell in the other to announce herself."

"A cane. Like yours, Nonna?" Zak asked. He looked at it with renewed interest.

"Like mine. Whenever she found children's stockings hanging up, she would fill them with toys and candy."

"Like Santa Claus!" the twins piped up together.

Nonna smiled. "Like Santa Claus." And oh, the nights she had waited for La Befana's appearance, hoping for a gift. A toy or wonderful fruit. She could almost touch the joy across the years.

"I'd still rather have Santa Claus than a dumb girl," Zak decided.

Alex intervened. "You know, guys, Santa Claus is called different names in different countries."

Nik eyed his dad. "You mean Santa's got an alias?"

"No," his mother quickly explained. "He's just called different things by different people."

"Jody Masters calls him a fake," Nik said.

There was always a Jody Masters, Derek thought. When he was a kid, his Jody Masters had been Michael Evans. He'd hated it when he'd discovered Michael was right. "Jody Masters doesn't know what she's missing," he said to the boys.

Zak seemed more than willing to agree. "You bet."

Dustin looked at Derek, uncertainty in his eyes. "You mean you believe in Santa Claus, Uncle Derek?"

Derek took the question in stride, wishing he were young enough again to feel secure and not question things. "Do I believe in miracles and a white-bearded old man who somehow finds a way to deliver presents the world over in one night?" Derek grinned. "You bet I do."

"That's all I wanted to know." Nik's expression was the picture of satisfaction.

It had been a long day. And a longer evening. There was a time when Nonna would have sat up until dawn, the last to go to bed. But those days were forever gone.

"I am very tired," Nonna announced. "I think I will go upstairs now." She rose slowly, leaning heavily on her cane.

Derek was on his feet instantly. "Allow me."

Nonna laughed like a delighted young girl as Derek lifted her in his arms. "Your grandfather used to pick me up like that," she told the others. "Whenever he was happy he would pick me up in his arms and spin me around."

"No spinning tonight," Derek told her, an affectionate smile on his face.

Alex took her cane and Nonna secured her hands around Derek's neck. "Good, I want to keep a clear head. Good night, everyone."

"Wait." Toni scrambled to her feet. She took the lantern from the floor and the cane from Alex. "I'll light the way for you."

She missed the others exchanging looks as she led the way to the staircase.

But she felt them just the same.

Chapter Eleven

"You'll be all right here tonight, Nonna?"

Derek looked a little uncertainly around the bedroom where Nonna had slept every day for the past fifty-nine years. Alex had come up right after dinner and started a fire in the fireplace for her, warding off the chill successfully.

Still, Derek didn't like leaving her alone like this. The power failure just made him that much more protective of her.

Nonna sat down on her bed and smiled at Derek's concern.

"I will be fine. I can still do what needs to be done, Derek. I am not that feeble yet."

He'd tripped over his own tongue again. Derek looked at the older woman ruefully, aware of the disapproving look Toni was probably giving him.

"I didn't mean to imply—"

"I know you did not." Dark sapphire eyes held his for a moment. "Go to your wife, Derek," she told him softly, gesturing toward the doorway where Toni stood. "She is the one who needs you."

Derek kissed Nonna good-night, then withdrew from the room. He couldn't help wondering if the comment had been just an offhand one, or if Nonna had been trying to tell him something.

Nonna didn't make offhand remarks, he reminded himself. Had Toni said something to her? Or had the woman just seen something that he was missing?

Damn it, he was building castles in the sky again, with no foundations under them. More than likely, Nonna had meant nothing more by her words than to say that every wife needed her husband.

Except for Toni. She seemed to be getting along just fine without him.

Holding the lantern aloft, Toni led the way down the hall to their room. It was five doors from Nonna's. Toni glanced at Derek over her shoulder. He had the oddest expression on his face. Had Nonna said something to him? Or was he having second thoughts about leaving the country?

Now, there was wishful thinking, she ridiculed herself. Of course he wasn't having seconds thoughts. He was positively eager to get away from her. He'd all but said that with his crack about needing half a world between them.

"What's the matter?" Toni opened the door to their room. It felt dreary and cold—as her life was without him. But that was something she was just going to have to get used to. "You look pensive."

"Nonna said you needed me." He walked into the room ahead of Toni. "Did you say something to her?"

Toni closed the door, then placed the lantern on the bureau. It cast eerie, haunting shapes on the walls and ceiling.

Or maybe, she mused, they weren't shapes at all but ghosts of their affection for each other.

She shrugged, both at her interpretation and at his question. "I thought about telling her the truth, but no, I didn't say anything to her."

The room was frigid. They needed to start a fire in here, he thought, looking at the small pile of wood beside the hearth. It was there more for show than use, since the house had long since acquired central heating. But it would do in a pinch.

Her admission caught him by surprise. "The truth? I thought the whole purpose of our being here, playing out this charade, was to spare her the truth."

Restless, cold, Toni prowled about the room. The drapes were still hanging open, admitting only a silvery shaft of what was left of the moon. She yanked them closed.

"I feel guilty. I hate lying. I always have. Ever since..." Her voice trailed off. There was no sense in bringing that up again.

He watched her move around aimlessly. Was she always going to remain a prisoner of that emotion? he wondered. Was what her father had done always going to color everything for her? Or was there a chance that she could finally shed that fear?

If he thought that there was a chance...

He let it go. No use spinning dreams, not tonight. "Ever since your father lied to you," he concluded for her.

Toni ran her hands over her arms. Though she had

thrown on her coat like the others, she still felt cold. Maybe it was the conversation.

"Yeah." She watched as the word came out on a visible puff of breath. "Maybe you'd better build a fire. It's really cold in here and besides, this lantern isn't going to last all night."

"Afraid of the dark?" he asked, mildly amused. Crouching down, he shifted the woodpile into the hearth, piece by piece.

Absently she nodded. "A little. Sometimes."

He could almost feel her shadow as it passed over him. Derek twisted around to look at her. "I didn't know that."

There was a reason for that. "It's not something I like admitting." It seemed like a fear a child would harbor, not an adult. "Besides, it's only when I'm alone."

He needed a newspaper to start the fire going. Rising, he observed, "You're not alone."

A smile curved her mouth, but there was no humor in it, no delight, no happiness of any kind. "Matter of opinion."

They were almost touching. There was something very sad in her eyes, Derek thought. Compassion stirred within him. And something more.

"I'm right here," he told her softly.

There was a coat and a jacket between them, as well as layers of clothing, yet she could feel the heat from his body. Or thought she did.

Maybe she wished it into being.

For just a moment, as the lantern light played along the long, sturdy planes of his face, she thought he was going to kiss her. She held her breath, waiting.

Hoping.

But then he turned away, reaching for the newspaper on the nightstand. He tore it into strips.

Best not to play with fire if you're unsure how to control it, she told herself. And kissing Derek here, in the dark, alone, was just asking for trouble. The kind of trouble that invited more of the same.

She stood behind him, watching as he crouched down again and tucked the papers between the pieces of wood. "How are you going to light a fire?"

By holding you in my arms and kissing you until we both ignite. The thought came from nowhere, and echoed in the recesses of his mind. It was probably a sign that he was going crazy.

In reply to her question, Derek dug into his back pocket and took out Joe's cigarette lighter. He held it aloft for her to see. "Joe gave me his lighter when the power went out."

She stared at it in disbelief. "Joe is smoking again? He swore to Annie that he'd quit." She remembered how long Joe had struggled to master the vice that had taken hold of him by the time he was fifteen.

God, she could be up in arms faster than any woman he knew. "Hold your horses," Derek ordered. "He hasn't started smoking again. But there's no reason to throw away a perfectly good lighter." He took another long strip of newspaper and twisted it into a makeshift torch. Lighting it, he applied the burning tier to the paper within the pile of wood. "You never know when it might come in handy." He smiled in satisfaction as the fire caught hold. "Like now."

"How did you know that? That Joe was just hanging on to the lighter and wasn't smoking again?"

That seemed a simple enough question to answer. "He told me."

Joe hadn't mentioned it to her. It occurred to Toni that there might be a lot of confidences her brothers shared with Derek that they didn't with her.

She looked at the back of his head. Her fingers itched to run through that mop of dark blond hair. He always did keep it a little too long. She caught her lower lip between her teeth, tempted.

Toni crossed her arms before her to keep from touching him. "You get along well with my family, don't you?"

"Yes, I do." He lit another strip and tossed it in. The fire was beginning to spread. He stared into the flame and saw only her. "I'm going to miss them."

And they him, she knew. "Well, just because we're getting a divorce doesn't mean you have to divorce my family."

He laughed shortly. That was a little too sophisticated for his tastes. "Makes it a little awkward at family gatherings, don't you think?"

Her head was beginning to hurt. Just like her heart, she thought. "Right now I don't know what to think. I think I'll just put thinking on hold for now. I'm too busy trying to warm up."

Tiny yellow flames were sprouting everywhere, playing hide-and-seek between the pieces of wood. "I've almost got the fire going."

She looked at him again. Remembering. Wishing.

You already have. You just don't know it.

The fire would warm up the room well enough, but the bed was on the opposite side. She looked at it, then at him. Debating.

"Um, in light of the situation, maybe we can share the bed tonight," she said, her voice a little shaky. She didn't want him to think she was asking him to make love with her. She was suggesting that he not freeze to death, that was all. "The floor's bound to be cold and we can, um, share the blankets."

Very slowly Derek dropped the last of the newspaper into the fire. It was now a healthy blaze and shouldn't go out until almost morning. He turned very slowly to look up at her. "And make our own heat?"

She drew herself up, her chin raised. "I didn't say that."

His smile came slowly, like molasses pouring out of a jug.

"No, but I did." He rose to his feet carefully, like a snake uncoiling. Like an emotion unfolding. His body was a breath away from hers. Less. "I'm feeling warmer already."

She swallowed before answering. Her throat was incredibly dry. Swallowing didn't help. "Me, too. Must be the fire."

His eyes were on her lips. The firelight made them gleam. "Must be."

She made a motion to reach for the poker to stoke the fire. She never completed it. "Want to play with it a little? The fire, I mean." The words dripped from her lips.

"We shouldn't." But he was already running his hands through her hair, knowing he had lost the battle that tonight he was too weak to even begin to wage.

She couldn't have moved from the spot, away from his hands, unless lightning had struck her. And there was very little chance of that.

Her eyes fluttered, half-closing as she felt his fingers along her scalp, tangling in her hair. "Maybe that's the draw of it, that we shouldn't."

She could feel his smile along her cheek, his breath

along her skin. Her own desire flared in her chest. "I don't think so," he said.

"Oh?" The word was half a moan. She felt her knees weakening. And all he was doing was touching her. Ever so lightly. "What do you think is the draw?"

"You." His eyes caressed her face, her body, her soul. "Me. Us."

She could feel her breath as it tried to work its way out of her lungs. Her breasts were tingling even though his hands were still layers away from her skin. Just holding her to him was enough.

Anticipation clawed up her body like tiny, light creatures with long fingernails.

"That about sums it up," she answered, each word quieter than the one before. *Love me, Derek, please love me. Make love with me, because there are no tomorrows left for us.*

He toyed with the button at her breast and slid it from the hole. The others followed, one by one. "Do you need your coat?"

Slowly she moved her head from side to side. "Not to sleep in," she murmured. And she was beginning to perspire.

The coat was off her shoulders and down her arms, pooling to the floor as if it had been a veil of gossamer rather than a practical, lined, all-weather coat.

As it fell away, she felt limp, yet energized. All sorts of sensations were running about, colliding and exploding within her, yet it was almost as if she was drugged, transfixed by the emotions she felt.

Transfixed by this man.

"Good," he told her, kicking it aside. "It gets in the way."

He was wearing a sheepskin-lined denim jacket, the

one that made her think of him as a cowboy. A sexy cowboy instead of a serious doctor. "How about yours?"

He dropped his hands away from her body, then spread them wide. "Feel free."

She did. She did feel free, she thought. Freer than she had felt in months. It was as if everything she was experiencing now had been hidden, kept under glass. Until this moment.

Her palms felt almost slick as she unbuttoned the heavy blue jacket, then pulled it from his arms. It resisted, the sleeves held prisoner by his sweater. She yanked harder, succeeding in peeling it away. Toni tossed the jacket in the general vicinity of the fourposter. It fell to the floor.

He was wearing the same pullover sweater he'd worn earlier, sitting across the table from her, but she looked at it as if she was seeing it for the first time. Seeing it and remembering.

"I gave you that, didn't I?"

When she hadn't mentioned anything earlier, he'd thought she didn't remember. He smiled at the ambiguous question. "You gave me a lot of things."

She shook her head. It wasn't just another gift. "I mean our first Christmas together, when we hardly had anything, I gave you that."

He'd worn it because of that. Because it reminded him of a happier time when there'd been no differences to resolve, no accusations between them.

"Yes. I thought it was rather appropriate for the holidays."

Something broke free within her. The last of her resistance died.

Toni burrowed her hands beneath his sweater, her

fingers splayed along his flat midriff. She caught her breath, as did he.

Slowly she slid her hands up. The hairs on his abdomen and chest tickled the palms of her hands. His sharp intake of breath sent delicious sensations racing through her. Racing in search of a goal line.

Suddenly she wanted to touch all of him, to press her naked body against his.

"Do you want to get closer to the fire?" She nodded toward it.

He wanted this to go slowly, but he was having trouble containing the ardor that was mounting within his veins. As he watched her eyes, he tugged her blouse out from her waistband.

"I already am." Hands spanning her waist, he brought her to him. And his mouth covered hers.

The room was spinning as she ran headlong into the kiss like a woman running to her last chance for salvation.

A muffled cry of joy escaped her lips. His mouth tasted of all things wondrous. Memories collided in her mind. Their first kiss, the first time they'd made love. The last time.

The kiss beneath the mistletoe that had told her she would never be over him.

And she never would.

Nor did she want to be. Not when loving him brought back all these memories

She wound her fingers in his hair, letting herself fall deeper into the kiss.

The rapture that took her just reinforced how much she'd missed him. How much she would miss him when this was all behind them and they would once again go their separate, distant ways. He to Africa and she to emptiness.

No, not emptiness. Not anymore. She was carrying his child. And that baby would always be an eternal reminder of his love.

But she didn't want reminders, not now. She wanted it all. She wanted this moment, no matter how tortured the future became because of it. Toni didn't care. She didn't care about consequences.

She wanted now.

Eagerness sprinted through her, vying with the desire to make this moment, this night, last for eternity. It had to.

She wanted so much! She wanted the rippling sensation of his lovemaking pulsating through her body. She wanted to feel him, to touch him, to make love with him. To him.

She wanted to possess, and to be possessed, one more time.

Derek felt the change in her instantly, from passive acceptance to aggressive participation. From loved one to lover.

It activated something within him, something dormant and almost half-savage that, away from Toni, he had buried and presumed, after a time, to be dead. But it wasn't dead—it was alive and demanding tribute. Demanding to claim what was rightfully his.

What should have always remained his, not barred from him by misunderstandings and polite words the civilized world prized. Things that he prized when he could think clearly.

But he couldn't think clearly, not now, not when she was so willing in his arms, so eager beneath his mouth. Not when she was nibbling on his lower lip, her hands roaming his body in that way of hers, and making him ache for her.

Clear thinking was for men who had never loved passionately.

And he had.

And did.

The room was warming from the heat of the fire in the hearth.

The aura around them was sizzling from the heat of the fire in their bodies.

Unable to contain himself, Derek stripped away her blouse, ripping the sides apart with one tug. Buttons were sent flying helter-skelter through the air and along the floor.

Toni heard one *ping* into the fireplace and thought distantly that it would get charred.

Just the way she was.

Her breathing grew ragged as she felt his hands along her breasts, molding her, possessing her. Eagerly she pulled off his sweater, throwing it somewhere into the darkness. She was almost vibrating with anticipation. The dark, dangerous look in his eyes excited her beyond words.

Her mouth left his and she slid her tongue along his chin, down his throat, along his Adam's apple. She felt it quiver, felt him stiffen against her. Derek gripped her arms as she went down farther, nipping, sucking, reclaiming. His heart was pounding against her and his breath was growing shallow. She felt rather than heard the groan in his throat as it echoed in his body when she flicked her tongue along his navel.

She was making him weaker than a baby. His grip tightened on her shoulders, but he was powerless to stop her. Didn't want to stop her. "You're getting ahead of me."

"I can't help it if I'm an overachiever." The words came out in a warm breath along his quivering skin.

With effort he brought her back up to him. His mouth sealed to hers again, he unsnapped her jeans, then slid his hands beneath her underwear, along her skin, cupping her to him.

The hard silhouette made her damp. Eager. Overjoyed. Her loins hummed.

She couldn't remember if he took her jeans off or if she did. It didn't matter. They were naked, together.

Dressed in desire and heat.

He lifted her, bringing her to the bed, his mouth on hers, his body primed and wanting. Hers was slick with anticipation of things she knew were to come.

Of ecstasy unclaimed and a sense of fulfillment shimmering just beyond her reach.

But not for long.

She grasped for it. And for him, wiggling her body around so that she was on top while he was trapped beneath her. No wrestler had ever been so willingly pinned in a match.

Once again she brought her lips to his torso, questing, drinking deep of rivers that had been prohibited to her. Her mouth, open and eager, was everywhere.

She was setting him on fire as surely as if she'd taken the lighter in her hand and applied it to him.

More.

He burned and continued to burn. There was no doubt in his mind that the flame she lit would be eternal. That whatever happened after this night, he would remember the way she was, the way she'd made him feel.

And the way he wanted her.

The heel of her hand pressing against his abdomen, Toni moved it downward a fraction of an inch at a time, until she had him.

Forever.

Deftly she cupped him in her long, cool fingers, her thumb moving erotically. Stroking.

Derek moaned. With his last ounce of resistance he dragged her back up until their bodies were level and his mouth found hers.

He could make love with his mouth the way most men couldn't with their entire bodies, she remembered thinking as she gave herself up to the sensations battering the ramparts around her.

And then, suddenly, he was over her, returning the torture she had rendered to him, nipping, gliding, suckling until she had to bite her lips to keep from crying out and waking up everyone in the house.

His tongue had found her core, teasing her to unbearable heights. Making explosions happen. Then bringing her up to another, just when she thought there was no more left within her to give.

She almost sobbed when he rose over her, poised, ready, and took her like the pirate in Annie's fantasies.

Like the man Toni would always love.

Chapter Twelve

Noises somewhere outside the perimeter of her consciousness intruded, attempting to rouse her. Toni resisted. She didn't want to leave the haven she was cocooned in. Instead, still three-quarters asleep and determined to remain that way, Toni moved closer to the warmth.

In slow increments, anatomy began to register. An arm closed protectively around her shoulders. A chest rose and fell in gentle rhythm. There was skin. Lots and lots of skin, moving very seductively against hers in the same gentle rhythm.

Arousing rhythm.

She struggled to pry her lids open. They felt as if they each had bricks sitting on them.

Derek.

Oh, my God, Derek!

Everything within her scrambled for cover, even

though she couldn't move a muscle. Her body was tucked into the niche that was formed by his side and his arm. A very muscular arm that held her in place like the point of a tempered steel sword.

Her sharp intake of breath woke him. That and the thudding sensation against his side, which was the pleasing combination of her heart beating and her breast moving as she breathed. He felt instantly aroused. And instantly content.

It hadn't been a dream like all the others that had haunted the corners of his mind in sleep, only to fade in the first morning light. It had really happened. He *had* made love with Toni during the night. All night. A long, glorious night where all the hurt feelings, all the loneliness had been placed on hold, banished from this tiny region like locusts from paradise.

Maybe, he mused, looking into Toni's wide blue eyes, still dusted with sleep, it was a first step. At least, he could look at it that way until something else proved him wrong.

He had a distant, sinking feeling that he probably wouldn't have to wait long.

"Morning." The greeting came out on a sigh as he cleared the sleep from his brain and his throat. Leaning over, he pressed a kiss to her forehead.

The way he always had when they woke up, she thought, a pang clutching at the pit of her stomach. He was acting as if they were still together. As if nothing had ever happened.

But it had. And a whole myriad of conflicts had burst forth that she couldn't move or erase with an evening of lovemaking.

Could she?

She tried not to slip into the kiss, into the secure

feeling it generated. It was all too easy to do. And all too startling to find yourself standing in space, with nothing beneath your feet.

"Morning," Toni murmured, gathering the sheet around her.

She was turning shy, he thought. That hadn't happened since their first time together. Maybe she was regretting what had happened last night.

The thought went beyond sadness and straight to hurt without passing Go, without collecting two hundred dollars.

Maybe he was wrong. Derek sat up, running his hands through his hair. He turned his head to look at her. "Regrets?"

Was he telling her that he was having them? She couldn't tell by looking into his eyes. She hated it when he shut her out this way.

"Why, you?" she countered.

She was making him dance and twist in the wind again. He curbed his annoyance. "No."

He bit the word off. She stared at him for a minute. Sure, why should he have regrets? He was a man. Men didn't have regrets after having sex. They only puffed up their chests and went on their merry way without looking back.

That wasn't fair, she admonished herself. Derek wasn't like that.

But none of this was fair. It wasn't fair that what had once seemed like such a perfect world had cracked down the middle, as fragile as an egg.

And it wasn't fair that she didn't know how to fix it, how to tape it together again. How to change what she was and to make him realize that she'd changed.

Maybe she couldn't change, she thought. A sliver of

a panicky feeling pricked at her. Maybe there would always be that tiny kernel deep within her that would wonder if he was straying.

She just didn't know.

"Me neither," she finally answered. Lifting a bare shoulder, she tried to be casual. "After all, we're both adults."

A smile curved his mouth, slipping along his lips like a panther stalking an unsuspecting prey. She didn't know whether to run for cover or stare in fascination. She chose the latter.

"I think you proved that more than adequately last night." He leaned over and tucked a strand of hair behind her ear. He toyed with pulling her sheet away and immersing himself in her again. "I didn't know a pregnant woman could be so flexible."

She drew back. Her stomach was beginning to churn. So much for thinking she was going to get a day's respite. Toni lifted her chin. "Why, how many pregnant women have you made love with?"

He sighed and shook his head. Same old, same old. "Conversation, Toni. I was just making idle conversation. Don't you recognize it?"

Oh, God, here it came. Her stomach lurched up to her mouth like a roller-coaster ride gone amok. She shook her head in response to his question. "All I recognize right now is that if you don't get out of my way quick, you're going to be very sorry."

She was getting really waspish. Why? He hadn't done anything to bring this on. Other than to love her. "Another mood swing?"

She kicked her feet out of the covers and swung them over the side of the bed. "No, another appearance of last night's meal."

Pressing her lips together, Toni pushed Derek out of her way and made a mad dash for the bathroom. She just barely had enough time to close the door behind her and fall to her knees.

The icy floor didn't even register until she was finished.

Gulping in snatches of air, she leaned her head against the bowl. The temperature announced itself with a shock. My God, it was cold.

She gasped in surprise as a blanket dropped from nowhere around her shoulders. Startled, Toni looked up.

Derek was standing over her, completely naked and oblivious to the cold. He rubbed her shoulders through the blanket. Circulation raced through her veins, doing double time.

"Are you all right?"

Toni nodded as the color slowly returned to her face. It had been sudden, but this bout of morning sickness seemed easier to take than the ones that had come before. Maybe she was finally getting her sea legs.

"As all right as a woman on the cusp of death can be, I guess."

She always did have a flair for the dramatic. Derek picked up a washcloth from the towel rack and wet it. "Here."

She pressed the cloth to her face, sliding it over one cheek and then the other. The shiver was involuntary. "It's cold," she murmured.

He thought of getting in under the blanket with her. After a moment they probably wouldn't notice how hard the tile was. But it was morning and there were things to do. Derek glanced out the tiny bathroom window. It was as if he was looking out into oblivion.

Or into his future without her.

He looked down at her. "The heater isn't working. Power failure, remember?"

"How can I forget?" She laughed ruefully. She looked down at her legs. "I think I'm frozen to the floor."

Taking the washcloth from her, he tossed it into the sink, then took hold of both her hands and hauled her to her feet. The blanket fell from her shoulders, pooling onto the floor as her body brushed along his. She shivered again, not so much from the cold as from the jolt that went through her.

His body was still hot. How was that possible?

"Aren't you cold?"

"No," he whispered, the sound curling her toes. "Are you?"

Her breath caught in her throat as he lowered his mouth to hers.

There was a knock on the bedroom door, shattering the moment. Something within her wept.

"Toni, Derek, are you awake?" Joe's voice came through the door like a bulldozer, plowing under what could have been.

Disappointment shimmered between them and then Toni pointed toward the shower. "Get in there," she whispered.

He didn't know whether to be amused or annoyed. "Toni, I'm still your husband. This isn't exactly an illicit tryst." But to make her happy, he picked up the blanket and slung it around his hips before crossing to the door. "What is it?"

"Can I come in?"

Derek shrugged, wondering what couldn't be said through a closed door. "Sure."

With an infuriated yelp, Toni dived for the bed and

cover. She made it under the comforter just before her brother opened the door.

"Are you crazy?" she cried to Derek.

"Sorry, it's been so long since I had a naked woman around, I forgot the drill," Derek quipped as the door opened.

Whatever was on his mind temporarily froze there as Joe looked from his brother-in-law to his sister. The fire had gone out and the room was as cold as all the others in the house, yet there they were, obviously without a stitch of clothing on.

The surprise on his face melted into a grin broad enough to encompass both of them. "Hey, you two back together again?"

You would have thought he'd won the lottery he was always buying tickets to. "No," Toni retorted quickly and with feeling, embarrassment reddening her face.

Out of the corner of her eye she saw the expression on Derek's face harden ever so slightly. Maybe she shouldn't have sounded quite so adamant.

"You didn't come knocking on our door to ask that," Derek said quietly. "What's the matter?"

"Is it Nonna?" Toni asked suddenly. "I knew we shouldn't have left her like that last night…" Guilt nibbled holes in her, especially since she had spent the night making love while her grandmother might have needed her.

"Oh, no, nothing like that," Joe said quickly. "We just need help in the basement." He looked positively sheepish. "Um, the bottom of the water heater's corroded." He directed his words to Derek. "There's about six inches of water everywhere, and it's getting worse."

Derek nodded. With the ease of a man who was completely comfortable with his own body, he dropped the blanket and tossed it onto the bed, then turned toward the bureau to get out fresh clothing.

The fact that there was clothing scattered in heaps around the room didn't escape Joe. He grinned again, his eyes coming in contact with Toni's. She dropped her head and sighed.

Jeans on, Derek jammed his arms through his V-neck sweater and pulled it down over his torso. "Have you put in a call to a plumber?"

There didn't seem to be much point in doing that. "I can call him, but unless he's riding a snowplow or a sleigh being pulled by eight tiny reindeer, I don't think he's going to get here." Joe gestured toward the window. "It's been snowing all night and everything's down." His grin broadened again. "But I guess you two wouldn't have noticed that."

She'd had more than she could take. "Joe, get your mind out of the gutter and take it out with you so I can get dressed."

"My mind's not in the gutter, Toni," he said to irritate her. "It's on the second floor. Third bedroom on the right."

Like a queen banishing a peasant, she pointed to the door. "Out." And then she threw a pillow at his grinning face for good measure.

"I'm going. I'm going." Hands raised in surrender, he backed out of the room. His laughter rang in the air in his wake.

Miserable, cold, Toni looked at Derek. Because it was at her expense, he probably enjoyed this. "You could have—"

He raised his eyes to her face. "What?"

What was the use? She wasn't even sure what she was going to say. "Nothing."

He drew closer, his eyes pinning her. "No, you were going to say something. What?"

All right, she'd put him on the spot. "You could have set him straight that we weren't getting back together." She held her breath, waiting to see what his answer was.

Broad shoulders more suited to a bricklayer than a pediatrician rose and fell in casual uninterest. "He's your brother. You tell him."

Then they weren't getting back together, she thought. His answer confirmed it. Confirmed that nothing had changed.

Except that she would miss him that much more when he left.

It was mutual, she reminded herself. She was leaving him, as well. And she had been the one to start it, not him.

And for that she was going to wind up paying for the rest of her life. Dearly.

"Do you feel all right?" he suddenly asked.

She looked up at him. He had stopped short of the doorway and was peering into her face. She moved back on the bed, though it made no real difference from where he stood. "What?"

"You have a strange expression on your face. Are you still sick?"

"Yes. I'm still sick." Being heartsick qualified as being sick, didn't it?

The doctor in him took over. "Why don't you lie down for a while?" Crossing to her, he felt her forehead. But it was cool and she wasn't flushed anymore.

She moved her head away from his hand. "The room spins when I do."

He smiled softly into her eyes. "Maybe it's the company."

Yeah, there's that, she thought. But she wasn't about to admit it. Not to him. Not when he could leave her so easily. She indicated the door with her eyes. "Joe's waiting for you."

"Right." Turning, he left the room.

It felt twice as empty when he did. With a strangled, helpless cry, Toni buried her head in the pillow.

"About time." Joe beckoned Derek to him as he came down the basement steps. "I thought maybe you'd decided to go back for seconds."

Derek laughed shortly. "Not unless I wanted my head handed to me."

Annie frowned. Everyone knew she hated to be kept in the dark about anything. It wasn't that she gossiped, she just had an insatiable need to know. Everything. "What are you talking about?"

"I'll tell you later," Joe promised. She muttered something in response, but he ignored her. He picked up a bucket and handed it to Derek. "Okay, start bailing," he instructed.

Annie laid a hand on Derek's arm, stopping him. "Joe, he's a doctor."

"And I'm a cop and Alex is the mayor's attaché," Joe recited. "And not one of us probably makes what the plumbers will after this blizzard gets through battering the city."

Joining them, Alex frowned as he refilled his pail. "This would go a hell of a lot faster if we had a pump." He looked at Joe.

"No power," Jackie observed. With a bucket on either side of her, she slowly went up the stairs.

Alex was still hopeful. "We could attach it to a generator."

"If we had one," Joe interjected.

Toni passed Jackie on the steps and turned sideways to make her way down. She clutched the banister for support. "How long is this outage going to last?" she asked Alex. He shrugged without looking in her direction. "Don't lift your shoulders at me," she protested. "You're the one with a job in the mayor's office. Make some calls."

"What do you want me to do?" he asked. "Call up the mayor and have him turn on the power for our house?"

Of course it wasn't that easy, but he could at least find out when the snowplows were coming through. "Sounds like a plan," she quipped. This was supposed to be a special Christmas for Nonna. It wouldn't be very special if they had to gnaw on a turkey that was frozen because they couldn't use the oven.

"Maybe to you. I don't think the mayor can do anything in this situation, Toni," Alex said. He filled another bucket and handed it to Derek.

"Big surprise," Joe murmured.

"Hey," Annie cut in, "this isn't the time to get into a political discussion. Bail, people, bail."

Derek laughed under his breath as he passed her, going up the stairs.

Pitching right in, Toni mused, her eyes following him. He did fit into this family, she thought. Almost more than she did.

"Hey, don't just stand there." Joe nudged her. "Get a mop."

She fisted one hand on her waist. "And just what are you planning to do?"

He gestured around at them. "I'm the coordinator. It's a dirty job, but someone has to do it."

She looked at the mop he had thrust into her hand, and then at him.

He knew her well enough to read her mind. "Don't even think it."

"Foiled again," Toni murmured, and got to work.

Between bailing and mopping, working together, it took them a little over an hour to remove the water heater and clean up the mess in the basement. The dank smell lingered and wafted up to the first floor, but there was nothing to be done about it now. Without electricity, the fans were useless, and leaving the windows open was only asking to borrow trouble. The storm had broken, but there was still snow falling, albeit lightly.

Straggling out of the basement single file, they walked into the kitchen and discovered that Josephine and Nonna had put together breakfast for them.

"How did you manage scrambled eggs?" Toni wanted to know.

"What, you never heard of camping out?" Josephine looked very pleased with herself. "I held a pan over the fire in the living room. The eggs did the rest. Eat," she ordered.

"Don't have to tell me twice," Joe said, filling his plate a second time.

"Maybe he's the one who's pregnant," Alex commented. Toni merely laughed.

"Well, at least *they're* enjoying it." Derek indicated the window that looked out on the backyard.

All four kids, having been served first while their parents worked, were outside now, playing in the snow with relish and abandon. Karen had temporarily forgotten her ascent into adulthood and was taking delight in pelting her brother with well-aimed snowballs. Dustin was having no luck escaping them no matter which direction he ran, or how fast.

"You know, if they ever let women on a baseball team..." Derek mused aloud, looking at Joe.

"Bite your tongue." Alex groaned at the very thought. "The world'll come to an end first."

Jackie raised her glass of orange juice in a toast. "Spoken like a true open-minded person."

"Hey, I never claimed to be broad-minded." His eyes glinted because he knew just what buttons to press to set his wife and sister off. "Except maybe in the strictest sense of the word." He leered, raising and lowering his brows at Jackie.

When she rose from the table, he reached over and pulled her onto his lap, nuzzling her neck like a newly infatuated teenager.

"Well, someone's feeling their oats," Joe observed. Storms had to bring out the romance in this family, he decided. He and Annie had had quite a night of it themselves, and from the looks of it, so had his brother, and so had Toni.

"That wasn't all I was feeling." Alex's laugh was wicked.

A blush crept up Jackie's cheek. "Hush," she admonished, but her heart wasn't in it. She caught Annie's eye and nodded. Annie gave her the high sign.

Alex missed that, but not the color on his wife's cheeks. He flicked a finger along one. "Hey, we're all adults here."

Joe slanted a look at Toni and Derek and grinned. "We sure are, aren't we, Toni?"

She looked at him pointedly. "Some of us are, at least."

Alex deftly changed the topic. "You going in to work today?" he asked his brother.

Joe shook his head. "I've got some time coming to me. I think I'll just call in."

"Sounds good to me," Alex agreed. "Mayor's off to the Bahamas and the council is just woolgathering, anyway."

Joe looked around the table. "Phones working?" he asked no one in particular.

Since no one knew, Toni rose and lifted the receiver on the kitchen telephone. A dial tone hummed in her ear. She held it aloft.

"And we have a winner," she announced.

Joe took a sip of his juice and wiped his mouth. "Okay, first things first. Toni, you get out the Yellow Pages and call around to see if any hardware stores in the area are open. If they are, see if they stock water heaters."

She frowned, exchanging looks with Annie. "Are you planning on installing it yourself?"

"Hey, I'm pretty handy if I have to be." He ignored his wife's soft laughter and Alex's snickering. "Besides, you think I'm going to let Mom hand over her money to a plumber?"

Alex leaned over to Derek. "This should be very interesting."

"Hey, you guys are going to help, aren't you?" Joe looked around the table.

"Is this the part where we say one for all and all for one?" Derek asked.

Alex sighed. "As long as it doesn't require crossing swords."

Toni merely shook her head as she began paging through the Yellow Pages. It had all the earmarks of being a very long day.

Chapter Thirteen

The city, working overtime, restored power to their section of town just in time to usher in the evening. A huge, audible sigh of relief was heard from adults and children alike. No one had been looking forward to a cold dinner. Now they wouldn't have to.

Alex laid down his fork after doing justice to his mother's pie twice over. "Although," he mused, casting a sidelong glance at his wife, "going to bed by candlelight does have its advantages."

"Who says you can't?" Derek countered. Alex looked at him quizzically. "Just keep the lights off and light the candles instead." He grinned at his brother-in-law. "Your choice."

"Sounds good to me," Jackie put in innocently. But there was a wicked look in her eyes that no one over the age of twelve missed.

''Why do you like candles, Mama?'' Zak asked, mystified.

''Because it's romantic, dork,'' Dustin answered before his aunt could. He gave his younger cousin a look of sheer superiority.

He might as well have been talking in a foreign language. ''What's ro-mantic?'' Nik asked him.

Karen made a face. ''It's that icky stuff grown-ups like.'' It was clear where her sympathies lay in the matter. As far as she was concerned, romance was for lame-brains and old people.

Toni caught Annie's eye and smiled. Maybe the girl wasn't growing up quite as fast as they thought she was. Toni could remember being twelve very clearly. All she wanted at the time was to beat her brothers to the top of the tree that grew in the backyard. She'd succeeded at thirteen, but by then her brothers had gone on to more worldly things. Girls. It wasn't until two years later that she'd had her first major crush.

Derek had been aware of Toni's every movement all day. It was as if all his senses had been heightened and attuned to her. He wondered what she was thinking and if any of her thoughts were of the night they'd spent. She'd had regrets this morning, but as the day wore on, she seemed more like her normal self, bossing her brothers around, joking with her sisters-in-law and playfully sparring with him.

He'd taken it as a good sign. Last night had just brought home how empty his life was without her. How empty it would be if he just let things go. He'd done it once in a moment of hurt and anger, and then seen the plan through. But not anymore. His mind was made up. He was going to give their marriage another try.

Now all he had to do was convince her and make her think it was her idea.

His mother-in-law was stacking dinner plates closest to her. "Need any help?" Rising, he started gathering dirty dishes on his end.

Josephine beamed. That man was staying in the family if she had to marry him herself.

"That's what I like, a man who isn't afraid to help out in the kitchen." As she passed Alex, Josephine thumped him on the head. "Wouldn't hurt you or Joe to volunteer, you know."

"Why?" Alex looked at his mother, smothering a grin as he rubbed his head. "Derek beat us to it." He covered his head when Josephine raised her hand again. "Okay, okay." Grabbing his plate, Alex pushed away from the table. "I guess we've got to show them how to do it right once in a while, right, Joe?" He pushed the swinging door open with his back.

Annie looked at Toni. "There's a wrong way to wash dishes?" she quipped as her husband followed his brother into the kitchen.

"Yeah, their way." Toni fluttered her eyelashes at Derek, who was carrying the remainder of the dishes out of the room.

Laughing at the look he gave her, Toni glanced toward her grandmother to see if she had noticed. Nonna had been very quiet during the meal.

The laughter ebbed away slowly as Toni wondered if there was anything wrong. The heat had been restored and, thanks to their combined efforts, so had the hot water. There was a brand-new heater standing in the basement, bountifully dispensing hot water to all corners of the house whenever it was needed. Triumphs notwithstanding, it had been a hell of a taxing day.

Nonna had helped her mother in the kitchen, preparing dinner once electricity had been restored. Had the excitement been too much for her?

Toni leaned over to her. Lowering her voice so no one else would overhear, she asked, "Nonna, are you all right?"

Nonna watched as the children left the table in a rush, bent on playing some new game that involved cartridges and something her grandson Alex had attached to the television set when they had arrived. She wished longingly that she had half their energy and a quarter of their time left.

She smiled at the concern in her granddaughter's voice. Antoinette was a good girl. "Never better. I am just absorbing all this." Her eyes scanned the room. "Enjoying it." Pride and love highlighted her eyes as she watched. "When I was your age, I was always rushing. There was always so much to do. The little moments, they slipped through my fingers and I cannot catch them back. I want to catch all this." Nonna turned her eyes to her youngest grandchild and scrutinized her face. "You are better."

Toni passed her hand reflexively over her stomach. She'd actually been able to eat dinner and not feel everything heaving up in revolt. With her, it hadn't been morning sickness so much as all-day sickness. But it seemed to be passing now that she was beginning to show a little. She supposed it was a trade off. "Yes, I am. I think I'm finally licking this morning-sickness thing."

"You are better," Nonna repeated with a small nod of her head.

Toni paused, seeing things in her grandmother's eyes. She didn't think Nonna was talking about morning sickness, but she didn't want to probe, in case the conversation turned down an avenue she wasn't prepared to walk. She didn't want to lie to Nonna any more than she already had.

"Yes," she agreed as Derek reentered the room. "I'm better."

"I thought so." Nonna was looking at Derek when she said it.

Derek watched her as she moved about the bedroom. Toni made him think of a hummingbird, furiously looking for a place to alight and unable to make up its mind. Since they'd entered the room five minutes ago, she had fiddled with the curtains, brushed her hair, arranged the toiletries on top of the bureau, turned down the bed, then looked unsatisfied with the results and fussed over it some more.

He could find only one reason for this flurry of nervous activity. And he didn't like it. Was she afraid of him?

Enduring it for as long as he could, he finally crossed to her and laid a hand on her shoulder. She stiffened, as if bracing herself for something. Damn it, she *was* afraid of him.

Determined to find out why, Derek turned her around. "What's the matter?"

"Nothing," she said too quickly, her voice too high. "What makes you think something's the matter?" She tried to shrug off his hand, but he didn't release her. Instead, he bracketed both her shoulders, holding her in place.

"The fact that you're behaving like the proverbial long-tailed cat in a room full of rockers, for one." And it seemed that he had been given the part of the rocking chairs.

Her mouth curved at the antiquated comparison. "Where did you pick that up?"

"Old movie. Someone I know used to love watching them." He remembered those rare rainy afternoons when they would curl up together on the sofa, a giant tub of homemade popcorn between them, and watch some black-and-white feature flicker on their tiny TV set.

Old memories beckoned to her. Toni could feel herself responding to him. "I still do."

He nodded slowly, his eyes on hers. "Nice to know some things don't change."

His gaze pinned her. She didn't try to move. "But other things do."

Derek sifted her hair between his fingers. It fell like dark rain. "Like you and me?"

"Actually—" she qualified her remark, her voice low, her emotions high "—I was thinking of me."

I've changed, Derek, I think I really have. For you. But how do I let you know? Saying it isn't enough. And yet, there's no way to show you.

Was she saying that she'd changed from the woman he'd fallen in love with, changed and evolved so that she needed to move on? He wasn't sure he could deal with that tonight. And so he chose the easy way out. The coward's way out. "Pregnancy does that to a woman."

Because he needed her tonight, needed her in the worst way, he was willing to humble himself. Willing to do anything to be with her.

Derek drew her into his arms and slowly swept the

hair away from her face. He brushed his fingers against her cheek, caressing it.

And making a bid for her soul.

She wasn't going to succumb to this, not until things were cleared up between them once and for all. Not until she told him what she wanted to say. She wasn't going to crumble like a cookie that had been dropped on the kitchen floor.

She wasn't.

The hell she wasn't.

Her heart pounding in her throat, in every viable part of her, Toni could offer no resistance when Derek lightly cupped her cheek in his hand and turned her face up to meet his.

Mesmerized, she couldn't have drawn her eyes away from his even if the world was ending. And it would, if he didn't make love with her.

Time stood still, a sentry just outside a door where entrance was forbidden.

The door just beyond opened. She ran in.

Toni felt the kiss before it ever became a reality. Felt it in every part of her body. Begged for it with every part of her soul.

Because only his kiss could erase her doubts and every thought from her mind. And she didn't want to think, not tonight. She just wanted to feel. Feel everything. His hands, his mouth, his lovemaking. And the wondrous sensations that they all created.

She wanted to feel like a woman again. Derek's woman.

Nothing else mattered.

The kiss deepened, taking her with it. She went gladly.

Toni dug her fingers into his shoulders, anchoring

herself not to the world, but to him. Going where only he could take her. Her body swayed into his, melting bonelessly and taking on whatever shape he dictated.

It was incredible. He felt both empowered and humbled to feel her like this against him. To feel the control he had over her. And, in having it, he was controlled himself. By it, by her. Because her vulnerability held him in the palm of her hand.

He would do anything for her. Protect her, defend her. Everything. Everything but give her up. It was the one thing he couldn't do. The one thing he didn't have enough strength to do.

Her softness engulfed him until he'd lost all identity. He was only the man who loved Toni, nothing more. They could put it on his tombstone and he would have happily, humbly died to accommodate it.

So long as he had this night.

Desires battered at him urgently as every single inch of her body made itself known to him. Without so much as a movement, she seemed to be flowing over him.

He caressed, fondled, worshiped, touching her through her clothes. The clothes didn't matter. Only she did, and she was there, beneath them. Just as her heart was there, beneath the emotions that she used as a barricade between them.

It was a barricade made of tissues and he was determined to tear them.

His breathing growing shallow, Derek tugged out the ends of her shirt from her jeans.

"I still haven't found all the buttons to the other blouse." The words came out in short, hot breaths against his mouth.

She felt his smile spread against her lips. "I'll go slower," he promised.

Anticipation shot through her very core, moistening her. "Not too slow."

She felt like exploding, like racing him to the place that was only large enough to cradle the two of them. It was a wonder that she hadn't jumped him already, she thought. He could turn her inside out with just a touch of his hand. Just the promise of his body.

Her willingness excited him, giving him a rush that was second to none. Hands that were capable of gently cradling a newborn trembled as he slipped free button after button down her blouse.

He was careful not to rip anything, but it wasn't easy, not with the degree of passion that simmered just beneath.

"Can't you get pullovers?"

Her eyes were fluttering shut. He was seducing her as his fingertips lightly skimmed along her breasts, along her midriff, undoing her blouse. She had to collect enough air together just to answer.

"I'll see what I can do."

The blouse hung open, a curtain parting, admitting only one to the performance about to begin. He paused, gathering the moment. Then, using the flat of his hands, he pushed the blouse from her shoulders. Skimming his palms along her breasts, he caressed her and reduced her to almost liquid consistency.

Encircling her in his arms, he flicked the clasp at the back of her bra just as her blouse gently floated to the floor. Ever so slowly, watching her eyes, he brought his hands forward again. And with it, the bra. It fell, unnoticed, to the side.

When those same palms brushed and rubbed against her nipples, a moan bubbled in her throat. Toni had to bite it back, afraid the others would hear. She stifled it, but it echoed loudly in her brain, like the cry of a banshee about to be set loose.

"I'm behind," she told him with effort. He was still standing there dressed.

His smile was gentle, soft. Inviting. "Not for long. Not if I know you."

And he did. He knew this woman, knew what existed at the very core of her. He could build from there. He had to. Life without her, even those two months, had been hell. Derek didn't intend to reside in hell forever. Not if there was any way he could prevent it.

He was right. There was no way she was going to lag behind. Like a woman possessed, Toni urgently pulled his shirt from his body and then pressed herself against his bare chest.

She shivered as the hairs lightly tickled her. Sighed in triumphant satisfaction as they ignited fires.

Almost in unison they set each other free of jeans, of underwear, and tangled their limbs, fitting together the way they had been created to do.

They never made it to the four-poster. It was much too far away.

Instead, they sank to the floor, wrapped in each other, exploring each other as if this was the very first time.

As if each was afraid there would never be another opportunity to do so.

He stroked her until she twisted and turned into his hand, eager to be taken up to the summit, to dive freely from there into the rivers below. Time and again he took her up and watched her face as she dived, ecstasy exploding in her veins.

And still there was more.

Derek anointed the length and breadth of her with openmouthed kisses that had Toni squirming and grasping for him. Wanting to return the favor. To return the torture.

He knew how to torture, she thought. And knew how to conquer. She was utterly, completely his and there wasn't a thing she could do about it.

He saw it in her eyes. And in seeing it he was firmly trapped there.

His mouth on hers, he grabbed her hair in his hands and came to her. As she lifted her hips to admit him, he sheathed himself and slowly began to move, approximating a timeless rhythm that belonged to only them.

And only now.

The cry she made echoed in his mouth and reinforced his weakness. He slumped against her, drenched, content to never move again and fully convinced that he couldn't, even if he wanted to.

Her head cradled against his shoulder, he felt as well as heard her sigh.

"Anything wrong?" he murmured against her neck.

She was exhausted beyond belief, but his breath still sent little shock waves through her. "No, everything's perfect."

If it was perfect, why did she sound so sad?

"But?" he prompted.

She sighed again before answering. It didn't help. The sadness wouldn't leave. "Too bad it can't remain that way."

He rose on his elbow to look at her. "And why can't it?"

"Because..." She couldn't put it into words. Maybe didn't want to put it into words. Not now. Later.

He fed the word back to her. "Because?"

"Because of a lot of things." It wasn't enough of an answer. She gave him more. "Because you're going to

Africa." She looked away. "Because you don't want this baby."

Is that what she thought? "I told you, I never said that."

He might not have said it in so many words, but omission spoke for itself. "But you never wanted any children." She wasn't going to have him lie to her, not when they were here like this, not after having made love. She raised herself up on her elbow. "Look at me and tell me I'm wrong."

Instinct told him to say she was, but he couldn't bring himself to lie to her. He valued the truth too much. "No, you're not wrong."

She sat up. Suddenly she felt very cold. She wrapped her dignity around her. "Well, then, I guess there's nothing left to say."

"No, there is." He had wanted to pick his time to tell her about Kevin. But he couldn't let it go like this— he couldn't have her thinking the worst. "There's a lot left to say. I have to tell you something."

Something froze within her as she looked at his eyes. "What?" she whispered, not knowing what he would say, yet afraid to hear it. Afraid that his words would forever separate them.

He gathered her to him, needing to feel the warmth of her body beside him as he spoke. It helped ward off the chill in his soul.

It had been a long time since he'd allowed himself to think of Kevin.

Derek had no idea where to begin. "I had a brother—"

She jolted, stunned, and stared at him. "You have a brother?"

He'd never mentioned any family at all. It was only

after she'd prodded relentlessly that he'd told her his parents had divorced when he was thirteen and he hadn't had much of a home life after that. They were both gone now. It hadn't been worth talking about, he'd told her. She'd felt shut out then, but not half so much as now.

"Had," Derek repeated, correcting her. "Kevin was three years younger than I was. He died of leukemia the summer I was twelve."

It still affected him. She could see it in his eyes. Toni reached out to him. "Oh, Derek, I'm so sorry."

"Yeah." He blew out a breath. "So am I. I was completely devastated by his death. So were my parents. Kevin's illness—Kevin's death—summarily tore up the fabric of our family. My parents were at each other's throats all the time, blaming one another, saying things they didn't mean, that they could never take back. And all that spilled out on me." It was, he thought, as if in their grief they'd forgotten that they had another child. "I never wanted to feel that again, what they had to feel as parents. What I felt, losing him." Even now, talking about it, took little pieces of him away. "It was the most awful feeling in the world."

He looked at her, wondering if she understood. Reaching out, he toyed with her hair.

"That was one of the reasons it took me so long to admit that I was in love with you. I didn't want to love, because if I loved, I could lose. And that was something I didn't know if I could endure. I took a risk with you because I couldn't help myself. But when it came to having children..." His voice trailed off as he shrugged.

"I couldn't do it, didn't want to do it. I thought by becoming a pediatrician, by treating children, I could somehow keep Kevin's memory alive, yet not get emotionally involved." He laughed ruefully at himself. "I couldn't do a very good job of that, either. Children, even other people's children, have a way of pulling you in. Of making you care about them." He raised his eyes to look at her. "And then you became pregnant and the point became moot." He saw the dark look in her eyes. "What's the matter?"

How could he ask that? Didn't he know? Didn't he know what he had just done to her, to their marriage?

"You had a brother and you never told me. You had pain, and you never shared it." She rose to her knees, barely suppressing fury. "You had the gall to be angry with me because I didn't trust you, because I didn't take you on faith, when you didn't trust me with this part of you?"

"You're angry—"

Fury almost exploded. "What gave you your first clue? Of course I'm angry—"

She scrambled to her feet. She wanted to throw on some clothes and get out of the room. Out of the house. She wanted to feel the cold wind on her face and to calm down. If she could.

Derek grabbed her wrist, stopping her. "It wasn't a matter of trust—"

Her eyes blazed. "Then what the hell would you call it?"

It was very simple. "Having a pain I didn't want to share."

And he thought there was a difference? "Just as bad. Worse." Toni fisted her hands impotently at her sides, then, frustrated, whacked the palm of her hand against his chest. He stared at her, stunned. She did it again. It didn't alleviate the feelings of frustration. "I'm your wife, damn it, or at least I was. Certain things go with the territory. Part of it is being there for the person when they need you—and knowing that they trust you to support them emotionally.''

He couldn't make heads or tails out of this. ''I hurt you.''

Was he really that dense? ''You're damn straight you did.''

She turned her head, afraid she would cry. If she did, they would be angry tears. But men were too dumb to know the difference, she thought in frustration.

He wouldn't let her turn away. Derek held her arms. ''Toni, I never meant to hurt you.''

With effort, she maintained her poise. The tears retreated. Toni lifted her chin. ''And I never meant to hurt you. But the hurt's there, isn't it?''

''Yeah, it is.''

She searched his face. He looked miserable. She softened, thinking of what he must have gone through. Her heart went out to him. ''So, what do we do now?''

He had no solutions. They'd thrown all the cards on the table. He had no idea if there was a winning hand there or not. He could only hope. But he was too tired now to sort it out beyond what they had already done.

''Go to sleep. Think about it in the morning. Want me to take the floor?''

In light of the way relations were between them at the moment, he fully expected her to yell yes and throw the blankets at him.

Suddenly bone weary and sick of arguing, Toni crawled into bed. Sitting up, she drew the covers around her and looked at him. ''I want you to shut up, come here and kiss me again.''

There was just no understanding the species. He

wouldn't figure her out even if he lived to be a thousand. But it comforted him to know that he was not alone.

He nodded, sliding in on his side. He slipped his arm around her and drew her to him. "I think I can manage that."

"It's a start," she murmured.

And maybe it was.

And maybe it was,

Chapter Fourteen

Derek wasn't sure what woke him up. Maybe it was the noise he heard coming from outside. Front or back, he couldn't tell. Or perhaps it was the warm smells wafting up from the kitchen that he would forever associate with this house. Maybe it was the slow, steady rattle of the radiator as it struggled to bring up enough heat into the room. It could even have been the fact that the room was flooded with daylight, courtesy of a hospitable sun that was doing its best to melt some of the snow that the blizzard had brought.

Or maybe it was the emptiness.

He rolled over, his hand spread, reaching for her. And found nothing. Just the way he had for the two long months he'd been in exile.

He took a deep breath, rubbing the sleep from his eyes with the heels of his hands.

"Toni?"

There was no answer. Derek dragged himself up into a sitting position and looked toward the bathroom. The door was standing open. She wasn't in there. Almost instinctively, he ran his hand along her side of the bed. It was cold.

Calculating the time it normally took her to shower and get dressed, that meant that she'd gotten up and left the room at least half an hour ago. Probably more.

He wondered if the empty place next to him was her final answer to last night. She'd been pretty angry about his keeping Kevin a secret.

Derek dragged his hand through his hair and tried to collect his thoughts, his feelings. They were scattered about like so many fallen leaves, blowing in the wind, swirling around each other without a set pattern. Without rhyme or reason.

Coffee. He needed coffee. Probably a gallon of it, barely refined, to set him straight and get him thinking clearly.

Clinging to the thought, he stumbled out of bed and headed for the shower. In med school and the grueling years that had followed, he had practically lived on the stuff.

On that and love.

The water hit him, hot and fast. He moved the dial toward Cold and felt his skin contracting in response as the needles of water turned icy. Every nerve ending sprang to attention. Good. It was waking him up. At least temporarily.

Derek showered in record time, then passed a razor over his face, shaving down only. Slinging the towel over the side of the shower stall, he went in search of something clean, or semiclean, to wear. Whatever batteries he was running on were almost drained.

He supposed he could get used to living on just coffee all over again. After all, he'd done it before. He jammed his legs into his jeans, remembering.

But that had been before Toni had burst into his life like a small, glowing sunbeam. Back then the confines of his life had been as close to Spartan as could be found outside a monastery.

He had made up his mind from twelve on not to care about anyone. He'd never been close to his parents, but he had worshiped the ground that Kevin had run on. And it had broken his heart when Kevin died.

Shoeless, Derek dropped to his knees to search for a pair under the bed.

There'd been no one to comfort him, no one to hold him when Kevin died. No one to understand how much he missed his brother. His parents had been too busy grieving and blaming each other. So he had withdrawn. Withdrawn into his world and made plans about how to live the rest of his life.

He found sneakers—his—at opposite ends of the bed. Triumphant, he gathered them up and remembered that he had yet to find socks.

The plans he'd made for himself hadn't included a wife or family. Or a rampant sunbeam with raven hair, sensual limbs and a lusty laugh that went straight to his core and unwound him like a runaway ball of wool tumbling down a hillside.

But she had come. And though he'd been captured, mesmerized from the very first moment, he'd tried to shut her out.

He could have saved his energy. There was no shutting Toni out. She seeped into every part of his life, like daylight creeping into a house whose shutters were too weak to keep it out.

Even now, as he thought of it, a smile curved his mouth.

He put on his last pair of socks and made a mental note to wash out the others.

Soon.

With charm and grace Toni had pulled him into her world, given him her family to call his own. The first family he had truly been part of. And he had taken to it the way a starving man took to his first feast.

He wasn't ready to walk away from the banquet table yet.

Or ever.

Glancing in the mirror, he ran his fingers through his damp hair. That would have to do. His comb was missing. Toni had probably misplaced it somewhere. Small price to pay for happiness.

And happiness was where he was bound. There was absolutely no way he intended to go through with the divorce. Not when they loved each other like this. Toni was right—he'd placed such an emphasis on trust, and yet he hadn't trusted her with his grief, with the essence of what made up his privacy.

He hadn't seen it that way, but now that she'd pointed it out, he knew she was right. He was willing to admit that. Willing to try again if she was. It was time for both of them to take down the barriers they'd constructed against getting hurt again.

He was more than ready.

Derek came down to the bottom of the landing, a warrior prepared to take the fort single-handedly and disassemble its ramparts one by one.

He was surrounded by the fort's reinforcements.

They seemed to come at him from all four sides, like

four jack-in-the-boxes, their timers all set to the same moment.

Zak grabbed his hand first. "Wow, you're finally awake. It's almost thirteen o'clock!"

"One o'clock." Karen corrected her cousin condescendingly.

He'd slept the sleep of the righteous, Derek thought, amused at the thought. The last time he'd slept until almost one he'd had a 103-degree fever and was in his first year in med school.

"Mama said not to bother you until you got up," Nik interjected.

"So we didn't." Zak raised his voice to get the last word in.

Karen assumed a superior air and frowned reprovingly at the twins and her brother. "I tried to keep the rug rats quiet."

"Yeah, right," Dustin hooted. "She was the one who kept running in, looking at the clock and sighing, 'Is he still asleep?'" He laced his fingers together under his chin and fluttered his eyelashes, pretending to be Karen. Karen punched him in the arm and he laughed. "She just couldn't wait."

If he didn't get some coffee soon, his brain was going to go into meltdown. When a quartet of children under the age of thirteen lost him, he was in a bad way. "Wait for what?"

Zak was tugging at his sleeve, trying to drag him to the nearest window. "There's lots more snow, Uncle Derek."

That was supposed to mean something to him, but he hadn't a clue as to what.

Nik looked up at him impatiently. "You said you'd

show us how to build a real good fort when there was enough snow.''

Zak was on his other side, talking faster than his brother. Derek felt as if he was wedged between twin stereo speakers, slightly out of sync and broadcasting at different frequencies. ''And we didn't bother you yesterday 'cause of the water heat and all.''

''Water heater,'' Karen corrected. She rolled her eyes dramatically. ''Can't these children get anything straight?''

Derek thought it was a great imitation of Bette Davis, but refrained from mentioning it. Karen probably didn't know who Bette Davis was.

Nik wasn't put off by the correction. ''Yeah, that. So can you?''

Zak was all but hanging off his arm. ''Can you, please?''

He might have been able to beg off from one, or maybe even two. But all four of them were looking up at him with almost identical puppy-dog expressions and pleading, eager eyes. Derek hadn't realized, until this moment, that they all had Toni's eyes. Eyes as blue as a crystal lake in the spring.

Would the baby have her eyes? Derek certainly hoped so.

Oh, what the hell. He didn't really have anything planned for this morning—this afternoon, he amended ruefully—except to plead for his life. That could be put on hold temporarily.

''Okay.''

Cheering, Nik grabbed for his other hand. ''Great. Let's go!''

Very firmly, Karen uncoupled her uncle first from Zak, then from Nik.

"He needs to get his jacket first, dorks," Karen admonished them when they turned pouty faces up to her. She in turn looked at Derek with an expression that was way too old for her years. "Don't you, Uncle Derek?"

She was going to be a first-class flirt, Derek decided. It seemed as if the bullpen was warming up. "Yes, that, too. But what I really need is coffee." Opening the hall closet, he took out his jacket.

Following behind him like a child's pull toy, Zak scrooched up his face. "Yuck, why coffee?"

"It's like engine fuel for grown-ups," Dustin told him, though the beverage held no attraction for him, either. He'd sneaked a little once or twice and thought that if he had the foul drink waiting for him in the morning, he'd sleep in all the time. "My dad can't even open his eyes without it."

Zak tried to envision his uncle with eyes that had to be pried open with coffee. "Really?"

Reaching the haven of the kitchen, Derek stopped. "I'll be with you guys in a few minutes." He waved them on to the back door. "Why don't you get started building it without me?"

"'Kay!"

"Hey, he asked me, not you."

"In your dreams."

"I can do it better than you can."

The door slammed four times as each ran out, determined to shut the door on the one who came after. Appropriate mothers winced and Josephine sighed deeply and shook her head. Nonna merely smiled and went on combining ingredients in a huge silver pot. Steam curled up from it, wafting toward him an aroma that was to die for.

As was the feeling he had for Toni. His eyes slid

toward her. He wondered what she was thinking. What she was feeling today. And if her feelings matched his own. He could only hope.

The warm smells of blending spices, breads and pastries reached their full potency. Drawn to the island where the coffeemaker stood, Derek felt as if he could remain here for hours, just inhaling. And maybe sampling now and again.

He reached for a mug. He supposed what he had to say to Toni *could* wait a little longer. After all, neither one of them was going anywhere. Even if the snowplows had managed to clear away some of the streets. Tonight was Christmas Eve and they were here for the duration.

What he was having, he decided, was a bout of cold feet. But the rest of him wasn't cold. Not when she smiled at him that way.

Picking up the coffeepot, Toni gestured toward his mug. This was the first morning in a long time that she hadn't had to visit the bathroom within three minutes of waking up. She was really getting into this routine of being pregnant, rounding belly and all. She'd spent the time propped up on her elbow, just looking at him. Looking and remembering.

And deciding things.

"Hi." She topped off his mug. "I hear you're going to build a fort." She and the others had heard nothing else all morning as the kids raced in and out of the house, anxiously awaiting Derek's arrival downstairs.

Derek slid onto a stool and held the mug with both hands. He took a long sip and his brain seemed to clear instantly. "Yeah, I promised."

Nonna turned from her pot. Reaching over, she patted his arm. "You are a good man, Derek." Josephine smiled at him over her mother's head. The others murmured their assent to Nonna's pronouncement.

Derek smiled to himself, taking another long sip. As the coffee wound into his stomach, his confidence grew. What did he have to be worried about? He had the rest of the family in his pocket. He couldn't have worked this better if he had planned. Toni would come around. And stay around.

He had to believe that.

He stared into the mug. The remaining liquid shimmered seductively at him, catching the overhead light. It reminded him of Toni's hair. He raised his eyes to her. And fell in love all over again. It was something he hoped would never stop happening to him.

Taking advantage of the audience that trapped her by its presence, he brushed a quick kiss to her lips. She was surprised, and then giving. Surprising him. Pleasantly so.

Josephine sighed. "Warms your heart, doesn't it, Mama?"

As it had from the very beginning, Nonna thought. "Yes, it does."

A large Christmas Eve meal was a tradition they had observed ever since Josephine could remember. Thank goodness the power had been restored to facilitate things. But even if it hadn't, she and the others would have found a way. Traditions were what cemented families together. Traditions like marriage. She blinked back a tear. It looked as if Toni was going to take her advice.

Sniffing, Josephine looked around at the others. Work had come to a standstill. "Well, the manicotti isn't going to stuff itself," Josephine announced with the air of a drill sergeant sending his men into battle.

Jackie and Annie grinned at her as they took up their assigned posts. Her daughters-in-law knew better than to be intimidated. But they also knew better than to ignore a direct order in the kitchen.

Glancing out the window, Derek saw that the kids were busy. He lingered a moment longer with Toni. "Where is everyone?"

She smiled at his wording. Her hands flew as she diced carrots into tiny squares with the flair of a swordsman. She would have been a hell of a surgeon if she'd gone that route, he thought.

"By everyone, you mean Alex and Joe?" Everyone else was either in the kitchen or playing in the yard.

He grinned. "Yes."

She pulled two more carrots from the bag and peeled them clean as she talked. "They decided to give going to work a try. I think they were getting cabin fever." All this closeness was driving her brothers crazy. "How about you?"

Compared to the hectic pace he was accustomed to, with rounds, patients and emergencies, this was a walk in the park. Power outage and broken water heater notwithstanding.

"I like the peace and quiet."

Suddenly the sound of raised voices was heard as an argument exploded and escalated in the backyard.

Whatever truce had been struck up was over. Toni grinned, walking to the sink to rinse off the vegetables. "You were saying?"

Derek got off the stool, draining his mug. "I think my minions are calling." Passing Toni to get to the back door, he handed her his mug. And snared one more kiss before leaving.

He was the only man she knew who could consume

scalding hot coffee as if it was ice water. With a shake of her head, Toni rinsed out his mug.

Placing it on the draining board, she stopped to watch him playing with her niece and nephews. This felt good, Toni thought. Very good. It was a moment to press between the pages of her memory, she mused, the way Nonna had told her to.

She was in the bosom of her family, anticipating Christmas, watching her husband play with the children. It didn't get any better than this.

Yes, it did. Next year at this time, there would be one more. Without realizing it, she pressed her hand over her swelling abdomen. And they would be right back here, all of them, anticipating the magic of Christmas.

She'd already decided to forget about the divorce proceedings. There were things they had to iron out, but she was more than willing to set up the ironing board and pull up her sleeves to do the work.

A man like Derek came along only once in a lifetime. She was glad that lifetime was hers, and she intended to make the most of the gift.

Right now she had to make the most of her job, or she'd never hear the end of it.

Heat in the kitchen rose as more and more pots were set on the burners, then shifted to the ovens. Top and bottom were full—with turkey, side dishes and enough pastries to make a baker thump his chest with pride. It represented the efforts of five women, working full-time. Toni had to admit she enjoyed giving vent to her creative side.

Just as long as it was only once a year, she thought, smiling to herself as she tried to place the salad in the refrigerator. As if there was going to be room for any salad, she mused. There was hardly any space left in the refrigerator.

Sighing, she began moving containers around, looking for enough space to accommodate the bowl.

"Toni!"

The urgent note in her mother's voice almost made her drop the bowl on the floor. Toni turned around.

Her heart constricted as she saw that the others had all clustered around Nonna.

She didn't even remember crossing the floor to her. Nonna was sitting on a chair, her face the color of the snow outside. Toni took her hand, holding it between her own. It felt icy to the touch.

"Nonna," she whispered fearfully, "what is it?"

Nonna's breathing was labored and she tried to wave away the concern. Her hand hardly swiped the air. "A great deal of nothing."

"I turned around and saw her sway. She almost fainted. She's having an attack. Oh, my God, she's having an attack." Josephine covered her mouth with both hands to keep the cry of anguish back. Annie put her arm around her, mutely comforting Josephine, her own eyes wide with fear.

Toni felt her grandmother's pulse. It was rapid and weak. Weak like the last flutterings of a butterfly before the fall.

Panic tightened within her, panic she saw mirrored in her mother's face. It was a struggle to allow the doctor to emerge between the heavy bars of emotion, but she didn't have the luxury of being the terrified granddaughter. That wouldn't do Nonna any good right now.

Her hand tightened around Nonna's, as if that could somehow anchor her to this life. That was all that mattered.

"Jackie, get Derek." She looked at her mother. "Who's Nonna's doctor?"

For a minute her mind was blank. "Dr. Fields." Josephine remembered suddenly. "But he's away. We were just there last week." She blinked away the tears that were threatening to come. "He said she was doing beautifully."

That didn't jibe with what her mother had told her when she called last week. "But you said—"

She broke off. The expression on Josephine's face told her that she didn't remember anything she had said, only that her mother was ill.

A blast of cold came in, and with it Derek. Jackie had remained outside, to keep the children from coming in and getting underfoot.

"What's the matter?" He was covered with snow. He stopped brushing the snow out of his hair and his features tightened when he looked at the women. Josephine and Annie stepped aside, leaving him room. He looked questioningly at Toni.

"Her pulse rate is high and she almost fainted," Toni told him.

Derek knelt beside Nonna, taking her pulse himself. Toni was right. It was rapid. But she looked alert and very composed. "Are you having any pains?"

Nonna paused before answering. "Maybe, just a little." And then she shrugged. "The others, they like to fuss too much."

"The others worry about you." He pivoted on his heel, turning toward Josephine. "What was she doing when she fainted?"

"Almost fainted," Nonna corrected gently.

"She's been on her feet all morning, Derek. And fasting. It's tradition to fast, but only she observes it." Josephine wrung her hands. Derek couldn't remember ever seeing her this distraught. "I told her she shouldn't fast at her age and that she was doing too much."

"But it is Christmas Eve tonight," Nonna observed to Derek. She leaned forward, gaining his ear. "I have always done too much, if you listen to Josephine."

He knew better than to get in the middle of this. "And this time, you will listen." Derek rose to his feet and picked her up in his arms. She hardly weighed anything at all. "I'm taking you upstairs, young lady, and giving you a once-over." As he began to leave the room, he looked over his shoulder at Toni. She looked paler than her grandmother, he thought. "Toni, get my bag."

Toni moved quickly, getting ahead of him before he reached the doorway. She raced up the stairs. Her heart was pounding double-time in her chest and she was afraid to form any thoughts.

She formed prayers instead.

Derek set aside his stethoscope. He'd given Nonna as thorough an exam as he could under the limiting circumstances. All her vital signs checked out and were extremely encouraging. The fluttering had ceased even before she'd had an opportunity to take the nitroglycerin tablets he'd packed with him on the outside chance that she would need the medicine.

As he listened to Toni talk to her, Derek opened Nonna's medicine cabinet and sifted through the bottles of prescriptions that stood there. Mevacor, Cardizem, Catapres, Antivert. They all had Nonna's name on them, and looked like neat little soldiers, all in a row.

Neat, unused soldiers.

He walked back into the bedroom and looked at

Nonna. "Toni, would you mind leaving us alone for a minute? I'd like to talk to my patient."

Toni looked at him sharply. What was he going to say to her that she couldn't hear? Nonna was her grandmother, not his.

"I think I should—"

"Listen to your husband," Nonna interjected, smiling to temper the words.

Toni shook her head and kissed the woman's velvety cheek as she withdrew. "You are entirely too old-world Italian, Nonna."

Nonna's smile widened, crinkling about her eyes. "Yes, I know. Now go."

Giving Derek a warning look that told him she wanted to know everything the moment he was finished, Toni stepped outside the room and closed the door behind her.

Chapter Fifteen

Derek stood for a moment, leaning his hip against the triple-chested cherrywood bureau, his arms crossed before him. He studied the tiny woman sitting up on the bed. An amused expression played on his lips. "You know, don't you?"

Her eyes were clear and guileless when they looked up into his. The jig, as her grandson used to say, was up. "About the divorce? Yes."

Everyone had gone to such lengths to deceive her. "But how…?"

As if there could be such things as secrets from her in this house. Nonna shrugged innocently. "I overhear Josephine on the telephone with Antoinette. I put things together. It is not hard."

Derek sat down on the bed beside Nonna, taking her hand in his. His admiration for her grew. "So you came up with this?"

That, too, had not been hard to do. She knew they both loved her, as she them. She nodded. "You came. Both of you."

"And you're not sick?" No piece of information could make him happier.

The shoulders moved again in a half shrug. "The heart, it flutters sometimes." Her smile was wide, conspiratorial, as she inclined her head to his. "When I first saw my Giuseppe, it fluttered, too."

She must have been something else when she was young. Derek wished he could have known her then. Wished she could have been his grandmother. In a way, he supposed now she was.

He nodded toward the bathroom and the medicine cabinet he had rummaged through. "How did you get all those pills?"

That, she felt, had been a stroke of genius on her part. "Selena's grandson is a—how you say? Pharmist."

"Pharmacist," Derek corrected. Selena was probably one of her cohorts. He was surprised at the revelation. "And he gave you these?" It was one thing to indulge an old lady, but another to freely dispense prescription medicines without a doctor's authorization.

"He gave me the bottles. And the little papers to put in front." She laced her hands together in her lap, momentarily looking contrite for his benefit. But she was happy, because she knew she had accomplished what she had set out to do—bring them together. "He typed the names in for me, too, but that I had to ask extra."

The little devil. So much for thinking her harmless. He had to bite the inside of his mouth to keep from laughing. "And what's inside the bottles?"

"Vitamins." She thought a minute, translating names

in her head to get the proper English sound. "Magnesium, potassium. The tiny pills are mine. The doctor gave them to me in case I needed them."

Which would explain the worn label on the one bottle at the end, he thought. "I've got to hand it to you, you're one smart lady."

His praise made her blush. He thought it charming.

"You live a long time, you learn a few things."

He was certain that in her case, that was a vast understatement. But she had gone to a cardiologist. There had to have been a reason. Derek got down to business. "What did the doctor say you had?"

"Angina. Just a touch." She qualified the word before he could become concerned. "He said it was nothing to worry about."

Derek tried to look stern and knew he failed miserably. If not for her, he and Toni would probably have just gone ahead with the divorce, stubborn and misguided to the end. Right about now, he would be packing to relocate to Africa.

"But you made us worry," he noted.

"To make you come here." Deftly she turned the tables on him. "You made me worry. I did not want to see either of you alone."

This time her hands went around his, as if to infuse him with her feelings, her thoughts. She wanted him to see himself and her granddaughter the way she saw them. As a couple who belonged together.

"There was never such joy in Antoniette's face until she was with you. And you, you had sad eyes when she first brought you to us." It had made her ache with sympathy just to look at him. "Your eyes were not sad anymore when you married her." She sighed, making a pronouncement. "It would be a sin for you not to be together."

He could accept that. Be grateful for that. It still didn't explain what had happened today. After all, with her insight, she could see that what had once been broken was mending. There had been no need to pretend to faint. That had been real.

"And in the kitchen now?"

That had been an annoyance, and she wanted to get past it. "It is warm, I get a little dizzy...." Her voice trailed off dismissively.

The door flew open. Toni stalked into the room, impatience and concern etched on her face.

This was taking much too long. What was he saying to her grandmother? Was he preparing her for something?

She glared at Derek. How dare he keep this from her? She didn't give a damn about doctor-patient privilege. That was fine when it came to other people, but this was Nonna. *Her* Nonna, and she had a right to know.

"I can't take it anymore. How is she?"

He'd forgotten that Toni was outside, waiting. Getting up, he slipped an arm around his wife's shoulders. "She's terrific. With any luck, this lady will outlive us all." He looked at Nonna. "Get some rest."

She was a little tired, but Nonna looked toward the doorway uncertainly. "But the cooking—"

"Will be taken care of, I promise you. You taught everyone very well," he assured her. Laying a hand on her shoulder, he gently pushed her back. It took very little pressure. "You can go down in half an hour. I'll take you myself," he promised.

Nonna sighed, content. "Well, with an offer like that, how can I refuse?"

He winked at her. "You can't." With that he shut the door behind him.

Josephine was waiting in the hall and pounced on him as he emerged. Derek told her the truth, that Nonna had had a little dizzy spell brought on by the heat, her lack of food intake and the excitement. She was resting and would be herself in no time.

Toni waited until her mother went back downstairs with the news. Then she dragged Derek into their room and firmly closed the door.

"Hmm, this looks intriguing," Derek murmured against her hair.

What had gotten into him? Her grandmother was sick and he was putting moves on her. She whirled around. "How is she, really?"

"Fine." How had he ever thought that he could survive without the scent of her hair softly wafting to him in the middle of the night?

That was the same tone he'd used with her mother. She wanted to know the truth. Toni blew out an impatient breath. "Don't toy with me."

The smile that curved his mouth was almost wicked. At the very least, it was disarmingly sexy.

"Oh, but I'd like to. So would Nonna." His fingers feathered along her neck, making her squirm inwardly. He could see it in her eyes. "Like me to toy with you," he added.

She took a step back. Any more of that and she wasn't going to be able to think straight. "What are you talking about?"

He laughed fondly, temporarily halting his assault. "She's a very foxy little old lady, your grandmother. This was all for show."

She didn't understand. "You mean she didn't almost faint?"

"No, that part's true." He saw the concern return and was quick to explain. "Close quarters, steam coming out of pots, lots of bodies in the room, taking up air. She got a little dizzy." His very tone dismissed it. "Under the circumstances, anyone might."

This wasn't getting any clearer. "But all those pills I saw..."

"Plants. Props." He still marveled at the lengths Nonna had gone to. Such careful planning. And all of it was for them. It felt wonderful to be that loved. To finally be within the bosom of a family that cared so much.

Toni could only stare at him. "Props? What are you talking about?"

"About vitamins in little bottles she had one of her friend's grandsons get for her." He laughed, shaking his head. "And we were all taken in by it. Good thing she didn't decide on a life of crime. She's got the face to get away with it."

She allowed relief to begin to take hold. "Then she really is all right?"

He nodded. "She has a touch of angina, but for the most part, her heart is very strong."

Toni's brows narrowed. "But why did she lie to us like that?"

"It's not lying," he corrected, getting into the spirit. "It's inventive truth. Nonna decided to put on a little drama to get us here for Christmas." He never had had that talk with Toni. But if she saw how important this was to her grandmother, maybe that was the leverage he needed to cement things. "She was hoping if we were together, pretending to be together, we'd naturally slip into the roles.'' The smile left his lips, to be replaced by a deeper, fuller emotion as he looked into her eyes. ''She was right.''

''Then Nonna knew?'' And here she thought they had done so well with their charade.

Toni was wearing tiny silver bells at her ears. He flicked one and set it spinning. ''Yup.''

Toni was still unclear on the details. ''But how? Mom said everyone kept it from her.''

Where there was a will, there was definitely a way. And Nonna had found it.

''Like I said, she's a crafty little old lady. She overheard your mother on the telephone with you. And she was right,'' Derek reminded Toni.

Toni blinked, lost again. ''Right?''

He nodded, slipping his arms around her. ''About us. I don't want to play games anymore.''

She desperately tried to sort out his words from her feelings. ''Then you want to call off the charade?''

He smiled. ''No, I want to call off the calling off. The divorce,'' he added when she just stared at him. ''I don't want this divorce, Toni.''

Neither did she. With all her heart she wanted to pretend it had never happened. But it had to be for the right reasons. If it wasn't, she couldn't live with it, and eventually, neither could he. ''If you're doing this because of the baby...''

Derek inclined his head, granting her that it had some bearing. ''Yes, but...''

A chill passed over her. It was exactly what she was afraid of. Exactly what she didn't want. She pushed him away. ''Well, I don't want you being noble. I can get along fine by myself. If you—''

He was going to have to find a way to talk more

quickly if he wanted to survive with her. He caught her by the arm before she could leave the room.

"There was a 'but' there and you're not paying attention. I'm doing this because I want to be there for the baby. From the first moment. But I also want to be there for you. For every moment." And he had never meant anything more in his life.

She thought of the reason she had driven him away. "What about trust?"

It was a noble sentiment, but it was a cold consolation prize all by itself. "Maybe I was a little overly sensitive. Maybe it is something you have to earn."

She thought of the way she had treated him. He hadn't deserved that sort of treatment. She knew that now. A man who was this wonderful to her family wouldn't just break her heart for a fling.

"A little at a time?" she guessed.

"A lot at a time." He didn't ever want to risk losing her again. Not over anything. Derek glanced down at his foot. "We could put a ball and chain around my ankle until you feel you can let me out into the world."

Her smile rose to her eyes. "No need. I know I can trust you." She wanted him to know she was sincere. "You're not like Daddy." She thought of what her mother had told her. Pity and absolution filled her. "And even he deserved to be forgiven when he was sorry."

Her words gave him hope. Very slowly he pressed a kiss to her neck and felt her pulse flutter. Like Nonna when she saw her Giuseppe for the first time, he remembered. "Only thing I'm sorry about is not firing Sylvia sooner. But I never knew."

She readily believed that. "No, you never knew. You're unassuming enough to let things like that just zip right by you. I should have realized that." It was hard to form coherent sentences when he was undoing her nerve endings, turning her to the consistency of the confection they were stuffing the cannolis with. "It was just...just when I saw her all over you like that—" Toni gripped his shoulders, afraid of sliding straight to the floor "—all I could think of was that I had lost you, and it broke my heart." She swallowed, focusing. "I hated you for that feeling."

That was all behind them now. And would stay there if he had anything to say about it.

"We've wasted time." He began to loosen her blouse. More buttons, he thought.

She shivered as his fingers brushed along her breasts. The bra in the way didn't make a difference. Nothing made a difference except Derek. "We shouldn't waste any more," she agreed.

"I'm also sorry..."

She spanned her palms along his taut belly, rubbing slowly, watching his eyes. "Yes?"

He had to get this out before they made love. "For not telling you about Kevin sooner."

Toni stopped for a moment, sobering. "That was major."

He laced his hands behind her, holding her close. This had to be explained once and for all before he could move on.

"Yes, it was. For me. It was something I kept bottled up because I thought that if it was bottled up, it wouldn't hurt me." His eyes washed over her face, searching. Imploring her to understand. "I wouldn't think about it. Losing you brought it all back to me." Very tenderly he pressed a kiss to her temple. When he thought of what he had almost allowed to happen...

"And then when you told me about the baby, all I could think of was how I felt when Kevin died. But if I had to do it all over again…" He paused, clearing his throat, clearing the emotions away. "If it were in my power to do it all over again, I wouldn't have missed a moment of Kevin's life."

Over the years Kevin's face had become a blur in his mind, but not his essences, not the best part of what had made up his brother. That would go on for as long as he did.

"He was an absolute joy." With all his heart, Derek wished that Toni could have known Kevin. And that he could have known his brother a little longer. "The best part of my life. Until I met you."

She couldn't speak for a moment. There were too many tears in the way. She brushed two aside as they slid down her face. God, but she did love this man. "So I guess that means we're back together again?"

He grinned at her, then kissed her until she felt as if her clothes would incinerate. "I guess so."

"And Africa?"

"Will stay halfway around the world. You're right, I can do just as much good volunteering at a free clinic. Charity does start at home."

She was never so glad to hear him agree with her. This was the best gift of all, to have him back in her life again. It really *was* going to be a merry Christmas after all. "When can you pack up and move in again?"

That was easy enough. "I never unpacked. My life was in a state of flux after you threw me out. I couldn't bring myself to put things away in the apartment." It had been just a shell of a place, somewhere to sleep and change his clothes, nothing more. "That would have made it permanent. And I didn't want to accept that."

Her fault. It was all her fault. If she hadn't exploded that way, if she had just let him talk to her instead of seeing her father all over again—

She threaded her arms around his neck. "Oh, God, Derek, I am so sorry."

He didn't want her apologies, he just wanted it to be over. "So we're both sorry and one cancels the other out." He could feel her body heating against him, could feel excitement rushing up to meet it. "Want to start again?"

She nodded. "Okay." Toni put out her hand. "Hello, my name's Toni D'Angelo, what's yours?"

Derek laughed, eschewing her hand and pulling her back into his arms. "Not that far back. Start at the good part."

"Oh, okay." Which was exactly what she had in mind. Toni turned her face up to his, anticipating the touch of his mouth, the feel of his hands.

The urgent knock on the door put everything on hold.

"Uncle Derek, are you asleep again?"

It was Zak. Or maybe Nik. Derek sighed, leaning his head against Toni's. "The minions are back."

She laughed. "I hear." She kissed him, one limb-loosening, bone-dissolving kiss to let him know what was waiting for him tonight. "This is just intermission."

It took him a moment to dislodge his heart from his throat. His hand was on the doorknob for support as much as to open it. "You bet it is."

They held the news until after dinner, when everyone was mellow or just too full to move. Except for Josephine, who insisted on clearing the table.

"Later," Toni said, taking her mother's hands and

leading her into the living room. "You can do them later."

Toni was acting very strangely, Josephine thought. "You know I can't enjoy myself unless everything is neat."

"Make an exception, just this once." She exchanged glances with Derek. He slipped his arm around her shoulders. "We just wanted to tell you that we're back together again."

"You were coming apart?" Nik asked, confused. No one answered him.

Josephine looked as if she was torn between elation and shock. She slanted a nervous glance at her mother.

Toni read the look correctly. "Don't worry." Toni winked at Nonna. "Nonna knows all about it." And bless her for that. "Nonna's known all along."

Nonna gave her daughter what might have passed as a smug look were it on anyone else's face. "Just because I am old does not mean I am stupid."

The room echoed with congratulations and a group sigh of relief. No one had wanted to be put in a position of choosing sides. Derek had been one of them almost from the very beginning.

"So, do you have to renew your vows or anything?" Annie wanted to know.

"No, the divorce isn't final." Toni looked up at Derek, rolling the thought over in her head. "But that sounds like a very nice idea."

He could read her mind, and it was fine with him. "When?"

Jackie couldn't think of anything more romantic. "How about now?"

Derek looked at her. It was a little late to go looking for a priest. "Now?"

"Sure, it's Christmas Eve," Annie said eagerly. She could just see them exchanging vows beside the tree. "What better time?"

"I think it's romantic," Nik piped up, trying out his new word.

Jackie laughed and tousled her son's hair. For once, he let her. He was too busy beaming.

Alex jerked a thumb at his son. "You heard what the authority said."

It was all very lovely, but there was just one little problem. "There's no one to marry us," Toni observed.

The more he thought about it, the more Derek liked the idea. To repeat their vows in front of her family. Their family. "We could marry each other," Derek suggested. They didn't need anything official. Just each other.

"I could do it," Joe volunteered.

"You?" Toni hooted.

"Why not?" Joe wanted to know. "I had a year at seminary school," he reminded her. That was when, influenced by his mother's cousin Dominick, he had flirted with the idea of becoming a man of the cloth. It had been a very short flirtation. "That should count for something."

"They threw you out, remember?"

"Worst year I ever spent," Annie confided to her mother-in-law.

The doorbell rang. Josephine left them to discuss their options and opened the door. Everyone turned when they heard the exclamation of joy.

"Look, look who's here!" she announced. Josephine hooked her arm through the visitor's and ushered in the darkly garbed man. "Cousin Dominick."

Toni and Derek exchanged looks.

"Sign?" Toni asked.

Derek grinned. "Looks like one to me."

"You're just in time," Josephine told her cousin.

"For some of Nonna's cannolis, I hope." Crossing to her, he warmly greeted his aunt, kissing Nonna on both cheeks.

"You can have all the cannolis you want," Josephine promised. "After you marry them." She waved a hand at Toni and Derek.

"I already married them," Dominick said. He looked at the other two couples in the room, wondering what was up. "I married all of you."

Josephine picked up a plate of cannolis from the coffee table and urged them on her cousin. "Just think of it as a reaffirmation."

Allowing one of Nonna's cannolis to tantalize his taste buds, Dominick was willing to think of it any way his cousin asked him to.

It wasn't like their first wedding. That had been filled to the rafters with family—hers—and medical school friends—theirs. Here there were only ten, not counting themselves or Dominick.

And yet, in its simplicity, it was the more beautiful of the two ceremonies. Josephine had turned out all the lights, save for those coming from the Christmas tree. Alex and Joe had lit candles, placing them about the room, and there was a warm glow coming from the fireplace. As well as from everyone in the room.

Annie had managed to form a bouquet out of the poinsettias Joe had brought his mother that afternoon. The look on Toni's face when Annie handed it to her had Joe swallowing his protest.

They stood beneath the mistletoe, where Derek had

first kissed her and where they had each realized that there was never going to be a life for either of them without the other.

Father Dominick said the appropriate words, though he knew they didn't need them. If anyone ever needed to be reminded of marriage vows, it certainly wasn't the couple before him.

He smiled as he closed his book. "And now, you may kiss the bride."

"Best part," Derek murmured, looking into her eyes.

"No," she countered as his lips touched hers, "the best is yet to be."

He let her have the last word, because he knew she was right.

Epilogue

"It's cold here by the window, Ma." Josephine placed a hand on Nonna's shoulder, hoping that the light touch would urge her mother away. Knowing that it wouldn't. Stubbornness had deep roots in their family tree. Still, she had to try. Nonna had been sitting here, in the chair that Dustin had moved for her, for the past hour.

Nonna patted the hand on her shoulder, but her eyes remained fixed on the scene beyond the window. The snow had long since obscured the curb. But she knew where it was, and whose car would soon be parked there. She had waited this long—she could wait a little longer.

"It is not so cold. Besides, I am waiting for Antoinette and Derek to come with the baby."

As were they all, Josephine thought. Alex had left for the airport to pick them up over two hours ago. They were due back any time now. She shook her head. It seemed almost impossible that so much time had elapsed, yet here it was, Christmas again, and the house was filled with the sounds of family and love. And this time there would be no need for pretending.

Josephine bent closer to her mother. She had flown out to be with Toni after the baby was born, but this would be Nonna's first glimpse of the child. "They're not going to come any faster if you sit here, watching for them."

"They are not going to come any slower, either. And it makes me happy to sit here. To have my face the first thing that they see when they walk up to the door."

"It'll be a frozen face if you're not careful." Josephine sighed. Surrendering, she took the dish towel she had slung over her shoulder and tucked it along the window sash. The slight breeze where the sash no longer met the casement was muted. She was going to have to get after Joe to fix that.

"Then it will freeze with a smile." When Josephine looked at her mother quizzically, Nonna pointed toward the window. Raising her eyes, Josephine saw what had widened her mother's smile.

"They're here!" Nik shouted. Sneakered feet pounded along the stairs like the thunder of stampeding elephants instead of one lone, eight-year-old boy. The sound echoed as Zak followed him down.

"I saw them first," Zak crowed, outshouting his twin.

Nik swung around. "Did not!"

Josephine silenced the heated debate. "Neither one of you did." Zak and Nik halted abruptly at her side, stunned that she had robbed them both of the honor of the sighting. "Nonna did." She gestured at their great-grandmother.

Her mother was already struggling to her feet, eager to greet Toni and Derek the moment they walked through the door. Eager to greet them and the latest member of the family. Her namesake.

"Boys, help Nonna," Josephine instructed, stepping out of the way. Dutifully the twins surrounded the woman they both adored and regarded with awe as ancient. They each took an arm.

Nonna smiled at them. "Ah, my faithful crutches. Here, let me lean on you."

And that was how Toni and Derek first saw her as they entered the house—standing to greet them with a twin beneath each arm.

"Got 'em!" Alex announced needlessly as he swung open the door. Standing aside, he stamped his feet to shed the clumps of snow from his boots.

The cold was still stinging Toni's cheeks. It rivaled the bittersweet sting she felt in her heart as she looked at her grandmother. She looked frailer than ever. And happier. "Hello, Nonna."

"Hello, my darlings." Nonna's eyes touched them both warmly, but briefly. They shifted eagerly to the bundle in Derek's arms. "Let me see her. Let me see my little Gina."

Derek gently lifted back the corner of the receiving blanket that covered his daughter's face. A few snow-flakes drifted onto the carpet. "Here she is, Nonna."

The baby blinked and gurgled as the rest of the family filled the room and crowded around them. Greetings melted in a chorus of oohs and ahhs, even from the twins. At eight months, Gina Warner had a head of thick black hair and snapping blue eyes that seemed to take in everything in her path. She looked like a doll come to life.

Nonna drew closer, her eyes fixed on the child's. She seemed to grow straighter and younger. The light tremor in her hand abated as she touched the baby's face. "She is beautiful."

Derek bent over and kissed Nonna's wrinkled cheek. "She has no choice. Her name is Gina."

Nonna glowed at the compliment. Her eyes shifted to her granddaughter. Antoinette looked happier than she had seen her look in a very long time. Joy swelled within Nonna's thin breast.

She leaned into Toni and confided in a whisper that everyone heard, "Your Derek, he still makes my heart glad."

Toni lifted her eyes to Derek's, thinking of what she had almost lost. "And mine, Nonna. And mine."

Gina Warner cooed, as if to confirm her mother's words, and the room filled with the sounds of laughter and love. And Christmas.

* * * * *

Dear Reader,

First let me wish you and those you love a joyous and romantic holiday. May it include snow if that's what you're dreaming of. As you'll see when you read *Father by Marriage*, I gave the novel's hero and heroine a glorious Colorado snowfall as my wedding present to them and the much-loved daughter who wasn't born to either of them.

Here in Florida we don't get snow, though one of my daughters swore one chilly Christmas Eve that it had snowed a little. And it did seem there was a thin coating of the glittery stuff on the trunk of my convertible. When I tried to write my name in it, however, it turned out to be frozen dew. In other words, ice!

I did see snow before any of my Illinois relatives did the previous year when the love of my life and I drove through a Colorado mountain pass during my quest to research the book. Since we'd stopped anyway to let some cowboys drive their cattle across the road at that relatively high elevation, I got out of the car and exulted in tramping around in it!

Here's hoping you have a fabulous holiday, whether it's spent on skis or under a palm tree!

Suzanne Carey

FATHER BY MARRIAGE
Suzanne Carey

Special thanks to Mr. Amos Cordova
of the Durango & Silverton Railroad,
Durango, Colorado, for his help with my research.
Though my heroine in *Father by Marriage* was
too distraught to appreciate it to the fullest, the ride
on a coal-powered train from Durango to Silverton,
high in the southern Rockies, has to be one of the
most spectacular and thrilling rides a person can take!

Chapter One

"I want you to find her...*whatever it takes.*"

Seated behind the massive, carved-oak desk that dominated his study at the famed Flying D Ranch, Colorado real-estate-and-mining magnate Wiley E. "Dutch" Hargrett drove home the demand with a blunt stab of his cigar. His craggy salt-and-pepper eyebrows bristled, giving the words added emphasis. Accustomed to twinkling affably unless there was serious business to discuss, his myopic gray eyes burned with fierce determination behind his spectacles.

It was to be a command performance, then.

His back to the sweep of mullioned windows that overlooked the multimillion-dollar spread's magnificent stands of aspen and ponderosa pine, tough, high-powered lawyer Jake McKenzie didn't answer for a moment. Tall, rangy, dark-haired, good-looking in a rugged, outdoor sense that clashed subtly with his expensive pin-striped suit, he exuded a restless, faintly disillusioned air, as if the life he'd made for himself with grit, intelligence and sheer hard work had failed to satisfy.

At the moment, his priorities included discussing several pending legal matters with Dutch and the lengthy vacation he was determined to take just as soon as he could clear his calendar. The very last thing he wanted was to mount a personal search for Dutch's granddaughter, Lisa, whom a private detective had been unable to locate.

Mildly, because Dutch was a personal friend in addition to being his firm's most important client, Jake responded that the firm of Fordyce, Lane and McKenzie wasn't in the business of locating missing persons. He and his partners weren't trained investigators. They left that sort of thing to the experts.

"Maybe another detective..." he suggested.

With the single-mindedness that had helped make him a millionaire several times over, Dutch shook his head. "I want you," he insisted.

Lisa was the result of a brief affair between Dutch's and his wife Bernie's only child, thirty-four-year-old Dawn Hargrett, who was currently serving prison time in North Dakota for cocaine dealing, and the late Clint Yarborough, who'd been fatally injured when a rodeo stunt he'd attempted had gone awry, and she was all the Hargretts had. Yet she might be living in squalor somewhere. They wanted her *home,* in Durango, with them.

"She was last seen in the company of her stepmother, Yarborough's widow, shortly after his death," Dutch continued, naming the small Texas town where Clint Yarborough's rodeo accident had taken place. "A couple of years earlier, Yarborough hit it lucky. He won a minor lottery prize of several hundred thousand dollars. Supposedly, he bought a modest ranch with his winnings…somewhere in northern New Mexico or southern Colorado. I guess he sank most of the money in it, or ran through his reserves pretty quick, because he went back to the rodeo circuit a couple of years later, and got himself gored by a bull. Dollars to doughnuts the widow and Lisa returned to the ranch, at least long enough to put it on the market. If you can find it, you can probably pick up their trail.''

Jake frowned. Having grown up poor on a small, down-at-the-heels ranch in southern Idaho and done some rodeo work himself to supplement his GI-bill-subsidized college and law-school tuition, he could sympathize with the financial difficulties Clint Yarborough had faced. As it happened, he'd met Clint once, at some fairgrounds or other, and rather liked the tall, taciturn cowboy with a face full of freckles and thinning, reddish hair.

Years later, after he and his increasingly successful law firm had landed Dutch as a client, he'd met Dawn Hargrett, as well. A spoiled, pouty Madonna-type used to getting her way with men, she'd propositioned him, then tried to get him in hot water with her father when he wouldn't cooperate.

She's a piece of work, all right, Jake thought with a wry purse of his lips—*trouble if she so much as looks in a man's direction.* In light of Clint's affair with Dawn, with whom he'd apparently cohabited less than a month, he wondered what kind of woman the lanky cowboy had seen fit to marry. *One with scruples and maternal instincts, I'll bet,* hc thought, *if she hasn't de-*

livered Lisa to the Hargretts and demanded a hefty finder's fee.

There weren't that many loving, principled women running around loose in the world, in Jake's opinion. In his heart of hearts, he suspected their scarcity was one of the reasons for his disillusionment.

"I don't see how I could go after your granddaughter, even if I wanted to, with the Blackwell project on the table," he objected.

Dutch dismissed the importance of the hostile take-over his mining conglomerate was trying to engineer with a negligent wave of his hand. "Brent Fordyce can handle it with a little advice from you," he answered. "Nothing much is going to happen for the next couple of months, anyway." He paused. "I'd offer you a bonus if I thought you'd accept."

Though he was scarcely in Dutch Hargrett's league when it came to material wealth, these days Jake had all the money he needed. On the other hand, his premier client's reference to a "couple of months" dangled in front of his inner man like a plum just out of reach. Lately, he'd been feeling burned out, fidgety...soul hungry. He needed a rest. More than that, a change of scene. Sufficient time to regroup, search for new meaning in life, get reacquainted with the kind of fresh air and mountain scenery that had been a hallmark of his youth.

Abruptly, he found himself abandoning the idea of a traditional vacation in favor of a genuine leave of absence from the firm. Rethinking his refusal to hunt for the older man's granddaughter, he regarded Dutch with a thoughtful air. "To tell you the truth, I could use a breather," he admitted. "Of course, you realize that if I took several months' sabbatical and agreed to search for Lisa during my absence, I wouldn't be available here in Durango, at your beck and call.''

His wish knocking on the door of fulfillment, Dutch was all ears. "Then you'll do it!" he exclaimed.

Jake had no intention of being bulldozed. "Hold on," he cautioned. "If I agree to go, my partners must be willing to take up the slack. *You'll* have to give me plenty of leeway. Refrain from leaning on me for instant results. The search will be part investigation, part respite from my regular routine and I plan to take my time with it. I won't be checking in with you every day. Or even every week. Still, I don't see why finding the girl should prove that difficult...."

What might have been a tear of renewed hope slid down one of Dutch's leathery cheeks and was quickly brushed aside. "My boy, I don't know how to thank you," he whispered.

Jake pretended not to notice the breach in Dutch's tough-guy demeanor. "There's no need to thank me until I locate her," he said. "Are you sure the detective you hired checked official property records in the counties where you believe Clint Yarborough may have bought his spread?"

Dutch shrugged. "He claims he did—that he couldn't find a trace."

The prospect of succeeding where the detective had failed was pleasing to Jake. "I gather I've got your word, then," he reiterated. "No nagging. No pressure. I can take all the time I need...and want."

"Yes to all of the above."

Getting to their feet, the two men shook on it, with equally firm handgrips.

"Naturally, I hope you won't take too long," Dutch added, reclaiming an inch or so of the territory he'd relinquished. "We haven't laid eyes on Lisa since shortly before Dawn's arrest. She was going on five then. Bernie and I want a chance to know her and love her before she's all grown up."

Jake's request that his law partners, Brent Fordyce and Harry Lane, fill in for him while he was on leave met with little resistance once he'd informed them he'd be doing the firm's most prestigious client a personal favor. The following afternoon, having cleared his desk and read the lackluster detective's report Dutch had handed him, he was packing for his trip.

For once, instead of stashing custom-made shirts, designer suits and silk ties in a supple leather garment bag, he was tossing jeans and flannel shirts into a beat-up canvas valise. Scuffed and curling up at the toes from several decades of wear, his oldest pair of cowboy boots awaited him.

As he removed his gold Tissot timepiece from his wrist and placed it in his bedroom safe for the duration, he smiled at the callused condition of his palms. Thanks to the work he'd done himself, finishing off the new log home and barn he'd built on a prime twenty-seven-acre parcel just outside Durango, his hands wouldn't give him away. Neither would the secondhand truck he'd been using to haul lumber and other building materials to the site. Or the watch with a cracked crystal and worn leather strap that had seen him through his tour of duty as an eighteen-year-old medic's assistant near the end of the Vietnam War.

In addition to being comfortable and well suited to his mood, his old, unpretentious duds would provide excellent cover for his purposes. People weren't always comfortable talking to lawyers or prosperous-looking strangers. If and when they met, he knew Holly Yarborough wouldn't be. Dressed like the dirt-poor cowpoke he'd once been, he could spin her a line about being an old friend of Clint's, down on his luck. Or pretend he was an odd-jobs drifter, looking for work, close to needing a handout. She wouldn't recognize him as the well-heeled enemy.

For some reason, though he knew next to nothing about Clint Yarborough's widow beyond the fact that she was thirty-four years old, a former first-grade teacher who'd married the father of one of her pupils and taken up ranching with him, he was intrigued by the prospect of meeting her. In part, he supposed, that was because of the anticipated thrill of the chase, in which he viewed Lisa as the prize and Holly Yarborough as his adversary. Yet the theory didn't totally explain what he felt.

Ironically, because they were on opposite sides of the fence, the *idea* of her appealed to him. Pledged to further Dutch's cause as both friend and attorney, he found her decision to raise the Hargretts' granddaughter by herself after her husband's death and steer clear of any entanglement with them somehow exemplary.

If she was deliberately keeping Lisa from Bernie and Dutch, as they suspected, it wasn't too difficult to guess her reasons. Dawn would be eligible for parole in just eight months. If she was released, the Hargretts would be all too likely to reunite her and Lisa if they could. Idolizing Dawn and blinding themselves to her faults, they might go so far as to place Lisa in her care. And that would be a disaster, in Jake's opinion.

Though his sense of fairness dictated that every ex-convict should be given a second chance, and he agreed wholeheartedly that the Hargretts deserved contact with their grandchild, instinct told Jake he and the unknown Holly were in accord about the dangers of Dawn's influence. Why'd you agree to search for Lisa, if that's how you feel? he asked himself ironically, retrieving his padded and hooded winter parka from the back of his closet in case cold weather set in before he returned. Have your ethics become that profit motivated?

He certainly hoped that wasn't the case. Relaxing a little into the beginning of his leave, he decided to take a wait-and-see attitude. Before reporting back to Dutch or setting a custody suit in motion against her, he'd check Holly Yarborough out as thoroughly as he could—attempt to see the issues of her stepdaughter's welfare the way she saw them.

Two and a half weeks later, at Honeycomb Ranch in a mountain-fringed valley near the small, somewhat isolated town of Larisson, Colorado, Holly Yarborough was cutting the wire fastenings from a bale of new shingles intended for the barn roof as she mentally grappled with a problem that seemed all but insurmountable. The previous afternoon, her hired man had quit, leaving her and Lisa to run the ranch alone.

During the past four years, two of them under Clint's tutelage and two on her own, she'd learned a lot about ranching. And that was just the trouble. She knew from experience that there were things a woman and a ten-year-old girl couldn't accomplish without help. I'll have to find a replacement if I'm to keep Honeycomb operating so Lisa can inherit it someday, she thought, grimacing with effort as the wire cutter in her gloved hand bit into the stubborn bindings.

Unfortunately for them, Clint's modest lottery winnings had long since vanished, and profits from the herd they'd been trying to expand into a sizable holding had been skimpy, at best. As a result, she couldn't afford to pay prospective help the going rate. To make matters worse, there wasn't anyone to whom she could turn for financial help. Both her parents had been dead for years. Her nearest living relatives were second cousins who lived on the east coast.

I'll die before I ask the Hargretts to bail us out, she vowed as the wire binding gave way, whipping across her denim-clad thigh. In fact, she wasn't even tempted. Since quitting her teaching career to marry Clint and settle on a cattle ranch with him, she'd loved his red-headed, freckle-faced daughter as her own. The two of them were very close.

There's nothing I wouldn't do for Lisa, she thought, straightening and pushing a stray wisp of blond hair out of her eyes. No sacrifice would be too great.

Clint's dying plea had only strengthened her resolve. As he lay gored by a bull in the back of the ambulance that was rushing him to the hospital, the man she'd married had begged her to keep his daughter away from her maternal grandparents.

"They'll take her from you...give her to Dawn," he'd warned, coughing up blood in his effort to speak. "And Dawn will ruin her. By the time she's fifteen, she'll be foul-mouthed...pregnant...on drugs. Thank God we put the ranch in your maiden name, so they won't be able to find you. Promise me, Holly...you'll raise her without their input."

Unknown to Holly as Clint's words echoed in her head, Jake was passing through Larisson, bringing involvement with the Hargretts straight to her door. Though he'd struck out in Texas, where no one seemed to have known Clint very well, or remember his wife and child, he'd done better in Taos, New Mexico. It was in Taos that Clint's now-deceased great-aunt had cared for Lisa while he'd traveled from one rodeo and dusty county fair to another, a single dad desperately trying to earn a living for them—there that Holly had taught school, making friends with her fellow teachers, who continued to nurture a warm regard for her. By asking around, Jake had learned Holly's maiden name and the fact that she'd married Clint in Chimayo, on the high road to Santa Fe.

Though nobody had been able to produce her current address, several people had tentatively pointed him toward Colorado and their information had been good. Earlier that afternoon, immersed in property deeds at the Bonino County courthouse, he'd turned up the name of one Holly Neeson and located the plat book that set forth the coordinates of her ranch. Incredibly, she and Lisa had been under their noses all along—less than sixty miles from the Flying D and his Durango law offices!

Content though Jake was with his own investigative prowess, which had left the detective Dutch had hired in the shade, he almost regretted running her to ground so easily. Still, he was whistling as he drove, more invigorated than he'd been in months. It would be tough to feel anything but fantastic on a day like today, he admitted, with the mission he'd undertaken verging on success, the early October sun dazzling the meadows and great drifts of aspen shimmering like yellow fire on the mountainsides. Yet he knew the lion's share of his excitement flowed from none of those things. In large measure, it derived from the unknown quantity of Holly

Yarborough herself, whom chance and Dutch Hargrett's stubbornness had placed directly in his path.

Since leaving Durango and spending more nights than not in his sleeping bag under the stars, Jake had transformed her into a legend in his imagination. The odds that she'd measure up caused his grin to broaden as he considered them. In the flesh, he realized, the woman who'd frustrated Dutch's efforts to find her could turn out to be ugly, mean spirited or both—a clone of the evil stepmothers found in so many fairy tales. At best, she was probably the feminine equivalent of commercially baked bread, bland and doughy in its mass-produced wrappers.

Grinning at his own perverse sense of humor, Jake glanced at the directions he'd jotted down and turned from the hard-surface highway he'd been following onto a dusty secondary road with a gravel surface. As usual, the truth probably lay somewhere in between. If he was a betting man, he'd wager the woman he sought would turn out to be as nice as her Taos friends thought, but no goddess in blue jeans. When they finally met, he'd be forced to consign the paragon he'd created to fill his need for romance and a woman who'd restore his faith in her gender to the scrap heap.

The shingles freed of their wire bindings, Holly hauled out the extension ladder and propped it against the wall of the barn nearest the second-story entrance to the hayloft. She supposed she ought to check out the plywood subroofing before fastening on Clint's carpenter's apron and dragging a bunch of shingles to one of the upper rungs. According to her former hired man, who'd ripped off the damaged shingles in the area that needed patching before going on a three-day drunk and quitting her cold, a sizable portion of it needed to re-placed.

About to clamber up for a look, she noticed a cloud of gravel dust mushrooming in the distance. Somebody was headed her way—probably the mailman. Though her mail usually consisted of a stack of bills she found difficult to pay, she decided to hike the quarter mile that separated her house and barn from the county-maintained highway and pick it up before continuing with her task.

To her surprise, the flag on her box was down. Her mail carrier had already deposited today's quota.

A couple of minutes later, Jake rounded a bend in the road that brought her ranch into view. To his aston-ishment, *there she was,* Lisa Yarborough's stepmother and the woman of his quixotic daydreams, a slim but shapely Scandinavian blonde whose sun-streaked hair was plaited in a single braid that fell between her shoul-der blades. Busy removing mail from her country mail-box, she glanced up at his approach.

Boy, were you ever wrong, Jake thought, apprecia-tively noting the rounded but slender curves that filled out her faded, five-pocket jeans and plaid flannel shirt as he stopped his dusty, beat-up truck a few feet from her. She's a far cry from witch look-alikes. Or store-bought bread. Your notion of a goddess in blue jeans wasn't so preposterous.

Her mail held in one tentative, ungloved hand, Holly Yarborough gazed at him with a puzzled frown, as if she were attempting to make out his identity.

"Excuse me, ma'am," he said, getting out of the truck. "I'm just passing through…looking for some kind of work. Would you happen to know of anyone around here who has a job open? Or some odd chores that need doing? Right now, I'd settle for food...a little gas money. Maybe a place to spend the night.''

Continuing to clutch her mail, which included another late notice from her mortgage company, Holly studied him. Rangy, big shouldered, with a narrow waist, muscular build and several stubby days' growth of beard, the stranger who had stopped at her gate in search of employment appeared to be down on his luck. His words only confirmed that impression. Yet something in his eyes, which were narrowed against the strong sunlight, begged to differ. For a drifter, he seemed to have a strong sense of himself.

After the long neutrality of her marriage to Clint and a two-year widowhood, she was undone by her strong reaction to him. Everything about him interested her. With a sudden, keen appreciation for detail, she found herself visually tracing the laugh lines that bracketed his mouth, and wondering how that mouth would feel pressed against hers. Sex appeal radiated from every inch of him.

A greater threat to her composure lay in his eyes. Sky mirrors of unadulterated blue, they seemed to gaze into her soul as if he expected to seek his fortune there. Yet she didn't harbor the slightest doubt that they'd registered every aspect of her physical self.

The sudden, gut-level tug was a new experience for her. From the beginning with Clint, her emotions had been gentle and sweet, not unruly and passionate. She'd never been swept off her feet by anyone.

How pretty and wholesome she looks, Jake thought, his jaded sensibilities quickening. More than he could say, he liked the long, pale lashes that shaded her eyes, the soft way her lips parted as she gazed up at him. With their short, clean-scrubbed nails, her hands were slim and capable looking. Her cheeks were lightly flushed, as if he'd unnerved her out of proportion to his question.

For her part, Holly needed a hired hand. This dark-haired stranger looked able. He didn't strike her as a potential thief or rapist. Yet she knew having him at Honeycomb for any length of time would be awkward if he kept undressing her with his eyes. Maybe it would be all right to let him stay for a day or two, she reasoned. *He could help me get a leg up on mending the barn roof and replacing some of the fencing.*

"Actually, I have a few things that need doing around here," she volunteered after a lengthy pause. "Mainly fencing, carpentry stuff. My hired man…is away just now. You could sleep in his trailer…stay a couple of days if you want. I'm a pretty good cook. Interested?"

The offer was tailor-made. If he accepted, Jake would be able to check her out—learn firsthand what kind of mother she was. He still wasn't sure what he would do with the information. As Dutch's attorney, he had a duty to serve the strong-willed older man's best interests. Yet he supposed a case could be made for them being synonymous with his granddaughter's. If things worked out the way he suddenly hoped they might, maybe he could serve as a go-between, effect a compromise of some sort.

Besides, he thought with a wry twist of humor that only glinted in his eyes, you'd be crazy to let a woman like Holly Yarborough slip through your fingers. To his appreciative eyes, she looked like a potential cure for what ailed him.

"That sounds good to me," he said, stifling any lingering scruples as he held out his hand. "This valley's a mighty pretty place. I'm Jake McKenzie—born and raised on a ranch in Idaho. I can start right now, if you want.''

He hadn't said where he hailed from now. Or asked if there was a man about the place. She gathered he knew there wasn't. At least the calluses she noted testified he was no stranger to physical labor. ''Okay, then,'' she answered, tentatively shaking hands with him and doing her best to quell the little shiver of excitement she felt. ''I'm Holly Yarborough. I live here with my daughter, Lisa. If you'll give me a ride up to the barn, I'll show you where to park your truck.''

''Great.'' He held the passenger door open for her.

A quick glance around the cab's interior as he took his place behind the wheel didn't tell her much—just that he didn't smoke or litter his surroundings with junk-food wrappers. Aside from a ballpoint pen, crumpled scrap of paper, cheap sunglasses and the beat-up valise he'd stashed behind the seat, it was devoid of personal effects.

During their brief ride up the dusty, quarter-mile track that separated her mailbox from the barn, Holly was glad his vehicle had a floor-mounted gearshift. Though his hand hovered close to her knee as he reached for it, the gear formed a kind of barrier between them.

She couldn't help noticing the long, lean thigh muscle that rippled beneath faded denim as he adjusted his pressure on the gas pedal. Or responding to the pheromone assault his proximity was mounting on her senses. She'd have to harden her heart before it got out of hand. Falling for a drifter—even a personable, good-looking one—was totally out of the question.

Like the place Jake had built himself on twenty-seven

rolling acres outside Durango, Holly Yarborough's ranch house was constructed of logs and situated near a creek. But there the similarity ended. Smaller and older, it had mortared seams, a steeply pitched roof that would allow snow to slide off easily in winter and a rough fieldstone chimney. An old-fashioned veranda ran the width of the simple, octagonal structure. On it, someone had placed a pair of split-ash rockers. There were crisp, white curtains at all the windows.

"The trailer's on the other side of the barn," she advised, getting out of the truck as he braked by the corral. "You can park there. I've got some iced tea in the fridge. Would you like some before we get to work?"

Jake nodded. The dusty roads had made him thirsty.

"I was about to check on some rotted subroofing on the barn when I walked down to get the mail," she added. "We can start with that this afternoon."

Apparently she planned to work alongside him. Well, who was he to complain? Her proximity would be pleasant even if she had two left thumbs. Parking as directed beside a sagging, diminutive house trailer that looked as if the wind would whistle between its seams as soon as the weather turned cold, he stuffed his keys in his back pocket and took a moment to check out its interior. He rounded the barn in time to meet Holly as she emerged from the house with two tall glasses and a frosty pitcher.

The tea was cold and lemony, the way he liked it. Taking a deep draught that quenched the sensation of road dust in his throat, he paused and finished it to the last drop. "Thanks, that hit the spot," he said as he returned the glass to her.

Fastening on the carpenter's apron she handed him,

he followed her up the extension ladder she'd propped against the barn. For the sake of his peace of mind, he tried not to stare at the shape of her denim-clad derriere too much.

The subroofing was rotten, as she'd said, and they had to knock out a sizable chunk of it. They were hard at work, patching the spot with fresh plywood, when another cloud of gravel dust arose in the distance.

"That'll be the school bus, dropping off Lisa," Holly said, pushing a loose strand of hair back from her forehead and scooting for the ladder. "I'll be back in a minute. I want to see how her day went."

From his perch, Jake watched as a traditional yellow school bus drew up beside the ranch gate to discharge a skinny, half-grown girl with a mass of carroty, flyaway curls. Clad in jeans, boots and a plaid flannel shirt, the child juggled a book bag, lunch pail and some sort of rolled-up artwork as she raced up the dirt track to where Holly waited by the corral for her. The enthusiastic hug they exchanged when they met caused his mouth to soften in approval.

A gangly, freckle-faced child who clearly knew herself to be well loved, Dutch's granddaughter wriggled free and held up her drawing. Watching them together, Jake was reminded of the warm way his mother had greeted him when he came home from school. Like his mom had been, Holly was a widow, struggling to hold a ranch together. At first glance, she appeared to be doing a fairly good job of it. Yet it was easy to see that mothering came first with her.

Careful, he reminded himself as he bent over his task. You can't afford to switch sides. The most you can do is see to it that she gets a fair shake.

Meanwhile, Lisa had become aware of his presence. "Who's that?" she asked.

Holly shrugged. "A man who came by this afternoon looking for work. I decided to let him help me with a few projects I need to finish before the snow flies."

Briefly continuing to squint at Jake, Lisa returned her gaze to Holly. "He doesn't look like Ernie or any of our other hired hands," she commented. "Is he going to stay?"

The question tweaked at Holly's sense of fate. Maybe he *would*. She wanted to hug herself at the thought. A moment later she was telling herself not to be ridiculous. The appealing, dark-haired cowboy who was pounding nails into her roof was nobody to her—just a passing stranger. He'd be on his way before the week was out.

"A few days at most," she answered, smoothing her stepdaughter's unruly hair as she ignored her goose bumps. "There are brownies in the cookie jar. Do you have any homework?"

Chapter Two

By 5:00 p.m., Lisa had finished studying her spelling words and completed her geography lesson. She hung over the corral fence, feeding carrots to a sprightly bay filly as she talked to it in a crooning voice. Both girl and horse seemed content with the interchange.

Glancing at her watch, Holly excused herself and climbed down the ladder to make dinner. Jake continued to hammer away until the subroofing portion of their task was complete. As he washed up afterward by the pump, he noticed Lisa watching him.

"Mighty nice filly," he said admiringly. "Is she yours?"

The girl nodded. "Her name's Comet. My dad bought her for me. He died in a rodeo accident when I was eight."

Jake wasn't quite sure what to say to that. Not responding, he finger-combed his damp hair.

"Do *you* like horses?" Lisa asked.

"Love 'em," he answered wholeheartedly, and then added a white lie, depending on whether you counted the string of saddle mares he kept at his place outside Durango. "I don't have one at the moment."

They were still talking when Holly appeared on the porch in a red denim apron to call them in to supper. She caught the tag end of Jake's comments to her stepdaughter as they approached.

"You might say horses are like people," he was saying. "They can smell it when you're afraid of them. And they'll take advantage. Some are bad eggs, not worth knowing. The good ones pay back all the trouble you have to take."

As Jake stepped inside with Lisa, his most cherished fantasies about home and hearth paled in comparison to the interior of Holly's house and the dinner she'd cooked. In contrast to the rapidly gathering dusk, her cozy living-and- kitchen area was bathed in the yellow glow of lamplight. He noted natural log walls, an island counter equipped with a gas stove and copper pots, baskets hanging from exposed overhead beams. Hand-braided rugs warmed the gleaming pine floors. A fire was crackling in her fieldstone fireplace, doubtless to ward off the evening chill.

But it was the meal itself that seized the greater part of his attention. Casually arranged on the blue-and-white patterned cloth that covered her round oak table, a trio of white ironstone serving dishes contained picture-perfect fried chicken, mashed potatoes and sweet corn on the ear. He spied a napkin-lined basket of what appeared to be flaky homemade biscuits. A blue pottery bowl held applesauce, something he hadn't eaten since he was a kid. A ravenous sensation of hunger he hadn't been aware of feeling earlier washed over him.

With a shy smile at him, Lisa slid into her place.

"You can sit here," Holly directed, motioning Jake to a chair across from the empty one that had been Clint's.

He was surprised and impressed by the moment of quiet that preceded the meal.

Apparently, it showed. "We're not what you'd call religious," Holly explained, briefly meeting his intense, blue gaze as she passed the chicken to him. "There isn't time, for one thing. But I think it's good to reflect at the end of the day on what we've accomplished, and what we're thankful for."

The drumstick Jake bit into nearly melted in his mouth. Ditto Holly's country gravy. Mostly silent as he devoured one of the best meals he'd ever eaten, he watched and listened intently as Holly and Lisa discussed what was happening on the ranch and went over her day at school. His initial judgment that they formed a close-knit family of two only deepened as the meal progressed. The question, *What can I be thinking of, stepping into their lives this way?* kept running through his head.

Pragmatic, let-the-chips-fall-where-they-may attorney that he was, he was more than a little uncomfortable deceiving Holly Yarborough. Yet from his own perspective, his presence in her house was a perfect fit. It was as if he'd been moving toward that circle of lamplight and that particular dinner table for most of his adult years, yearning for what they could give him, though he couldn't have described his lack.

Now he sensed what he'd been missing, though he still couldn't put it into words. I'll be damned if I'll walk away in the name of professional ethics, he rationalized. I have a couple of weeks, maybe even a month, at my disposal and my motive is good—checking out the kind of parenting Lisa has received. If I hadn't found them, somebody else would have. Because of my personal relationship with Dutch, I'm better equipped than they would be to ease the inevitable transition, help work out a compromise that will benefit everyone.

Of course, he realized there'd be a price to pay, whether he confessed the truth about his identity now or later. Once Holly found out who he represented, they'd find themselves on the opposite sides of a very high fence.

For her part, though she did her best not to let it show, Holly was engaged in an emotional tussle of her own. Following Clint's death, she'd vowed to devote her energies to running the ranch and raising Lisa rather than getting romantically involved with someone new. The girl's early years had been a hodgepodge of temporary abodes and shifting caretakers, exacerbated by the struggle between her unmarried parents, that could have set her on a less-than-fortuitous path. Now she had a stable home. Friends. A parent she trusted. Holly didn't plan to let anything rock the boat.

The limited array of bachelors, divorced men and widowers in Larisson Valley had made her resolve easy to keep. Now the sensual tug of a man she'd just met was threatening to undermine its foundation. Though she barely glanced at Jake throughout the meal, she was acutely aware of his scrutiny, his energizing but disturbing male presence.

It was Lisa's turn to clear the table and do the dishes, together with any pans that hadn't already been washed during the cooking process. To Holly's surprise, as she sat down at her desk to go through the afternoon mail, Jake voluntccred to help. With Lisa washing while he wielded a dish towel, they made short work of the task, laughing and talking as they went.

He has a natural affinity for kids, she decided, watching them. Plainly captivated by so much attention from a fascinating stranger, the girl was recounting an incident that had taken place on her school playground earlier that week, and asking Jake's advice. She misses her father, but it's more than that, Holly knew. Like me, she's hungry for the presence of a man in the house. There are some kinds of support only a nurturing male influence can provide for a girl.

However likable and friendly he might be, no temporary hired man could fill that gap for Lisa. A genuine father figure was needed. Sighing, Holly affixed stamps to the couple of envelopes she'd addressed and got to her feet. "I'm going to take these out to the mailbox," she announced. "I'll be back in a moment."

"Can I call Jane when I'm finished with the dishes?" Lisa asked.

"Provided you keep the conversation to half an hour. You need to spend some time on your science project, remember."

Her stepdaughter nodded dutifully. "Okay."

By now, it was fully dark. The night was clear, lit by a quarter moon and what seemed a billion stars. Walking to the mailbox and back—a half-mile jaunt—freed Holly of some of the sexual tension that had been bothering her. She fully expected that, by the time she returned, Jake would have left the house for his temporary digs. To her chagrin, he was waiting for her in the porch shadows.

"Could we talk for a moment?" he asked, gazing down at her from his six-foot height as he leaned against one of the rough pine columns that supported the roof.

His speech was awfully cultivated for an itinerant ranch laborer. "I guess so," she conceded, waving him to one of the split-ash rockers and taking the other. "What about?"

Jake cleared his throat. "I glanced inside the trailer where I'm supposed to sleep before going to work on the barn, and I couldn't help noticing that your former hired man cleared out lock, stock and barrel," he said. "To all appearances, he's gone for good. I was wondering if—provided my work is satisfactory—I could have his job on a more permanent basis."

In Holly's view, he was rushing things. Yet she couldn't argue his point. She needed him. Unfortunately, she'd barely been able to scrape up Ernie Townsend's minimal wages from week to week. At the moment, her budget was so strained that even that late, unlamented hireling's stipend was beyond her means.

"I can't afford to pay you much more than we agreed on for temporary work," she hedged. "At most, sixty dollars a week. Plus lodging and all the food you can eat. From what little I've seen, you're a hard and capable worker. You could do a lot better than that someplace else."

Jake thought how much he enjoyed sitting there, rocking on the porch with her. He wondered if she'd let him get to know her better. "I like it here," he said with a quixotic shrug. "Money isn't everything. With nobody but myself to think about, I can afford to be choosy, I guess."

It sounded as if they had a deal. "All right, if that's how you feel about it," she responded, stifling the misgivings that arose from her lack of knowledge of him. She hoped her strong attraction to him wouldn't plague her too much.

"I like to get an early start," she added, daring to hope he wouldn't quit after a couple of weeks as so many others had, though she almost wished he would. "Breakfast's at 6:30 a.m., so Lisa and I can have plenty of time to eat and talk before she catches the bus."

As Jake's sojourn at Honeycomb Ranch neared the end of its first week, Holly found herself waking up each morning with growing apprehension and excitement. Thursday was no exception. Burrowing for several drowsy seconds beneath the smooth cotton top sheet, patchwork quilt and down comforter that graced her four-poster bed, she stretched and yawned, testing the heightened body awareness his presence in her life had evoked. A voyager returned unwillingly from her travels, she clung to the tattered remnants of dreams that drifted through her head.

That most of the dreams had been about Jake, she had little doubt. She'd remembered snatches of them, in which she and her dark-haired, sexy hired man had gone exploring in the north pasture on horseback, or tumbled into the hayloft and, accidentally, each other's arms.

Disturbing to her peace of mind once she was fully awake, they had a tenuous foothold in reality, she guessed. Once their roofing project was completed, she and Jake had begun the lengthy task of replacing fence posts and stringing fresh barbed wire along Honeycomb's north boundary. They'd also spent an afternoon forking several truckloads of hay into the barn for winter use.

Whatever work they happened to be doing seemed to occasion physical closeness. Now and then, there was a brush of actual contact. The day before, after removing her gloves to eat a sandwich from the brown-bag lunch they'd carried with them, she'd reached for a hammer and collided with his hand. The air between them had fairly crackled with electricity as their eyes had met and held. For what had seemed aeons, she'd felt herself drowning in lake blue depths.

According to her windup alarm, it was 6:00 a.m. Time to get up, throw on some clothes and make breakfast. She could hear Lisa puttering about in the next room, getting ready for school. Before long, Jake would come whistling in the door.

His presence in our lives has forced me to remember that I'm a woman, with fantasies and a need to be touched, she conceded, throwing back the covers and sliding barefoot onto the cool board floor beside her bed. Until he appeared, I was satisfied with ranching and mothering. Now it's not enough. All the same, she had responsibilities. She didn't plan to let things get out of hand with him.

Having showered and washed her hair the night before, she needed less than a minute to shimmy into underwear, jeans, a turtleneck and a plaid flannel shirt. Her feet were quickly encased in woolen socks and cowboy boots. A few licks from her hairbrush and the long, blond hair she could almost sit on was smooth and gleaming. Plaiting it in its customary braid, she hesitated before the round, oak-framed mirror above her dresser. She didn't usually wear makeup. Yet maybe a little lipstick wouldn't hurt....

She was dishing up oatmeal, scrambled eggs, ham, cinnamon rolls and warm fruit compote when Jake rapped lightly at the door and sauntered in. "Hi, sunshine," he greeted Lisa, taking what had quickly become "his" seat at the table. "Morning, Miz Yarborough. It's a little bit nippy out there today."

Soon the aspens would be past their peak. The year was turning downward, toward winter, the loneliest season of all on a ranch when you didn't have someone to love. "All the more reason to keep after that fencing," Holly retorted and then wished she hadn't spoken so brusquely. To date, Jake McKenzie had behaved like a perfect gentlemen. The least she could do was make polite conversation with him.

Seemingly oblivious to any lapse of cordiality on her part, Jake helped himself from the steaming array of serving dishes and dug in. "These eggs are done just right," he commented.

"Thank you." Aware it was for his benefit she'd put on lipstick that morning and begun cooking elaborate meals on a daily basis for the first time since Clint's death, Holly bit into a piece of toast.

It seemed Lisa had noticed the changes, too. "Know what, Holly?" she asked suddenly. "You've been fixing cowboy breakfasts ever since Jake came, the way you used to do for Daddy."

The innocent observation caused Holly's cheeks to flush. She couldn't avoid the quizzical look Jake shot in her direction. "I *did* promise you good food as part of your wages," she told him a trifle defensively.

He grinned, the deepening laugh lines that bracketed his mouth devastating in their attractiveness. "Nobody can say you haven't delivered," he assured her in his smoky voice.

A moment later, she was off the hook. The conversation had turned to a problem Lisa was having with one of her classmates at school. "Every afternoon while we're waiting for the bus, Tommy Danzig grabs my book bag and runs off with it," the girl complained, glancing from Holly to Jake and back again. "Jane and some of my other friends try to help me chase him. But it doesn't do any good. I never get my stuff back until the very last second. I'm always afraid Tommy will dump it in the creek or something, and I'll get blamed for wrecking my schoolbooks."

As befitted his lack of standing, Jake remained silent, waiting for Holly to speak.

"Have you told Mrs. Allen about it?" she asked, referring to the girl's fifth-grade teacher.

Lisa shook her head.

"Maybe you should, sweetheart."

"I don't want to be a tattletale," Lisa protested.

As Holly poured more coffee without advancing an alternative solution, Jake decided to put in his two cents' worth. "You might have to take your mom's advice if the problem keeps up," he said diffidently. "But maybe there's something else you could try first. It sounds to me like that boy wants your attention, not your books. If you stop giving it to him—just shrug your shoulders and turn your back when he runs off with your stuff—all the fun will go out of his little game. He might just give up without a fight, and quit bothering you."

It was light out by the time they finished breakfast. A short time later, the bus was collecting Lisa at the ranch gate. Having trucked enough fencing supplies up to the north pasture the previous afternoon to last them through that day's labor, Holly and Jake decided to make the trip on horseback. Clearing the table and putting the dishes in to soak while he fed the chickens and readied the horses, she met him a few minutes later by the corral.

He'd saddled Brandy, her paint, and Clint's chestnut, Dasher, for himself. "Let me give you a hand," he offered.

Thanks, I don't need it was on the tip of her tongue. Instead she responded with a simple, "Thank you," and accepted an assist into the saddle.

Jake didn't need anyone to tell him that his display of manners was partly an excuse to touch her. He couldn't seem to keep his hand from brushing negligently against hers as he handed her the reins. God, but she was good to look at—all gold, pewter and honey with that corn-silk hair and those big, gray eyes, her tanned but dewy skin. He kept wanting to touch her and being forced to stay his hand.

Yet she didn't wear makeup except for the modest touch of lipstick he'd noticed for the first time that morning. Had she put it on for him? More smitten with Holly than he'd been with anyone for as long as he could remember, he could only speculate.

As they headed out, with Holly leading the way toward the foothills of the San Juan Mountains, which bordered her ranch to the north, he gave the chestnut its head. Instead of drinking in the scenery, his gaze was riveted to the compact bounce of Holly's seat in the saddle, the way her slim, denim-clad thighs gripped the sides of her mount. Red-blooded male that he was, he couldn't help but wonder how it would feel to have those thighs gripping him.

But it wasn't just looks and a dynamite figure that drew him to Holly Yarborough. Nor was it the kind of sexy, sophisticated teasing most of the women he'd dated had mastered so well. From what he could determine, she was far too genuine to play that kind of game. When she laughed and teased, he guessed, her laughter would come straight from the heart.

Silently leading the way, Holly reflected that the fencing project was much larger than she'd anticipated. Aside from the work they'd done on the barn and checking on her herd, they'd spent most of their time just trying to make a dent in it. I'll need Jake till the middle of November, at least, she thought. And realized her concern over securing her pastures wasn't her only motive for thinking so.

The tall grass of the north pasture was still damp from the passage of rainy weather the night before—the day bright and breezy, cool enough to require a jacket as they set to work. In the distance, swift-moving, patchy clouds skimmed snowcapped peaks. Intense drifts of aspen shimmered like yellow fire on the lower slopes.

"Beautiful up here, isn't it?" Holly said as they paused to share the steaming hot coffee she'd packed in a thermos.

"You bet." Jake's endorsement resonated with the emphasis of sincerity. He wanted to add, *So are you*, but held his tongue. He doubted if that kind of compliment would improve his standing with her very much.

"Is it anything like Idaho?"

"Quite a bit. The peace of it settles into a man's empty places."

Even as he spoke, Jake could feel himself relaxing a little more from the heady, high-wire atmosphere of his lawyer's existence. With each day he spent at Honeycomb, it seemed, he moved deeper into Holly Yarborough's simple but satisfying life of physical labor, fresh air and mountain vistas, and further away from the commitment that had brought him to her door. Annoyed that it should have arisen, he deliberately pushed all consideration of the conflict loyalty to his client was sure to generate from his head. If I have anything to say about it, he thought, for the next month or so I'll live in the present tense.

Sipping her coffee as she regarded him, Holly puzzled over what kind of man he was. He certainly didn't talk like your average ranch hand or a common drifter. Was he running from the law? Or some scandal in his past? A terrible failure or blot on his record? Supposedly he'd grown up on a ranch and his familiarity with the work seemed to back up his claim. Maybe he inherited the one where he lived as a boy, she speculated, and lost his shirt. Unless she learned how to make cattle pay, and quickly, the same fate would unfold for them.

Meanwhile, the chemistry between them was strong. Mesmerized by the mystery of Jake's past almost as much as she was the strong sexual energy that emanated from him, she lectured herself that it would be crazy to succumb. God knew what kind of historical baggage had arrived with the man in his dusty red truck. Yet the fact remained that she sorely wanted him.

Even a temporary fling was out of the question. For one thing, lovemaking outside of marriage was against her principles. For another, she had Lisa to think about.

That night at the supper table, her redheaded stepdaughter had news for them. She'd tried Jake's suggestion about how to handle Tommy Danzig and, to her astonishment, it had worked.

"When Tommy did his thing, I just looked at Jane and shrugged," she reported with a pleased and satisfied air. "We turned our backs on him and walked in the opposite direction. After a minute or two he followed us and shoved my stuff at me. 'Here's your dumb old book bag—I don't want it, anyway,' he said. Jane and I just laughed at him. He looked awfully…''

She hesitated, casting about for the proper word.

"Sheepish?" Jake suggested.

Lisa nodded. "*Right.* I don't think he'll bother me again. If he does, I'll tell everyone it's because he likes me. And that'll *totally* embarrass him.''

"Sounds like a winner," Jake said.

I'd never have thought of advising her to do what Jake did, Holly admitted to herself as she watched them exchange self-congratulatory grins. Yet, as a former teacher, I'm supposed to be an expert in handling schoolyard confrontations. Apparently her new ranch laborer had a gift for strategy in addition to his ability to entrance females of all ages. It was clear Lisa thought so.

With each day that passed, Holly's stepdaughter and the dark-haired cowboy who'd taken up residence in her hired man's trailer seemed to cement their growing friendship a little further. I shouldn't find it so surprising, Holly thought. Lisa needs a father figure. In the absence of one, she probably can't help latching onto the first charming stranger who takes an interest in her.

Maybe that's what *she* was guilty of—daydreaming about Jake because he was the only man available. But she couldn't get the explanation to stick. Slipping on her down parka, she went outside to sit on the porch while Jake and Lisa finished washing and drying the supper dishes. Huddled in her jacket, she gazed at the chilly, star-filled evening and tried to decide what to do. Firing him was out of the question. He didn't deserve it. Besides, she needed him too much.

Hugging herself against the cold but unwilling to go

back inside until he and Lisa were finished, she jumped a little as he came out on the porch and asked if he could sit a spell.

They were co-workers in addition to being employer and employee. Plus they ate all their meals together. "Be my guest," she heard herself answering him.

He was wearing his lightweight denim jacket over a ragged sweater and flannel shirt, and suddenly she worried that it wasn't warm enough. "Some of my late husband's things are still boxed up in the attic," she revealed. "I'm sure there are several winter parkas in the mix. Clint was tall, like you. If you'd like one of them, I'm sure it would fit...."

Touched by her generosity, Jake reached across the space that separated them to pat her hand. "Thanks, but I have one of my own in the truck," he said.

The sensation of his skin against hers was electric for both of them. To cover her response before it could lead to something even more unsettling, Holly changed the subject. "You said you were born and raised on a ranch in Idaho," she reminded him. "Was it your parents' place? Why'd you leave it?"

Abruptly, she was prying into his past. Well, he'd expected it at some point. He realized he'd have to tread carefully. "Vietnam," he answered, letting the single word stand in for his experience in that once-tortured country.

"You were there."

"During the last days of the war, as an eighteen-year-old medic's assistant."

She was silent a moment, digesting the information. So that's where some of his self-possession comes from, she thought. Maybe even some of his rootlessness. "You didn't go back to Idaho afterward?" she asked.

He'd try to give her the straight scoop on his life insofar as he could. "Not for long," he answered. "Mom passed away of cancer a few months after my return. The ranch was sold to cover her debts."

Apparently, his mother had faced a good deal of trouble keeping her head above water as a rancher, just as Holly did. For some reason, the revelation made her feel closer to him.

"I'm sorry," she said simply.

"It was some years back. I'm over it."

"What about your dad? Where was he when all this was taking place?"

"He died of a heart attack when I was eleven."

Jake's early history had paralleled Lisa's, with the exception that his mother, not a stepparent, had finished the job of raising him. But that didn't explain the life he'd chosen for himself.

"Once the ranch was sold, you hit the road...opted for the life of a traveling cowpoke, is that it?" she asked, trying to understand. "Didn't you ever want to settle down? Get an education and a decent job? Maybe even buy a place of your own?"

He'd have to lie or answer her question with a question. He supposed that was the price of his quest to find Dutch's granddaughter. By now, of course, it had become something far more complex.

"What's wrong with traveling around, working only when you choose or necessity forces you to?" he parried. "You see a lot of pretty country...meet some mighty interesting people that way."

She didn't reply and for several minutes neither of them said anything further as they rocked and listened to the cries of migrating geese that were seeking nighttime cover.

By portraying himself as a drifter, Jake decided, he'd been truthful in a larger sense. He *had* been drifting for quite a while—from one legal victory to another without being fired up by any of them...and from woman to woman without finding love. Ironically, by the act of seeking what *would* matter to him he'd placed it beyond his grasp.

"Tell me about you," he said. "Where did you grow up?"

Holly shrugged. "There isn't much to tell. I'm a native of northern New Mexico. I've lived there most of my life, with the exception of the four years I've spent here and another two in Alaska. My parents took a fling at homesteading when I was Lisa's age. Or perhaps I should say my father did. We went against my mother's wishes. He was determined to make his fortune on the last frontier."

"And did he?"

She shook her head. "We came back poorer than when we left. To make matters worse, his insistence that we move had soured their relationship. They divorced shortly after our return to New Mexico."

So she knew what it was to be the child of warring parents. Maybe that was why she'd tried so hard to make a home for her late husband's little girl...and done a damn fine job of it, in his opinion.

"What brought you here, to Larisson Valley?" he asked. "Ranching's not a common occupation for a single woman."

"As you must have guessed from my remark about the clothes, if you hadn't earlier, I'm a widow," she replied. "Lisa and I didn't get into ranching on our own. When we bought this place, her father was still with us."

Gently, Jake pressed her to elaborate. He wanted to hear the story from her point of view.

Leaving out Dawn Hargrett's identity and making no mention of Lisa's grandparents, Holly told him about teaching school, meeting and marrying Clint and becoming her pupil Lisa's stepmother. Clint's lottery winnings, his dream of ranching and his fear that Lisa's mother would try to reclaim her as he lay dying were among the things she related.

It was only when she'd finished that she stopped to ask herself if she'd told a stranger too much, and wonder what had prompted her to do so. She only hoped she hadn't extended a clue to their whereabouts through him to someone who knew the Hargretts. She supposed the likelihood of that was minimal.

As he'd listened, Jake had been forced to admit her perspective on who ought to be raising Lisa had considerable merit. Dawn *was* a threat to the stability of the girl's upbringing. It was also becoming increasingly clear that to cut Lisa off from Holly would be to separate her from the only mother she could remember.

Now, sensing the discomfort betrayed by her silence, Jake attempted to minimize it by changing the subject. "You have to wonder what brings two people from different backgrounds and beginnings to the same dot on the map so they can share their journeys," he mused. "Take you and me, for instance. The odds of us meeting were slim to nonexistent. And yet we did."

Holly wasn't sure how to answer him. She only knew he'd raised a lot of questions in her head, at a time when she needed to focus unswervingly on raising Lisa and paying her bills.

"I couldn't begin to tell you," she answered, getting

to her feet. "Meanwhile, it's getting colder by the minute out here. I'd better say good-night."

With the cultivated manners that had her questioning his claim to be a drifter, Jake got up, too. Suddenly they were standing very close together. Holly's pulse seemed to flutter in her throat. Overwhelmed by the stab of desire his nearness evoked, she was rooted to the spot. She doubted if she could move or speak.

His six-foot-plus frame looming in shadow against the moonlit backdrop of the yard, Jake gazed down at her. How lovely she is, he thought. And how innocent— seemingly untouched, though she was a married woman. With all that was masculine in him, he longed to enfold her, press his mouth against hers.

He almost lost it when her lips parted as if in anticipation. Raising his hands as if to grasp her and pull her to him, he quickly dropped them again. She gave a little sigh, betrayed by a plume of frosty breath.

"Good night, Miz Yarborough. See you in the morning." Giving her his customary salute, Jake headed for his trailer.

As she watched him go, Holly told herself to be grateful for her narrow escape. Simultaneously, she continued to puzzle over the mystery he represented. Though he wore threadbare clothes, knew ranching and had work-roughened hands, Jake McKenzie was smart and—she was willing to bet—educated, not to mention the sexiest man she'd ever met. What was he doing at Honeycomb, upsetting her emotional applecart while he worked for peanuts?

Chapter Three

Going inside, Holly sat down at her sewing machine to finish a corduroy skirt she was making for Lisa. Before long, she was ready to fit it on the girl in front of an oval pier glass that stood to one side of her sewing area. Her pincushion at the ready, she made several adjustments to her handiwork and then set about stitching them into place as her stepdaughter went back to reading her new Judy Blume novel in a nearby chair.

Though she did her best to concentrate on the task at hand, she couldn't seem to get Jake McKenzie and her attraction to him out of her head. A half hour later, she placed the skirt atop her workbasket to be hemmed the following evening. "Time to put the book away and get ready for bed, Leez," she said.

"Okay, Holly." With a hug and kiss that plainly indicated Holly's affection for her was mutual, Lisa trooped off to do her bidding.

Still aching for Jake's kiss and in the mood for some pampering, Holly decided to draw herself a bath and have a good, long soak as soon as Lisa was finished in the bathroom.

A few minutes later, Lisa had completed the nightly routine of brushing her teeth, washing her face and putting on her pajamas. "Okay if I read another chapter?" she coaxed. "I'll do it under the covers so if I get tired I can just turn out the light."

Sometimes Lisa reminded Holly of herself at the same age. She smiled indulgently. "You sold me, pumpkin. Another fifteen minutes."

Changing to a light blue chenille robe that was slightly oversized on her slender frame, Holly went into the bathroom and ran a tub full of scented bubbles. She even lit a couple of candles and turned on the portable radio she kept on a shelf below the medicine cabinet. She was about to drop the robe and slide into the suds when she thought she heard Lisa calling her. Though it turned out that she was mistaken, she decided to leave the door open partway, just in case.

"Ahh," she murmured, sinking into a mound of bubbles that billowed to her chin. "This is pure indulgence."

No doubt the heated water and subtle scent of her bubble bath were part and parcel with her sensuous stretching when she awoke from her early-morning dreams—second-class substitutes for lying warm and cosseted in Jake's arms. Well, what if they are? she reasoned as the strains of one of her favorite movie themes filled the air. They're good for what ails me...and a whole lot more sensible than the alternative.

Outside in his trailer, which was cramped, chilly and lonely, Jake was restless with unacted desire. Try as he would, he couldn't get his thoughts to quit running in circles. *You should have kissed her when you had the chance,* he scolded himself. *You know you wanted to. Right,* his sensible side responded in a sarcastic tone. *And get hustled off the property. I didn't realize you were ready to leave just yet.*

The fact of the matter was, he wanted to see her again. *Tonight.*

With a little rush of satisfaction and energy, he recalled their need to get additional rolls of barbed wire from town before they could continue with their fencing project. On the way, they could drop Lisa off at school. She'd get a kick out of it, and they wouldn't have to get up so early. Deciding to use the reminder as an excuse to talk to Holly right then, he put on his jacket.

Several lamps were still lit as Jake approached the house. When rapping lightly at the door didn't bring an answer, he tried it and found it unlocked. After a moment's hesitation, he entered. The kitchen and living areas were deserted. However, a radio was playing, probably in one of the bedrooms. Somebody was still up.

Glancing toward the pier glass where Holly had fitted and pinned up the hem of Lisa's skirt, Jake sucked in his breath. By chance, the mirror was positioned at just the right angle to the open bathroom door to give back Holly's reflection as she got out of the tub. *She's like Venus rising from the sea,* he thought, his body responding with swift desire.

God but she was beautiful to him! A soft pink against the creamy flesh tones of her skin, her nipples stood erect from the bath and colder air of the room as she patted the last traces of bubble bath from her body. Unconfined in its usual braid, her glorious Scandinavian-blond hair formed a wavy, damp halo about her head and shoulders. Jake couldn't help noticing that the patch of coarser curls between her thighs was the same Nordic shade.

"What are you doing, Jake?" Lisa's voice asked, causing him to jump with a guilty start.

Aware Lisa was up, Holly wrapped her towel more closely about her body and shut the bathroom door to finish drying herself.

Meanwhile, Lisa was waiting for an answer. "You saw Holly without any clothes on," she accused in a low voice. "You were staring at her in the mirror."

His arousal mercifully having subsided, Jake turned to face the girl. "I didn't mean to," he replied. "It just happened."

Clearly Lisa wasn't buying the explanation. "The way you were looking at her," she persisted, condemnation in her tone. "It wasn't right."

Jake knew he had to do something—fast—or there'd be hell to pay, not just for his own sake, but for the girl's. Sitting down on the arm of the chair where Lisa had been reading earlier, so that they were about the same height, he met her censure face-to-face.

"You're too young to understand fully," he said, keenly aware he was short on experience when it came to interpreting adult feelings to children. "But I'll try to explain. To a grown man, the female body is a work of beauty. I wasn't spying on Holly. But, when I saw her like that, I felt admiration. And great reverence."

It wasn't the whole truth, but it was true. For Lisa it seemed to be enough. "Okay," she said, granting him unspoken absolution. "I guess I get it."

With a sigh of relief, Jake tried to hurry her back to bed.

"What's reverence, exactly?" she demanded, prolonging the moment.

So this is what it would be like to have a kid of my own, Jake thought. He kind of liked the notion. "An attitude of honor and respect," he answered. "I honor and respect Holly. By the way, I came back to tell her we need to get more fencing first thing in the morning. I thought we could drive you to school on the way, if that's all right with her."

Jake was gone when Holly emerged from the bathroom a few minutes later with her robe knotted about her waist. But she'd heard his voice. She knew he'd been in the house. She wanted to know what had been going on. "What was Jake doing here?" she inquired from the doorway of Lisa's room.

Back in bed, with her down coverlet and one of Holly's grandmother's quilts pulled up to her chin, Lisa passed on Jake's message about the ride to school and the fencing.

Holly wasn't satisfied. Though to her knowledge he hadn't been standing opposite the bathroom door, something in Lisa's eyes confirmed that there was more to tell.

"What else should I know about this?" she prodded.

Lisa blinked. "I thought I heard someone come in. When I got up to see, he was watching you dry off...in the mirror."

Goose bumps of desire and excitement raced over Holly's skin even as outrage swelled in her breast. With her stepdaughter gauging her reaction, she tried to quell them both.

"You mean...he was just standing there, staring at me?" she asked.

Lisa nodded. "When I asked him what he was doing,

he said he didn't mean to spy on you. That he saw you by accident. He said a grown man thinks a woman's body is beautiful. That he looks at it with respect…I mean, reverence. 'I honor and respect Holly,' he said."

Awash in conflicting emotions, Holly couldn't seem to find the right words to answer her.

"Did Jake do something wrong?" Lisa asked worriedly.

"Not intentionally," Holly said, certain Jake couldn't have known she was bathing and unwilling the girl should get the wrong message from what had occurred. "It was just an accident. I should have locked the outside door."

As she put on her nightgown and climbed into bed, Holly had to admit the tenor of Jake's explanation to Lisa had hinted at a basic decency on his part. Unfortunately, it also confirmed that he found her attractive. With everything that was womanly in her, she longed to bask in his admiration, taste the pleasure of nestling naked in his arms.

His remarks further strengthened her impression that he was very sophisticated for a cowboy. Though Clint had been capable of similar emotions, he wouldn't have been able to articulate them that way. Who *is* Jake McKenzie? she asked herself for the second time that evening as she switched off her bedside lamp. And what does he want from me? Though she had some idea how to respond to the latter question, she'd begun to feel a full-fledged answer to the former might shake her to her roots.

Man-woman tension between Jake and Holly over what she'd mentally dubbed "the bathtub incident" was at its zenith the following morning as they dropped Lisa off at school, bought the wire and a few other supplies and returned to work on the ranch. Her worst moments came when she met his eyes as she welcomed him to the breakfast table and, later, as they drove her step-daughter to Beamish Elementary in Larisson. Jake had offered to take the wheel. To her chagrin, she'd found herself wedged between him and Lisa, because the girl was getting out first. Thanks to the limited space in the cab of her truck, their denim-clad thighs were pressed tightly together.

At the feed-and-hardware store, which was her source of wire, she noticed the proprietor, sixty-two-year-old Harlan Matthews, eyeing them speculatively. *You never brought any of them other fellas who worked for you into town,* his raised eyebrows seemed to suggest. *This one's smooth...and just the right age. Anythin' goin' on?* By afternoon, she suspected, the valley's party lines would be humming with gossip about them.

She was quiet, almost morose, as they returned to Honeycomb and bounced up a rutted dirt track that led to their current work site along the north boundary. Finally, unable to stomach the way she was hugging the passenger door and answering his conversational gambits in monosyllables any longer, Jake apologized to her.

"I gather Lisa told you I intruded on your privacy last night," he said, casting a swift, blue-eyed glance in her direction as he drove. "I want you to know I'm sorry...that it was in no way deliberate on my part."

Trapped by his forthrightness and gentlemanly request for her pardon, Holly had no choice but to grant the forgiveness he sought. "As a matter of fact, she did tell me," she admitted, thawing noticeably. "Let's forget it, okay? There wasn't any harm done. I never thought you came back to ogle me on purpose."

They both knew he'd have looked his fill if Lisa hadn't discovered him. Nevertheless, as a result of clearing the air, things were more comfortable between them as they set to work. I doubt if it was a big deal to him the way it was to me, Holly thought as she un-rolled a length of wire and held it taut so Jake could hammer it to one of the fence posts. With his looks and come-hither personality, he's probably seen more naked women than he can count.

They were interacting a bit more easily by the time Lisa rushed to greet them on their return to the barn at the end of the workday.

The girl was practically jumping out of her skin with excitement. "Holly...Jake! Look at this!" she ex-claimed, waving a flyer, which she eagerly handed to her stepmother.

The flyer, a bit crumpled from being stuffed in Lisa's book bag, had been distributed at her school that after-noon to remind valley residents about the annual Lar-isson Valley Fall Dance. Traditionally involving mostly square dancing, though there were ballroom numbers, too, it would be held a week from the upcoming Sat-urday, at the hay barn on the Cunningham ranch. Three years ago, Clint, Holly and Lisa had attended as a fam-ily, and he'd waltzed his daughter around the room. Holly knew it was a big deal—one of the girl's fondest memories.

As she read the flyer and passed it to Jake, her step-daughter was jumping up and down impatiently. "Can we go?" she begged. "*Please, please, please!* Since Dad died, it's been all work and no play for us. It's time we had a little fun!"

Though part of her recognized the truth of Lisa's statement and longed to say yes, Holly hesitated. The prospect of sitting on the sidelines for most of the evening with the valley's elderly, widowed population wasn't a very appealing one. "I don't know, Leez..." she answered, feeling a little selfish.

"You know you want to! Jake can come along so you'll have somebody to dance with. Right, Jake?"

While he might enjoy gazing at her naked form if the opportunity arose, in Holly's opinion, Jake probably had a woman or two stashed away for whenever he was in need of loving. He wouldn't want to waste time dancing attendance on his prissy employer, who couldn't be beguiled into the sack.

"Naturally, your free time is your own," she murmured, giving him a rueful look. "I wouldn't dream of imposing...."

"I'm not much of a dancer. But I'll be happy to go if Holly wants me to," he told Lisa, cutting off her excuse at the knees.

"Then it's settled!" Lisa was exuberant.

Holly shook her head. "Not so fast. I haven't decided yet."

Washing up at the pump, Jake strained his ears to hear their conversation as they turned and walked together toward the house. To his way of thinking, Holly didn't need him to dance with her. If there were any red-blooded men alive and well in Larisson Valley, she wouldn't lack for partners.

When he joined them a short time later at the table for a dinner of flaky biscuits, homemade chili, cabbage slaw and warm chocolate-chip cake, he gathered Holly hadn't made a commitment yet. With a bit of questioning by her stepmother, Lisa confessed the reason for her unbridled enthusiasm during the meal. She had a crush on one of her schoolmates.

"Not Tommy Danzig?" Holly teased, naming the former book-bag thief.

The girl wrinkled her nose. "It wouldn't be Tommy if he was the last boy in the world."

"Who, then?"

"Promise not to tell *anyone?* It's Jason Cunningham. Don't you think he's cute?"

Watching them together, Jake remarked to himself what a good stepmother Holly was. Without fanfare, she invested herself in things like fully engaged conversation and making Lisa's favorite desserts. It was easy to see the girl felt pampered and loved, even on a shoe-string budget. It occurred to him that his blond employer was a lot like his late mother, whom he'd greatly admired. Funny, but the comparison didn't stop him from wanting her.

Unable to get a firm answer from Holly about attending the dance, Lisa turned to wheedling Jake. He promptly repeated his willingness to go, but claimed he didn't know how to dance. "I'm just an ignorant cow-poke," he said with a grin. "If I tried to dance with Holly, I'd step on her toes."

Lisa shook her head in mock disgust. "What you guys need is *practice,*" she muttered inelegantly, her mouth full of cake as she jumped up to switch on the radio and turn the dial to a country-music station.

With Lisa's encouragement, while the girl did the dishes, Holly allowed Jake to sharpen his supposedly nonexistent dancing skills by dancing with her. At first they practiced square-dance moves. Though Jake pretended confusion and clumsiness, Holly had the strong impression he was bluffing.

Then the program's deejay aired an oldie known as the "Tennessee Waltz," and Jake took her in his arms. "I think maybe I could dance to this one," he whispered in his rough, deep voice.

For Holly, the sensation of being held in Jake's arms—even under such far-from-compromising circumstances—was dizzyingly erotic. Her cozy, familiar surroundings seemed to recede in soft focus, like the background elements in a romantic film. Only peripherally was she aware of Lisa pausing with a dish towel and serving platter in her hands to stand and stare at them.

Though she was sorely out of practice, somehow her feet managed to follow Jake's lead. Her left hand resting on the hard but vibrant muscles of his shoulder through the thin barrier of his worn plaid shirt, while her right was firmly grasped by warm, callused fingers, she caught a subtle whiff of after-shave she'd have sworn didn't come from the five-and-dime.

Every neuron in her body was firing at peak intensity as if she was experiencing *her* first crush. Instead, she feared, she was taking part in the first scary-sweet moves of a full-blown love affair. It was a relief, if something of a letdown, when the number came to an end and the station's announcer cut to several advertisements.

"Thank you, ma'am," Jake remarked, making her a courtly little bow as he relinquished her.

With Lisa still watching them, Holly struggled to maintain her cool. "My pleasure," she answered.

He gave her one of his bad-boy grins. "Waltzin' in the kitchen can be kind of fun," he allowed.

"But it's not the first time, is it? That you've waltzed, I mean…in the kitchen or otherwise."

The laugh lines beside his mouth deepened. "Not

quite," he admitted, inviting her to share his amusement at being caught posturing. "But I can honestly say I've never enjoyed it as much."

"Ah-hem!" Loudly clearing her throat, Lisa made a bid for their attention. "So...are we going to go or what?" she asked, tilting her curly red head to one side. "According to the flyer, we have to let the Cunninghams know this weekend."

Though Holly drew out the moment as much as possible, she knew when she was licked. "I suppose we could," she answered.

"Yesss!" Abandoning her task, Lisa threw her arms around Holly's neck. "My turn to practice with Jake," she announced excitedly. "When I danced with Daddy, my feet didn't touch the ground."

Holly laughed. "That's because he was carrying you, pumpkin."

Volunteering to finish the dishes while Lisa took a turn around the room with Jake, she kept an eye on the proceedings. She couldn't help but admire the way her tall hired hand gently instructed the girl in all the right moves while continuing to pretend a lack of expertise.

At Lisa's insistence, Holly and Jake danced together again before they said good-night, so she could watch and pick up some additional pointers. Afterward, on the way from the house to his less agreeable digs behind the barn, Jake paused and leaned against one of the oversize, nearly bare cottonwood trees that shaded the yard. Holly hadn't bothered to draw the living-room curtains. He could see her and Lisa moving about in the yellow lamp glow.

This is what I've needed, he thought, an expression of longing coming over his face. Hard work and pleasantly tired muscles from working on a ranch that's not a rich man's plaything. Open country. Stars to gaze at undimmed by city lights. A pretty, decent woman to get slowly, sweetly under my skin. Just to let time unfurl and nature do its handiwork.

He wasn't ready, yet, to think about the sad truth that the pretty, decent woman who consumed his thoughts and made him want something more than a passing fling with her would probably refuse even to speak with him when she learned why he'd sought her out.

The remainder of the week passed in a blur of effort and anticipation. Meanwhile, the weather had turned warmer, ushering in a final burst of Indian summer. Already, in the foothills, the aspens were loosing showers of gold doubloons with every breeze, while at higher elevations, they stood amid the dark green winter sentinels of ponderosa pine like slender, naked ghosts.

On Friday evening, to rein in Lisa's excess energy and give her something to do while they waited for the dance to roll around, Holly floated a dinner-table suggestion. What about a picnic? They could take the horses, head a little way up into the foothills. When Lisa promptly invited Jake, she had to admit that was just what she'd been hoping would occur.

"You needn't go if you'd rather not," she told him perversely, unwilling to seem too eager. "As we agreed, Saturday afternoons and Sundays are your days off. I know this country like the back of my hand. We'll be fine, just the two of us."

As Lisa flung her a killing look, Jake considered her statement. Was she simply trying to be fair to him? Or attempting to slow the progress of a relationship that was getting too sticky for her taste? Whatever the case, he didn't plan to humor her.

"I haven't been on a picnic since I was eight," he responded. "I accept your invitation."

They left shortly before noon the following day, after seeing to it that the chickens and other livestock were cared for. As they wound up the cottonwood-lined creek, picking their way among boulders, fallen tree branches and the occasional low-lying, muddy pool, a rolled-up, Indian-patterned blanket was tied behind Holly's saddle. Beside Jake, Dasher lugged a hamper of sandwiches, potato salad, cookies and fruit, plus a thermos each of coffee and lemonade.

With Holly in the lead, astride Brandy, and Lisa following on Comet, Jake brought up the rear. Energized by the prospect of getting to know Holly better, he whistled in his contentment. None of them were related by blood or marriage. Yet it's as if we're mother, father and daughter, he thought.

Though it was cool enough that they required light jackets, the day was heartrendingly beautiful, especially in light of the fact that winter was just a few weeks away. Overhead, the sky's azure bosom provided ample pasture for flocks of fluffy white clouds. Leaves rustled as they skittered over the loose stones beneath their horses' hooves, and blew across their path like the omens of snowflakes.

Before long, the first real snow would fly, grainy as soap powder, dusting the hay bales and settling on Holly's windowsills. Would Jake be gone by then? she wondered. Would she have just her memories of him?

As they climbed, past grazing cattle and a few nimble-footed elk, an eagle circled briefly overhead. Above the yellowing grass and some pinkish red weed Holly couldn't name, green-gold chamisa lifted its autumn blooms in brushy clumps.

An hour or so into their ride, they came to a padlocked gate that separated Honeycomb Ranch from the public lands of the San Juan National Forest. Opening it from the saddle with a key that she'd remembered to thrust into her pocket, Holly waved her companions through, and shut it behind the three of them. After that, their climb grew steeper. However, it wasn't long before they reached the meadow she had in mind. From it, a vista of snowcapped peaks opened up. There was a broad outcropping of rock they could use as a picnic table.

"I'm hungry," Jake announced as they tied their horses to several saplings, giving them ample rope to graze. "Let's eat."

"Me, too!" Lisa chimed in.

Holly smiled as she unsnapped the leather bindings that held her blanket roll in place. "So what's new?" she teased, striding over to their dining spot and spreading the blanket so he and her stepdaughter could unload their meal. "You two are always starved, no matter how much I feed you!"

The "you two" and "always" of her statement implied a unity and depth in their relationship that was almost familial, she reflected as they dug into the food. Yet Jake had been part of their lives for just a few weeks. A drifter, he couldn't be counted on to stick around for long. Was she making a big mistake by letting him penetrate their circle of two that way—setting herself, and worse still, Lisa, up for a disappointment?

That the girl had grown inordinately fond of him, she had little doubt. Watching the two of them together only confirmed it. As they munched their sandwiches and demolished generous portions of the applesauce-raisin cake Holly had baked, Lisa listened avidly to Jake's story of a picnic in the woods with a part-Indian companion who'd worked for his mother when he was about her age. According to him, he and his mentor had gathered and trapped their food and cooked it over an open fire. They'd also spent the night in the woods.

Though Holly judged the story to be a tall tale, Lisa hung on every word. "Will you teach me to trap for my dinner, the way Johnney Red Deer taught you, in case I'm ever lost in the woods?" she begged, caught up in the romance of his adventure.

His mouth curved slightly. "If you insist. Sure you want to skin and cook a squirrel? Or a chipmunk?"

Realizing what was at stake, Lisa made a face.

"I think she's changed her mind," Holly suggested.

When at last they were finished, Holly and Jake put away the leftover food and stretched out on the blanket to gaze at the distant mountains while Lisa gathered a bouquet of the wildflowers that grew among the meadow's yellowing grass and weeds. At Holly's prompting to share a little more of his past, Jake told a few stories from his rodeo days. He admitted to having met Clint on one occasion.

"Tall, redheaded guy, as I remember," he said.

She nodded, trying to imagine the two of them together.

"He was one of the best," Jake added. "Somewhat older than me. I looked up to him."

When she asked how long he'd been in rodeo, he equivocated. "Too long," he responded, rolling over on his side to gaze into her eyes. "I decided to get out while I was in one piece."

She had to bite her tongue to keep from telling him he was still in pretty good shape.

Lisa saved her from herself by insisting they play a game of tag. Designating herself as "it," and the slab of rock they'd picnicked on as "home base," she closed her eyes and counted to twenty while Jake and Holly scattered. The high-spirited free-for-all that followed had them screaming with hilarity, particularly when Lisa managed to tag Jake and he caught Holly in the next breath. Holly ended up on the ground with Jake and Lisa piled on top of her.

Fully invested in the spirit of the game, Lisa jumped up screaming, "Holly...you're it!" and ran away as fast as her legs would carry her.

Jake didn't move. His breath warm and seductive against Holly's ear, the weight of his upper body crushing her breasts, he lay there looking at her. One of his denim-clad knees rested between her thighs. She could feel his manhood stiffen, the secret gateway to her womanhood quiver in anticipation as he pressed against her.

God, but she's beautiful, Jake thought as he smoothed a loose strand of hair back from her forehead. So honest and natural—sweet as honey in the comb. I could die of wanting her. On fire to kiss her, he started to lower his mouth to hers.

The moment coincided with Lisa's discovery that they hadn't moved. "C'mon, you guys," she yelled in exasperation, returning to tug at them. "You're not supposed to wrestle. Holly, it's your job to *chase* us!"

Her cheeks flushed, Holly wriggled to an upright position and did her best to comply with Lisa's instructions. Both relieved and wistful that she and Jake had been interrupted before they could kiss, she was careful not to look too directly at him. Within minutes, she was calling a halt to the game. A mass of clouds had rolled in from the west, threatening rain as they transformed the day from bright to gloomy.

Nobody said much as they saddled up and headed back to Honeycomb. Even Lisa looked thoughtful. Hoping the girl was tired rather than upset by what had nearly turned out to be an embarrassing episode, Holly decided nothing of the sort could be allowed to happen again. She'd have to speak to Jake. If he couldn't keep his distance, he'd have to look elsewhere for employment.

When they reached the barn, she offered to help Lisa carry the picnic things into the house while he saw to the horses, then asked the girl to put the food away by herself as they entered the kitchen. "I've got to run outside and check on something, okay?" she said.

Jake heard her approach from Comet's stall, where he was rubbing the filly down and currying her. Was Holly on her way to read him the riot act? Or did she want precisely what he wanted?

His employer's classic, unadorned features were a study in mixed emotions when she appeared. "I need to talk to you," she asserted, standing closer to him than prudence might have dictated.

Jake put down the currycomb and towel he was using with a deliberate gesture. "I don't see why," he answered, "when words won't solve the problem."

A moment later, his mouth was consuming hers.

Chapter Four

An explosion of fireworks illuminating the dim and dusty stall, Jake's kiss carried Holly beyond protest. All thought of ordering him to keep his distance fled. Instead of just dreaming about the possibility, she was in his arms. Demanding but gentle, his hands explored her body through the slender barrier of her clothing. Exacting a similar privilege, she held him close.

He smelled wonderful, like saddle leather and straw, the piny tang of cool mountain air against heated skin mingled with the expensive-smelling after-shave she liked so much. She wanted to drink him in. Savor him like the finest brandy. With all that she had and all that she was, she wanted to breathe his every breath.

She didn't retreat when his tongue teased her lips apart in imitation of the deeper communion he so obviously wanted. Or cavil at his flagrant seeking. Half-delirious with pleasure, she caressed the corded muscles of his back and shoulders. Though it had never happened that way with anyone, she was damp inside her jeans with wanting him.

Comet's soft blowing as she nuzzled the incomprehensible humans who were wrestling in her stall brought Holly to her senses. You can't do this, she ordered herself in panic, appalled at the ease with which she'd tumbled from her lofty defenses. Jake is a stranger. Your hired hand. You have responsibilities. This doesn't *mean* anything to him.

With Holly nestled in his arms, Jake was storming heaven's gate. What a wonder she is! he exulted, half-drunk with the privilege of caressing her. So ladylike and sweet, yet passionate as a lioness. A month of Sundays in her bed wouldn't be enough. A rover where women were concerned up to that point, he realized to his delight and consternation that he'd never be sated with her crushed-berry lips, the trim but rounded shape of her buttocks. Compelled by everything that was male and randy in him, he longed to sweep her beyond reason. Together, they'd mount the footholds to paradise.

Thoughts of forever were knocking at the threshold of his consciousness as he drew back sufficiently to rain little kisses on her face and neck. "Holly...Holly...can you possibly know what you do to me?" he whispered.

I know what you do to *me,* she thought. You cut me loose from every mooring of sanity and prudence. It has to stop! Pushing hard, with her palms splayed against his chest, she managed to extricate herself from his embrace.

"Probably not," she answered as he stared at her in surprise. "I'd rather you didn't share the gory details. What happened just now was as much my fault as yours. But it can't be repeated...not even to the limited extent that it occurred up on the mountain this afternoon. I have a ten-year-old stepdaughter to think about.''

Astonished, Jake didn't answer her.

''I came back out here to tell you that,'' she persisted. ''I want your word that, in the future, you'll keep your hands to yourself.''

Tight-lipped and still hot with desire, Jake regarded her with narrowed eyes. If she kicked me off the ranch, it would serve me right, he acknowledged—not for kissing her, but for the deception I'm practicing. Perverse as always, he vowed not to let that happen if he could help it. With Holly, he'd discovered something that, previously, he'd only dreamed about.

''You're the boss,'' he said at last in a quiet voice. ''You call the shots.''

Her victory a hollow one when it came to the heart, Holly turned and strode back to the house. A short time later, his truck hurtled up the driveway in a cloud of dust. With a sinking feeling in the pit of her stomach, she wondered if he'd cleared out for good. Pride laced with fear kept her from checking his trailer to see if her guess was accurate.

When he didn't return by breakfast, she decided they wouldn't see him again. At once the life she'd made for herself and Lisa seemed dingier—a soul-empty place.

When Lisa asked where he was, she received a terse answer. ''Sunday is Jake's day off,'' she informed the girl in a tone that didn't invite dialogue. ''What he does with it is none of our affair.''

After two thoroughly wretched nights spent tossing and turning in her bed, Holly wanted to fling her arms around Jake's neck when, on Monday morning, he showed up at the breakfast table. Reason kept her from going for it. Though Lisa gabbed his head off and hung on his every sentence, she and Jake barely exchanged two words. They remained uncommunicative with each other as they returned to the fencing project a short time later. Everything about his carriage and deportment suggested he wouldn't try to kiss her again. Ironically, her yearning for him only strengthened.

That week, as they raced to finish their work before the first heavy snowfall, they prepared to attend the dance. Having brought nothing but work clothes when he set out on his leave of absence, Jake settled for the best shirt and jeans of the lot. Holly made Lisa a red velveteen dress with a lace collar. She took in a flowered challis one with long sleeves and piqué ruching she'd worn when Clint was courting her. Thanks to all the exercise she'd gotten during the past several years, running the ranch without much help, it was too big for her.

At last, Saturday rolled around. The red disk of the sun was slipping behind the mountains, leaving a slowly fading swath of magenta-tinged clouds as, bathed, brushed and dressed in their best clothes beneath winter-weight parkas, Holly, Jake and Lisa assembled beside Holly's truck. Like lovers who recently have quarreled, Holly and Jake sought each other's eyes, then glanced away.

It had been like that all week. Meanwhile, they were late getting started. "Want to drive?" Holly asked, her breath pluming on the frosty air as she held out her keys.

Jake's shrug was nonchalant. "If you want."

Watching them, Lisa was clearly aware they weren't on the best of terms. Yet their estrangement didn't seem to bother her. Scrambling into the middle position in the truck's cab so that she acted as a physical buffer between them, she chattered enthusiastically about the evening ahead.

The huge Cunningham ranch, one of the more prosperous in the valley, was a thirty-minute drive from Honeycomb. By the time they reached it, a sea of trucks and four-wheel-drive vehicles surrounded its corral. Atop tall poles, the yard lights were blazing. A scarecrow made of straw and a huge pile of pumpkins had been set up beside the half-open barn door, which was festooned with welcome streamers in an array of fall colors. The sounds of fiddling, square-dance calls and bursts of laughter greeted them.

Inside, the festivities were already in full swing, lit by the cheerful glow of electrified lanterns that had been strung from the barn's rafters and along the edge of the hayloft. Pausing briefly to ask Holly's permission, Lisa quickly ran off to join several of her schoolmates, including her best friend, Jane Tornquist. The granddaughter of Holly's closest neighbors, Emma and Lars Tornquist, Jane was spending the school year in Larisson Valley while her parents were on temporary work assignment in Saudi Arabia.

Though she was happy to see Lisa enjoy herself, Holly couldn't help feeling self-conscious about arriving with her attractive hired hand in tow. It was almost as if they were dating. Painfully aware his presence might set tongues to wagging, she made a beeline for the Tornquists, who were sipping cider from paper cups and chatting with some other neighbors as they watched the dancers. At least she could count on them to understand.

"Lars, Emma...Tom and Sandy...I'd like you to

meet Jake McKenzie, who's been helping me fence the north pasture," she said, coloring slightly at the friendly but curious way they and the Tibbetts, the couple who ranched the property just south of hers, looked him up and down as they greeted him.

"Happy to meet you, Jake," Lars responded, his Scandinavian accent pronounced and his eyes twinkling behind wire-rimmed glasses as he pumped Jake's hand. "Holly's one of our favorite people, and she's long been in need of reliable help. I hope you plan to stay awhile."

"Any friend of Holly's is a friend of ours," Emma added.

A bit more reserved, the Tibbetts took turns shaking hands with him.

Returning everyone's hello with his usual firm grip and wry flash of smile, Jake didn't volunteer any more information about himself than absolutely necessary.

"I hear you helped Holly fix the barn roof," Tom Tibbetts commented.

Jake nodded. "It was our first project."

The men had been talking about the price of beef and government subsidies. After briefly questioning Jake about where he was from and probing his credentials as a ranch hand, they resumed their discussion of the topic. Sandy Tibbetts excused herself to speak with some friends. Taking up the slack, Emma recounted an anecdote involving Jane and some kittens that had taken up residence in the Tornquist barn.

Her hand inadvertently brushing Jake's as she listened to Emma's story, Holly stole a quick glance at him.

Wanna dance? his blue eyes inquired. *Or will our practice in the kitchen go to waste?*

Nothing would have pleased her more than to take a turn on the dance floor with him. Unfortunately, she didn't trust herself to follow where it might lead. Their firestorm of a kiss a week earlier had taught her just how fragile her self-control *was* where he was concerned. She was also afraid of the gossip it might generate.

When she didn't encourage him with either word or look, he volunteered to get them some cider.

"Thanks, that'd be nice," Holly answered, regretting her qualms the moment he strode away from them, long and lean in his faded jeans and worn cowboy boots.

As soon as he was out of earshot, Emma moved closer. "So *that's* your new hand," her motherly neighbor said in an approving tone, gazing after him. "Lisa has described him to us. She said he was smart and fun...a very hard worker. But she didn't tell us how handsome he was!"

In Holly's estimation, Jake was the sexiest man on the planet. Old clothes and the occasional stubble of beard he sported only emphasized his looks by contrast. Yet she shrank from agreeing with Emma's appraisal. The proprietary thrill she felt at the praise her neighbor had lavished on him only added to her ambivalence.

"For the record, he sleeps in the old trailer next to the barn," she responded a trifle defensively. "Our arrangement is strictly business. He needed a job. And I needed help. It was that simple. There isn't any gossip circulating about us, I hope."

The corners of her mouth curving, as if she thought Holly protested too much, Emma gave her arm a reassuring pat. "Not to my knowledge," she said. "People around here know you too well to think you'd do anything scandalous. It's just that seeing you with a good-looking man the right age for you makes me realize how young and pretty you are...and how long it's been since you lost Clint. To my way of thinking, it's time there was a man in your life again.''

Surely you're not suggesting I take up with an itinerant laborer, Holly wanted to retort, and then hated herself for thinking such disparaging thoughts. She glanced up as a respectable, fortysomething widower from Stony Creek approached and asked her to join him in a lively square-dance number. Eager to put paid to her conversation with Emma and prove to the world at large that she was a free agent, she quickly accepted.

Thus it happened that, when Jake returned with cups of ice-cold cider for them, she was dancing. From what he could tell, she appeared to be enjoying herself. Scowling, he set her cup aside. Though he did his best to evince a polite interest in Emma Tornquist's murmured commentary as he sipped at his own beverage, his eyes didn't leave Holly's face.

Finally the widower returned her to her friends. He'd promised to call the next number. Not pausing to ask permission, Jake put down his cup and tucked his hand possessively through her arm.

''My turn,'' he insisted. ''If you're thinking of refusing me, don't...unless you want to start a fuss.''

Convinced everyone in the Cunninghams' oversize hay barn must be staring at them, Holly complied with his ultimatum. She was unsmiling, a little stiff, as they took their places in one of the circles that was forming. Once the fiddling started and her erstwhile partner began calling out the moves, however, she couldn't maintain her standoffish air. The music was too infectious, the feel of Jake's fingers gripping her waist through the fabric of her dress too welcome. She quickly learned that his skill as a dancer far surpassed his claims. Before long, they were exchanging amused, friendly glances as they strove to heed the caller's somewhat mixed-up instructions.

Things got exponentially a lot more serious when the widower from Stony Creek introduced a set of slower, ballroom-style numbers and they nestled more closely in each other's arms. For Holly, it was like kissing Jake in Comet's stall all over again, though their lips didn't meet. As if they'd been created for just that purpose, their hips moved in unison. Aching for the contact, their thighs brushed wantonly together.

It's as if we could make love right here in the Cunninghams' hay barn with my friends and neighbors looking on, yet not be impeded in our fulfillment, Holly thought, her heart pounding like a wild thing in her breast as she shut her eyes and pressed her cheek to his. *I should pull back. Conduct myself with greater decorum. Yet that's not what I want to do.* With everything that was womanly and willful in her, she longed to blend and merge with her tall partner until every trace of the individual boundaries that separated them had ceased to exist.

For Jake, her sudden softening, her melting into him, was more than his self-control could abrogate. Tugging her closer as his body responded with a passionate rush he couldn't quell, he let his thoughts fly past the deception that had brought him to her doorstep and dared to fantasize some kind of solution for them. *To her*, he knew, *he was a mendicant cowboy, down on his luck and not necessarily to be trusted. If he could talk her into forgiving him once she knew the truth, maybe there was hope for them.*

By the end of the set, he was temporarily indisposed.

Resting one hand casually on her shoulder, he positioned Holly in front of him so that she screened his recovery while the crowd applauded the musicians, who'd been drawn from the local population. Fully cognizant of what he was doing and none too eager to share her knowledge with the world, Holly cooperated, her face a study in ambivalence.

Another round of lively square-dance numbers was about to start. "Do you want to dance again?" Jake asked, aware her former partner had completed his stint on stage and was headed in their direction.

Her defenses in a shambles thanks to the intimacy of their turn on the dance floor, Holly couldn't muster the fortitude to reject him. If people wanted to gossip, she'd let them. On the other hand, she couldn't abandon her most cherished principles. Unless she wanted to end up in bed with Jake, sans marriage, or—God help her— agree to tie the knot without careful consideration of what that would mean, she needed to cool things herself.

"Maybe we'd better sit this one out," she suggested.

I hope that means you won't be dancing with your admirer, either, Jake responded silently. Glancing about for Lisa, he spotted the girl wistfully tapping her toe on the far side of the dance floor. Clearly, she was yearning to participate. It didn't look as if she stood much chance. True to form, most of the boys her age were wrestling and talking among themselves—giving their female classmates a wide berth.

Jake couldn't help thinking of the way Clint had danced with his daughter shortly before his death, and wondering if the girl was remembering it, too. He turned back to Holly. "Mind if I ask Lisa, then?"

Surprise and gratitude lit her face. "Jake...*would* you?"

"I'd be happy to," he said.

Walking her back to where the Tornquists continued to watch the dancers, Jake crossed the barn and made Lisa a little bow. Holly looked on as surprise and pleasure washed over her stepdaughter's face. Their heights as dissimilar as the contrasting colors of their hair, the shabbily dressed but dashing man and skinny redheaded schoolgirl took their places.

The first real snow of the year was falling an hour and a half later as, zipped into their parkas and toasty warm in the heated cab of Holly's truck, they drove back to Honeycomb with Lisa wedged between their bodies. Though at first the girl couldn't seem to stop talking about the evening's events, particularly the envy and excitement of her girlfriends when Jake had danced with her, it wasn't long before her lashes were fluttering lower and she was resting her head on Holly's shoulder. A country-western ballad was playing on the radio and, with a quiet glance at Holly, Jake turned down the volume.

How I wish things were different, Holly thought, enjoying the luxury of letting him care for them. Though none of us are related by blood, and I'm Jake's employer, not his lover, it's as if the three of us are in the process of becoming a family. If I shut my eyes and let my imagination carry me away, I can almost picture us kissing Lisa good-night and retiring to my room, snuggling cozy and secret beneath my down coverlet.

Envisioning them married and making a life together was jumping the gun, of course. She didn't know anything about Jake you couldn't discover by working side by side with a man for almost a month. And he hadn't volunteered much. I'd give anything if he were a local rancher...someone I'd known and trusted for several years, she thought, instead of a hired hand with a questionable past who turned up penniless on my doorstep. If the former were true, he could court me and rumors wouldn't fly. Everyone in the valley would know and approve of him.

For his part, though he felt the pleasure of their growing bond as keenly as she did, Jake was busy wishing he'd met Holly some other way—*any* way but the one he'd so brilliantly engineered. The fact was, she was beginning to mean a great deal to him. And his goose would be cooked with her the minute she learned whom he represented.

Damn it, he thought, trying not to grit his teeth in his frustration. I owe Dutch loyalty...both as his friend and as his attorney. And I genuinely support his right to interact with his granddaughter before she's all grown up. But I shouldn't have to throw away the best thing that's ever happened to me for his sake. There ought to be a way I can do right by him without spoiling my chances and torpedoing what Holly and Lisa have built together.

Unfortunately, he couldn't think of one that wouldn't leave him out in the cold. The possibility that Holly might end up there, too, with Dutch persuading a judge his blood tie to the girl ought to take precedence over the stepparent relationship she'd so lovingly nurtured, had begun to haunt him.

Too soon, from his point of view, they arrived at Honeycomb. Though the lights in the truck's cab came on when they opened the doors, letting in a blast of cold air, Lisa didn't fully wake. Lifting and carrying her into the house, Jake hung around in the kitchen while

Holly helped the drowsy girl undress and tucked her into bed. When she reappeared, he got to his feet, hat in hand, to wish her a subdued good-night.

"The dance was fun—thanks for inviting me," he said.

Silent a moment, she gazed up at him. Had she missed something? He sounded so somber—almost as if he were bidding her goodbye. "I had fun, too," she answered at last. "Don't mention it."

I don't know what to do, Jake agonized a minute later, his head down and his boots leaving a distinctive trail of footprints in the snow as he made his way to his cramped and chilly trailer. *I can't keep working beside her every day and not kiss her, hold her, want to make love to her. Yet she'll kick me off Honeycomb for good if I tell her the truth.*

The following Saturday would be Halloween. Midday temperatures that had hovered in the mid-forties dropped to the low thirties and snow fell with increasing frequency as Holly and Jake struggled, beginning Monday, to finish the fencing project they'd inaugurated in more clement weather. Meanwhile, Jake's trailer, with its drafty seams and inadequate space heater, was freezing. After spending several nights fully dressed, shivering in his sleeping bag beneath several layers of blankets, he asked in desperation if he could camp on the kitchen floor, beside the fireplace.

Unable to refuse what she considered a reasonable request, Holly agreed with mixed emotions. It didn't surprise her that letting him sleep under her roof only made her longing for him more intense. She tried to sublimate it by planning and working on Lisa's Halloween costume, a Native American squaw outfit—to little effect.

Their proximity had a equally devastating effect on Jake. As they pounded fence posts and strung wire bundled to the nines, or hauled hay in the truck to outlying pastures for the stock, he longed to kiss her ruddy, increasingly chapped cheeks and shelter her from the frigid north wind inside his coat. Lacking any outlet for his passionate, protective urges, he began to find his attraction to her something of a torment. Worry over their inevitable clash when he told her the truth, coupled with a nagging sense of guilt over his failure to inform Dutch of his granddaughter's whereabouts, were having him for breakfast.

Though it seemed like months had elapsed instead of days, finally the week was over. Quitting time on Friday found Holly waiting behind the wheel of her truck in swirling snow as Jake got out and opened the barn door for her. A moment later, she was driving inside and turning off the engine.

He's got the manners of a diplomat and the physique of a cowboy, she thought, helplessly drawn to him as he held open the cab door for her. He didn't step aside and, perforce, they were standing very close.

It was now or never. "I suppose you heard—the Tornquists are holding a Halloween party for Jane and her girlfriends from school at their house tomorrow night," she announced tentatively. "Since there are miles between neighbors in the valley and kids can't trick-or-treat from door to door…"

Jake tilted his head slightly to one side as he regarded her. Was she advertising the fact that she'd be home alone all evening? Somehow he doubted it. "Lisa mentioned it once or twice," he said.

"Well, umm…" She paused. "Lars has a lodge meeting in Pagosa Springs tomorrow afternoon. He'll be back late. Emma was wondering if we could come over to help. You don't have to go, if you don't want. It isn't a requirement of your job or anything. Of course you know Lisa would love it if you did."

Her ambivalence was painfully clear to him. What about you? he countered silently. Would *you* love it? "I was thinking of driving into Pagosa Springs myself tomorrow evening for a little R and R," he said indifferently. "But it's nothing I can't cancel. I don't mind driving over with you if you think I could be of help."

Though Jake's backhanded acceptance of her invitation drove a speculative stake of jealousy through Holly's heart, the evening turned out well. A somewhat incongruous sight with her springy red curls as Sacajawea, guide to Lewis and Clark, Lisa won a prize for the most authentic costume and aced the apple-bobbing contest. Jake was in demand—in part because several of her friends remembered him as the man who'd asked her to dance at the Cunninghams' party. But it was his unsuspected talent for telling ghost stories that won him the most points with Lisa's classmates.

"Know what?" Emma whispered to Holly as they set out mugs for hot chocolate and a huge tray of homemade doughnuts. "Your Jake would make a good father. He's got Jane and Lisa and all their friends eating out of his hand."

Forced to agree, provided he was capable of commitment, Holly wasn't about to admit it to her well-meaning neighbor. "Emma, please!" she protested, twin spots of color flooding her cheeks. "He's not *my* Jake…simply my employee. I don't even expect the situation to be permanent."

As if he'd planned it that way on purpose, Lars returned home from his meeting as the doughnuts and hot chocolate were being served. "I see I arrived at the proper moment," he joked, winking at Jane's friends and giving his wife a pacifying kiss on the cheek. "Good to see you, Holly...Jake. You got that fencing finished yet? Let me know if you need any help."

With Lars ensconced in his favorite easy chair, everyone settled down to munch and sip and listen to a final tale of the supernatural delivered by Jake in deliciously sepulchral tones. When at last it was over, and parents began arriving to pick up their daughters, Jane and Lisa put their heads together. A moment later, Lisa was begging for permission to spend the night.

"Jane can lend me a pair of pajamas and a robe," she cajoled earnestly. "Pretty please with sugar on it, Holly...say yes!"

Jane was tugging at her grandfather's hand. "Tell Mrs. Yarborough it's okay...that Lisa won't be any trouble," she begged.

Smiling as he filled his pipe, Lars took his time about answering. "It would be our pleasure to have Lisa as our guest," he affirmed at last in his courtly, old-world way. "Tomorrow's Sunday. I'll bring her home first thing in the morning, Holly, so you won't have to come after her."

A quick glance at Emma revealed that the spontaneous arrangements were fine with her. Somewhat reluctantly, because giving them her stamp of approval meant she and Jake would sleep under the same roof without the mediating influence of Lisa's presence, Holly gave in.

"Looks like you've got me outnumbered," she told her stepdaughter with an indulgent shake of her head.

"You can stay...provided you promise to get some sleep and don't keep Mr. Tornquist waiting tomorrow when he's ready to bring you home. Don't forget...you have chores to do that got shunted aside while you were talking on the phone to Jane and putting on your Indian makeup this afternoon."

Without Lisa's chatter to provide a distraction, the drive back to Honeycomb was quiet in the extreme. Tonight, Holly thought with a little shiver that was more excitement than cold, there'll be no ten-year-old to tuck into bed. Jake won't go trudging off to his trailer. We'll sleep alone under the same roof—with just a wall separating us.

Parking the truck inside the barn where it would be more likely to start in the morning if the temperature dropped, they headed toward the porch. A single lamp had been left burning in the living room. Unlocking the front door, Holly preceded Jake inside. Her keen awareness of the quandary their relationship had become sharpened perceptibly when he didn't wish her a routine good-night or move to fetch his sleeping bag from behind the couch. The charged quality of the atmosphere between them all but forced her to say something.

"Would you like a cup of coffee to chase away the chill?" she asked, pulling off her boots as she attempted to keep the unsteadiness she felt from surfacing in her voice. "I have some decaf that won't keep us awake...."

In the play of shadow and light that revealed the room's familiar furnishings, Jake's eyes had taken on their smoky look. "Wanting you keeps me awake," he answered.

A moment later, they were in each other's arms.

Chapter Five

During their absence at the Tornquists' party, the carefully banked blaze in Holly's fireplace had almost gone out. She kept her bottled-gas furnace set at sixty-five degrees to save on fuel bills. Yet she and Jake didn't feel the chill that was gathering in her living room. After so much yearning, they were making their own heat.

Bold but subtly questioning, his tongue parted her lips. A little sigh signaled her willingness to continue as she slipped her arms about his neck. Like it or not, this cowboy with a dubious past was the man for her. They were alone in the house, hidden from prying eyes. In that sequestered, unfettered moment, second-guessing her heart's desire wasn't on her agenda.

Running his hands down the slender curves of her body the way he'd wanted to do since the moment he'd set eyes on her, Jake was dumbfounded by her cooperation. Was the wholesome blond rancher who'd seemed so out of reach really kissing him back like a house afire? Or was he simply dreaming it? God knew, since their ill-fated skirmish in Comet's stall, he'd pictured it happening often enough.

He couldn't ignore the possibility that he was courting danger. With each fresh liberty he took, he might goad her further than she was willing to go. Prodding her past the point where she'd slap his face and order him off her property was the last thing he wanted. He had to take the risk. Faint heart never won a thing that mattered to you, he thought with a twinge of fatalism, slipping his hands beneath her sweater to claim her breasts.

Holly's gasp of delight was smothered against his mouth. Erect beneath the stretch-lace fabric of her bra, her nipples telegraphed inflammatory messages to her deepest places. Helpless to withstand them, she let wave after wave of sensation wash over her.

Passion was a river overflowing its banks and she was a leaf on its current. With all the generosity that had gone begging until he'd appeared at her gate, she longed to connect with Jake in every way possible, make her tall, bewitching ranch hand an unconditional present of who she was.

She surprised them both by pulling her sweater over her head. A moment later, she was unhooking her bra's front clasp and sliding its straps down her arms.

Jake's breath caught in his throat to see Holly revealed that way. His arousal intensified. Pliant, exquisite, too perfect for a man who hadn't always been selective in his choices, she stood naked to the waist in a nimbus of lamplight—a virgin in spirit, he guessed, despite her widowhood, whereas he'd known too many women without learning anything of substance from them.

With her, he'd immerse himself in life's mysteries, cede his carefully guarded separateness. Aware at some subliminal level that loving and winning her could heal the malaise that had afflicted him, he responded by taking off his shirt and positioning her against his chest.

So sweetly calculated to inflame her ardor, the gesture blew her away. Operating solely on instinct, she insinuated herself against him. In such proximity, his readiness to make love to her wasn't any secret.

Gray eyes blurring into blue, they kissed. Nipple seduced nipple. Half out of his head, Jake tugged her closer. He was trembling with his need for her.

Would she let him make love to her? Too hot not to pursue an answer, he dared to unzip her jeans. When she didn't object, he dragged them down her hips, raining blunt, adoring kisses on her neck as he helped her step free of them. Her cotton bikini panties came next, to be discarded with her socks in a little heap.

Pale as the dusting of snow that lay on Honeycomb Ranch in contrast to the outdoor tan that lingered on her face and arms, the smooth curve of Holly's buttocks was his to caress. Her nest of coarse, Scandinavian-blond curls awaited his fingertips.

To Holly, the corded muscles of Jake's biceps and the erect manhood that pressed against the front of his jeans were nothing short of breathtaking. She ached to bury her face against the tangled mat of crisp, dark chest hair that plunged toward his belt in a narrowing seam, draw down his zipper and learn his shape with her fingertips.

It would be their first time together. Despite a storm of longing that cried for immediate gratification, Jake wanted it to be special. Lifting Holly in his arms, he bypassed the couch and carried her into her bedroom.

They didn't switch on a light. Like frost, like opals, moonlight spilled across her down coverlet, barely illuminating the honeyed wood tones of her log walls and beamed ceiling. Their eyes gleamed black in the shadows it didn't penetrate as they gazed at each other.

Drowning in awe, Jake held Holly close. He was on fire with wanting her. "Tell me what you want," he whispered.

Everything you have, her heart clamored. *Nothing less will be enough.*

Flickering to the bed in anticipation of what they'd do, her gaze was caught and held by a throw pillow Lisa had painstakingly embroidered for her the previous Mother's Day. To The Best Holly In The World, it proclaimed mischievously in uneven block letters. Misgivings seized her, though she tried to quell them. The daughter Clint had placed in her care deserved better than the action she was contemplating.

"Jake...we can't make love," she whispered.

Was she making some kind of joke? If so, it wasn't funny. "Surely you're kidding," he said after a moment.

Turning her back on what they both wanted would be the hardest thing she'd ever had to do. To her regret, she didn't have any other choice. "I have a stepdaughter who trusts me to honor the principles I'm instilling in her," she tried to explain. "If I go against them behind her back I'll never forgive myself."

His thoughts in turmoil, he set her on her feet. "What am I supposed to say to that?" he asked. Aware his tone was harsh with disappointment, he quickly softened it. "Lisa's gone for the night," he added more reasonably. "She'd never have to know."

Though his willingness to deceive her stepdaughter hurt, Holly didn't hold it against him. What had transpired between them had been her doing as much as his. From a cowboy down on his luck who'd talked her into hiring him, Jake McKenzie had turned into the man she loved.

She hadn't previously admitted her feelings, even to herself. As the discovery sank in, she struggled to deal with the situation at hand. "Jake," she begged, adding as she felt him tense further, "please try to understand. I can't give myself to you the way you want...not because I don't want it, too, but because we aren't married. I don't believe in sex between unmarried people."

Was she saying she wanted to marry him? Somehow, Jake doubted it. She might crave him physically, even enjoy his company. But under the circumstances she'd never consider him husband material. In her eyes, he felt certain, he was nothing more than an itinerant ranch hand, here today and gone tomorrow. He wouldn't merit her trust.

What a fool I was to approach her under false colors, he thought. Yet he knew she wouldn't have let Dutch Hargrett's lawyer get within ten feet of her. "Do you mean to say," he asked softly, his passion fading, "that, after getting all worked up, we're just going to say good-night?"

Holly was on the verge of tears. There were names for women like her. *Tease* was one of them. Yet she'd never intended anything of the sort. "If you're willing, we could hold each other under the blankets," she proposed.

About to dismiss the notion out of hand and argue

forcefully for what he wanted, Jake didn't want to cause a rift between them. He guessed that was just what would happen if he pressed his case. Against his will, he was forced to admire her strength of principle. Meanwhile, it was tellingly clear that her feelings mattered a great deal to him.

"Don't cry, darlin'," he soothed, wrapping his arms around her and gently stroking the satin skin of her back and shoulders. "For tonight, holding you will be enough."

Abjectly grateful, Holly nestled close.

The room was bone-chillingly cold. Yet Jake didn't want her in a nightgown. Before she could make a move to cover up, he tugged off his boots and kicked them aside, dropped his jeans and undershorts on the braided rug beside her bed.

Her eyes devouring his nakedness, Holly didn't protest. Since their return from the Tornquists' party, a bridge had been crossed. Getting into bed and holding back the coverlet for him, she welcomed him into her embrace.

After so many weeks of pretending he was just an employee, she would sleep with Jake. Share her body heat with him. Inhale his skin-scent. Unlike the typical roving cowpoke she'd believed him to be, he hadn't stormed out, left Honeycomb for good when she'd refused to make love to him. *He'd stuck around.*

Her head pillowed on his shoulder, Holly knew what his forbearance had cost. The price had been equally compelling for her. What will happen tomorrow and the next day? she wondered as the first wisps of dreams loosened her hold on events. Will I be able to make my convictions stick? Meanwhile, Lisa would be back in the morning. Their every action would be chaperoned.

For his part, though the pleasure of cuddling Holly naked was deep, Jake's thoughts had returned to the basic quandary that was consuming him. I've got to set things straight with her, he vowed, clear the way for us to have a relationship.

The question was, how to do it. He knew without having to be told that, for Holly, the truth about who he was and who he represented would be abhorrent in the extreme. At minimum, she'd order him off the property. In all likelihood, she'd refuse to speak to him. It was anyone's guess whether, over time, her position would soften. Now that he knew her better, he feared it would prove unyielding.

Eight hours later, sunlight was streaming in the window. Emanating from a slight distance but getting closer, a noise disturbed the tranquility of Holly's room. Her eyelids fluttered open. Drowsily, she decided that it was coming from a pickup truck. From what she could tell, it was approaching the house.

Beside her, Jake was sleeping peacefully.

Lars! she realized, sitting bolt upright. He's returning Lisa as promised!

Hurling herself from the bed as if she'd been propelled by a slingshot, Holly tore into the living area. Her jeans, sweater and underwear lay on the floor in a wrinkled heap.

Not pausing to catch her breath, she dragged them on and scooped up Jake's sweater. "Here...get dressed!" she ordered him in panic, racing back into the bedroom and shaking him by the shoulders. "Lars is arriving with Lisa! We can't let them catch us like this!"

Blinking the sleep from his eyes, Jake complied as quickly as he could. He was in the kitchen, an overnight stubble of beard shadowing his jaw as he rebuilt the fire, when Lars rapped lightly and entered, assuming a welcome.

Jane and Lisa were with him. While Jake put on the coffee and tried to make intelligent conversation in his groggy state, Holly hung back in the bedroom, furiously brushing and rebraiding her unkempt hair. As quickly as possible, so that it would seem she'd been up for a while, she reentered the kitchen carrying a load of laundry in a wicker basket and bid her visitors a cheery hello.

Jake's sleeping bag wasn't in its usual place, but that was probably for the best. There wasn't any reason for Lars to suspect he'd slept with her. Its presence beside the hearth would only invite speculation. The way her stepdaughter was chattering away with Jane, she doubted the girl would sense anything was amiss.

To her consternation, she realized suddenly that Jake was barefoot. His boots were probably under her bed! Clearly he hadn't walked to the house from his trailer that way. If he noticed, Lars would realize they were sleeping under the same roof.

So far, her neighbor seemed oblivious. Given enough time, though, he'd spot the inconsistency, she guessed. So would Lisa, the moment Jane left, or Jake had to perform some outdoor task. He could hardly fetch his missing footgear from her bedroom.

To Holly's relief, neither scenario materialized. Finishing his coffee, Lars announced it was time to go. He parried the girls' usual request for more time together with his customary good nature.

"Jane has some cleanup tasks to perform before we can drive to Pagosa Springs to spend Sunday with relatives," he explained with a smile. "You know, Lisa, you and Jane will see each other again in less than twenty-four hours, on the school bus.''

That made it roughly twenty-four hours until she and Jake were alone again at Honeycomb. What would happen then? Murmuring something about having forgotten to strip her bed, Holly removed Jake's boots from her room under cover of a pile of sheets. She managed to slip them to him as Lisa was waving goodbye to her friend.

The close call had Holly rethinking her behavior. If she hadn't awakened at the sound of Lars's truck, Lisa would almost certainly have discovered them in bed together. Despite the fact that nothing had happened, she'd been wrong to sleep with Jake.

When he tried to kiss her by the barn later that morning, she sidestepped his embrace.

''What's wrong?'' he asked, though her rejection didn't surprise him much.

Holly had difficulty meeting his eyes. Somehow she managed it. ''I enjoyed what we ended up doing last night…as much as you seemed to,'' she confessed awkwardly. ''But I don't think we should do it again. If we hadn't awakened in time, Lisa would have caught us. I'm a parent in addition to being a woman with desires and urges. I won't conduct an affair in the house where my stepdaughter's growing up. Lisa's real mother was a tramp. *I* plan to set a good example for her.''

For what seemed an eternity, he didn't speak as he regarded her from beneath the brim of his cowboy hat. Then, ''It's your call to make, Holly,'' he rejoined in a monotone.

Determined to have her as he watched her slim, somewhat melancholy figure retreat to the house, Jake decided he might as well drive into Larisson and phone

Dutch. He'd been thoroughly negligent about calling in progress reports. Though he didn't intend to inform his friend and client that he'd located his missing granddaughter, the brief absence from Honeycomb would help clear his head.

Holly watched his truck head up the driveway with regret and foreboding. After what had happened, she couldn't blame Jake for seeking out a change of scene. She only hoped it wouldn't be permanent.

Jake quaffed a soft drink from a vending machine as he dialed Dutch's private number from a phone booth at Larisson's only gas station.

The older man's energy level soared perceptibly on hearing his voice. "Jake, my boy!" he cried. "I hope you're calling with good news. We have a room all decorated and waiting...."

Assailed with guilt over the double deception he was playing out, Jake was forced to betray Holly or lie to Dutch. He chose the latter course. "Take it easy, old friend," he said, applying the brakes to Dutch's enthusiasm as gently as he could. "I haven't found Lisa yet. But I've got a new lead...."

Never an easy man to thwart, Dutch staged one of his minor explosions. "Damn it!" he swore. "You've been gone for ages! When am I going to see some action?" There was a pause. "Don't tell me there's a woman mixed up in this...."

The irony of Dutch's wild guess was like a kick in the stomach for Jake. "Not in the way you're insinuating," he said hastily. Afraid the older man would put two and two together, he strove for an audible shrug. "It's been a while since we talked, that's all," he related. "I decided to check in, and—"

Impatient though he was to recover his granddaughter, Dutch had other worries. "Good thing you did," he interrupted. "I need you back in Durango…yesterday."

By now, Jake had begun to feel his real life was based in Larisson Valley with Holly and Lisa rather than in Durango, with his fancy new house and successful law firm. Uncertain how he was going to resolve the tangled mess his life had become, he quickly extracted the reason for Dutch's statement.

After a year of motions and bargaining, the Blackwell case—an important civil suit Jake had been handling prior to his departure—had suddenly reached the trial stage. Dutch had insisted one of his partners could handle it when that had suited his purposes. Now that push had come to shove, however, he wanted his most trusted counsel at the helm.

"Surely you can give up a few days of your leave as a favor to me," he wheedled.

Assessing the consequences of temporarily abandoning Holly at that juncture in their relationship, Jake tried to stall. "Can't it wait?" he backpedaled.

Dutch's answer was unequivocal. He planned to meet with the opposition in the morning in a last-ditch attempt to settle out of court. He wanted Jake there. "Where are you?" he asked.

Though Jake declined to name his exact location on the grounds that his sabbatical wouldn't be worth mud if it got out, he admitted to being a three-hour drive away.

"Terrific!" Dutch answered. "Bernie and I will expect you for supper. Try not to be late."

The evening meal at the Hargrett estate was served at 6:00 p.m. sharp. Jake answered that he'd do his best to make it. Returning the pay-phone receiver to its cradle, he reflected that resolving the Blackwell matter would take several days. He'd have to let Holly know he needed some personal time and hope she understood.

Returning to the ranch to inform her was out of the question. For one thing, it would take too long. But that wasn't his only reason. If they talked face-to-face, he might break down and tell her the truth.

He dialed her number with mixed emotions. After four rings, the answering tape came on. She and Lisa had probably gone outdoors. Anxious to depart so he could discharge his responsibilities to Dutch and return to them, he decided to leave a message.

"I, uh, have to go away for a few days on personal business," he mumbled by way of explanation. "Sorry if it interferes with the work. See you."

A chill gripped Holly an hour or so later as she listened to his cryptic message. Filled with regret over the way she'd handled their conversation by the barn that morning, she quickly put her own spin on the situation. Frustrated by her rejection, Jake had left to find himself another woman.

To Jake's chagrin, his informal meeting with Dutch's adversaries the next morning turned out to be a lost cause. The case would go to trial on Tuesday and last well into the next week, he guessed. He didn't have a prayer of convincing Dutch he didn't need to stick around and handle it.

As Holly fumed and wept, picturing him with a rival, Jake's trial proved the axiom that the wheels of justice turn slowly. Unable to explain his absence in a way that would make sense to her, he couldn't bring himself to call again.

She was suffering the torments of the damned by the

time that, unknown to her, the trial entered its second week. Somehow, she managed to maintain an upbeat, unconcerned front for Lisa, who missed Jake and kept asking when he'd return.

Alone in her room each night after her stepdaughter had gone to bed, it was a different story. In her agonized recriminations, Jake played alternating roles. Sometimes she saw him as an innocent man whom she'd willfully misled. Then her mood would shift, and he'd become a bounder who'd mocked her virtue by seeking a less principled playmate.

By the time a second week had passed, she was positive they wouldn't see him again. She was at the height of her misery the second Saturday after his departure when Emma called. Her nearest neighbor was breezy but curious. Lisa had mentioned Jake's absence more than a week earlier. Had he returned yet?

Holly's toneless "No," told the tale in a nutshell.

Emma was silent a moment. "There's quite a bit of snow on the ground after last night," she observed. "But the roads are clear. Why don't you and Lisa come over for cherry pie? There's someone here I'd like you to meet."

A bit listlessly, Holly agreed for Lisa's sake.

The someone in question turned out to be the Tornquists' younger son, Nels, a single geologist about Holly's age who specialized in oil exploration. A younger, blonder version of Lars with Emma's thousand-watt smile, he was both friendly and courteous.

"Can you believe it?" He beamed as he, his parents, Holly and the girls consumed generous slices of Emma's pie at the latter's sunny kitchen table. "I'm off work for three whole weeks!"

"Tell them why," Lars prompted indulgently.

His gaze meeting Holly's, Nels explained that he'd be on location in Siberia for six to eight months. Because of the anticipated rigors of his assignment, his employer had granted him compensatory leave. Lacking anyone special in his life, he'd chosen to spend most of the time with his parents.

"For once, I'll be here on Thanksgiving to wrestle Jane for the wishbone," he said, giving his niece a wink. "Will you and Lisa be joining us, Holly?"

"Please do," Emma chimed in. "We'd love to have you."

If Jake doesn't return, Thanksgiving will be a world-class downer, Holly thought. Celebrating with the Tornquists would make it bearable. "Thanks, we just might take you up on that," she said.

The visit with Emma, Nels, Lars and Jane was obviously great fun for Lisa and went a long way toward distracting Holly from what was bothering her. Though she was still depressed over Jake, she went along with Nels's suggestion that they drive into Larisson and see a movie while Jane and Lisa remained at home with his parents.

Meanwhile, in Durango, Jake had won his case. Announcing his verdict late Friday afternoon, the judge had found in favor of Dutch's company. Free to return to Honeycomb, Jake had decided to crash at his place north of town for the night. With the trial behind him, he'd needed some time to think.

Though he'd come to several conclusions—for instance, acknowledging the fact that he was serious about Holly and wanted to make a life with her—he hadn't been able to think of any way to tell her the truth about himself. His conflict-of-interest problem where Dutch was concerned was still a major obstacle. He couldn't stop worrying about Lisa's future. By now he was convinced that her primary place was with Holly, though he thought she ought to know her grandparents.

Driving a stretch of the partly snowpacked highway that led to Silverton in his sleek Mercedes early Saturday afternoon as a tension-relieving exercise hadn't helped much. In the absence of easy solutions now, he was packing a few things to return to the simpler life of Larisson Valley—a heavier coat, several more sweaters, a new toothbrush.

About to leave with them stashed in a beat-up suitcase from his post-Vietnam days, he hesitated and crossed the thickly carpeted floor of his bedroom to his concealed wall safe. Moving aside a framed oil painting of cowboys in the Tetons, he dialed the combination and retrieved what he wanted.

Pausing to gaze at the worn gold band set with a row of five small garnets that had once belonged to his mother, he slipped it into one of his billfold's inner pockets. The ghost of a smile tugged at the corners of his mouth. He might not get what he wanted. But his inner man knew what he was shooting for.

Moments later, whistling a popular country-western tune slightly off-key, he was in his beat-up red truck, starting the engine. Eagerness to see the two people who mattered most to him in the world lent impetus to his foot on the gas pedal as his old truck burned up the miles that separated them. Buoyed by the hope that things would be all right, his spirits plummeted when he reached the ranch to find nobody home. Where were Holly and Lisa? Since the weather had gotten nippy, they'd usually spent their Sunday afternoons doing

mother-daughter things like cutting out dress patterns
and making cookies.

Letting himself in with the spare key he knew Holly
kept wedged in a crevice between some logs at the back
of the house, he went directly to the telephone. If any-
body knew their whereabouts, it would be Emma Tornquist.

Holly's motherly neighbor answered on the second
ring. "Jake, where *are* you?" she exclaimed. "Back at
Honeycomb? Yes, Lisa and Holly were here. As a matter of fact, Lisa still is. Holly went to a movie in Larisson with our son, Nels."

Jake was caught off guard. He hadn't realized there
was a Nels Tornquist. "Any idea what time they'll be
back?" he asked, unable to keep the frown that drew
his brows together from coloring his question.

If she caught a note of jealousy in his voice, Emma
didn't remark on it. "Nels and Holly are coming in the
door right now," she answered. "She and Lisa should
be home in a little while."

Unaware of Jake's return, Holly let Lisa, Jane and
Nels talk her into staying for homemade pizza, which
was almost ready to come out of the oven. It was only
later, after everyone had eaten their fill and she volunteered to help Emma clear the table that the latter had
a private chance to talk with her.

"Your hired man's back," the older woman whispered with a smile.

Jolted from her despondency, Holly felt as if she'd
received a mild electrical shock. *Jake,* she thought,
yearning toward him with all her strength, though her
trust was tarnished by doubt over what she'd convinced
herself was his defection.

"What makes you think so?" she asked, not quite believing it. "He wasn't there when we left."

Emma gave her arm a reassuring pat. "He phoned just as you and Nels were coming up the driveway," she answered. "He sounded awfully anxious to see you."

If he's so anxious, Holly thought, why did he stay away so long? It crossed her mind that he might have come back for the remaining wages she owed him. If that's his only reason, she speculated, he won't stick around long.

When she told Lisa about Jake's return as they drove home, the girl was ecstatic. "Wow...cool!" she exclaimed. "I told you he'd come back, Holly. He *likes* living with us at Honeycomb."

A bundle of conflicting emotions as they turned off the county highway and headed up the driveway toward their house, Holly didn't answer. She wasn't sure she wanted to see Jake. How could she bear to look him in the eye—and imagine him with another woman?

He'd left his truck parked directly outside the front door instead of in its usual place behind the barn. Though the lapse argued for the eagerness Emma had attributed to him, Holly refused to see it that way. No doubt he's poised for a quick departure, she thought, wounding herself with the prospect.

The moment she brought the pickup to a stop, Lisa bounded out of the cab and ran like a champion sprinter for the house. Holly followed at a more decorous pace. Pausing to stamp the snow off her boots on the porch before entering her kitchen-and-living area, she was just in time to see her stepdaughter hugging Jake.

Freshly shaved, clad in faded jeans and a reindeer-patterned sweater she didn't remember seeing on him, he was all man and just as beautiful as she remembered. God, but she wanted him. The sad truth was that, whatever he'd done during his two weeks away from her, she loved him every bit as much.

She didn't plan to indulge her craving. Or to share her feelings with him.

The top of Lisa's head, with its exuberant mass of carroty curls escaping from a knitted cap, came to the midway point on Jake's chest. Her arms were twined about his waist the way she'd once wrapped them about Clint's. "I'm soooo glad you're back, Jake," she confessed, her feet all but dancing a jig of welcome as she continued to embrace him.

"Me, too, pumpkin."

The laugh lines beside Jake's mouth flashed deeper as he swept off the cap to ruffle Lisa's hair, then vanished as he met Holly's gaze. She was a sight for sore eyes, if not a sore heart. *What's your relationship with Nels Tornquist?* he wanted to ask. *Is he the competition I have to face?*

Thanks to the way he'd gone off and left her without a decent explanation, he didn't have the right. "I'm back," he announced, stating the obvious. "Do I still have a job?"

A wave of relief broke over Holly, mixed with anger that he should continue to define their relationship that way. She shrugged. "I still need help," she answered with a take-it-or-leave-it expression, turning away to hang up her parka in the coat closet.

Chapter Six

At Lars and Emma's insistence, Holly, Lisa and Jake would have Thanksgiving dinner with them. Plagued by unresolved suspicions about what her dark-haired ranch hand had been doing during his two-week absence from Honeycomb, Holly was ambivalent about including him. Yet she didn't feel as if she had much choice. She could scarcely leave him at home on a day that epitomized good cheer and feasting to dine alone, on cold cuts. For one thing, Lisa wouldn't hear of it. And, for another, she cared about him too much.

Never one to lack information about a rival or the opposing side in a lawsuit, Jake knew Nels would be present to vie for Holly's attention. Though he hadn't met the blond geologist, a man he'd probably like under any other circumstances, he'd heard about him from Lisa.

He knew Nels would be leaving for Siberia in a week

or so. Since the assignment wasn't permanent, the pending absence didn't set his mind at rest. As he sat beside the fire in Holly's cozy living room his first week back, helping Lisa with her math homework, he couldn't seem to stop imagining what might happen when Nels returned. Or keep from paying close attention to Holly's side of her phone conversation with him.

Finally, on a day of leaden skies and falling temperatures, he had his chance to evaluate Nels in person. Dressed in their best casual clothing, which for him was his reindeer sweater and freshly laundered jeans, they were seated across from each other at the Tornquists' dining room table.

Between them lay a groaning board of sumptuous-looking food, including a perfectly basted turkey and roast venison with wild rice, plus all the trimmings, including homemade stuffing, scalloped corn, candied sweet potatoes and an array of Lars's favorite Swedish delicacies. On a nearby sideboard reposed the expertly made mince and pumpkin pies Holly had baked earlier that day while Jake had completed their daily chores, along with one of Emma's famous lingonberry tortes.

As grace was said and the meal got under way, Jake couldn't help noticing that most of the Tornquist son's attention was focused on the slim, blond rancher he wanted for his own. Confining her answers to nods and monosyllables, she smiled noncommittally at Nels in the candlelight.

She seemed to have more to say to Emma, Lars, Lisa and Jane—even the Tornquists' hired men, Hank Jeffries and Charlie Gutierrez—than she did to Jake. In truth, she barely glanced in his direction, though once or twice, when he least expected it, he caught her studying him.

When at last everyone was stuffed to the gills and conversation had begun to lag, Hank and Charlie excused themselves and went outside to tend the stock. Holly, Nels and Lars volunteered to clear the table and do up the dishes in order to give Emma a well-deserved rest. At a prodding glance from Holly, Lisa and Jane quickly offered to help.

"You can count on me, too," Jake said, starting to stack a pile of sticky dessert plates.

Emma forestalled him with a gentle touch. "Come...talk to me," she requested, leading him toward the living room and a pair of wingback chairs that stood on either side of the Tornquists' massive stone fireplace. "If you don't, there won't be an inch of elbow room left in the kitchen. And I'll be bored to death."

As he parried Emma's seemingly offhand questions about his life prior to his arrival at Honeycomb, Jake strained to catch snatches of the lively conversation that was going on in the kitchen. He groaned silently when, once the dishes were finished, Holly and Nels emerged in search of their coats and boots.

"We're going to take an after-dinner walk," Nels explained.

Getting to his feet with every intention of accompanying them, Jake was promptly waylaid by Jane and Lisa, who had talked Lars into playing a card game called Push, and wanted a fourth at the table. With Lisa smiling up at him expectantly, he couldn't say no.

"Sounds like fun," he declared, deciding to make the best of the situation.

Assailed by a stiff north wind and snow as fine as soap powder, Holly and Nels didn't go far. At his suggestion, they paused on the lee side of the Tornquists' massive barn beneath some evergreens.

"I wonder if it's this cold in Siberia," Nels said facetiously.

"Colder, I would think," Holly answered in all seriousness, bracing herself for some kind of declaration.

He didn't keep her waiting long. "As you know, I'm leaving tomorrow," he said. "I'll be gone for at least six months...maybe eight. That's quite a while and I was wondering if you'd write to me. As you've probably guessed, I'd like the chance to know you better when I return."

He was so nice, so uncomplicated. Unlike Jake, an open book. Before gazing into the latter's devastating blue eyes and hiring him to help out on her ranch, she'd probably have encouraged Nels. Now she couldn't. The change in outlook spoke volumes about her feelings.

He was waiting for an answer.

"Nels," she said gently, holding up a hand to stop him when it looked as if he'd interrupt, "I like you a lot. But I'm afraid exchanging letters would be pointless. I'm in love with someone else...a man I'll probably never marry."

Absorbing the rejection, Nels regarded her quietly for a moment. "It's Jake McKenzie, isn't it?" he said. "I saw the way he was looking at you during dinner. You do a better job of camouflaging your feelings than he does."

An experienced judge of human nature thanks to his years as a trial lawyer and business negotiator, Jake assessed the look on Nels's face when they returned to the house and breathed a sigh of relief. There was still hope for him.

His observation was to sustain him during his continued exile from Holly's confidence as Christmas approached. Meanwhile, it had begun to snow in earnest. In addition to her usual chores, Holly was up to her neck in Christmas preparations. From the moment she'd become Lisa's stepmother, she'd always tried to make the holidays special for the girl. This year, in addition to ordering her a Sony Walkman she could ill afford and baking eight varieties of cookies, she was secretly making Lisa a complete wardrobe for her cherished Barbie doll.

Each evening, when his day's work was done, Jake pitched in, warming their housebound evenings with humorous tall tales as he whittled an amusing collection of wooden ornaments. Enchanted with his stories and manual dexterity, Lisa hung on his every word and demonstration of wood-carving skill.

As Holly gazed at the proximity of their bright and dark heads from her place at the sewing machine, where she was hemming a set of napkins for Emma, she had to admit they'd grown thick as thieves. *He's the dad she's so sorely missed and needed,* she acknowledged. *I just hope that, when he decides to disappear again, it won't be too hard on her. She's already had to grieve the loss of one father.*

Compounded of longing and unrequited glances, her own relationship with Jake remained in a holding pattern. Though the estrangement caused by his unexplained absence had eased a bit, nothing of substance had been resolved between them. *If he doesn't tell me where he went and with whom, I'll always wonder,* Holly thought. *I'll never be able to place my trust in him.*

Even if they could get past the questions raised by his disappearance, she could think of other barriers to a serious relationship with Jake. First and foremost was her belief that principle couldn't be tailored to suit one's

whims and desires. You either believed in something or
you didn't. That being the case, she couldn't make unmarried love with him, whether or not Lisa was likely
to be scandalized.

Try though she would to fathom them, Jake's feelings
remained a mystery to her. He seemed to be biding his
time, waiting patiently for her to forgive his absence,
change her mind about him. She had the odd but per-
sistent feeling he was leaving something unsaid. *I wish
he'd spit it out, whatever it is, even if it confirms my
worst fears about him,* she thought one chilly evening
as their eyes met over the large white pine they'd cut
down and dragged into the house to serve as their
Christmas tree.

Polite, even friendly, but impassable as a wall without a door, the emotional standoff between them persisted through a tree-decorating session in which the
three of them wrestled the majestic pine into its stand
and hung its aromatic branches with strings of popcorn
and cranberries, Jake's carved whimsies and Holly's
fanciful if somewhat more traditional collection of ornaments.

Acquiring a life of its own, their arm's-length posture
survived mornings of bitter cold as they hauled fodder
to the stock, cocoonlike evenings of hot chocolate and
Christmas carols on the radio.

Then, on a Saturday morning two weeks before
Christmas, a fierce winter storm began to move across
northern New Mexico and southern Colorado. Out until
4:00 p.m. distributing emergency feed to the cattle,
many of which had huddled in a small box canyon for
protection from the wind, Holly and Jake returned to
the barn to discover that, though the other horses were
fine, Lisa's beloved filly, Comet, wasn't herself. Usually

bright and inquisitive, her eyes were dull and apathetic looking. She suffered from a runny nose. The food they'd placed in her trough that morning hadn't been touched.

His dark brows drawing together, Jake stroked the filly's nose and patted her neck. Her hide seemed uncommonly warm to the touch. "I think she's coming down with something," he speculated. "Maybe we ought to take her temperature."

By now, Holly was frowning, too. Ducking into the unoccupied stall she'd converted to a tack-and-supply room, she got out an equine thermometer and a jar of petroleum jelly. "Steady her, will you?" she asked, approaching Comet's hindquarters.

The thermometer measured Comet's temperature at 102.5 degrees. Normal range for a horse was between 99 and 101 degrees. She definitely had a fever.

"Put some rubbing alcohol and water in a bucket—fifty-fifty—and give her a rubdown, will you?" Holly requested. "I'm going into the house to call the vet."

As she trudged toward her front door through blowing snow, Holly saw to her relief that a four-wheel-drive vehicle had left rapidly blurring tire tracks in the driveway. Lars had managed to bring Lisa home from her Friday-night sleepover with Jane. She wouldn't be marooned at the Tornquists' if the storm turned out to be as bad as weather forecasters were predicting.

Accustomed to spending every spare moment on Christmas crafts as the holiday approached, Lisa had flopped listlessly on the sofa. A new book by one of her favorite authors lay by her side, unopened. The hooded parka and mittens she'd worn to school the day before had been unceremoniously dumped in a nearby chair.

About to lecture her about the need to put her things away, Holly thought better of it. Instinct told her something wasn't right. "Hi, pumpkin...did you have a good time?" she asked instead, dropping a kiss on the girl's forehead.

Lisa shrugged. "Uh-huh," she said, sounding less than enthusiastic. "We made chocolate-chip cookies with Christmas sparkles."

And ate a few too many, Holly surmised, in addition to giggling and telling secrets half the night. "That sounds like fun," she said. "Sure you're feeling all right?"

"I'm okay."

Heading for the phone, Holly dialed the vet's number. To her chagrin, she got his message machine. "Ted, this is Holly Yarborough," she said after the beep. "It's roughly 4:30 p.m. Comet's running a fever. I know the weather's bad and you're probably busy, but could you possibly stop by on your way home? Or call? I'll be waiting to hear from you."

Lisa was at her elbow as she put down the receiver. "What's wrong with Comet?" she said urgently.

Holly placed a reassuring arm about the girl's shoulders. A strong believer in leveling with children when they asked for information, she conveyed the filly's temperature to her stepdaughter. "That's not terribly high," she explained. "But it isn't normal, either. I've got Jake sponging her down with cool water and alcohol."

Lisa's forehead was puckered with worry. "Can't we give her some of the antibiotics Dr. Ted gave you to put in the refrigerator?"

"Not without talking to him first."

"What if we can't reach him?"

"Then we'll decide."

The girl's eyes flashed with something of their customary purpose. "I want to help take care of her," she said, tugging on her boots.

Pocketing the portable phone, Holly accompanied Lisa back to the barn, where Jake was continuing to sponge the filly. After the relative heat of the house, the barn felt icy cold. While Lisa fussed over her beloved pet, stroking her neck and whispering in her ear, Holly swept an area free of straw and plugged in a space heater. With adequate precautions and someone around to keep an eye on it, sparks shouldn't be a problem, she thought.

Some twenty minutes later, the portable phone in her pocket shrilled. It was the vet, Dr. Ted Stephenson. "I got your message," he said in a harried voice. "Sorry, but it looks like I'm not going to make it over to your place this evening. I'm at the Masters ranch, near Antelope Crossing, about to conduct an emergency operation on Archie Masters's prize bull. The roads at this end of the county are close to impassable. What seems to be the trouble?"

Without wasting words, Holly described the filly's condition. "Sounds like equine flu," Ted Stephenson said. "I doubt if it's serious. Do you still have the penicillin I gave you? What about the tetracycline capsules?"

"Yes to both."

"Go ahead and give her fifteen cc's of the former. One of the capsules, too. It'll give her a boost."

Struggling back to the house through ever-deeper drifts and a steadily falling curtain of white, Holly removed a two-hundred-and-fifty milliliter bottle of penicillin from her refrigerator. The disposable syringes and tetracycline capsules Ted Stephenson had given her were on the top shelf of her spice and condiment cupboard. Pausing to take a jar of peanut butter from one of the other shelves, she filled a syringe with penicillin and returned the bottle to the refrigerator. A moment later, with her head bowed in the wind, she returned to Comet's stall.

Lisa winced slightly as Holly injected the penicillin directly into Comet's neck muscle. "Doesn't that hurt?" she asked.

Jake ruffled her hair. "No more than a pinch," he soothed.

His steadiness and affectionate way of dealing with Lisa will be sorely missed when he moves on to greener pastures, Holly thought. And that's not all. A hole will be torn in my heart big enough to accommodate a Mack truck.

Pushing down her personal feelings, she fished the tetracycline tablet from her pocket and removed the peanut butter jar's twist-off cap. "Here, Lisa…you can feed her the capsule," she said, intent on giving her stepdaughter something positive to do. "Just roll it into a nice, thick gob of peanut butter and offer it to her the way you would a carrot or piece of apple."

Accustomed to receiving treats from Lisa's hands, the filly took the tetracycline and peanut butter despite her lack of appetite. "Good job," Jake praised the girl. "When you become a vet someday, we won't have to call Dr. Stephenson. We'll have our own Dr. Yarborough right here on the premises."

The remark, which alluded to Lisa's dream of studying veterinary medicine, gave Holly fresh food for thought as Jake went back to sponging the filly's coat. Was it possible he planned to be around when Lisa was grown? Don't kid yourself, the skeptic in her scoffed. He was just trying to make her feel better.

Around 7:30 p.m., Holly took Comet's temperature again. It had dropped six-tenths of a degree. Though it was too soon to say so with any certainty, she appeared to be on the mend. Meanwhile, Lisa was drooping.

"Sure you're okay, baby doll?" Holly asked, smoothing the girl's unruly hair. "It's getting late. Do you want something to eat?"

Encouraged though she clearly was by the filly's progress, Lisa shook her head. "I'm not very hungry," she confessed. "I have a stomachache."

A worried glance passed between Jake and Holly. "Let me feel your head," Holly instructed.

Lightly pressed to Lisa's forehead, Holly's sensitive inner wrist confirmed her fears. Her stepdaughter had a fever. If she wasn't mistaken, it was in excess of one hundred degrees.

"Not you, too!" she said in alarm, zipping Lisa's parka up to her chin and tightening its drawstring hood about her face. "We've got to get you into bed at once. And call the doctor."

Outside the storm had gotten worse. Howling out of the north, the wind had buried the lane that connected the house with the county highway beneath an arctic terrain of snowdrifts. When they peered outside, they could barely make out any identifying landmarks.

Jake unplugged the heater. "I'll carry her," he volunteered, wrapping Lisa in a saddle blanket and scooping her up. "Grab hold of my jacket, Holly. I don't want us to get separated."

When she'd gone to fetch the antibiotics for Comet, Holly had left the kitchen lights on. Though their yellow glow wavered from moment to moment, occasionally disappearing altogether for a few seconds, it served as a beacon through the blinding curtain of snowflakes. In places, the drifts were up to their knees, making progress difficult. Clutching Lisa to his chest and sheltering her face from the wind, Jake slogged forward. Holly was right behind him, holding tight to his parka hem.

No previous sense of gratitude could compare with the one she felt when they reached her front porch. Wresting the door open against a particularly powerful gust, she stood back for Jake and Lisa to pass. The girl was whimpering as, like some kind of snow-encrusted guardian angel, he carried her to her room.

"Is it your stomach, sweetheart?" Holly asked, close behind him as he lowered her gently onto her bed.

Lisa nodded.

"Where does it hurt?"

Grimacing, the girl indicated her right side. Thoughts of appendicitis flickered through Holly's head. She dismissed them as borrowing trouble. Lisa's ailment was probably flu. It was making the rounds at her school.

"I'll undress her," she said to Jake, throwing off her jacket and unzipping Lisa's. "Get me some aspirin and a glass of water from the bathroom, will you? We're also going to need a bowl of ice water and a washcloth."

Tears of self-pity slipped down Lisa's cheeks as she swallowed the aspirin and Holly dressed her in a flannel nightgown. With several pillows plumped beneath her head and the covers pulled up to her chin, she didn't protest when Holly wrung the washcloth out in the ice water and bathed her forehead. "That feels good, Mommy," she whispered.

To Holly, Lisa's use of the familial term indicated just how sick she was. "That's good, pumpkin," she answered. "We'll have that nasty fever down in a little while. Take over for me, will you, Jake? I need to get in touch with the doctor."

She wasn't really surprised—just dismayed—when she discovered the phone was dead. Hopefully the company linemen would have it operating in the morning. In the meantime, they were on their own. Returning to Lisa's bedside, she signaled Jake without words that her effort had been unsuccessful.

Several nervous hours ensued, as Holly sponged her stepdaughter's overheated skin and Jake battled his way back and forth to the barn to check on the filly's progress. By 10:30 p.m., Comet was almost back to normal. In contrast, Lisa was verging on delirium. The right side of her stomach was swollen and rigid, arguing for Holly's discarded diagnosis.

"We have to do something, Jake," she said desperately, sharing her fears as she joined him for a moment out of Lisa's earshot. "But what? We can't call the doctor. And the roads are drifting over. Weather Service bulletins on the radio are urging people to stay indoors. If we try to drive her to the hospital in Larisson, we'll end up in a ditch…freeze to death beside the road someplace."

They could pack her in snow and hope her swollen appendix would shrink a little, Jake supposed. It was a radical solution, and maybe it wouldn't be needed. Holly's mention of the radio broadcast had jogged something in Jake's memory. "Wasn't that a shortwave set I saw in the attic when I brought down the storm windows?" he asked.

Holly wanted to kick herself. "Of *course!*" she acknowledged. "How could I have forgotten it? Clint bought it for exactly this sort of emergency. Unfortunately, I don't know how to operate it."

Jake did. Having learned to use a similar piece of equipment in Vietnam, he managed to reach a friendly ham operator who patched them through to the local emergency room. From what they told him about Lisa's condition, a doctor there agreed. Lisa probably had appendicitis.

"Our emergency chopper is out on another case. I'll dispatch it to you as soon as possible," he said. "Meanwhile, keep up what you're doing. You have good instincts."

With Jake's help and constant sponging, Holly was able to get Lisa's fever to recede somewhat. But she was still very hot. Abruptly, a message crackled on the shortwave set. "Be ready to evacuate your daughter in fifteen minutes."

Zipping Lisa's parka over her nightgown, they wrapped her in a blanket. As the rescue team's arrival time approached, Jake carried her to the door while Holly put on her own coat and mittens. *Dear God…let my little girl be okay,* Holly prayed as they waited for the rescue team. *And thank you for Jake. Without him, we might not have made it.*

Holly, her stepdaughter and the dark-haired ranch hand she loved fused in a three-way hug as the chopper came roaring out of the blizzard to land near their doorstep. Seconds later, the pilot and a medic were jumping out with a stretcher. "We won't need this," the latter said, handing the blanket they'd wrapped around Lisa back to Jake as he and his partner strapped the girl in place. "We have plenty of our own."

"Mommy?" Lisa asked, wide-eyed. "You're coming with me, aren't you? Please say yes.…"

"Of course I am," Holly answered, daring the rescue team to contradict her.

The pilot glanced in her direction. "You're Mrs. Yarborough, the mother, right?" he said distractedly. "You can ride along." He nodded at Jake. "Sorry, we don't have room for him."

So quickly that it made her head spin, Holly was strapped into the emergency craft beside Lisa. She grasped the girl's hand and held it tightly, willing her appendix not to burst. Coming to life and whirling ever faster in the maelstrom of white, the helicopter's overhead blades began to emit their characteristic *chop-chop*. The engine noise was deafening as they lifted off the ground, rising straight up, like an elevator.

On the ground below, Lisa's blanket covering his head and shoulders to protect him from the driving snow, Jake was waving at them. "Don't worry," he shouted. "Lisa's going to be okay. I'll join you in town as soon as the roads are passable."

Wind snatched the words from his mouth. With all the din and the rapidly expanding distance, Holly guessed, she couldn't have caught them, anyway. Yet in her heart, she sensed their drift. Without him, this evening could have been far worse than it was, she thought again, leaning over to kiss Lisa's forehead.

Rushed to the surgical suite at Larisson Hospital for an emergency appendectomy, Lisa was transferred following her operation to a postanesthesia room. She was still groggy when Holly was allowed briefly to visit her. But her eyes were open.

"I'm going to be okay...aren't I, Mommy?" the girl asked.

This time it was Holly who had tears in her eyes. She

didn't let them spill. "Absolutely good as new, pumpkin," she promised.

"You're going to stay right here?"

"The nurses can't watch over you properly if I'm in the way. If you need me, I'll be right down the hall, in the family waiting area."

Crashing on the Leatherette couch in the impersonally furnished lounge, Holly sorely missed Jake's presence. Now that Lisa was going to be all right, she'd given herself permission to shake a little. She wanted to rest her head on his shoulder—draw comfort from his strong, enveloping presence.

After checking on Lisa a second time, Holly returned to the waiting room couch. This time, she fell into an exhausted sleep. She didn't stir when a passing orderly returned and threw a spare blanket over her.

When she opened her eyes around 6:00 a.m., the snow seemed to have stopped. To her astonishment, Jake was there, a stubble of shadow beard darkening his chin, slouched in one of the armchairs with his back to the window. He was still wearing his outdoor parka, though he'd unzipped it. His long legs in their faded jeans were stretched out before him.

"So you're awake," he observed, getting to his feet.

Stiff from the cramped space where she'd been sleeping, Holly struggled to a sitting position. Though she was overjoyed to see him, her first thought was for her stepdaughter.

"Lisa?" she asked, rising also.

Jake gave her a tired smile. "Awake. And feeling much better. She's been assigned to a regular patient room. You can visit her if you want."

Relief coursed through Holly in a flood. "Thank God!" she exclaimed.

Courtesy of insights gained during the harrowing night they'd shared, the rift between them seemed the height of foolishness. Without compromising her responsibility to Lisa, she decided, she could lean on him for as long as he chose to stay around. She loved him, after all. If she didn't, she'd be sorry later. Propelled by instinct, she sought the sanctuary of his embrace, threading her arms around him beneath his worn, down-filled jacket. With a feeling of coming home, she blended into his body warmth.

Jake was totally undone. "Ah, Holly..." he whispered. "You can't possibly know how much I've longed to hold you this way."

Seconds later, their lips were meeting hungrily, greedily, easing their mutual deprivation. How had they managed to stay apart so long, when they needed each other so much?

When Holly learned the truth about his reasons for showing up on her doorstep and asking her for a job, Jake knew she'd be furious with him. He might find himself out in the cold again. Yet his defenses were down, his sense of practicality at a low ebb, thanks to the long, difficult night they'd just endured. He could think only of his need for her.

"Marry me," he begged, speaking words he'd never spoken to anyone. "Holly, darling...I love you so much."

Chapter Seven

He was her hired hand. And the man she loved. She knew everything about him. And nothing. Reason suggested she'd be crazy to marry him—a man with no money of his own and seemingly no ambition except, possibly, to gain a stake in the ranch Clint had put in her name with the express purpose that, someday, she'd bequeath it to Lisa.

The thought wasn't worthy of him and, instinctively, Holly knew it. Yet she had to protect her stepdaughter's interests. In addition, she still didn't know where Jake had gone when he'd been absent from Honeycomb those two weeks. *Had* there been another woman in his life during the time she'd known him? Did he have an ex-wife and children someplace?

She couldn't bring herself to ask. Stalling, she took refuge in a question. "Are you...serious about this?" she asked.

It was Jake's moment of truth. Though he'd never entertained the idea before, marriage with Holly was something he'd come to want with all his heart. With the thought, the burden of his deception grew heavier. If he told Holly who he really was and what he was doing in her life, she'd refuse to marry him. She'd almost certainly kick him off her property. Yet she deserved to know the truth.

As tired as he was, and more bereft of his acute facility for predicting what others would do than at any time he could remember, he managed to convince himself that, once they were engaged—no, wed and happy together—her spasm of anger on learning the truth would quickly play itself out.

We're perfect for each other, he thought. Not to have a life together would be criminal. I want to make her heart sing again, as she has mine.

"I've never been more serious about anything in my life, darlin'," he said, his untold secret a lump in his throat as he traced the shape of her mouth with one gentle fingertip.

Aching at the tempered sweetness of the gesture and bursting with love at his declaration, Holly had sufficient unanswered questions to be scared to death. Putting them on hold, she withdrew a little. "Mind if we talk about this a little later?" she asked. "Right now, I want to check on Lisa."

Eager as he was for an answer, Jake wasn't offended. "Okay by me," he said. "Mind if I tag along?"

Holly slipped her hands into his larger ones. "Of course not," she answered. "After last night, Lisa and I owe you a great deal. I know how much you care about us."

The girl's surgeon had just finished examining her

when they entered her room. "Ah, Mrs. Yarborough," he said. "I'm glad you're here. This young lady of yours is doing just fine. If there aren't any complications, she'll be free to go home day after tomorrow." He paused, glancing at Jake. "I take it you're *Mr.* Yarborough," he said.

Lisa giggled at the misnomer, though it caused her to clutch her side. For her part, Holly was blushing. She was grateful for Jake's nonchalance as he shrugged off the question. In her opinion, most men wouldn't have.

"I'm Jake McKenzie," he told the surgeon in a friendly tone, declining to explain his relationship to them.

As expected, Lisa got a little teary when it was time for them to go. Still, raised on a ranch, she knew from experience that they had to return home and check on the animals.

"You'll call and let me know how Comet's doing, won't you, Mommy?" she asked.

Holly bent to give the girl a hug. "Of course I will," she promised. "By now, she's probably yearning for some of the carrots and apples you always give her. Since you can't take care of that today, Jake and I will do it for you."

Though Jake's proposal and Holly's delay in giving him an answer were on both their minds as they got into his truck and started for home, neither of them brought up the subject. He'd decided to give her as much time as she needed, now that he'd spoken his piece. And, sensing that, she'd decided to take it. As a result, their scraps of conversation were confined to the storm and the massive pileup of snow on both sides of the highway.

Their route took them past the Tornquist ranch, where

sixty-five-year-old Lars was attempting to plow his driveway. As a by-product of the effort to make way for traffic, the county snowplow had thrown up an eight-foot-high barrier of white at his gate. He was obviously having a difficult time removing it.

Meanwhile, Jake's truck had Holly's snow blade attached to the front. He'd had to borrow it in order to make it out of her driveway once the highways were clear.

"Mind if I stop and help?" he asked. "I can run you up to the house for coffee with Emma while you wait."

It was the sort of neighborly thing folks did for one another in the valley, and sweet of Jake to offer. Holly had worried a bit about Lars overdoing it of late. Besides, she was only too glad of the chance to talk with Emma, who was a kind of surrogate mother to her.

"That's a great idea," she said.

Clearly guessing Jake's purpose when he dropped Holly off at her door and, making a U-turn, returned to the spot where Lars was working, Emma threw open her front door before Holly had a chance to knock.

"How nice of Jake to stop and help," she said, welcoming Holly into her house. "Snow removal is such hard work and Lars isn't getting any younger. Come…let's talk in the kitchen. I've got the coffee on."

They settled at Emma's maple dinette, which fitted cozily into the embrace of a large bay window. As promised, the coffee was steaming hot as Holly's neighbor poured it into blue willow china cups. So were the double-blueberry muffins that had just emerged from the oven.

As they sipped Emma's steaming brew, Jane wandered in from the family room. "Where's Lisa?" she asked. "Why didn't you bring her, Mrs. Yarborough?"

The question prompted a complete rendition of the previous night's events, ending with Holly and Jake's visit to Lisa's hospital room a short time earlier. Holly left out just one newsworthy detail—Jake's marriage proposal.

In response, Emma was shaking her head. Jane was wide-eyed to learn about her best friend's illness. "How awful that must have been for Lisa!" the girl exclaimed when Holly fell silent. "Would it be all right if I called her, Gram? I could ask the nurse to give her a message if she's sleeping or something."

"The phones are working again?" Holly interjected.

Emma nodded. "They came back on around 8:00 a.m. Okay with you if Jane phones the hospital?"

Holly gave her permission. A minute or so later, the distant murmur of Jane's voice reached them as she spoke into the telephone receiver in her bedroom down the hall. Apparently, Lisa was awake and able to take calls, because Jane settled in for a lengthy chat.

"So," Emma remarked, turning her attention back to Holly, "you had quite an adventure during the storm. After hearing about what happened, I'm going to insist we get a shortwave radio."

Holly nodded her approval. "I think that would be a good idea." She paused. "Emma…I was, umm, wondering about something."

Her curiosity clearly aroused, the older woman regarded Holly expectantly.

On the verge of asking for Emma's opinion of Jake, Holly took a different tack. "What did the girls eat Friday night? Lisa said she and Jane made chocolate-chip cookies. How many did they eat?"

Emma rolled her eyes. "Quite a few more than I would have allowed them to, had I known about it.

Once the cookies were out of the oven, I went to bed. Lars was up, doing book work, but he didn't pay much attention to them. Neither of us had a clue until Saturday morning, when I saw how few cookies were left.'' She smiled. "Kids Jane's age can be quite a handful for grandparents!"

"Do you think their gorging could have caused Lisa's appendicitis?"

Emma shrugged. "I doubt it, though I suppose an overload of sweets could have made it worse." Hesitating, she regarded Holly silently for a moment. "Why do I have the feeling you want to tell me something important?" she asked.

Feeling as if her friend and neighbor was adept at reading her mind, Holly decided to level with her. "Jake has asked me to marry him," she said, keeping her voice down so Jane wouldn't overhear.

Emma's round, weather-beaten face creased in a smile. "How wonderful! I'm so happy for you," she said, reaching across the table to squeeze Holly's hand. "Naturally, I can't help wishing it could have been Nels. But I never really expected that. It's easy to see you and Jake love each other."

Had they been that obvious? Holly blushed. "I haven't given him an answer yet," she admitted. "I have some doubts. To begin with, I know next to nothing about his past. Frankly, it worries me that someone as smart and capable as he seems to be has contented himself with the life of a wandering ranch hand. If ranching is what he loves, why hasn't he found a way to buy a place of his own? Doesn't he have any ambition? I hate myself for thinking such thoughts. But it *has* occurred to me that he might see me and Lisa as a means to advance himself."

The worst was out and Emma didn't seem shocked. Instead, she appeared thoughtful. "You know him better than I do, dear," she said at last, throwing the question back into Holly's lap. "But it seems to me that a man's behavior is the best road map of what's in his heart. Jake's been good...*to* you and *for* you. He clearly dotes on Lisa. And he seems like a solid person. Anyone can have reversals in their life, and maybe he did. If you have questions, why don't you put them to him?"

Holly was afraid that if she aired her reservations to Jake, it would be all over with them. Despite the paucity of his assets, she suspected, he was a proud man. Wounded over her failure to trust him, he might walk out of her life for good. And that would kill her. She didn't know what to do.

A short time later, Jake and Lars came in to stoke up on coffee. The four of them talked awhile—mostly about the storm, the possibility that they might need to airlift feed if additional snow fell before a thaw and the need for the Tornquists to get a shortwave radio. Though Emma's eyes held a new benevolence as she gazed at Holly and her dark-haired cowboy, she didn't betray by word or deed that she knew about Jake's proposal.

At last, Jake got to his feet. "We'd better go home...check on the animals and have breakfast," he suggested.

Holly quickly agreed.

The phone was ringing as they stomped the snow off their boots on her front porch and entered the house. Plaintive as a calf that had been separated from its mother, Lisa's voice came over the line when Holly picked it up.

"Mommy?" her stepdaughter said. "You sound so

far away. I'm feeling awfully lonesome. And it doesn't hurt anywhere…at least, not much. Do you think I could come home early?''

"I'm not sure, baby doll," Holly replied. "We don't want to do anything that would impede your recovery. I suppose I could phone your doctor this afternoon and explore the idea.''

"*Would* you?" The girl's words positively jumped with enthusiasm. "It's so boring up here! And the food isn't very good. How is Comet doing?''

Forced to report Jake had been helping Lars plow his driveway and they hadn't been out to the barn yet, Holly signaled him it was likely to be a lengthy mother-daughter conversation.

She hadn't given him the semblance of an answer yet. But Jake was hopeful. Giving her an indulgent grin, he volunteered to see to the animals by himself.

Some twenty minutes later, after promising Lisa for the second time that she'd call the surgeon's office, Holly managed to end the call. She and Jake desperately needed something to eat. With the exception of several blueberry muffins at Emma's, neither of them had eaten since Saturday noon, when they'd taken a break from distributing feed to wolf down some hot coffee and a couple of ham sandwiches.

Taking a quick shower and putting on fresh jeans and a clean sweater, she returned to the kitchen, where she whipped up an omelet and the chicken-fried steak she'd planned to serve the night before. As she dished them up on a pair of heated plates and placed them on a serving tray covered with a blue-and-white striped dish towel, she paused to reflect that things had changed dramatically between her and Jake. Like it or not, his proposal and confession of love for her had caused her to lower her guard.

The way he'd helped and protected them the night before also had a lot to do with it. Love is more action than declaration, she thought. That being the case, what can I do for him?

The answer came from the deepest, most instinctive part of herself. *You could learn to trust him.*

Tugging on her boots and zipping up her parka, she carried the meal she'd repaired out to the barn. "Breakfast...with a little of last night's unmade supper thrown in," she announced with a smile that didn't quite hide the excitement and uncertainty she felt.

Jake emerged from Comet's stall. His beardroughened face in shadow, he looked dead serious. For most of the night after she and Lisa had left in the chopper, and again during their drive back to Honeycomb that morning, he'd agonized over the secret he hadn't shared with her.

Characteristically, he was determined to get what he wanted, come hell or high water—a home with her and her little girl. Gently taking the tray from her hands, he set it aside on a bale of hay and took Holly in his arms.

"Say you'll marry me," he demanded, crushing her to him in a fierce embrace. "Life without you wouldn't be worth a damn now that I know what we could have together."

Briefly his words stirred her fears that he might be trying to take advantage of them even as they deeply warmed her heart. Which way of looking at things would win out? For Holly's inner woman, there wasn't any contest.

"Though I wasn't willing to admit it earlier, I love you, too," she confided. "If you're serious about making a life with us, I'd be proud and happy to marry you.''

To her, he was just a down-at-the-heels cowboy. Unlike most of the women he'd previously known, she'd acknowledged her love for him without knowing anything about his Juris Doctorate or considering his tax bracket. Meanwhile, with her valiant heart and high standards, her sweet, giving nature, she was the biggest prize a man could want.

Ecstatic, humbled, he pushed down the guilt he felt over deceiving her about his connections to Dutch and crushed her mouth with his. Beneath her jacket and the sweater she'd pulled on without bothering to fasten on a bra, his big, calloused hands were caressing and claiming her. Erect and ready to prove his love, his manhood was pressing against her lower stomach.

Holly's response was like an avalanche. From deep within, a tide of longing welled up, crying out to be satisfied. *What does it matter if we're not married yet?* she rationalized. *We soon* will *be. I don't want to wait to welcome him inside me, become his lover in every sense.*

This time, it was Jake who tugged them back from the brink. She was ready to give him everything. And he couldn't let her do it.

''What's wrong?'' she asked, the dark velvet of her pupils swallowing up the gray of her irises.

The answer to her question was there in his face. ''Nothing, my dearest darlin','' he whispered, encircling her tightly as he kissed the tip of her nose. ''I just think we ought to defer making love out of respect for your feelings. Of course, that means you'll have to marry me pretty damn quick.''

It was what she wanted, too. ''What would you say

to Christmas Eve?'' she suggested, feeling incredibly sheltered and cherished as she smiled up at him. ''That's less than two weeks from today.''

''I can't think of anything I'd rather do than marry you at Christmas,'' Jake said.

More kisses followed, hot but careful not to nudge past the boundaries they'd set. At last, stomach hunger got the better of them. Laughing together over their tendency to forget practical matters when they were in each other's arms, they carried the breakfast tray back into the house. Thanks to their neglect, the omelet was a congealed mess. However, the steak was salvageable. Reheated, sliced thin and doused with barbecue sauce from the refrigerator, it made excellent sandwiches.

When she phoned Lisa's surgeon that afternoon, Holly learned that he'd stopped by to see the girl again. ''She's mending nicely,'' he related. ''But then children usually bounce back from these things. Of course, you know she's angling to come home early. This afternoon's still out of the question, but tomorrow's a possibility, provided you have the time and inclination to wait on her hand and foot for a couple of days.''

With Jake available to tend the stock, Holly felt free to accept. She phoned Lisa with the news, apprising Jake of her decision at the dinner table. ''Naturally, that means less privacy for us,'' she admitted. ''But with Lisa so lonesome and feeling better…''

Savoring a mouthful of Holly's spicy Taos chili, Jake patted her hand. ''You did the right thing,'' he said, the laugh lines deepening beside his mouth. ''The way you light my fire, we *need* a chaperon.''

Though Jake managed to keep his promise to himself, they did several things that evening they wouldn't have dreamed of doing if Lisa were around. Adding several logs to the fire and dialing a mellow "oldies" station on the radio, he settled on the couch with Holly in the curve of his shoulder. As they kissed, talked and kissed some more, they planned to hold their wedding at home and discussed whom to invite. Since her closest family members were second cousins she hadn't seen since the third grade, Holly's contingent would consist of neighbors and friends. To her chagrin, Jake claimed he didn't have anyone in mind.

"Like you, I don't have any close family," he explained. "And few true friends, if you want the truth. None of them live around here. I'll be happy if it's just us, Lisa, the Tornquists, and anyone else you want to invite."

It would have to do. Willing to take him without some of the blanks filled in, Holly worked up her courage to ask what she considered to be two essential questions. Had Jake been married before? Ever fathered a child? Or children?

His answer was no to both questions. "Though I never found anyone I wanted to marry until I met you, I always thought I'd like being a husband and father someday," he said, lifting Holly's left hand and lightly pressing it to his lips. "Being around you and Lisa has only confirmed that feeling a hundredfold. Though we'll be a family cobbled together by happenstance, with a child who isn't related by blood to either of us, I can't imagine being part of one that would be more satisfying to my soul. I'll be honored to be Lisa's father by marriage—and your husband in every sense."

In honor of Holly's principles, she and Jake didn't make love that night. Yet they agreed it would have been asking too much of them not to sleep together. Outside, the temperature had dropped into the single digits and, with Holly still saving on heating costs, the room was positively polar. Yet they didn't suffer from any lack of warmth. Deep in each other's arms beneath Holly's down coverlet and several layers of woolen blankets, they luxuriated in each other's body heat as they kissed, touched and fantasized about what the future might hold.

With her most pressing questions about Jake's past laid to rest and no idea of the secret he was keeping from her, Holly's imagined scenarios were all of blue skies, sunlight and summer weather, horseback riding in the mountains with the man and girl she loved. As they had on a fall day in the not-so-distant past, they'd picnic within view of snow-covered peaks, run laughing through a meadow full of wildflowers.

Afterward, they'd come home, eat, listen to music on the radio as she sewed, Jake whittled and Lisa read or worked on one of her craft projects. Lovers at last, she and Jake would sleep together. Though her fantasy was a simple one—not what most people would consider glamorous or exotic, she suspected—it sounded like heaven on earth to her.

Happier than he'd ever dreamed possible, Jake couldn't stop thinking in a more somber vein. What would Holly do when he finally was forced to tell her the truth about himself? Would she ever forgive him for his deception? *She has a right to know what she's getting into, and with whom,* his conscience argued. *If you don't tell her* now, *her trust in you is sadly misplaced.*

Aching to reveal the truth and, in the best of all possible outcomes, receive her forgiveness, he couldn't bring himself to take the risk. Though he upbraided himself for his lack of courage, he decided to wait until after they were married before broaching the subject. Once we've spoken our vows, it'll be harder for her to kick me out, he reasoned. Yet he knew that the longer he waited, the greater his offense would be, the heavier his burden.

He was also thinking about Lisa and the need to make her feel safe and loved in their new arrangement. As he and Holly dressed for the trip into Larisson to pick her up the following morning, he advanced the somewhat courtly notion of asking the girl's permission to marry her.

"You mean...propose 'daughtership' to her?" Holly asked, a dimple flashing beside her mouth.

Jake grinned, too. His blue eyes betrayed only a minimal worry that he might be rejected. "In a sense, the three of us will be marrying one another," he explained. "I want Lisa to be as enthusiastic as we are about our new life together."

Holly's redheaded stepdaughter was dangling her legs over the edge of her hospital bed, fiddling with some paper dolls one of the nurses had given her, when they arrived. "You're here!" she exclaimed in delight, jumping to her feet and giving Holly a hug. "Did you remember to bring my clothes?"

"Here they are," Holly answered, handing Lisa the duffel bag she used for her overnights with Jane. "By the way...as soon as you're dressed, Jake would like to talk to you about something."

About to dash into the small adjacent bathroom so she could change into her jeans, sweater and parka as fast as possible, Lisa hesitated. She glanced from Jake to her stepmother. "What about?" she demanded, clearly sensing something important was at stake.

"The fact that I want to marry Holly." To Lisa's obvious astonishment, Jake went down before her on bended knee. "I won't do it without your approval, pumpkin," he said. "Could you handle having me as Holly's husband...and your new stepdad?"

Lisa gaped at him. "You already asked her, didn't you?" she speculated, recovering. "And she told you *yes.*"

Jake nodded. Beside him, Holly held her breath.

Again there was silence. "It wouldn't be like you were taking my real dad's place, would it?" Lisa asked slowly.

"No, it wouldn't," Jake agreed.

"But...you could have a spot of your own."

His heart turned over at the girl's wisdom. "It's what I want, sweetheart," he whispered. "More than anything."

Like the sun at its zenith, dispelling dark clouds, a smile lit her freckled countenance. "Then it's okay with me," she said shyly. "In fact, I think it's a cool idea."

Seconds later, the three of them were caught in a fierce embrace.

Chapter Eight

When they phoned Emma with the news, she responded with delight and an invitation. "Have the ceremony at our house," she suggested. "We have more space. A bigger Christmas tree, thanks to the height of our living room. And several dozen candles left over from our celebration of St. Lucia's Day. You'll be able to concentrate on getting married without the burden of entertaining. Afterward, Lisa can stay over with Jane, so you'll have a proper wedding night."

Though at first they protested that it would be too much work for her, ultimately Jake and Holly accepted. They had to agree that the huge stone fireplace in the Tornquists' living room, which was always elaborately decorated at Christmastime, was the ideal backdrop for their exchange of vows.

Following the snowstorm that accompanied Lisa's airlift to the hospital, the weather turned sunny, dry and cold. Jake assumed a greater role in caring for the animals and performing maintenance tasks around the ranch while Holly concentrated on getting ready for the wedding and finishing up her Christmas presents. In her spare moments while Jake was out-of-doors, she was fashioning a bulky sweater for him from a deep blue yarn that matched his eyes.

By now, her long-legged cowboy had won her trust in addition to her affection. After two lonely years spent running the ranch without Clint's help and raising Lisa on her own, she'd found a man to love. And what a man he was—tall, sexy and remarkably nurturing. Each time they kissed, his mouth seared her very soul. Over and over, as she imagined them setting a seal on their love, the yarn would slacken in her fingers.

She had wedding preparations to complete, though Emma would be in charge of the hostessing. First and foremost, she needed a dress. What she *had,* as a typical hard-working rancher, was a closet full of jeans and sweaters, and not much money in her bank account. Still, she had an idea in mind that was both affordable and full of sentiment.

Near the end of Lisa's first week home, as the girl napped on the living room couch with the novel *Black Beauty* open beside her, Holly disappeared into her bedroom and lifted the lid of her grandmother's cedar chest. Yes…there they were, Grandma Peterson's wedding dress and veil, preserved in layers of tissue beneath a stack of hand-embroidered tablecloths. The former Mabel Torgilson had wed Olaf Peterson in 1928, five years before giving birth to Holly's mother, and the white, ankle-length dress reflected it.

Made of clinging silk peau de soie over a matching slip in a whisper-weight version of the same fabric, it had long sleeves and a modest neckline decorated with seed pearls. The veil was attached to a head-hugging satin cap, also decorated with pearls and trimmed with hand-appliquéd swirls of silk soutache braid. She hadn't worn them when she and Clint had pledged their troth before a justice of the peace, considering them too formal for that occasion, and she'd regretted it ever afterward.

Now she had another chance.

To be married in the flapper-era outfit would be to carry on a family tradition, as her mother had worn it, too. It would also save her money she could ill afford to spend. It can't be allowed to matter that Mom and Dad's marriage ended in divorce, she thought. Mine and Jake's won't, and that's what counts. Though the arbiters of such things might have considered her grandmother's gown hopelessly dated, Holly thought it exquisite. To her, the echoes it summoned of other times and places only added to its mystique.

When she modeled it before the pier glass in the living room, it fit as if it had been custom-made for her. Taking off the cap and veil, and unbraiding her hair so that its waist-length tresses descended in waves about her shoulders, she surveyed herself again. With her hair loose, the ensemble took on an almost medieval air. Humming a ballad the musicians had played as she and Jake had danced together at the Cunninghams' party, she regarded herself with pleasure. I'll wear my jeans to drive to the Tornquists' so my bridal garments won't get wrinkled, she thought.

Jake wouldn't see her in the outfit until she put it on in one of her neighbors' guest bedrooms. But he heard about it from Lisa. Realizing it would mean a great deal to Holly if he dressed appropriately for the occasion as well, he made a quick trip into Pagosa Springs to buy a suit off the rack. Though he was tempted, he could hardly step forward to claim her hand in one of the custom-made suits that was currently languishing in his Durango closet. If Holly asked how he'd managed to afford the dark jacket and slacks he bought in a men's discount store, he decided, he'd simply tell her that he'd saved up his paychecks.

The problem of her wedding attire resolved, Holly turned her attention to Lisa's. It, too, proved to be a frugal, easy choice. The red velveteen dress she'd made the girl for the Cunninghams' party was perfect. Despite the clash of shades with Lisa's mass of carroty curls, the dress looked good on her. And she loved the color. I wonder who we can get to take some photographs, Holly mused, imagining the tableau they'd make. Maybe Tom Tibbets can do it. I've heard he's handy with a camera.

At last, it was Christmas Eve—the fourth shortest day of the year. From first light, the sky had been cloudy and gray. Now, as they made their final preparations, the sun was setting behind a bank of darkening clouds. A light veil of snow began to fall. Initially so fine that they were barely visible, the snowflakes grew huge and lacy, like children's paper-lace cutouts.

Plagued by a mild case of nerves, yet at bottom secure in the knowledge that her marriage to Jake was meant, Holly had packed her best underwear, nylons and pearl earrings in an alligator-embossed train case that had belonged to her as a girl. Her gown and veil were on padded hangers, carefully swathed in plastic dry-cleaner's bags.

She'd splurged on a pair of white satin, low-heeled slippers for herself and a gold locket for Lisa, who might feel left out if she didn't have something new, as well. I hope the spring calving is good so our finances won't be so tight, she thought as she smoothed her grandmother's wedding gown through its transparent covering. Lisa deserves a treat now and then. Maybe we'll do better with Jake to help out from now on instead of a series of uncaring drifters.

"Holly...hurry up! We're going to be late!"

An excited tug from Lisa's hand accompanied the urgent request. Unlike her stepmother, the girl had elected to wear her best for the brief journey, though she'd bowed to circumstances and tucked her black patent flats into her overnight bag. She was ready except for the act of putting on her coat—and fairly dancing with impatience.

Gathering up her things, Holly followed Lisa into the living room and promptly caught her breath. Instead of his usual jeans, sweater and flannel shirt, which were the extent of his wardrobe as far as she knew, Jake was wearing a dark suit, white shirt and tie. A pair of black tooled-leather cowboy boots she hadn't seen before peeked out from beneath his trouser legs. He'd tucked a sprig of her namesake botanical in his buttonhole.

Smiling at her astonishment, he gave her a little salute.

"Where...where did you get that outfit?" she stammered, too smitten with the way he looked to articulate what she felt.

Casting a twinkling, blue-eyed glance at Lisa, who'd clearly been in on the secret of his upgraded wardrobe, he kissed the tip of Holly's nose. "I saved my pay and went on a little shopping spree," he claimed.

"Well, you look wonderful."

The blue eyes got merrier. "Thank you very much."

By now, Lisa was bundled to face the elements. Zipping on their parkas and scooping up several gaily wrapped Christmas presents for Emma, Lars and Jane, Holly and Jake followed her out the door. The soles of their boots squeaked on the tightly packed snow as they hurried to Holly's truck, which Jake had dashed out earlier to leave warming in the driveway.

When we return home, we'll be married, Holly thought, overwhelmed by the powerful love and closeness contained in the cab of her modest pickup as they settled in for their brief journey. Though she couldn't prove it in any objective sense, she felt certain she was the luckiest woman in the world.

As always at Christmastime, her neighbors' ranch house was ablaze with St. Lucia candles, the warm glow of firelight and what seemed a hundred strings of Christmas bulbs. The bulbs were twined about an oversize, aromatic Christmas tree. Positioned beside the massive stone hearth that would serve as the backdrop for their wedding vows, it filled the air with its strong evergreen scent. Christmas carols were playing softly on the stereo.

They were a few minutes late. Holly barely had time to duck into one of the guest bedrooms to dress before the first guests arrived. As she shed her jeans, she silently thanked Emma for setting out every item she conceivably might want—lotion, tissue, a pincushion full of pins, even a pair of panty hose in her slender size in case she snagged the stockings she'd brought.

Taking off her sweater and putting on her nylons and lacy garter belt, Holly removed her wedding slip from its protective covering and shimmied it over her head. The dress came next, cool like its matching undergarment from the brisk December air.

For once, she'd decided, she'd wear makeup. Before putting on her veil, she sat on the padded bench at the dressing table to smooth on a light blusher and add a trace of mascara, a dab of lipstick. Next came her pearl earrings, which were shaped like tiny teardrops. Unfastening her braid, she brushed out the heavy blond length of her hair so that it fell liquid about her shoulders.

Last of all, she settled her cap and veil into place. As she did so, her eyes caught and held those of her alter ego in the mirror. Tonight, you and the handsome cowboy who appeared at your gate in October will be husband and wife, she acknowledged with a little shiver of happiness.

She could only imagine the ecstasy of making love to him. Her sexual encounters with Clint—the only ones she'd known to date—had generated more relaxed togetherness than heat. Happy enough, she'd never known soul-deep contentment. From the kisses she and Jake had exchanged, she knew her experience with him would fall into a completely different category.

By now, the chatter of guests in the Tornquists' living room had reached an expectant pitch. Tapping lightly on the door, Lisa slipped into the room. Her mouth opening to deliver some message or other, she stopped dead in her tracks and stared. "You're so beautiful, Holly!" she said after a moment.

Her heart overflowing with love for the world at large, Holly held out her arms. For once the girl hesitated to come into them. "I don't want to crush your dress," Lisa protested.

Holly shook her head. Though Lisa hadn't grown to the maturity of birth beneath her heart, she considered the girl to be her own in every other sense. Lisa and Jake would form a similar bond, she hoped. "Don't you know I *want* it to have that kind of crease, sweetheart?'' she asked.

The hug they exchanged was heartfelt, an unspoken vow that the charmed circle of Holly's love for her husband-to-be would always include Lisa and bring them even closer together. Emerging from it, the girl announced that the Tornquists' minister had arrived. ''We're ready to start,'' she said, sounding serious and extremely grown-up. ''If you are, too, I'll tell Mrs. Baake she can play the wedding march.''

Imogen Baake, the minister's wife, had been enlisted to play the Tornquists' upright piano throughout the service.

Taking a deep breath, Holly didn't answer for a moment. It was her last chance to back out, if that was what she wanted. I've only known Jake a couple of months, she thought. And, though he's told me a few stories about his boyhood and tour of duty in Vietnam, much of his history is still unknown to me. Whenever I've tried to get him to fill in the blanks or discuss the string of jobs he's held, he's found a way to shrug off my questions. What am I doing, marrying him?

On the verge of a belated panic attack, she remembered Emma's words of wisdom. Hadn't her motherly neighbor opined that a man's actions were the best key to what was in his heart? And hadn't she agreed with that assessment?

From his first afternoon at Honeycomb, Jake had been decent, loving and protective of both of them. Without knowing every detail of his past, she could afford to trust him. ''You can tell her I'm ready,'' she directed.

Jake was talking with Lars by the fireplace when someone switched off the stereo. Wide-eyed at the gravity of what they were about to do, Lisa slipped her hand into his. Emotions fierce and tremulous pierced him to the quick as Imogen Baake began to play the age-old processional.

Somewhere beyond the sudden quiet that swept the guests, a door opened. Holly appeared in the shadows of the bedroom hall. After a slight hesitation, she entered the living room. The buzz of admiring whispers that greeted her caused twin spots of color to bloom in her cheeks.

In her antique dress, with her unbraided hair cascading about her shoulders, she was so fresh, so radiant, that Jake's heart turned over in his chest. As he stepped forward to take her hand and lead her back to the fireplace, he could scarcely believe his luck. What had he done to deserve such happiness, the love and trust that were shining in her face?

God knew he loved her with all his heart, that he was ready a thousand times over to shed his bachelorhood like a worn-out coat. Yet by his failure to tell her the full truth about himself and the mission that had brought him to her door, he'd violated her trust. How did you let things get this far? he asked himself. But he knew the answer well enough. If he'd told her everything, the love they shared would never have had a chance to blossom.

He'd just have to beg her forgiveness at the appropriate moment. Maybe I can make it up to her by forcing Dutch to see how good she is for Lisa, he kidded himself, his hand tightening about Holly's as they faced the minister. Maybe the family we're cementing today won't have to fall apart.

Holding out her hand to Lisa, Holly drew the girl against her side as Elton Baake began to read the wedding service. Though Jake's voice nearly broke with emotion when it was time for him to say his vows, hers floated clear and true into the pine-scented hush that filled the Tornquists' living room. But it was Lisa's, "Yes!" when—per their instructions—Elton Baake asked if she took Jake and Holly to be her parents till death did them part that carried the day.

"Did I do something wrong, Mommy?" the girl whispered, embarrassed at the indulgent ripple of amusement her response had evoked.

Holly shook her head. "You were perfect, pumpkin."

Seconds later, the minister was asking Jake for the ring. Assuming Jake couldn't afford to purchase one, Holly hadn't brought up the subject. They'd said nothing about a ring to the minister. Now she gaped as her groom retrieved a worn gold band set with garnets from his pocket.

"With this ring, which was my mother's wedding band, I thee wed," he said with unabashed sentimentality, causing her eyes to mist.

There wasn't any way he could have sized the ring for her finger. Yet it fit as if it had been custom made for her. *Jake, Jake,* she thought, lifting her gaze to his. *Can you ever forgive me for doubting you?*

Goose bumps brushed Holly's skin as the minister pronounced them husband and wife. It was time for their nuptial embrace. *How big, how solid, Jake is,* she thought as she put her arms around him and offered up her mouth. *A rock that will see me through any trouble. The beloved object of my desire.*

Though it held just a hint of the passion she knew ran hot in him, Jake's swooping confiscation of her mouth was all-consuming. Its warmth flooded her soul, easing its places of greatest loneliness. *You are loved,* it seemed to promise. *Whatever lies ahead, we'll weather it.*

How long they stood there, communing in a way that blurred the physical and the spiritual, she couldn't have said afterward—just that time seemed to stand still and the room might as well have been empty of wedding guests.

Lisa's urgent poke in their ribs returned them to their senses. "You guys are embarrassing me," she whispered.

The most sacred moments of the ceremony having passed, the guests applauded when Jake widened his embrace to include the blushing ten-year-old. In response, they hugged some more, the three-way tie that united them in an almost tangible presence.

"Time for a toast," Lars proposed in his mostly Americanized Swedish accent and suddenly the ceremony was complete. Several of Holly's neighbors had offered to tend bar, and champagne corks quickly began popping. Without consulting them, it turned out, the Tornquists had provided enough of the celebratory beverage for several rounds of good wishes. Even Lisa and Jane got tiny sips.

Our married life has begun, Holly thought wonderingly, her earlier tension evaporating into smiles and hugs as friends and neighbors surrounded them to pump Jake's hand and kiss her cheek. Behind them, Christmas lights sparkled on lavishly decorated boughs. Gradually the crescendo of talk and laughter intensified. As Emma and Lars invited everyone to partake of the caraway-and-onion meatballs in sour cream and other Scandinavian delicacies that waited on the buffet, Imogen Baake began to play traditional Christmas carols.

Singing and even a bit of dancing followed, along

with the pleasurable opening of wedding gifts. However, the reception wasn't scheduled to run very late. The Tornquists and their guests had last-minute preparations to make for their own family celebrations of Christmas. Besides, Holly and Jake were eager to start their honeymoon.

Her veil removed and carefully placed inside her train case along with her satin slippers, Holly pulled on her cowboy boots and zipped her parka over the top half of her wedding dress. In that outlandish getup, she hugged Emma and Lars good-night. "Thank you, *thank you both*... for everything!" she exclaimed, barely able to contain the enormous gratitude she felt. "What you did for us was so wonderful...."

"It was our pleasure, dear." Emma beamed. "It's good to see you so happy."

Lars nodded in agreement, his weather-beaten face creasing in a broad smile. "We benefited, too," he claimed. "We'll always own a little piece of your happiness."

The acceptance and friendship Holly's neighbors had accorded him—for the man he was, not the money and credentials that had seemed so important to everyone he'd met in his legal career—thoroughly touched Jake's heart. Together with Holly's and Lisa's affection, they'd brought him solidly to earth in a place he'd begun to call his own. If only he could keep them....

He'd move heaven and earth if that's what it took. His only fear was that, once he leveled with Holly about his relationship to Dutch, his boundless love for her might not be enough.

"Emma, Lars...I'll never be able to repay you for your kindness," he said soberly.

"Yes, you can." Lars gave his shoulder a squeeze. "You can take good care of this special lady."

With hugs and kisses for Lisa and anyone else who wanted to get into the act, they were off, hurrying toward Holly's pickup and their one-night honeymoon.

While they'd been speaking their vows, the front that had brought their earlier snowfall had passed, leaving behind clear skies, a pale winter moon and falling temperatures. Thanks to Jake's careful maintenance, the pickup's engine roared to life immediately. "C'mere," he growled, flipping on the heater, though he didn't activate the blower immediately. "I want you where I can feel you, Mrs. McKenzie."

It was what Holly wanted, too. Cold in her grandmother's wedding dress despite the warmth of her parka, she burrowed against him. She'd been wild about him from the first and now he was her husband.

Their ride home, over snow-dusted country roads, was swift, its progress barely impeded by numerous kisses. Before many minutes had elapsed, they were passing through Honeycomb's gate. Sheltered by its bare cottonwoods, the house waited, a single lamp burning in its living room window.

Fresh snow coated Holly's front steps. Though she was wearing cowboy boots, Jake wouldn't hear of letting her step in it. "You're my bride and I'm going to carry you over the threshold," he insisted.

She was shivering as he set her on her feet just inside the front door. "Darlin', you're cold!" he said worriedly. "Here… let me warm you."

"That sounds wonderful. I want you to do it—"

The rest of her words were muffled by a kiss. "What did you say?" he prodded.

"I want you to do it in our bed."

Tonight and every night from now on, they would share the same sleeping space, the same coverlet. Ardently but tenderly, Jake led her through her bedroom's open door. In anticipation of their lovemaking, Holly had dressed her four-poster with fresh, eyelet-trimmed sheets. Since they wouldn't wear nightclothes, her goose-down comforter topped several warm woolen blankets.

Tugging back the bed covers to make a place for her, Jake helped her out of her parka and cowboy boots first. Usually so graceful and capable, his big hands were awkward as they fumbled with the fragile, fabric-covered buttons of her dress.

"Here...let me help..."

Making a more adroit job of it, she finished taking off the dress and laid it over a chair. More with excitement than cold, she shivered again as she freed herself of its matching slip.

Jake wasn't sure of the cause. "We've got to get you under the blankets," he insisted.

"Not in my underwear."

Unhooking her bra and garter belt, and peeling down her filmy stockings, Holly allowed Jake to remove her panties. The brush of his fingers on her naked thighs ignited little fires in places the cold couldn't touch.

A moment later, she watched from the bed with the covers pulled up to her chin as he took off his things. How beautiful he is, how economical in motion...like some great, wild stallion, she thought, the hot interior place where she wanted him warming and opening a little more as her gaze followed the uneven seam of dark hair that pointed downward from his chest to his taut readiness. To think he wants me...that he let me put a halter on him. Before he could reach for them, she threw back the covers, offering herself.

The gesture was like a goad to Jake, who'd spent too many nights alone in his trailer and sleeping bag, wanting her. Getting in beside her, he pulled the blankets over them like a tent. They'd be joined at last, fused in ecstasy and body heat. First, though, he wanted to hear her helpless cries as he gave her a foretaste.

On Holly's mouth, his was like an avalanche—kissing, tasting, owning her moist depths tongue to tongue. But that was only the beginning of what he wanted. From there, his hot, damp nuzzling descended via her throat and creamy shoulders to the upturned mounds of her breasts.

They'd been starving for each other and now, it seemed, he planned to eat her up. Already her nipples stood like miniature volcanoes in their arousal. A little moan escaped her as he licked one tight, pink bud and then fastened wetly on it, to suck as if he'd draw the last ounce of sweetness from her body.

One of his callused thumbs teased her other nipple, flicking it back and forth with such seductive restraint that little stabs of longing pierced her body. Their deep, erotic connection with the place where she wanted him most was instantaneous.

Big with his craving for her, he insinuated himself against the blond-tufted mound that guarded her womanhood. Within its sanctuary, she'd gone liquid with expectation. "Jake...oh, Jake...I love you so much. Please...come into me," she begged, feverishly caressing the broad muscles of his back and buttocks.

It was what he'd longed to do from the moment they met. But he wouldn't go for it yet—not until he'd given her a preliminary ride to glory and assumed protection.

"This way first, darlin'," he coaxed, his dark head disappearing beneath the blankets as he moved downward to insert his tongue in her velvety folds.

She shivered with delight as he positioned himself between her legs. Because he was *Jake,* the blue-eyed cowboy her heart hadn't been able to resist, the simple act of granting him that degree of familiarity increased her pleasure a hundredfold.

Yet it wasn't what surprised Holly most. Overwhelmed by the upward spiral of sensations he was evoking, she quickly realized the flutters of gratification and relief she'd achieved on rare occasions with Clint were about to be surpassed the way a candle flame is outstripped by a forest fire.

Meanwhile, for the first time in Jake's life, another person's fulfillment mattered more than his own. In his experience, a woman couldn't be hurried and, bent on satisfying Holly's most sensuous claims, he maintained an exquisitely slow, provocative pace. Paradoxically, a part of him regretted the seasoning he possessed to exercise in her service. How I wish I'd never known another woman, he thought, his nostrils filled with the unique perfume of her arousal. And that she'd never had another husband. How glorious it would be to approach this equinox for the first time together.

To Holly, the unknown women who'd figured in Jake's past no longer mattered a whit. From this night forward, he was hers, and that was all that counted. Tangling her fingers in his thick, dark hair, she let herself tumble beyond reason, the last vestige of self-control.

With Jake, she found, she didn't have to strain for completion. Or *try* to do anything. All he asked was that she lose herself completely in his affection. Carried up, up, up by the most intimate touch she'd ever known, she kept thinking she could go no higher. Yet against all logic she felt her delirium intensify.

Instinctively, she lifted her lower body from the bed as she reached the breaking point. Seconds later she was dissolving in ecstasy. Instead of stimulating her mildly, the way her previous experiences had, the paroxysm of shudders that claimed her threatened to sweep her away. Heat rushed to her face, a ruddy sensation, as if her body's thermostat had gone completely berserk. Only subliminally aware that she was moaning, she clung to the man she loved as he moved upward to cover her.

"Ride it to the end, darlin'," he urged. "Don't stop until you reach the last ember."

Safe in his love, she dared to accept. At last, she quieted. Her thighs ached pleasantly. Her face was buried against his neck. "Jake," she whispered at last, filled with love to bursting, "it's over. I want you inside me...where you belong."

They were just beginning to explore what the night could hold. Absorbed in pleasuring her, Jake had felt his arousal subside a little. Now, at her passionate request, it reintensified. He was a cannon primed for shot, a loving sword seeking the depths of its scabbard.

Too easily, the tangible result of his longing could make her a baby. Though the notion thrilled and delighted him, he didn't want it to happen yet. They needed time to be newlyweds first—enough time for him to set things straight. The last thing he wanted was to trap her with that kind of connection.

Having allowed the weed of his dissembling to flourish, he'd have to stifle his conscience a little longer or ruin his wedding night. Shifting his weight, he reached for a foil packet he'd placed in the top drawer of Holly's nightstand that afternoon. A heartbeat later, sheathed in protection and forgetfulness, he was riding high against her body for maximum contact as he led her back to paradise.

Chapter Nine

Their bodies sated and their passion for each other temporarily quenched, Holly and Jake were deep in slumber when car doors banged and tires crunched on the snow outside their window. It was fully morning. A bunch of people, from the sounds of things, were making an awful din. They seemed to be beating on pots and pans and shaking cowbells. Somebody was actually playing a harmonica!

Rubbing the sleep from her eyes, Holly surfaced for a look. *"Ohmygod!"* she exclaimed in panic. "Jake...wake up! We're about to have company!"

Struggling awake, her groggy-eyed husband confirmed that she wasn't imagining things. When they scrambled into jeans and sweaters without bothering to put on underwear and hurried barefoot to the front door, they were greeted by Lars, Emma, Lisa, Jane and a gaggle of laughing neighbors. Several of the men were carrying the wedding presents they'd left behind at the Tornquist ranch the night before.

"What...what's this all about?" Holly stammered as her stepdaughter hugged her about the waist.

"Ain't you ever heard of a shivaree?" a wizened rancher who lived to the south of them responded with a grin. "It's a fine old Colorado tradition. We couldn't let you off the hook just because it happens to be Christmas!"

Their recollection of the good-natured hazing newlyweds sometimes received partially restored, Holly and Jake hastened to make their visitors welcome. While she set out trays of Christmas cookies and a kuchen she'd made the previous day for their breakfast, he put on the coffee and reconstituted several cans of frozen orange juice. Before long, everyone was gathered about her island counter, laughing, talking and munching.

Waking up a little more and exchanging a loving glance with Jake, Holly felt her satisfaction deepen. The three of us are going to be so happy together, she thought, looking forward to the moment when Jake would try on the sweater she'd made and Lisa would unwrap her Barbie-doll wardrobe.

It was only after their guests had gone and they were cleaning up the dirty dishes that a shadow fled across her contentment. Jake and Lisa had been drying while she washed and, for several moments, her new husband let the towel he'd been using dangle unused from his fingers. He seemed to be staring at the freshly washed coffee cups that were piling up in the dish drainer without really seeing them as a troubled expression drew his dark brows together.

It was early January. Having made love in their room after Lisa had gone to sleep for the night, Holly and

Jake were dozing. At least, Holly was. Though he'd never been happier in his personal life, Jake was wide-awake, agonizing over the problem of telling her the truth about himself.

Except for the time he'd spent in Durango winning Dutch's case, he'd been absent from his legal firm for more than three months. Even stretching things, his sabbatical was up. His most lucrative client would be getting impatient. Dutch being Dutch, he'd want an answer—soon. If he didn't get one, he was liable to come looking for them. Yet Jake was afraid to level with Holly. What thc hcll was he going to do?

Peripherally aware he was wakeful and restless, Holly opened her eyes. She snuggled closer. "Anything wrong?" she asked.

He couldn't bring himself to seize the opportunity that beckoned. Instead, he settled for halfway measures. "I was thinking about Lisa and the other side of her birth family," he said. "I know you've told me that her mother's no angel. But what about her grandparents? They might be decent folks. It seems to me that she and they deserve a chance to know one another."

From a plateau of peace and tranquility, Holly's mood plummeted to one of irritation. "Whose side are you on, anyway?" she asked, giving him a speaking look.

"Yours. And Lisa's." He turned on his side to face her, the expression in his blue eyes disturbing. "I'm only trying to think of what's best for her."

As if *I* haven't done that since the day I married her father, Holly thought. "Maybe you didn't understand when I told you about my promise to Clint," she said, swallowing her impatience. "Lisa's mother neglected her. She was sexually promiscuous. And she did drugs. She's in prison now because she was convicted of selling them. On his deathbed, Clint begged me to keep Lisa away from her—and her parents.''

Jake felt as if he were arguing a court case under false pretenses. In fact, he was, he supposed. "What did *they* do to deserve his mistrust?" he asked, stifling his scruples and proceeding, anyway. "Are they drug dealers, too?"

Holly resented his interference in what she considered her personal business. Her mouth had taken on a set, rebellious look. "On the contrary," she conceded reluctantly, "they're wealthy, respected business people.''

"Then I don't see—"

"According to Clint, they spoiled Lisa's mother rotten from the time she was a toddler. And you see how that profited them. Unfortunately, the potential for harm is a lot greater than the likelihood that they'd spoil Lisa, too. My greatest fear, as was Clint's, is that—when her mother's released from prison—they'd let her spend unsupervised time with Lisa...maybe even hand that innocent child over to her.''

Jake was silent a moment. Knowing Dawn as he did, he could sympathize with Holly's predicament. Yet he'd embarked on making a point he hoped would soften her up for his eventual confession of his standing in the situation. Lawyerlike, he pursued his original line of questioning.

"As her guardian, you could put a stop to that, couldn't you?" he asked, knowing full well that Holly had no official status where the girl was concerned.

Holly grimaced. "Not if they got a judge to give them custody. As Lisa's stepmother and Clint's widow,

I don't have the legal standing of blood relative. I'd probably lose if push came to shove. I don't think I mentioned it before, but they tried to take Lisa from Clint when she was six, based on the argument that he was an unfit parent. At the time, his great-aunt looked after her whenever he was absent on the rodeo circuit. The petition argued that, as a single, working father, he couldn't devote enough time to her care.

"We started dating shortly after that, and then he won a minor lottery prize. I quit teaching to marry him and their argument fell apart. A month or so later, the court ruled in his favor."

Having filed the suit himself, Jake knew everything about it there was to know. In representing the Hargretts, he'd only done what he was paid to do. They deserved representation as much as anyone. Nonetheless, he was abjectly grateful that Holly had forgotten the name of the law firm involved. Similarly, he blessed the fact that it was dark in the room and she couldn't read his discomfort.

"Did you ever think Clint married you so that he could keep Lisa?" he asked, covering his tracks.

Calming down a bit, Holly took the question at face value. "It may have crossed his mind that it would be an advantage," she admitted. "But he honestly loved me. Of that, I've never had any doubt."

Their discussion ended on that note and they were soon drifting off to sleep. Yet, the following day, Holly could sense that something was bothering Jake. Unknown to her, he was anguishing over the need to make a clean breast of things. Eventually he'd have to do it, of course. And when he did, he stood to lose her.

Meanwhile, it was past time for him to call Dutch. Midmorning, though he still hadn't decided whether he'd tell the older man the truth or continue to prevaricate, he announced he was driving into town on a variety of errands. He got the shock of his life when he dialed Dutch's private number from the wind-buffeted pay phone at the local gas station.

"So you finally decided to call," his old friend and client hailed him sarcastically while he was still trying to decide what tack to take. "Damn thoughtful of you. Too bad you're a little late. I've traced the area where you've been calling from. It's only a matter of time before I locate my granddaughter myself. Thanks to Brent Fordyce's help, I have a court order demanding her stepmother produce her so a judge can rule on her custody."

For once, Jake was speechless.

"Handle this...or I will," Dutch threatened.

Too shaken even to think of informing his hard-nosed client about his marriage or the job he'd taken at Holly's ranch for the purpose of checking her out, Jake admitted he'd pinpointed Holly's exact whereabouts. "I'll take the matter up with her this afternoon," he promised, aware his words might be a death knell to everything he held precious.

"You'd damn well better," Dutch emphasized.

Holly was bundled to her ears, forking bales of hay into the bed of her pickup preparatory to servicing the herd, when he returned to Honeycomb.

"Come into the house.... I have to talk to you," he greeted her without preamble, a strong north wind all but snatching the words from his mouth.

As his wife and intimate partner, Holly knew at once that something was terribly wrong. Unerringly, her female instinct fastened on the gray areas of his past. A problem had arisen from one of them with the potential to drive them apart.

Leaning her pitchfork against the pickup without a word, she preceded him into the house and made a pot of coffee. Thank God Lisa's at school…that she doesn't have to hear this, whatever it is, she congratulated herself.

"Okay," she said, turning to Jake with steel in her eyes. "Let's have it. I don't think I can take the suspense."

He didn't know where to start. Beginning, middle or end, his story would be excruciatingly painful to her ears. "Tell me you love me first," he pleaded.

It was going to be really bad. "You know I do," she replied unequivocally.

Try though he would, Jake couldn't think of any further reason to delay speaking the truth. He might as well get it over with and take his chances. "The day I turned up at your gate," he confessed, "it wasn't by accident."

A chill feathered down Holly's spine. Who had sent him?

She had her answer a moment later. "The fact is, I'm not your average wandering cowboy," he admitted when she didn't speak. "I'm Dutch Hargrett's attorney and I agreed to help him find his granddaughter. From what little I knew of you, I thought there might be another side to the story, and when I saw you, I knew there was. I needed fresh air and a breather from the life I led, and I decided to stick around—document what kind of mother you were. I didn't consciously plan to fall in love with you."

For Holly, each word that fell from Jake's lips was like a bullet aimed straight at her heart. She seemed to freeze until it was as if she'd metamorphosed into a statue made of ice. To her shame, she'd fallen in love with Jake and married him, when all the time he'd been making a fool of her. His protestation that he'd fallen in love with her, too, fell on rocky ground.

"In other words, Dutch knows where we are," she said at last, desperately trying to cope. "Will you be serving his court papers on me yourself? Or will a sheriff's deputy come knocking at my door?"

Her helpless feeling of being a moth pinned to paper was painfully obvious to Jake. Whatever I try to do to help her straighten out this mess, she isn't going to forgive me, he thought. Not if I beg till my hundredth birthday.

"By tracing my calls to him from the pay phone in town, Dutch learned Lisa is in Bonino County," he admitted. "But he doesn't have her specific address. Before he discovers it, we've got to put our heads together...."

Heartsick and gripped by the most debilitating anger she'd ever experienced, Holly was seized by a fit of shivering. She refused to let Jake touch her, let alone take her in his arms. By tricking her the way he had over something he knew was of paramount importance to her, he'd betrayed everything she'd held dear in him.

"Was there some reason you had to romance and marry me to carry out your research?" she asked, putting the width of the island counter between them. "No...don't answer that. Surely, as an attorney, you recognize a rhetorical question when you hear one. For the record, there isn't any 'our' or 'we' anymore. You may be my husband in the eyes of the law, but as far as I'm concerned we no longer have a relationship. I want you out of here in the time it takes to pack your stuff."

Though he argued and pleaded, protesting his love for her, Jake couldn't change her mind. She flatly declined to discuss the options he thought they still had in dealing with Dutch. She wanted a divorce. It was that simple, that heartrending.

"Make it an annulment," she stormed. "I ought to be eligible for one, don't you think, since you married me under false pretenses?"

Surrendering the field with an eye to doing battle another day when her shock and outrage had lessened seemed the better part of wisdom. With a clenched jaw and a host of self-directed recriminations, Jake retrieved his belongings from Holly's bedroom closet and put on his coat and gloves.

"Couldn't we at least talk about this a little more?" he asked, his blue eyes filled with the pain of her rejection as he lingered just inside the front door. "I *love* you, Holly. And I always will. I'm on your side—and Lisa's—despite my loyalty to Dutch...."

By now, Holly's anger was like a stone, taking up the space in her chest usually allocated to her heart.

"Because of you and what you did, your client has a crack at taking Lisa away from me and placing her under Dawn's influence," she answered in a wintry voice. "Both of our lives are up for grabs. With you on our side, we don't need enemies."

She was dry eyed as she watched Jake tramp through the snow by the corral and get into his truck. To be sure he left and didn't double back, or so she told herself, she stayed at the window until he'd driven through the gate. It was only when she turned away and discovered she couldn't find a comforting spot anywhere in her beloved ranch house that the tears began to flow.

Once they started, there seemed to be no stopping

them. Great sobs racked her frame, causing her breath to come in ragged gasps as she lay facedown on the bed where Jake had prostrated her with so much pleasure and sheltered her in what she'd believed was his undying love.

All the time she'd been falling for Jake and, later, telling herself how lucky she was to be building a new life with him, he'd been cheating on her in the most profound way imaginable. Why, oh, why couldn't he simply have come and checked me out, if his job required that of him? she asked herself. Being hunted down and handed to the Hargretts on a silver platter would have been bad enough. Why did he have to make me love him? And put me through the travesty of a wedding ceremony?

Though her eyes were puffy and sore, she managed to pull herself together—even to formulate some provisional plans by the time Lisa got off the school bus and trudged up the driveway. Unwilling to thrust the girl headfirst into the controversy that was shaping up, but well aware she eventually would have to be told the reason for Jake's absence, Holly drew her down on the sofa by the fire and put a loving arm about her shoulders.

"Pumpkin, I have some bad news," she said, hastily adding at Lisa's look of alarm, "Take it easy. Comet's all right. This is about Jake. He's gone…this time for good. If we see him again, it'll be in a courtroom."

Lisa stared. "You mean…you guys are getting a divorce?" she croaked. "But…but…you just got married! Jake *loves* us. He wouldn't walk out on us. I *know* he wouldn't!"

With a show of calm and poise she didn't actually possess, Holly patted the girl's shoulder. Somehow, she had to make sure Lisa wasn't permanently affected by what had taken place. The fact that she was dying inside couldn't be allowed to take precedence.

"He didn't leave of his own accord," she admitted. "I threw him out. Early this afternoon, he told me the truth about why he came to Honeycomb. Instead of the cowboy he pretended to be, Jake is a lawyer hired by your Hargrett grandfather. There's every chance he'll help him file suit to gain your custody."

Expecting fear on Lisa's part, Holly was prepared to deal with it. She hadn't bargained for the volatile blend of anger and anxiety the girl displayed. Seemingly oblivious to the very real possibility that she and Holly might be separated, Lisa focused on Jake's departure and what she clearly felt was Holly's mishandling of a lovers' quarrel.

"Jake would never leave us without a good reason," she reiterated, her thrust-out jaw defying Holly to contradict her. "What did you do to make him mad at us?"

Though Holly tried a second time to explain who Jake really was and what his reason had been for showing up at Honeycomb, it only seemed to make matters worse. As a result, she and Lisa were at odds for the remainder of the afternoon—a fact which added considerably to her emotional burden. Genuinely close and accustomed to being on an even keel with each other, they kissed and made up at dinnertime. But the problem between them was far from resolved and Holly knew it. She had only to meditate on the tenor of her stepdaughter's next remark to have an inkling of what lay ahead.

"I've been wondering..." Lisa said as they did the dishes. "Why would it be so bad for me to meet my grandparents? They might turn out to be like Mr. and Mrs. Tornquist. And Jane loves them."

Without running down the Hargretts, who were—after all—Lisa's blood relatives, Holly did her best to make the girl see what was at stake. "If a judge gives them custody, they'll take you away from me," she said. "You'll go to live with them and I won't get to see you anymore. But that's not the worst thing that could happen. When your mother gets out of jail, they might turn you over to her."

Having heard about Dawn from Clint, Lisa made a face. "I don't want to be taken away from you, Holly," she said, putting down her dish towel and snuggling close. "I just wish Jake would come back—that things could be the way they were. It was almost like having a dad again."

In an effort to distract the girl from their troubles, Holly offered to take her into Larisson to see a movie she was enthusiastic about. When they got into the truck, however, the engine wouldn't start. Though Holly peered under the hood, she was no mechanic. She couldn't diagnose the problem. Returning to the house, she phoned Lars, who held his tongue when she volunteered the news that Jake was gone and promised to come over in the morning for a look.

Lisa sighed when she learned that they'd be staying home, after all. "Jake could have fixed the truck for us," she muttered rebelliously, driving yet another nail into Holly's heart.

In a somewhat acerbic tone, Holly reminded her that Jake was out of the picture for good. "We got along without him before," she said, "and we can do it again."

Usually so even tempered, Lisa answered with a sharp retort. "Jake's not a quitter any more than my dad was," she asserted. "He loves us, and he'll be back for us."

Each time Jake tried to phone her from Durango, Holly hung up on him. A week later, a fresh-faced sheriff's deputy from Larisson served her with the expected formal notice of a custody hearing. It was to be held in three weeks, in a Durango judge's chambers. Adding insult to injury, Jake had personally signed her copy of the petition in his capacity as Dutch Hargrett's attorney. "Holly, please contact me so we can work something out," he begged in a separate, handwritten note that arrived the same day via her regular postman.

With Jake's help, Dutch Hargrett was going to take Lisa away from her. She didn't have the financial resources to stop them. She couldn't keep herself from panicking. As she paced the floor after Lisa had gone to sleep, she remembered Clint had put keeping Lisa from the Hargretts first and preserving Honeycomb for her future second.

The situation called for desperate measures. Putting any notion of seeking an annulment or divorcing Jake on the back burner and blinding herself to the reality that what she was envisioning qualified as contempt of court, she came to a momentous decision. We'll run to Alaska if we have to, she thought. Dutch Hargrett and his daughter aren't going to shape Lisa's life if I have anything to do with it.

Recalling that the Tornquists had wanted to expand their own spread by buying Honeycomb before Clint had come along and offered most of his lottery winnings for it, she phoned them while her stepdaughter was at school. When Emma told her to "C'mon over," she drove to their ranch and laid her troubles in front of them.

Characteristically, they asked what they could do to help.

"Buy Honeycomb from me," she answered, "for whatever you consider a fair price. The money will allow us to make a fresh start somewhere Jake can't find us."

Devastated by the news that the man who'd seemed so right for her had turned out to be allied with the enemy, the Tornquists hesitantly advanced the theory that running away from problems never solved anything. When she was adamant about selling, however, they agreed to rent the ranch for six months and run her cattle with theirs. If she still wanted to sell at the end of that time, they'd buy the ranch and its herd from her.

Packing up their clothes, she announced to Lisa that they were going away for a little while. She'd taken a temporary job as a cook at one of the spreads north of Pagosa Springs to make some sorely needed cash. While they were gone, the Tornquists would care for their cattle and horses.

It would mean changing school districts for the rest of the year, at least, and Lisa didn't want to go. She missed Jake and she would miss her friends. She didn't want to leave her filly and her life at Honeycomb. Yet this time the storm for which Holly had been bracing herself never materialized. In the final analysis, it appeared, Lisa loved and trusted her even when she was skeptical.

In Durango, the court date passed and Holly didn't appear. To forestall a warrant being issued for her arrest,

Jake took it upon himself to get the case continued. Though it was an out-and-out lie, he told the judge the parties were negotiating.

For at least a week, Holly hadn't answered her telephone. Heartsick over the mess he'd made of things, Jake decided to drive down to Honeycomb and try to persuade her to give him another chance. Together, he believed, they could come to a solution that would benefit everyone.

To his dismay, he found the place deserted. Even the horses' stalls looked as if they hadn't been inhabited for several weeks. Pausing outside the barn with the collar of his sherpa-lined jacket turned up against the wind, he let the loneliness of the place wash over him. The life they'd begun together so lovingly was gone. So was everything that mattered to him.

Several minutes later, he was hightailing it to the Tornquist ranch in search of information regarding Holly's and Lisa's whereabouts. To his frustration, though they still treated him like a friend, Emma and Lars refused to tell him anything.

Returning to Honeycomb, he let himself into the house with the key Holly had given him after they were engaged. The cedar chest containing her grandmother's wedding gown and other family treasures was still there, in the bedroom they'd shared. If he knew her, she'd be back for it before leaving the area.

It was Friday afternoon and he had a lonely weekend to waste. He decided to hang around. She and Lisa can't be too far away, he reasoned as he lay on the bed they'd shared, staring at the exposed ceiling beams. They're probably staying with friends. They'll be back, if only to get the rest of their things and say goodbye to a place they loved.

Unfortunately, it was a serious situation. By absconding with Lisa in defiance of a court order, Holly had flouted the law. She was risking arrest. I've got to find her, he thought. And fast...before this thing explodes in her face.

While Jake was holed up at Honeycomb, Dutch and his wife, Bernie, happened to lunch with friends at a favorite Durango watering hole. Among the locals at the next table was the judge who'd been assigned to hear Lisa's custody case. They belonged to the same country club. When Dutch stopped to chat after they'd finished their meal, he learned something interesting. The continuance had been Jake's suggestion.

Jake returned home on Sunday night to find an angry message on his answering machine. "Get your butt over here before I file a grievance with the bar association," Dutch's voice growled. "I want to talk to you about representing my best interests."

The session that followed in the older man's private office at the Flying D wasn't a pretty one. Reaming Jake out every which way to Sunday, Dutch vowed he'd have Holly arrested. "In case you didn't know it, Judge Markey is a friend of mine," he harrumphed. "He won't hesitate to issue a bench warrant on my behalf."

"You know where Holly is?" Jake asked, keeping a cool head. "I don't. She's gone from Honeycomb Ranch. And her neighbors won't tell me her whereabouts."

To his astonishment, Dutch did. A detective he'd dispatched to the valley on Saturday had stumbled across someone who, by chance, knew exactly where she was working.

Somehow, Jake had to save Holly from herself. He demanded to be told the details. "I swear to God I won't spirit her away or cooperate in anything illegal," he said when Dutch demurred. "Instead, I'll pick up Lisa for you. She can stay here, at the ranch, until the custody dispute's settled."

Irritably, though he betrayed a glimmer of satisfaction, Dutch agreed. When pressed, he revealed that a man who worked as a wrangler for one of Holly's neighbors had seen her in Pagosa Springs, buying large quantities of groceries. Partly out of curiosity and partly because he'd always admired her from a distance, the man had followed her back to the Lazy S, a huge commercial cattle spread owned and operated by a conglomerate. Incredibly, she was working there, as a cook in the bunkhouse mess.

The desperation to which he'd driven Holly made Jake wince. However, he'd promised Dutch he'd pick up Lisa and he'd keep his word. Ironically, though she'd hate him, it might keep the woman he loved from landing in a jail cell.

"I'll get right on it," he pledged.

Dutch gave him a caustic look. "Unless I miss my guess, you're sweet on Holly Yarborough," he observed. "If you weren't, you wouldn't have compromised your integrity to this extent."

That night, Holly dreamed of Jake and awoke with a heavy heart. She put a cheerful face on things as she saw Lisa off on Monday morning at the school bus stop. It would be her afternoon off and, keenly aware the girl wasn't happy in her new environment, she impulsively promised to pick her up at the end of the school day. Instead of Lisa sitting through the long bus ride home while Holly sat around and twiddled her thumbs, they'd go shopping in Pagosa Springs and eat hamburgers out as a special treat.

Somewhat lackadaisically, Lisa accepted. A short time later, Holly was hard at work, preparing a hot lunch plus a cold buffet supper the ranch hands would consume in her absence, when she was struck by a sudden sense that something was amiss. I hope to God Lisa hasn't been injured in a playground accident, she thought. That's about all I'd need to go crazy at this point.

The stress of hanging around until the Tornquists were ready to buy the ranch was getting to her, she supposed. Pushing down her uneasiness, she cleaned the kitchen and returned to their private quarters to change clothes. At the appointed time, she was waiting in her pickup outside Lisa's school, watching a steady stream of youngsters in winter clothing come flooding through a gap in the chain-link fence.

Her uneasiness returned when no redheaded ten-year-old in a turquoise parka with a navy-and-white stocking cap pulled down over her ears came running to meet her. Is she making me wait because she's mad at me about something? Holly asked herself. Or did one of her teachers ask her to stay after for a moment?

Worried, she decided to find out. When a quick search of Lisa's classroom and the area near her locker didn't yield any sign of her, she was on the verge of panicking. Spotting the girl's teacher as the latter emerged from the principal's office, Holly hurried over to her. "Where's my daughter?" she said. "She didn't come out with the other children."

The woman blinked in confusion. "I thought you knew, Mrs. McKenzie," she said a bit defensively.

"Lisa's father picked her up a few minutes early, for a dental appointment."

Incredibly, Jake had run them to ground again. Shivering like a hunted animal, she asked the woman to describe Lisa's male parent. The teacher's hesitant string of adjectives fit Jake to a T. He had Lisa. And he was taking her to the Hargretts.

"What was he driving?" Holly asked as calmly as she could. "A dusty red pickup?"

Lisa's teacher shook her head. "A silver-gray Mercedes. Is anything wrong?"

Without pausing to explain, Holly demanded to know what time they'd left. Seconds later, she was racing for her truck. Jake and Lisa were on their way to Durango with a ten-minute lead. If she broke every traffic law in the book, she might be able to catch them. Exactly what she planned to *do* if she succeeded didn't enter into her reckoning.

She'd gone just a short distance out of town when, suddenly, she was slamming on the brakes. A silver-gray Mercedes had caught her eye. It was parked near the gas pumps at a discount station on the lefthand side of the road. With the discovery came a break in traffic. She made a screaming U-turn.

Lisa was inside the car. "Get in...quick!" Holly ordered, reaching across the pickup's front seat to open the door on its passenger side.

Wide-eyed, Lisa did as she was told.

"Where's Jake?" Holly asked as they sped away.

"Inside the gas station."

Paying for gas, no doubt, Holly thought half-hysterically. In his haste to snatch Lisa, apparently, he forgot to check his gas gauge. Too bad he isn't wasting precious minutes in the rest room.

With a powerful car at his command, he'd be after them in a shot. On impulse, Holly turned into a run-down motel's parking lot and drove around to the side, where they'd be mostly hidden from view. Her evasive strategy didn't come a moment too soon. A heartbeat later, they were watching Jake's Mercedes speed past.

"He said he loves you—that he's trying to head off trouble for everyone," Lisa ventured.

Holly grimaced at what she considered a trumped-up excuse. "He sure found a funny way to do it," she answered bitterly. "He must have known I'd be out of my mind with worry when you turned up missing that way."

Hoping Jake would lose their scent, she decided they'd spend the night at the motel. Tomorrow, if the coast was clear, they could retrieve the few possessions they'd brought with them to the Lazy S. A quick stop at Honeycomb for family mementoes, and we'll be off, driving north through the mountains toward a fresh start in Alaska, she thought.

They'd be sitting ducks if they did either, she concluded the next morning, with a somewhat frayed night's sleep under her belt. The keepsakes at Honeycomb were the only things she cared about. Emma and Lars could send them to their new address.

In the interim, she had to select a route. With mountainous country on all sides, she didn't have many alternatives. Abruptly, the ghost of a smile played about her mouth. Our best bet is to drive *toward* Durango, and go on from there, she decided. Jake would never expect it.

Following a sleepless night filled with worry and calculation, Jake was trying to get inside her head. If I were Holly, and as blindly committed as she is to saving Lisa from Dawn, I'd do the least anticipated thing and head for Durango, he thought. He decided to drive that way and hope for the best.

Forty-five minutes later, Holly and Lisa were passing the Durango city limits. Because of seasonal activity on the nearby ski slopes, the town was crawling with tourists. They quickly found themselves in a traffic jam.

Jake's right behind us—I *know* he is, Holly thought, praying the riveting fear she felt wasn't communicating itself to Lisa. Desperate to keep moving amid cars that were bumper-to-bumper, she made a wrong turn and was forced to backtrack. Stopped at a red light, she looked in the rearview mirror and spotted a silver-gray Mercedes.

There were a lot of red trucks in the world, including the one Jake owned. It was possible he hadn't seen them yet. What could she do? They were near the parking lot for the popular "smoke and cinders," coal-powered train that ran between Durango and Silverton. On impulse, she turned into the lot and paid an attendant to park. The train was about to depart and, without any coherent plan in mind, she caught hold of Lisa's hand. Together, they ran to the depot, where she bought two tickets, and hurried aboard, two fugitives in a mob of skiers.

Jake hadn't noticed Holly's red truck. Biding his time in the traffic, he happened to glance toward the train parking lot, which was more than three-quarters full. In his opinion, it would provide excellent cover for someone seeking to escape detection.

On impulse, he turned in, too. Several minutes passed before he located Holly's truck. To his chagrin, it was empty. They're on the train! he thought. Just then, the engine's whistle blew two short blasts. A column of smoke issued from its smokestack.

The train was about to pull out! Sprinting, he arrived at the track just seconds too late to jump aboard. He'd have to follow them in the car. His heart pumping like the engine's pistons, only harder, Jake forced himself to relax. Now that he knew where they were, he had plenty of time. He'd collect them at their destination.

Chapter Ten

Though they'd been expecting it, the train's sudden departure caused Holly and Lisa to lurch forward in their seats. From her position next to the window in the second-to-last car, Holly shuddered to see Jake standing there. Clearly he saw *her*. Having escaped him for the moment, they were every bit as trapped as if his lean, powerful fingers had just closed about her wrists like handcuffs.

So familiar, he seemed almost a stranger in his dark slacks and top-quality, sherpa-lined leather coat. His eyes were just the same—bluer than blue and intent on getting what he wanted. In the fleeting glimpse she got of him, with Lisa's reflection superimposed on it in the glass, she sensed frustration, anguish, tenacity. The man she'd loved, married and slept with so briefly was used to winning. If and when he succeeded in reuniting

Dutch with his granddaughter, would he consider Holly's refusal to accept him anyway much of a loss?

With a Mercedes at his disposal, Jake would be waiting for them at the Silverton station. Meanwhile, her truck was parked in Durango. If somehow they managed to evade him in Silverton, should they try to hitch a ride back, and reclaim it? Or hop a bus for some destination farther along their route? If she chose the latter option, they'd be reduced to the clothes on their backs and what little money she carried in her purse.

She would do whatever it took to keep her promise to Clint. Chugging slowly through the town with its plume of smoke hanging overhead like grayish lace, the train gradually picked up speed as they passed a series of low-lying rural properties along the river. A few elk were grazing among the cattle. The highway—a straightforward ribbon of concrete—paralleled the tracks on the left. They could see the Mercedes beside them, keeping pace.

Their first glimpse of snowcapped peaks came twenty minutes to the north. Farther along, the tracks crossed a railroad bridge over the highway. Their path and Jake's diverged. While the highway took a high-altitude route, blasted from the shoulders of mountains, the train would chug up a narrow, winding river gorge, stopping for water once along the way. People lived near the water stop, and that meant a road. Would Jake be waiting for them there? Or would he continue onward, knowing he had them exactly where he wanted them?

Lisa chose that moment to slip a hand into hers. Though her lower lip wasn't quivering, there was an unhappy, confused look on her face. "Couldn't we trust Jake, Mommy?" she asked. "He loves us. He wouldn't try to make us do something that wasn't right."

I wish we could, Holly thought. Unfortunately, our entire relationship with him was built on a lie. Unable to think of an answer that wouldn't violate the girl's assumptions about the man she'd placed in Clint's stead as a father to her, she didn't say anything. Instead, she simply shook her head and hugged her stepdaughter close.

Beneath the train, which seemed to hang over the gorge, water tumbled over rocks. Snow glistened. Aspens shivered in their nakedness. As they continued to labor upward, Holly switched seats with Lisa and shut her eyes to the spectacular scenery on either side. Doing her best to let go of the tension that was eating her up, she lost herself in the squeak and groan of wheel flanges, the wail of the train's whistle, the clacking of its wheels over the rails. It was only a matter of time until Jake caught them. To all intents and purposes, she'd lost.

Hope revived as, some three hours later, they pulled into the station at Silverton. Retrieving their luggage and gear from the overhead racks, the skiers prepared to alight at the mountain-ringed resort. With so many people getting off at once, maybe Jake will lose us in the crowd, Holly thought.

While he was elbowing his way in search of them, they could be making their getaway on the other side of the railroad cars! Grasping Lisa's hand, she raced with her to the caboose, where souvenirs and hot chocolate had been sold during the trip. A quick look around informed her that the coast was clear. Hurriedly climbing down the steps, they crossed behind the caboose and took off, running as fast as they could.

When they reached Silverton's main street, which was overflowing with skiers and tourists on holiday, she

hesitated, then turned left. Beyond the panoply of tour-
ist-oriented shops, she spotted a small coin laundry. Perhaps there was a telephone.

Dashing inside with Lisa in tow, she found one, complete with phone book. Rapidly scanning the tattered
yellow pages, she started to dial the number of a bus
company that advertised ski tours. If they could nab a
pair of extra seats…

"Not so fast." Reaching past her, a strong hand sev-
ered her connection. With a sick feeling in the pit of
her stomach, Holly turned to face the man she'd married
and thought she knew. At close range, he was every bit
as handsome as she remembered—and ten times more
authoritative.

"You have no right to take Lisa…or power to arrest
me," Holly said.

Jake's fingers tightened. "On the contrary. I'm an
officer of the court. And you're a fugitive from justice."

The other women in the laundry were staring. "You
want me to call the police, honey?" one of them said.

Slowly, Holly shook her head. Jake had won. It was
that simple. If he was to be believed, she was in im-
minent danger of arrest. To retain any chance of seeing
Lisa from time to time, let alone raising her the way
she'd promised Clint she'd do, she'd have to cooperate.
Ceasing all protest, she allowed him to lead them back
to the station, where he was double-parked.

With an uncommunicative ten-year-old sandwiched
in between them as if he were still driving her truck
and living with them at Honeycomb Ranch, Holly and
Jake exchanged few words on the return trip. Instead,
they were lost in their private thoughts. Why, oh, why
didn't he take Lisa away last fall? Why didn't he show
his true colors, when he first came looking for us, Holly

asked herself miserably. Why did he have to hang around and make me fall in love with him? Dissemble to the point of asking me to marry him?

On their way to the Hargretts' ranch, Jake pointed out a handsome log home and barn on what Holly would have termed a "dude ranchette" or weekend property. "That's where I live," he said negligently, as if he doubted she or Lisa would be interested. "I did a lot of the carpentry and plumbing myself."

Maintaining her wall of silence, Holly didn't answer him. But she was undeniably curious. Despite the money he'd probably saved by taking on some of the work himself, the house, its outbuildings and land had cost him a pretty penny, she guessed. It had become increasingly clear to her that, whatever his start as a "dirt-poor rancher's son" in Idaho, he'd been quite successful. When she'd characterized him as a man used to winning, she hadn't been far from the mark.

He didn't say anything more as his big silver car ate up the miles that separated them from Dutch's place. All too soon, he was lowering the power window on the driver's side to punch in a numerical code on a keypad that was mounted on a pole to the left of an electronic gate. The gate itself was framed by tall stone pillars and a high electronic fence.

Somewhere, a computer processed his combination and the gate swung open to reveal a winding driveway. At its end, amid ponderosa pines, junipers and aspen, stood the huge, somewhat ostentatious pseudo-Victorian mansion that belonged to Lisa's grandparents. Having imagined it many times, Holly had never expected to set eyes on it. Now she was being brought there against her will, like a miscreant to justice.

A uniformed butler opened the front door for them

before they had a chance to press the bell. Immediately behind him were the Hargretts, who'd abandoned whatever pursuits had been occupying them to greet their granddaughter in the mansion's marble foyer.

"Lisa, darling! You've come home to us!" sweet-faced Bernie Hargrett exclaimed, rushing forward to throw her arms about the shy youngster.

A smile of satisfaction and pleasure splitting his craggy countenance, Dutch joined them in a three-way hug. Obviously overwhelmed by so much affection from people who were, in essence, strangers to her, Lisa remained a passive participant. Watching them, Holly bit her lip. Unless she could convince a judge that she was a better parent than two blood relatives who obviously loved her and could give her everything she wanted, she realized, she had lost.

Keenly aware of her pain and the fact that he'd been its instrument, Jake lightly squeezed her shoulder, the words *It'll be all right* somehow inherent in the gesture. Flinching as if she'd been struck, Holly moved away from him. Don't even try to smooth over what you've done, she retorted silently. You can never make it up to me—*never* make it right.

Rebuffed, Jake hid his feelings behind a guarded expression.

For all her wealth and access to designer clothes and beauty treatments, Bernie Hargrett looked every inch the cozy grandmother. In a tense situation that rendered Dutch's business acumen useless, it was she who empathized with their discomfort and took charge of the situation.

"You two and Dutch will want to confer," she told Jake and Holly softly before her more combative husband could bark out the kind of orders that would raise hackles all around. Her bright eyes rested on Holly's face. "Would you mind if I took Lisa to the kitchen for some cookies and hot chocolate?" she added, asking permission just as if Holly weren't at a serious disadvantage and the Hargretts, at least for the moment, in the driver's seat.

From a reluctant accomplice, it turned out, Lisa had become Holly's staunchest defender. It was clear from the look on her face that she wouldn't go willingly without her stepmother's okay.

Holly gave it, feeling she had little choice. A moment later, Bernie was gently leading the girl away and Holly was staring after them. "Okay, Mrs. Yarborough, Jake...what do you say we step into my office and talk things over," Dutch suggested.

Closeted with Jake and Dutch in the latter's study, which overlooked forested, snow-clad grounds through a sweep of mullioned windows, Holly felt like a wild animal caught in a trap. She could chew off her paw and escape, a cripple, as forest creatures sometimes did. But not if that "paw" was Lisa. She'd fight Dutch to the finish for her stepdaughter if that was what it took.

Despite the real-estate-and-mining magnate's initially soft-spoken manner, fireworks quickly erupted in the session. Holding forth from behind his massive desk, Dutch spoke eloquently of grandparents' rights. He demanded to know why Holly had ignored a court summons. "A proper parent for a ten-year-old wouldn't flout the law that way," he lectured her.

His pious words provoked a storm of countercharges from her, most of them focused on Dawn Hargrett's drug addiction, criminal record and demonstrated unfitness as a parent. "You raised her," she accused, unintimidated by his glowering expression. "What kind of parent does that make *you*, I wonder."

About to blast her with a retort, Dutch was silenced by additional blistering words from her mouth. "Maybe I shouldn't have run out on the court summons," she admitted, disarming his most serious charge. "But what would you have done in my place? Obediently lay your head on the chopping block of so much money and influence?" Her emphasis was derogatory as she glanced at Jake. "You and your *lawyer* here used subterfuge to hunt me down and invade my privacy. Today, he kidnapped me on your behalf. I wonder what a judge will say to that!"

At least she didn't tell Dutch about our marriage, Jake thought. If his volatile client found out about *that* before he had a chance to settle things, he might find himself facing disbarment proceedings.

"Hold on," he said, finally going on the offensive. "I didn't invade your privacy, Holly. True, I came looking for you. And hung around so I could check you out as a parent. What was I supposed to do—serve you with court papers? Or send you a telegram? I didn't know your address. As for your supposed kidnapping…"

Her tone frozen but smoking, like dry ice, Holly faced him. "It took place. Lisa was a witness."

"It's Lisa we have to think about…Lisa we're here to discuss." The words were Dutch's. Biting down on an unlighted cigar in an obvious attempt to regain his cool, he fixed Holly with a baleful stare. "You're damn right I sent my attorney after you, young lady," he said. "If he 'kidnapped' you, as you put it, he did you a favor. A sheriff's deputy would have arrested you and thrown your butt in jail."

Offended by his manner toward her, Holly didn't

speak. Jake chose to bide his time as he tried to call his keen negotiating instincts into play. Filling the vacuum, Dutch went on to speak of improved rehabilitation techniques and his hope that Dawn would emerge from her prison experience a new woman, finished with drugs for good and ready to take on adult responsibilities.

"Whatever her progress, my wife, Bernardine, and I are ready to do our best for the girl," he pontificated. "A child should be raised by blood relatives, if at all possible. Despite your history with her and her father, Mrs. Yarborough, you can't claim any kind of kinship with my granddaughter."

His monologue fueled Holly's worst fears. Fond parents that they were, if the Hargretts were successful in winning Lisa's custody, they'd hand her over to Dawn just as soon as she was released. She was highly insulted that Dutch should dismiss the loving bond between her and Lisa so lightly just because they weren't genetically related. Didn't he realize some of the best families didn't rely on kinship for the bond that united them?

"Are you through spouting off?" she demanded bitterly when at last he fell silent. "If so, you should know a couple of things. I love Lisa every bit as much as if I gave birth to her. And I'll die before I willingly hand her over to you so Dawn can corrupt and abuse her. You may have physical possession of her at the moment, thanks to Jake and most of the money in Colorado. But I'll fight you to my last penny and my last breath, even if that leaves me bankrupt and homeless!"

Unused to being told off by anyone, let alone a slender, financially strapped young woman, Dutch had gone red in the face. He all but leapt out of his chair. Desperate to defuse the growing animosity between his premier client, a man he liked despite his abrasive qualities, and the woman he loved but clearly stood to lose, Jake stepped physically between the two of them and attempted to mediate.

"I agree with a lot of what Dutch has said," he confessed to Holly, braving what he knew would be her scorn and distaste. "Grandparents do have rights. And that's as it should be. In most cases, they're assets to their grandchildren. Despite Dawn's bad behavior, it wasn't right or fair that he and Bernie missed out on Lisa's early years. They should be part of her life today...."

Stung by his implied criticism of her failure to notify the Hargretts of Lisa's whereabouts, Holly muttered that she'd only been honoring Clint's deathbed request.

"Be that as it may," he answered, "I agree with you on some points, as well. In my opinion, allowing Dawn unsupervised visitation with Lisa would pose a serious risk. Though, of course, we all hope for the girl's sake that her mother can be rehabilitated, the statistics on recovering addicts are mixed. Only time will tell in her case."

Turning slightly, he addressed himself to Dutch, who'd plainly gone ballistic over the implied criticism of his daughter. "Until the verdict on her recovery is in, caution on Lisa's behalf is mandatory," he continued. "Meanwhile, I can vouch firsthand for the fact that Holly has been an excellent mother. She and Lisa are extremely fond of each other. It's my hope that some sort of compromise can be reached."

Holly's mutinous expression clearly stated, *Don't do me any favors.* In her opinion, any arrangement that gave even partial custody to the Hargretts was too dangerous even to think about.

Used to calling the shots and relying on Jake to back him up, Dutch was getting increasingly steamed. Aware of his feelings, Jake sensed a compromise might be more easily reached if they agreed to a brief cooling-off period.

"What would you say to taking a break in our discussion?" he asked, including Holly in the question. "In court, it's difficult to predict which way a judge will go, and some form of shared custody agreement, arrived at in advance of a hearing, might prove advantageous to both sides. We could give the matter some thought this afternoon…meet again after supper prepared to discuss practical measures."

Deferring to Dutch first, he got a qualified grunt of approval—for the cooling-off period, at least. He could only hope his remark about the unpredictability of judges would sink in once the mining-and-real-estate tycoon had time to reflect.

Holly gave the idea her blessing, though she was seething. She needed time to plan and Jake was offering her that. She might as well take advantage of it. Nonetheless, she was still furious with him. The moment they were out of Dutch's office, she let him have it with both barrels.

"If you know Dawn, and I gather that you do, you know shared custody would pose the same risk as handing Lisa over to the Hargretts completely," she raged. "She'd still be subject to Dawn's influence. To think I believed you actually cared about my stepdaughter! Like a fool, I saw you as a father figure for her, when all along you were only interested in doing Dutch's bidding and furthering your own cause with him! In my opinion, you're lower than low. How dare you sit in judgment on me after the intimate deception you pulled?''

Fortunately for them both, perhaps, a maid hesitantly intruded on their acrimonious tête-à-tête. ''Mrs. Hargrett hopes everyone will eat together in the dining room this evening,'' she said. ''Dinner will be served at 6:00 p.m. In the meantime, you and Lisa have been assigned a twin-bedded guest room on the second floor, Mrs. Yarborough. If you would care to go upstairs and rest, Lisa will join you in a little while.''

Disposed to trust Bernie Hargrett somewhat, thanks to her friendly, noncombative manner on their arrival, and concerned that she and Lisa not be separated, Holly accepted. She turned to Jake. ''Does this meet with your approval?'' she demanded sarcastically.

Answering her with a look, he asked the maid for his jacket and went outside to pace the length of the Hargretts' snow-lined driveway and think about options. As he did so, Holly was similarly pacing in her room, an ultrafeminine boudoir tastefully decorated in shades of pink. She'd managed to calm down somewhat by the time Lisa arrived with tales of a ''kitchen bigger than our whole house at Honeycomb'' and the palomino mare that was waiting for her in the Hargrett stables.

The expected seduction of Lisa by the Hargretts' largesse was already under way. Though it hurt like a stiletto in the solar plexis, Holly did her best not to take her feelings out on the girl. Instead, ''I thought you liked Comet best of all horses,'' she reminded gently.

Following a moment's reflection, Lisa agreed that was indeed the case. But, ''I like the idea of a palomino, too,'' she admitted sheepishly. ''If we aren't going to see Comet anymore...''

''I *guarantee* we're going to see her again,'' Holly

vowed, painfully aware of the tactical error she'd made in separating the girl from her familiar, much-beloved surroundings.

Lisa's questions about her grandparents and what would happen next in her life weren't quite as easy to handle. To Holly's surprise, despite the overwhelming stresses of the situation in which they found themselves—or perhaps because of them—both she and Lisa managed to nap.

Holly slept the longest. She awoke finally, in early evening, at the sound of a light tapping on her bedroom door. A glance told her Lisa's bed was empty.

"Jenny's helping Lisa with her bath and a change of clothes in another suite," the maid who'd led her upstairs earlier explained, naming a fellow domestic, when Holly answered the door. "Mrs. Hargrett said you're welcome to use the adjoining bath and any of the clothes that have been placed in the dressing room for your use. She thought you might like to freshen up before joining everyone else in the dining room."

It was already 7:15 p.m. Aware she'd have to hurry, Holly thanked the maid and shut the door. Having slept in her clothes the previous night, she immediately searched the dressing room closet. Dawn and I must be about the same size, she meditated ruefully as she pawed through a generous selection of sweaters, skirts, slacks and dinner dresses. To her relief, none of the garments appeared to have been used. Indeed, some of them still sported their expensive price tags.

In Holly's opinion, the outfits had been bought for Dawn by her doting parents and rejected because they were too conservative. Though she hated to borrow any of them, or to accept favors of any kind from the Hargretts, she was even more put off by the notion of bathing and wriggling back into her soiled clothing. Selecting a plain navy blue wool challis dress and matching leather pumps, she decided to capitulate.

Though the food was delicious, dinner with the Hargretts in their magnificent, crystal-chandelier-appointed dining room was awkward for Holly, to say the least. Jake's blue eyes blazing across the table into hers and Dutch glaring at her from its head didn't help. For her part, Lisa was silent, wide-eyed, clearly nervous over the hostility she could sense in the room but curious, too, about her newly acquired grandparents. Of the assembled diners, only Bernie seemed at ease as she graciously kept the conversation flowing around the shoals of everyone's displeasure and unhappiness.

Before he aired the ideas he'd formulated during his lonely walk, Jake decided, everyone needed a good night's rest. "I've been thinking, and it seems best to me that we resume our earlier discussion in the morning, rather than going at it again tonight," he suggested.

To his surprise, Dutch concurred. The look Holly gave him intimated that, if she never spoke to him or Dutch again, it would be too soon for her.

When at last the group around the Hargretts' dining table broke up, he took her aside in the hall to issue a demand and a warning. "If you want Lisa to sleep in the same room with you tonight, you'll have to promise you won't attempt to run off with her under cover of darkness," he said. "I guarantee the gloves will come off if you try anything of the sort."

Aware of the security fence that surrounded the Hargrett estate, Holly condescendingly gave her word. A short time later, Bernie kissed Lisa good-night and walked her to Holly's room, then joined Dutch in the sitting area of their private suite.

"Honey…I just learned something from Lisa I think you ought to hear," she said gently, resting one hand on his knee as she joined him on the sofa in front of their wide-screen television set.

Immediately, Dutch was all ears.

"Our granddaughter says Jake and Holly were married on Christmas Eve," she confided. "Did you know about that? If so, you never mentioned it."

Chapter Eleven

His already florid complexion flushing a dangerous beet color, Dutch blistered the sitting room walls with his choicest scatological terms. Pausing to remind Bernie that he wasn't angry with *her,* he stormed out of the room and ordered Evans, the family butler, to find Jake at once. "I want him in my office in five minutes!" he decreed. "No ifs, ands or buts!"

Guessing that his irascible client had somehow learned the full extent of his relationship with Holly, Jake braced himself for a firestorm as he complied with Dutch's summons.

He got exactly what he expected. From his position of authority behind the fortress of his desk, Dutch called Jake every name in the book. Accusing him of being a traitor to his obligations, he threatened a malpractice suit.

Irate as Dutch was, he managed to find a crumb of

comfort in the situation. "Unless I'm misguided as sin," he gloated bitterly, "you're poison to Holly Yarborough now. Maybe I should call her Holly McKenzie. If so, I doubt if she'll be using the name for long."

Jake didn't let his client see how much that likelihood hurt him. "I plan to change her mind about me," he answered with as much equanimity as possible. "Just as I plan to change yours. Somehow, we've got to deal with the fact that you and Bernie spoiled Dawn rotten...that you're still tempted to give her the benefit of the doubt when a child's welfare is at stake. I guarantee you Judge Markey will consider it."

About to escalate the hostilities a notch, Dutch struggled with his famous temper and appeared to win. Abruptly, he sagged a little in his chair. "You're right, son," he admitted in a tone that told Jake he was back in the older man's good graces. "We failed with Dawn, though the latest reports from her rehab counselor at the prison are hopeful. We're just selfish enough to want another chance with our granddaughter. What do you suggest?"

Breakfast was served buffet-style in a plush but tweedy dinette-and-family-room area that was dominated by a huge stone fireplace. Homesick for her own ranch as she filled her plate before the crackling blaze in a heavy sweater and never-worn pair of Dawn's jeans, Holly did her best to ignore Jake's unspoken hints that he wanted time alone with her.

Patently fast friends with Bernie, though she'd known her less than twenty-four hours, Lisa was chattering away about their planned trip that morning to the Hargrett stables and kennel. Reluctant to interrupt and be the odd woman out, Holly opened one of the glass sliders and took her plate of cheese strata, bacon and fruit out on the adjoining redwood deck. Placing it on the broad, comfortable railing, she rested her elbows beside it and stared pensively at a spectacular view of the nearby mountains as she tried to imagine what the future might hold.

She tensed when Jake joined her a moment later.

"We need to talk privately," he said, doing his best to ignore her obvious distaste for him. "Dutch knows about our marital status. Even so, we've managed to work out a compromise you might be willing to accept."

Holly's skepticism was evident in her deep sigh, the helpless shrug of her shoulders. Having spent the night under the same roof with him but in a separate bed, she was furious with herself for missing him—and with him for delivering her into Dutch's hands.

"Go ahead, tell me about it," she answered, making no attempt to be gracious. "You will, anyway."

So close that their shoulders all but brushed, Jake didn't make a move to touch her. "According to the terms we worked out, you and I would have custody of Lisa with visitation rights reserved to Bernie and Dutch Hargrett," he explained. "In return, they'd agree in writing not to allow Dawn time alone with her unless you gave your explicit permission."

Incredulous, Holly bit her lip. He hadn't finished yet.

"You may not be disposed to believe it," he continued. "I can hardly blame you. But the truth is, Dawn's counselor at the prison has given her a glowing report. Dutch showed me a copy of it. And it appears to be legitimate.

"Since entering a special program for drug offenders a year and a half ago, she's improved her behavior one hundred percent. She's reportedly recognized the factors that caused her to turn to drugs in the first place, and volunteered her understanding that staying away from them in the future will be an arduous, day-to-day struggle. She's enrolled in a parenting class for inmates at her request.

"As you might imagine, Dutch and Bernie are overjoyed at her progress. However they recognize that the odds against long-term recovery from an addiction like hers are formidable. And that they're more than a little prejudiced where she's concerned. They're prepared to let you decide when—or *if*—Dawn qualifies for time alone with Lisa. You'd have the arbitrary right to withhold your permission for as long as you see fit if you aren't thoroughly convinced of Dawn's rehabilitation and fitness as an alternative parent."

Jake paused, half-afraid to phrase the question that hovered on the tip of his tongue. "Mind telling me what you think about what we're suggesting?" he asked.

Stunned, Holly could scarcely believe Jake had wrung such far-reaching concessions from Dutch. Before quizzing him about how he'd managed it, she felt compelled to clear up her soaring confusion about one of the conditions he'd set forth.

"What do you mean, 'you and I' would have custody of Lisa under your plan?" she asked. "Aside from being Dutch's attorney, how do you come into it?"

By now they'd completely abandoned their breakfast plates. Courting danger, a small brown wren had alighted and darted forward to share their feast.

"Aside from being Dutch's attorney, I'm still your husband," he reminded her. "I expect to continue in that capacity. Despite what you may think of me, I love you deeply, Holly. And I love Lisa, just as if she were my own child. I want to salvage the life we promised to share on our wedding day. Fortunately for both of us, Dutch trusts me to see to it that any out-of-court agreement we reach is equitably carried out."

Something painful Holly couldn't articulate twisted in her gut. "And if we don't stay married?" she asked, unwilling to admit, even to herself, how much she still loved him. "Supposing I want a divorce. And the freedom to raise Lisa without your help."

Somehow, Jake had known she'd seize on that point. "You're right," he conceded with the greatest of reluctance. "Fair's fair. My presence or absence in your life shouldn't make a difference."

Her eyes narrowed even as, deep inside, she registered his unhappiness. "But it does...doesn't it?" she asked.

Painfully, because he'd vowed not to lie to her again and he knew it was another way of losing her, he answered, "Yes."

Something closed in her face. "I'll have to think about it," she said.

Jake was silent a moment. "You realize this isn't totally about Lisa or her grandparents—that it's also about *us*," he said at last. "For what it's worth, I'm ashamed that I didn't tell you the truth about why I was there, at Honeycomb, right from the first. But in a way you might not understand or forgive, I don't regret it. If I *had* told you, I'd have been your adversary. We'd never have gotten to know each other."

At least she didn't turn him down flat. "As I said, I'll have to think about it," she reiterated, her voice bereft of any discernable emotion.

Jake did his best to smother his disappointment. "I'll leave you, then, so you can get on with it," he responded, picking up his plate and going back into the house.

Alone on the deck after he'd gone, Holly let the remains of her breakfast congeal on her plate. Outfitted with a pair of suede hiking boots that also belonged to Dawn, which she'd adjusted to fit by adding a second pair of socks, she decided to go for a walk.

As she strolled through the trees toward a little knoll, shivering despite the strong winter sunlight, she tried to sort through the muddled thoughts that were competing in her head. Despite her animosity toward him, which by now was ebbing, she still loved Jake with all her heart. The chance he'd offered to recapture the life they'd begun to share a shining possibility within her grasp, she grieved that he hadn't given her much of a choice.

If she refused to cooperate with the plan he'd conceived, she could lose Lisa and be forced to default on her promise to Clint. In her book, that was coercion. If she succumbed to it, she feared, her feeling of helplessness would always poison their relationship, just as her parents' relationship had been poisoned when her father had insisted that her mother accompany him to Alaska against her will.

Ultimately, though her mother had caved in to his demands, the divorce she'd attempted to stave off by doing so had come about, anyway. What on earth was she going to do?

To her surprise, the tracks of the Durango-Silverton Railroad were visible in the distance, through an opening in the trees. As she watched the morning train make its way up the valley preparatory to its long climb along the gorge, she reflected that she'd liked Alaska. Unlike her mother, she'd been sorry to leave it. In fact, the

years she'd spent there as a child had been among the
most colorful and exhilarating she could remember.

There was a lesson in the thought and, abruptly,
Holly knew what it was. *Why fret over solving a problem you don't have?* she asked herself joyously. Your
mom didn't want to go to Alaska. But you want to keep
Lisa and stay married to Jake. What's stopping you?
Pride? Your late mother's unhappy life? Your infernal
stubbornness?

She still didn't like the fact that Jake hadn't been
honest with her. Yet it was obvious to her by now that
he'd suffered greatly for it. Secure in his love, she could
afford to lay the matter to rest. The way things had
worked out, she doubted he'd ever be so rash again!

Racing into the house with a little explosion of happiness and energy, she burst uninvited into Dutch Hargrett's study, where one of the maids had told her he
and Jake were in conference. "I've decided to accept
your proposal," she announced, looking from Lisa's
grandfather to the man she loved.

While Dutch's craggy but affable face lit up, Jake's
was a study in mixed emotions. He'd been thinking
about the coercion angle, too. "Sure this is what you
want?" he asked.

Holly's smile was positively luminous. "You *and*
Lisa?" she exclaimed, putting her arms around him so
lovingly that his anxious frown relaxed into a grin.
"You'd better believe it. To my way of thinking, that's
the bargain of the century!"

Bernie chose that moment to tap lightly on her husband's office door and enter. "Everything okay in
here?" she asked.

"Couldn't be better." Dutch beamed.

Jake's response fell into the nonverbal category. With

profound relief and humility over the second chance
he'd been given, he was thoroughly kissing the woman
he loved.

With his law practice situated in Durango while
Holly and Lisa were still emotionally tied to the ranch
Clint had bought for them, Jake and Holly still had a
few things to settle. Fortunately, he didn't expect it to
be all that difficult. Having learned a thing or two during his sabbatical and their time apart, he was planning
some permanent changes in his life-style that would co-
incide with theirs.

Walking arm in arm with Holly down the driveway
where he'd ambled in solitary reflection the day before,
he told her how much he'd grown to love Larisson
Valley and Honeycomb Ranch.

"The prospect of being a real rancher again, not just
a tenderfoot with a weekend place, is more enticing to
me than you can imagine," he confessed. "Viewed in
the context of daily physical labor and fresh air, the
gorgeous scenery I've come to take for granted and—
most importantly of all—loving you and watching Lisa
grow up, my life as a lawyer in Durango can't compete."

He wanted to live at Honeycomb with them! Though
she was spilling over with happiness, Holly's forehead
crumpled a little. "I don't want you to give up your
legal career entirely," she objected, halting to gaze up
at him.

Putting both arms about her waist, he reassured her
as he tugged her close. "I've thought about it, and I
want to remain a partner in Fordyce, Lane and Mc-
Kenzie. I just plan to take fewer cases. If things work
out the way I want them to, I might spend a few days
a month here in Durango—maybe even a week or two

now and then. But I can do a lot from Honeycomb via fax, telephone and computer. We'll need to expand the house a little, to make room for an office, my law books and a fax machine.''

''Oh, Jake…'' Holly's exclamation was part joy, part distress. She wanted to expand the house, too, so they could have a baby. But…

For once, Jake was oblivious to her mood. ''I'm ready to go back today if you are,'' he told her.

A lump had formed in Holly's throat. ''I hate to tell you,'' she said, ''but the Tornquists are renting the place.''

His response was a grin. ''Not to worry,'' he soothed. ''We can easily straighten that out. If I know Lars and Emma, they'll be so happy you and Lisa are happy that they'll tear up the lease forthwith.''

Back at the house, they told Bernie and Dutch about the decisions they'd made. Business clients as well as longtime friends of Jake's, they listened with qualified approval and a high degree of self-interest.

''What about us?'' Dutch asked at once when finally he was able to get a word in edgewise. ''Now that we've found her again, we want to spend some time with Lisa. We won't be able to do that if you take her back to Larisson Valley this afternoon.''

In Jake's opinion, matriculating at a third school in as many months would be a disaster for the girl, particularly in view of all the confusion and upset she'd just endured. Despite the new horse and other treats that were in the offing for her in Durango, he guessed, she'd want to return to Honeycomb with them.

''I've been thinking about that, and I may have come up with a solution,'' he said. ''First, we'll be back in Durango for the hearing next week to finalize our custody arrangement. But that isn't all. You have a motor home, don't you? As I recall, it's fairly luxurious. Why not come down to Honeycomb for Lisa's birthday? She'll be eleven in just three weeks. You could stay as long as you wanted."

Simultaneously, Bernie and Dutch turned to Holly. Their faces held an identical question.

Realizing he'd made free with an invitation before consulting her, Jake deferred to the pretty Scandinavian blonde who was nestled in the curve of his arm.

Assured of the Hargretts' discretion where Dawn was concerned, she sparkled up at him. "I think it's a great idea," she said. "It just occurred to me that, when school lets out in the spring, she could come to Durango for a month or so. Jake and I could use some time alone—a kind of second honeymoon."

Lisa was elated when she learned the news. Hugging Holly first, she turned to Jake. A moment later she was nestled in his arms. "I guess this means you're my new dad-by-marriage...for keeps," she whispered.

For his part, Jake was thinking he couldn't have a daughter who was any dearer to him if she'd sprung from his own genes. If he and Holly had a baby girl someday, his daughters would be two peas in a pod when it came to his heart.

"You'd better believe it, sweetheart," he answered, his exceptionally gruff tone betraying the depth of his tenderness.

A phone call to Lars and Emma catching them up on the news easily persuaded them to vacate the lease Holly had signed. Though she, Jake and Lisa remained at the Hargrett estate for lunch, by early afternoon they were in the Mercedes, heading home to the ranch they loved.

As they approached the Tornquist place, Jane was getting off the school bus. "Oh, *please!*" Lisa squealed. "Stop! We haven't seen each other for so long...."

Minutes later, they were having coffee and home-made doughnuts in Emma's cozy dinette while the two girls fairly danced around them with merriment. Following a barrage of congratulations and expressed happiness all around, it was decided Lisa would spend the night with Jane so the lovers' reunion wouldn't be interrupted.

"Just think...we'll be going to the same school again!" Jane rejoiced as she and Lisa disappeared down the hall to exchange confidences in her room.

As she and Jake continued home without their favorite ten-year-old, Holly recalled a loose end that hadn't been satisfactorily knotted. "There's just one small thing that still bothers me," she divulged.

Jake threw her a worried glance. "And that is?"

"I have a hard time understanding how you could pick up Lisa at school and make off with her without letting me know. Didn't you think I'd be sick with worry?"

Jake's tension evaporated. "Ah, but I didn't," he said. "As far as I knew, she was supposed to take the school bus home—a half hour's ride at the very least. She didn't tell me any different. I was phoning you from that gas station to tell you what had transpired when you caught up with us."

If it hadn't been for his generosity of spirit, he might have gotten away with Lisa's abduction. Instead of ending up together at the Flying D, where they'd been able to settle their differences, they might have met again in a courtroom. The outcome—and their subsequent lives—could have turned out vastly different.

"Thank heaven you're a principled softie at heart," Holly whispered, planting a warm little kiss on his neck. "Jake McKenzie, you easygoing lawyer, you...I love you so much."

Honeycomb Ranch welcomed them with its snow-covered meadows and distant mountains as if they'd never left. It was their home and would continue to be, at least until Lisa was grown. They could plant their roots deeply, without the fear of unspoken conflicts haunting them.

Their physical reunion started the moment they'd unlocked the front door. Unbuttoning Holly's parka, Jake slid it down her arms. "I want to touch you...worship you all over, darlin'," he said, running his hands down her body.

Dawn's heavy sweater and stiff jeans were in the way. "That goes for me, too," Holly answered, unwilling that the slightest barrier should separate them. "Don't you think we're a bit overdressed?"

The problem wouldn't be difficult to resolve. Pausing to adjust the furnace controls, which Holly had set at a chilly forty-five degrees prior to her departure, Jake lovingly drew her toward their bedroom.

Preoccupied though she was with what they were about to do, she sensed instantly that something was amiss. Seconds later, she realized that the down-filled comforter she used as a bed cover was rumpled, as if from the imprint of a body. She was positive she'd left it neat.

"Somebody's been in the house," she proclaimed worriedly.

Jake flung her a contrite look. "You're right," he said. "Somebody *has*."

"You?" she asked in surprise.

He nodded. "I drove down over the weekend, hoping to put things right. And you weren't anywhere to be found. I stretched out on the bed to wait for you. Somehow..." He shrugged. "I don't know. Lying there, where we'd made love, made me feel closer to you, I guess."

All the affection he felt for her, all the longing, reverberated in the offhand confession.

"I'm here now," she whispered.

Seconds later, they were wriggling out of their clothes and climbing under the covers with nothing but their skin to separate them. How have I managed without this man? Holly thought in amazement as Jake's mouth blazed a sensuous trail to worship her breasts. He's in my pores, in my bloodstream. As the years go by, we'll be more and more a part of each other.

For once, she wouldn't let him bring her to culmination first. Instead, they'd reach the heights together. "I want you in me from the beginning," she asserted. "Just as deep as you can get."

Though it had been intensely satisfying between them since their wedding night, their reunion sparked their most earth-shattering coitus yet. Relief entered into it, but it wasn't the only cause. In a way they'd only grasped at earlier, they were truly married at last, journeying soul to journeying soul, locked in a profound embrace.

Thrusting high against her body, so that her face was buried against his chest hair and their sexual contact was exquisite, Jake primed the pump of their ascent. It wasn't long before Holly was fluttering at the brink and dissolving in a maelstrom of pleasure that seemed to implode and implode until she was at one with the universe.

Jake followed in seconds, unaware he was invoking her name like a blessing. At last they quieted. Heat radiated from their bodies, compounding itself wherever they touched.

With Honeycomb's animal population still in the Tornquists' charge, there were no chickens to feed, no horses to curry. They could go to sleep if they wanted, though it was still daylight.

As Holly surrendered to the urge, Jake thought of Clint, the man whose untimely death had made all this possible for him. If your spirit's around somewhere, you can rest easy, old buddy, he whispered mutely to his predecessor. I love them both more than life and I'll take good care of them. I know how utterly damn lucky I am to have the love and trust of Holly and your daughter.

Someday soon, they'd make a little brother or sister for Lisa to love.

As if she'd sensed the desire he hadn't articulated to her yet, Holly sighed contentedly in her sleep. Her seeming awareness of what he was thinking caused the corners of Jake's mouth to lift. She was his alter ego, wasn't she? His treasure and his beneficence. Why should he be surprised if, on some subliminal level, she knew the loving thoughts that drifted through his head.

* * * * *

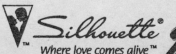

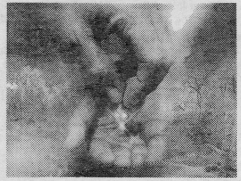

New from

a sperm bank mix-up sets a
powerful executive in search
of the woman who's...

Don't miss any of these titles from
this exciting new miniseries:

WHEN THE LIGHTS WENT OUT...,
October 2001 by Judy Christenberry

A PREGNANT PROPOSAL,
November 2001 by Elizabeth Harbison

THE MAKEOVER TAKEOVER,
December 2001 by Sandra Paul

LAST CHANCE FOR BABY,
January 2002 by Julianna Morris

SHE'S HAVING MY BABY!,
February 2002 by Raye Morgan

Available at your favorite retail outlet.

Where love comes alive™

Visit Silhouette at www.eHarlequin.com

SRHBB

*H*ugh Blake,
soon to become stepfather to
the Maitland clan, has produced three
high-performing offspring of his own. But
at the rate they're going, they're never going to
make him a grandpa!

There's *Suzanne*, a work-obsessed CEO whose Christmas spirit could use a little topping up....

And *Thomas*, a lawyer whose ability to hold on to the woman he loves is evaporating by the minute....

And *Diane*, a teacher so dedicated to her teenage students she hasn't noticed she's put her own life on hold.

But there's a Christmas wake-up call in store
for the Blake siblings. Love *and* Christmas miracles
are in store for all three!

Maitland Maternity Christmas

A collection from three of Harlequin's favorite authors

Muriel Jensen
Judy Christenberry
&Tina Leonard

Look for it in November 2001.